America's enemies, be warned: the
than a wounded and cor

Praise for *VIN*

and his electrifying #1 *New York Times* bestsellers featuring
CIA superagent Mitch Rapp

THE LAST MAN

"Flynn's best work yet. Tight, right and dynamite."

—*Minneapolis Star Tribune*

"A great read . . . hard to put down. The action is non-stop and well paced. An incredible and captivating novel."

—*Blackfive*

"Absolutely first rate. . . . Flynn fans will not be disappointed."

—*Men Reading Books*

"Read every book in the [Mitch Rapp] series . . . they're too good to put down! Five stars, all day, every day."

—*A Little Bit of R&R*

"Flynn, master storyteller that he is, skillfully navigates the reader through twists and turns . . . while setting up the next intriguing volume."

—*Book Reporter*

"Filled with action, deception, corruption, and a whole lot of ass-kicking."

—*Arms Vault*

"*The Last Man* will play out well for people who are just politically savvy enough to believe that our government may very well be doing things right at this moment that we believe only other governments are capable of."

—*Good E-Reader* (5 stars)

"Vince Flynn has never been better"
(*The Providence Journal*) than in this powerful #1 bestseller of a
young Mitch Rapp on his explosive first mission. . . .

KILL SHOT

"Nail-biting."

—*Good Reads*

"Flynn is a master—maybe *the* master—of thrillers in which the pages
seem to turn themselves."

—*Book Reporter*

The #1 blockbuster from "the voice of today's postmodern thriller
generation" (*The Providence Journal*). . . .

AMERICAN ASSASSIN

"There is a reason Flynn is #1 on the bestseller lists."

—*The New York Post*

"Captivating."

—*Glenn Beck*

"Terrific."

—*The Toronto Sun*

And don't miss these "complex, chilling, and satisfying"
(*The Cleveland Plain Dealer*) Mitch Rapp thrillers!

Pursuit of Honor   *Extreme Measures*   *Protect and Defend*

Act of Treason   *Consent to Kill*   *Memorial Day*   *Executive Power*

Separation of Power   *The Third Option*   *Transfer of Power*

Vince Flynn "demonstrates that he truly understands the psyche
of the enemy" (*Book Reporter*) in his "exciting, Ludlum-like series"
(*Booklist*)

Also by Vince Flynn

THE
LAST MAN

A THRILLER

VINCE FLYNN

POCKET Books

New York   London   Toronto   Sydney   New Delhi

 Pocket Books
A Division of Simon & Schuster, Inc.
1230 Avenue of the Americas
New York, NY 10020

First Pocket Books export edition April 2013

POCKET and colophon are registered trademarks of Simon & Schuster, Inc.

For information about special discounts for bulk purchases, please contact Simon & Schuster Special Sales at 1-866-506-1949 or business@simonandschuster.com.

The Simon & Schuster Speakers Bureau can bring authors to your live event. For more information or to book an event, contact the Simon & Schuster Speakers Bureau at 1-866-248-3049 or visit our website at www.simonspeakers.com.

Designed by Dana Sloan

Manufactured in the United States of America

10 9 8 7 6 5 4 3 2 1

ISBN 978-1-4767-4403-2
ISBN 978-1-4391-0053-0 (ebook)

*To all of my teachers and coaches at
Saint Thomas Academy who taught me that
to succeed in life, you need to raise the bar, not lower it.*

ACKNOWLEDGMENTS

To my agent and friend Sloan Harris, for another smooth contract negotiation; you always come through. To Kristyn Keene at ICM, congrats on your promotion, and to Shira Schindel, who will be taking over for everyone's favorite assistant. To Chris Silbermann, for a stellar job negotiating the extension with CBS Films. To Lorenzo Di Bonaventura and Nick Wechsler, for inching the movie ever closer to reality. I wish I had your patience. To Rob Richer, who continues to enlighten me on espionage, terrorism, and geopolitics. You truly are one of the good guys.

To my editor and publisher Emily Bestler, thank you for fifteen years of a great partnership and more to come. To Kate Cetrulo and Caroline Porter at Emily Bestler Books, for taking care of all the details I miss and gently reminding me that I need to hand in my homework. To Jeanne Lee, you never disappoint. Thanks for another great cover. To Al Madocs, my goal is that one of these years I will not have to put you in the acknowledgments, but for now, I'm sorry, yet again, for putting you through the wringer. To David Brown, of all the people I work with, no one makes me laugh more. You are a joy to work with, and so is Ariele Fredman, who we all know really runs the department. To Judith Curr and Louise Burke, thank you for all your continued support. To Carolyn Reidy, for one of the smoothest, most business-minded contract negotiations that I have ever been involved in. It is an honor to still be part of the Simon & Schuster family after fifteen years.

Thanks to a lot of prayers and great medical care, I'm feeling better than I've felt in years. To all the friends and family in the Twin Cities and beyond who have continued to support my family through prayers, well wishes, and great kindness, I am humbled. To Dr. Bill Utz and Dr. Eugene Kwon and the amazing people you work with—cancer sucks, but somehow you make the journey enjoyable. To Dr. Douglas Olson, my radiologist, you are in my prayers every day. To my friend Dr. Mike Nanne, I am in awe of your courage. To Misty Mills, Paul Hesli, Leslie Vadnais, Jodi Bakkegard, and Cristine Suihkonen, for all that you do for my family.

To my darling wife, Lysa, who has always been wise beyond her years, thank you for giving me some of that wisdom when I really needed it. Now if I could just get some of that grace from you, I'd really have things moving in the right direction. You are my favorite thing about life.

THE LAST MAN

CHAPTER 1

JALALABAD, AFGHANISTAN

THE four dead men were lined up on the living room floor of the safe house. Mitch Rapp started with the one on the left. The bearded face, the dark, lifeless eyes, and the dime-sized bullet hole that marked the center of the man's forehead were all expected. One bullet, nice and neat—the way Rapp would have done it. The next two bodyguards looked the same, including red pucker marks in the center of their brows. The fourth Afghani was a different story. He'd been shot through the back of the head. A quarter of his face was now a jagged crater of flesh, blood, and bone. The exit wound told him the man had been shot by something a lot bigger than a 9mm—probably a .45 caliber with ammunition that pancaked and tumbled for maximum damage. There was nothing about this mess to give Rapp any assurance that things would be fine, but this last little twist cracked open the door on something he did not want to consider.

Rapp set the troubling thought aside for a second, tried to imagine how it had gone down. The early signs pointed toward a well-coordinated assault. The perimeter security had been breached; phone line, cameras, motion sensors, heat sensors, and even the pressure pads had all been taken off-line. The backup connection through the satellite dish on the roof had also been disabled. Whoever had attacked the safe house had the knowledge and skill to hit the place without setting off a single alarm and alerting the quick-reaction force less than a mile away at the air base. According to the experts at Langley this was never supposed to happen. Four years earlier they had claimed the safe house was impregnable against any threat that the Taliban or any other local group could come up with. Rapp had told those same experts that they were full of shit. He'd never seen an impregnable safe house for the simple reason that people had to come and go.

As with most CIA safe houses, this one was intentionally bland. There was no American flag flown out front and there were no snappy Marines standing post at the main gate. This was a black site where the more unpleasant aspects of the war had been coordinated. Langley didn't want any official records of the comings and goings of the drug dealers, warlords, arms dealers, local politicians, police, and Afghan Army officers who were on the take.

The house looked like your run-of-the-mill two-story blockhouse in Jalalabad. There were quite a few upgrades that made it unique, but from the outside it looked dingy and run-down just like all the other houses in the neighborhood. The cinderblock wall that surrounded the property was coated with a special resin designed to prevent it from exploding into a million pieces and shredding the house in the event of a car bomb. The simple-looking front door contained a one-inch steel plate and a reinforced steel frame. All of the windows were bulletproof Plexiglas and the high-tech security cameras and sensors were concealed so as to not attract the attention of the neighbors. Langley had even taken the unusual precaution of buying the houses on each side and moving in the bodyguards and their families. All to protect one man.

Joe Rickman was the most cunning and brilliant operative Rapp had ever worked with. They'd known each other for sixteen years. At first Rapp didn't know what to think of him. Rickman was pure vanilla. There wasn't a single physical characteristic about him that was memorable. At five-feet-ten he was neither tall nor short. His mousy brown hair matched his dull brown eyes, and his weak chin completed the bland lines of his roundish face. On the rare occasion that you heard him speak, he was never animated and his voice was pure monotone—the kind of thing that could put the most restless baby to sleep.

Rickman's forgettable face allowed him to blend in and those who met him were almost underwhelmed by his presence. For Rickman that was just fine. Much of his success was built on fools underestimating him. He'd worked for the CIA for twenty-three years and it was rumored that he had never set foot inside headquarters. Only a few months earlier Rapp had asked him if the rumor was true. Rickman responded with a soft smile and said that he'd never been invited.

At the time, Rapp took the comment as a self-deprecating attempt at a little levity. Later he realized Rickman was dead serious. Rickman was one of those people who were tolerated only during tough times— usually war. For the last eight years he'd run America's clandestine war in Afghanistan. More than a billion dollars in cash had passed through his hands. Most of it was used to bribe people into playing on the right team, but a fair amount of the money was used to kill enemies and for a laundry list of other unpleasant things that went with the territory. People back at Langley didn't want to know what Rickman was up to. They only wanted results, and that was something Rickman was exceedingly good at. Underneath Rickman's bland façade was a cunning mind that was perfectly suited to the duplicitous, infinitely complicated world of espionage.

Rapp understood the tinge of fear in his boss's voice when she'd called him a little over two hours ago. When the morning guards showed up, they had discovered the bodies and the absence of Joe Rickman and had immediately immediately alerted John Hubbard, the CIA's Jalalabad base chief. Hubbard rang his boss in Kabul and the shit rolled uphill from there. Rapp received a call from CIA Director Irene Kennedy while he was sitting down for breakfast in the big mess hall at Bagram Air Force Base. He had just arrived in-country the previous evening on a high-priority mission that was now on hold. Kennedy passed along what little information she knew and ordered Rapp to grab the next Blackhawk to Jalalabad. Rapp didn't argue. He and four of his team members made the trip and were on the ground in Jalalabad before nine in the morning. Hubbard met them with a three-SUV convoy and a security detail and they rolled to the house.

Langley would want Rickman back, but Rapp got the strange feeling that all things considered, they would prefer the black-ops boss delivered in a body bag. It would be impossible to keep the kidnapping a secret. Rickman's operational knowledge and reach was too vast to ignore. Entire teams would already be gathered at Langley, working around the clock to assess the damage. If Rapp didn't find Rickman quickly, then complex, expensive operations would have to be unwound or assets would start showing up in morgues all across the Middle East, Southwest Asia, and beyond. Sooner or later Congress would get wind of the disaster and they would want answers. For a good number of people back at Langley, the only thing worse than Rickman spilling the Company secrets to an enemy would be Rickman testifying before Congress.

Rapp had a long and somewhat complicated history with Rickman. He respected the man, but it had taken a while. Rapp was considering how he would handle a possible order to eliminate Rickman when the towering Hubbard approached.

"This shit is really bad."

Rapp nodded. "It's about as bad as it could get."

Hubbard rubbed his bald head and asked, "How in the hell are we going to find him?"

"At this point I'm not sure." Rapp knew their chances for success were remote, but they had to start somewhere. "This is going to get really nasty, and if you don't have the stomach for it, Hub, I suggest you go back to the base and lock yourself in your office."

Hubbard studied Rapp for a moment and then nodded. "You don't have to worry about me getting all sensitive on you. I've been over here for two years. I've seen all kinds of crazy shit."

Most of that "crazy shit" was stuff done by the enemy. This time they would be the ones crossing the line. "I know you have," Rapp said, "but trust me, if we're going to get him back we are going to have to be more ruthless than you can imagine, and if at any point you start to have doubts, that's fine, step aside, but I need you to promise me you'll stick your head in the sand and keep your mouth shut."

Hubbard gave him a nervous smile. "I can do a Sergeant Schultz when I need to."

"Good," Rapp replied, even though he had his doubts.

"So where do you want to start?"

Rapp returned his attention to the row of dead men. "The bodyguards."

Hubbard turned his six-foot-five-inch frame toward the row of men and pursed his lips. "I think we can rule these four out."

Rapp focused on the man with the cratered face. An inside job was the obvious conclusion, but the bodyguards were all hardened Northern Alliance types. It was possible that one of them could have been bribed into giving up the crucial information on the security system, but unlikely. If one of them had turned, however, it was also possible that the Taliban, or whoever was responsible for this, had decided to kill the inside man as soon as they got what they wanted. The wrench in the works was that Rapp was pretty certain the Taliban had nothing to do with this. He pointed at the man missing part of his face. "Focus on this one. I want to know everything there is to know about him . . . especially his family. Do his parents or wife or kids have medical problems? Does he have a drug problem? Anything you can find."

"And the other eight?"

A team of interrogation experts from D.C. were in flight but not expected to land for another thirteen hours. "If you have the manpower, you can get started with them, but I doubt they'd hang around after something like this. What would you do if someone gave you a pile of cash to betray your buddies and a man like Rick?" Rickman's first name was Joe, but everyone who worked with him called him Rick.

"I'd run."

"That's right." Rapp pointed to the man who'd been shot with a .45 caliber. "Focus on this one for now."

"So you think the Taliban turned him?"

Rapp ignored the question for the moment and asked, "Who moved these bodies?"

"What do you mean?"

"The bodies," Rapp said as he pointed at the row of four. "They weren't shot here. Look at the blood on the floor. They were dragged here after they were killed." Rapp pointed at the stairs. "One of them was dragged down from the second story."

Hubbard shrugged. "They were lined up like this when I got here."

"Did the bodyguards move them?"

"Not that I know of. Do you want me to find out?"

"In a minute." Rapp looked toward the front door where one of the bodyguards was standing post with an AK-47 gripped in both hands. "The neighbors . . . did they hear or see anything last night?"

"No. Not a thing."

"No signs of forced entry?"

"Not that we've discovered, but they wouldn't need to force their way in if one of these guys were helping them."

"So no forced entry . . . four bodyguards . . . four headshots . . . four dead men. Anything about that seem unusual to you?"

Hubbard thought about it for a moment and said, "Not sure what you're driving at."

Rapp pointed at the bodies one after another, saying, "Nine-millimeter, nine-millimeter, nine-millimeter, .45 caliber, and my bet is they were all fired from suppressed weapons. Pretty accurate work. Good fire discipline. Look at the walls."

Hubbard did a 360-degree turn and said, "What about them?"

"You see anything?"

"No."

"That's the point. You ever seen the Taliban operate like this? Four shots, four hits, and not a shot more. The Taliban likes to get the lead out. You know their MO. They would have rolled up on this place with three or four trucks and started unloading RPG rounds at all three buildings. This place would be riddled with bullets. This was done by pros."

Hubbard made a sour face and then nodded. "Yeah . . . you're right. The towelheads like to blow shit up. This is more like something our guys would do . . ."

Hubbard kept talking, but Rapp had stopped listening. The idea that U.S. Special Operators had been involved was something he hadn't considered and something he didn't want to consider. From the moment Rapp had heard Rickman was missing, there was a gnawing fear that he was about to head down the rabbit hole. Rickman excelled at his job for the simple reason that he could think five, ten, fifteen, even twenty steps ahead of the enemy, and everyone else, for that matter. There had been many times when Rapp didn't understand what the man was up to because he wasn't smart enough to follow Rick's thinking.

"How about those assholes from the ISI?" Hubbard asked.

Rapp had considered the less-than-loyal members of the Pakistani Intelligence Service. They would be on the list as well as others. "Don't forget the Iranians, the Russians, and the Chinese." And there was one other possibility that Rapp wasn't quite prepared to mention.

"My money's on the ISI. This is just the kind of bullshit they'd pull."

A thought occurred to Rapp. "Where's the dog? That big frickin' Rottweiler that never left Rick's side?"

"Ajax . . . he died a month ago."

Rapp was surprised by the news. "What was wrong with him?"

"Don't know. Rick was pretty bummed out, though. Dog got sick, he took him to the vet and had to put him down. I think Rick said it was cancer or something like that."

One of Rapp's team members came down the stairs with a disturbed look on his face. The man had blond hair and blue eyes and was pushing fifty. "Not good," was all he had to say.

Rapp looked at Scott Coleman and said, "Please tell me you're talking about something other than the safe. Tell me the safe is untouched and all the cash, drives, and laptop are safely tucked inside."

Coleman shook his head. "All gone. Completely cleaned out."

Even though Rapp had expected it, he had held out some hope that he could give his boss a piece of good news. "Shit, I need to call Irene and let her know." Rapp reached for his phone, but stopped upon hearing a commotion at the front door.

CHAPTER 2

ABDUL Siraj Zahir admired himself in the mirror. At forty-eight he was an old man in his country. Even among the common people it was difficult to make it to manhood. In Zahir's line of work the challenge was much greater. He was a warrior, like his father and his father before him. His father and all three of his older brothers were dead. His father and the two oldest brothers had been killed by the Soviets and the third one had died at the hands of the Northern Alliance. Zahir had learned from their mistakes. Afghanistan was a brutal country where the only person you could really trust was someone from your own village. Beyond that, loyalties were an ever-shifting, complicated game.

Zahir had learned that to stay alive he had to be brutal and vigilant. He knew that some described him as sadistic and paranoid, and he wore that as a badge of honor—the more people who feared him the better. In Afghanistan, fear ruled. If you couldn't get men to fear you, you became a target. Zahir didn't want his life to end the way it had for his father and brothers, so he stoked the fear. It wasn't always easy, but had found that he was good at it.

Zahir pulled down on his gray uniform blouse, snapped his fingers, and then held out his arms. His aide rushed forward with Zahir's shiny black leather service belt. He buckled it around his boss's ample waist, made sure it was straight, and then stepped out of the way so Zahir could admire himself in the mirror. Zahir smiled at his reflection. His weapon was a still-unfired .40 caliber Smith & Wesson. The fact that Americans had given it to him for free made ownership all that much more delicious. He'd spent most of the last decade killing Americans, and now he was on their payroll.

Zahir noticed something wrong with his beard and moved closer to the mirror. His irritation was directed at a patch of gray that he had missed. He grabbed a bottle of black dye from his desk and inserted a small brush. After a few applications the gray was gone. Zahir smiled at his fine-looking beard and placed his hands on his hips. He looked good in his uniform. It was a little tight around the waist, but in Afghanistan his expanding middle section was a sign that he was a prosperous man.

Afghanistan was a unique place. It was like a petri dish for the survival of the fittest. Historically it had always been a harsh country; hot summers, cold winters, and rugged geography had shaped a breed of extremely tough people. For the last three decades a state of near-constant war had only heightened the selection process. Being physically strong was no longer enough. One had to be adept at reading the ever-shifting alliances that had shaped and reshaped the power structure of the isolated country. The Soviets had to be appeased and then the Americans and their Pakistani partners, who sponsored the crazed Wahhabi fighters from across the Persian Gulf, who in turn led to the Taliban and their enemies the Northern Alliance and a long civil war. Then the Americans and their coalition showed up and swept the Taliban from power in a matter of months.

Abdul Siraj Zahir had been able to look into the future on that day more than a decade ago and understand that the Taliban would be back. American airpower and their advanced weaponry had given him doubts along the way, but Zahir knew the Afghan people, and more important, the devout Muslims who represented the base of the Taliban. They would die to the last man before they let these godless people beat them. Zahir also knew that the Americans were too self-conscious to hunt the Taliban down like the dogs that they were and exterminate them.

So Zahir played them all against each other and never forgot the fates of his father and brothers. He held on to his little enclave southeast of Jalalabad and changed sides as many times as he needed to to survive. Zahir neither loved nor hated his country. He didn't think in those terms. He lived in this particular part of the world, like most of its people, because he had been born here. He considered himself to be an above-average intelligent person with a very good understanding of what motivated people and, more important, what they feared.

Despite his ability to sense the shift, winds of power, the most recent gigantic twist was something that even he had been unable to predict. After he had killed countless Americans, and taken their money, the fools had come to him with a job offer—a legitimate job offer. Not simply a bag of cash as they had done in the past for certain information. They wanted him to become commander of the local police force. He thought it was a trap, of course, but then he learned that other lions like himself had been offered and taken similar positions in the Afghan Police. It was a new push the Americans were calling the reintegration program.

He had been on the job for just six weeks, and he was already lining his pockets with bribes from local businessmen. The Taliban was a concern, of course. They would after all eventually work their way back into power, but not for a few more years, and in the meantime, Zahir would play both sides against each other. He would work for the Americans, take their money, and keep the Taliban informed of what they needed to know.

As always, the most important thing was to stay one step ahead

of seen and unseen enemies. Zahir had long ago surrounded himself with fiercely loyal people. There wasn't a man in his inner circle
whom he had known for fewer than ten years, and they were all from
his village. They were of his tribe, and in return for their loyalty he
protected their families. Zahir never spent more than two nights in
the same place, and even with his newfound legitimacy he continued
his old ways. Part of the reason was that he had four wives. They all
needed his attention, but it was beyond that. The axiom was extremely
simple: They couldn't kill him if they couldn't find him. Nights were
always the most dangerous. That was when the American killers
hunted. They used their optics advantage to harass and assassinate his
countrymen.

For many years now Zahir had avoided sleeping at night. He always made sure he was awake from midnight until one hour before
sunrise. That was the preferred time that the American dogs liked to
attack, so he stayed awake and on the move. He would then sleep in
the mornings and conduct business in the afternoons and evenings.
This morning, however, was different. After only a few hours of sleep,
Pamir, one of his most trusted men, had awoken him with a startling
piece of news. There was a rumor sweeping through the back alleys of
Jalalabad that a notorious American had been snatched from his for-
tress. Mr. Rickman was a very important man who had made many of
Zahir's countrymen extremely wealthy. Unfortunately, Mr. Rickman
had also spent a great deal of his time and money trying to kill Zahir.
There had been many close calls, but Zahir had always managed to
stay one step ahead of him. Now that Zahir was in a position to finally
receive some of the cash that the American was so famous for handing
out, someone had grabbed him.

Zahir had been silently berating himself all morning for not coming up with the plan first. With his newfound influence it was just the
type of operation he could have pulled off. Having been beaten to the
prize, however, he would now be forced to adapt. If the last thirty years

had taught him anything, it was that out of chaos came great opportunity, especially to those who were bold and ruthless.

In the reflection in the mirror, Zahir saw Pamir enter. The man did not wear the uniform of the Afghan Local Police. He had always been more suited to lurking in the shadows. "What have you learned?"

Pamir inclined his head slightly and said, "More Americans are at the house. I was told they flew in from Kandahar this morning and were driven to the house by the tall American."

"Hubbard?"

"Yes."

Zahir snorted. The CIA's local man was no match for him. It would be easy to manipulate him. "Was Mr. Sickles with them?"

"No."

This surprised Zahir. He had found it very pleasant to work with Sickles. It had been easy to pick up on the fact that Rickman and Sickles did not get along. Sickles had told him to stay well clear of Rickman. Had told him that the man was someone he had no control over, but still Sickles was the CIA's top man in Kandahar. "These new Americans . . . any idea who they are?"

"No." Pamir shook his head. "Only that there were six of them."

"Security?"

"Three Humvees . . . one normal, one with a 50-caliber turret, and another with a grenade turret."

"And men?"

"Eight total. They control each end of the street."

Zahir snorted again. They would never stop his police vehicles. He would push right past them. Turning to Raashid, his lieutenant, he asked, "Are the men ready?"

"Yes, sir."

"Good. Have everyone get in the vehicles. I want to make a show of force."

Pamir asked, "And what would you like me to do?"

"Keep looking for him and report to me the second you learn anything useful."

Pamir gave a slight bow and left. In his outer office, Zahir was happy to see more than a dozen men strapping on their new bulletproof vests and checking their weapons—all courtesy of the United States of America. *What a bunch of fools,* he thought to himself. The Americans were going to learn a very hard lesson over the next few months.

CHAPTER 3

A GROUP of men in Afghan Police uniforms were trying to push their way into the house. Rapp looked on with irritation as a man with an oily black beard berated the CIA bodyguards. The man's beard was obviously dyed. So much so that he looked like a silent-movie actor playing a pirate. To his right, he heard Hubbard muttering to himself. The only thing Rapp could make out were the words "This is not good."

"Who is he?" Rapp asked.

"Commander Abdul Siraj Zahir. ALP."

ALP stood for Afghan Local Police. "What's his story?"

"Up until six months ago he was an insurgent. More of a crime boss, really. Extorted and kidnapped in every village between here and the border, and now with the new reintegration program the geniuses in Kabul have seen fit to put him in charge of the local police."

The info clicked and Rapp remembered the name. Zahir and his group were responsible for a good number of the roadside bombs in the area. "Was he on Rick's payroll?"

"They were working on it." Hubbard motioned to the guards at the door and said, "It's all right. Let him in."

With obvious displeasure on his face, Zahir pushed his way past the guards and approached Hubbard, Rapp, and Coleman. He focused his attention on Hubbard and unleashed a torrent of expletives that were meant to punctuate his less-than-stellar view of Hubbard's abilities and his view in general of Americans.

Rapp took a step back, his dark eyes dissecting this strange man who had so rudely forced his way into the safe house. The bombastic behavior and bluster were not entirely unexpected, but something else was. The fact that Hubbard was letting this piece of human refuse walk all over him. Rapp reminded himself that Hubbard didn't have the luxury of flying under the radar as he did. He had to report to his boss in Kabul, Darren Sickles, who was more concerned with appearances than results. Sickles had to work side by side with the alphabet soup of U.S. agencies and departments that had come up with the touchy-feely reintegration program. The consensus with the foot soldiers in the Clandestine Service was that Sickles didn't back them up. Rapp was willing to bet that this unhealthy and unproductive style of cooperation had something to do with Sickles.

When Zahir was done berating Hubbard he turned to Rapp and Coleman and asked, "And who in the hell are these two? Why wasn't I called about these murders?"

Never one to run from a fight, Rapp squared himself so he was within striking distance of the police officer. Even though the man looked over fifty he was probably in his early forties like Rapp. Unlike Rapp, though, he was pudgy and out of shape. He had a little potbelly and that ridiculous shoe-polish-black beard.

Hubbard started to answer but Rapp reached out and grabbed his arm. Turning his eyes on the Afghani, Rapp said, "Who I am is none of your fucking business. As to why we didn't call you, that should be obvious. You're a thug and a piece of shit."

Zahir's face flushed with anger and he began to stutter.

Hubbard put up his hands and said. "Commander . . . what he's trying to say is that it has been a very busy morning and that we were about to call you."

Rapp kept his eyes on Zahir but directed his ire at the Jalalabad base chief. "Hub, shut up. That's not what I was about to say. I was about to tell this little yellow turd that I know exactly who he is, and if he has a half a brain he'll get the hell out of here before I shoot him."

"How dare you speak to me in such a way." Zahir stepped back and began clutching at his big leather holster for his sidearm.

From the right inside fold of his jacket, Rapp produced his Glock 19 in an easy, fluid motion. Zahir was still struggling with the flap on his holster when he looked up to find the square black frame of Rapp's gun in his face.

"I want you to listen to me," Rapp said in an easy tone, "and I don't want you to say a fucking word until I'm done."

Coleman had already drawn his gun, a big H&K .45 caliber, and maneuvered to cover the other two police officers who were just one step inside the doorway. The safety was already off and he spoke to the officers in Pashto, telling them to keep their hands where he could see them.

Rapp pressed the gun into Zahir's face just under his nose. "Here's what you need to know. I'm not some State Department weenie, or some two-star corporate general who thinks the best way to advance my career is to kiss your terrorist ass and get the hell out of this place so someone else can come deal with all you assholes again in twenty years. I'm the guy they call when the shit hits the fan. I'm the one they bring in to get results because they know I don't play by the rules. I know who you are. I know you've killed plenty of GIs and you've tormented and kidnapped your fellow citizens for your own profit. You're a bully and a piece of shit and you're the kind of guy who I actually enjoy killing. Normally I don't put a lot of thought into the people I shoot, but you fall into a special category. I figure I'd be doing the human race a favor by ending your worthless life. Add to that the fact that I'm in a really bad mood. In fact I'm in such a shitty mood that putting a bullet in your head might be the only thing that could make me feel better."

Rapp studied the man for a moment and then tilted his head toward his right shoulder as if he thought there might be some other way to deal with him. "In the interest of fairness, though, I suppose I should give you a chance to convince me otherwise."

Zahir's chest was heaving as he struggled to get his lungs working. His eyes nervously darted between Hubbard and this crazed man sticking a gun in his face. He'd been around plenty of killers and felt he could tell the difference between the pretenders and the men who meant what they said. This man had the look of someone who clearly meant what he said. The only lifeline that came to mind was the person who had negotiated Zahir into leaving behind his lawless ways.

"Mr. Sickles is a good friend of mine," Zahir sputtered. "He is a very good friend. He is a very important man. He will be very upset when he finds out about this."

Rapp's instincts were right. The Kabul station chief had put this goon in a position of power. "Darren Sickles," Rapp said, with contempt dripping from each word, "is important in his own mind, but that's about as far as it goes."

"He is the CIA's man here in my country!"

"He's an idiot, and the fact that he put you in a police uniform pretty much proves the point, so you're going to have to come up with something better than Darren Sickles."

Zahir licked his dry lips and struggled to find something that would make this American reconsider his vile threat. After an uncomfortably long silence, nothing had come to mind, so Zahir forced a smile on his face and retreated a step. "I think it would be best if I left."

Rapp grabbed the man's uniform shirt. "That's not an option. You either come up with a way to show me you might be useful, or I'm going to blow your brains all over the floor."

Zahir's eyes showed hope and he said, "Useful?"

"That's right."

"I can be extremely valuable."

"I'm listening."

"I know many people . . . I know many things. I can get you anything you want." Zahir's nature allowed him to go only so far, and he quickly added, "For the right price, of course."

"The right price," Rapp said, amused by the comment. "I'm going to tell you how this is going to work and that's only if you can prove to me that I should let you live. You're not going to get paid a dime. The only thing you'll get from me is your life, which I would assume is fairly important to you."

"It is very important to me, but I am not a wealthy man."

"Stop talking about money. You're boring me and if you bore me enough this negotiation will be over and you'll be dead."

"Tell me what it is you want me to do. I will do anything."

Rapp thought about Rickman. The truth was, very few people knew what the man was up to. In a general sense Kennedy and a few others knew his operational orders, but in terms of specifics, Rickman had left them in the dark. Zahir might be able to pull back the curtains on some of those details. "The man who lives here, you know him?"

"Mr. Rickman . . . very much. Yes. We were good friends."

"Let's not get carried away. Why did you decide to come here this morning?"

"I was driving by and I saw Mr. Hubbard's mercenaries. It looked like there was something wrong, so I stopped to investigate."

"Do I look stupid, Abdul?"

"No," he answered quickly. "I did not say that."

"Then tell me the real reason why you stopped." Rapp watched the man fidget. He was clearly trying to figure out a way to shade the truth. Rapp's patience was nearly gone, so he took his pistol and tapped Zahir on the top of his head. "I know lying is like breathing to you." Rapp shook his head as if he were admonishing a child. "You need to fight that. It's going to get you killed."

Zahir rubbed his head with his right hand. "I heard a rumor."

"What kind of rumor?"

"That something had happened to Mr. Rickman."

"Keep going."

"That something very bad happened. That he was missing."

"And you learned this how?"

Sharing information without getting something back was very foreign to Zahir, so he lied. "One of my men saw Mr. Hubbard leave the base in a panic. I started to make calls and soon found out that something was wrong at Mr. Rickman's house."

"So you were concerned for Mr. Rickman."

"Yes."

"And that's why you showed up here acting like a jackass and threatening people."

"No, I was concerned."

Rapp glanced at his watch. It was eight minutes past ten in the morning and he had a growing list of priorities that needed his immediate attention. Zahir, as disreputable as he was, might indeed have some use. Rapp made a quick decision. "Here's what we're going to do. You will work for me. You will find out who grabbed Mr. Rickman and you've got forty-eight hours to come up with the answers I need. If you fail me you're a dead man."

Zahir once again tried to retreat. He needed room to think and he couldn't do that with a gun in his face, but it did no good. The American simply followed him. Zahir's eyes pleaded for Hubbard to give him a reprieve. He didn't receive any help so he reverted to what he knew best. "How much will you pay me?"

Rapp laughed, but there was no levity in it. "I'm not going to pay you shit. In fact I'm going to do the exact opposite. If I find out you're fucking me, I'm going to text your photo to every jerkoff with a gun in this town and on the other side of the border as well, and I'm going to put a five-hundred-thousand-dollar bounty on your head. And if you think about heading for the hills I'll have a Predator on you twenty-four seven. If you make a call, if you step into the clear for a second I'll shove a Hellfire missile up your ass and blow you to hell."

To Zahir, the threat was all too real. He had used the CIA to decimate his own enemies by giving up their locations and phone numbers. The drone strikes were very effective. After a little consideration Zahir realized that at least for the moment he had no choice but to go along with this man. He slowly nodded his head and said, "I will see what I can do."

"If you want to live, you'll do more than that." Rapp lowered his gun and said, "Give me your phone."

Zahir scrambled to retrieve the phone from the breast pocket of his blue-gray uniform shirt. He surrendered it to Rapp, who handed it to Hubbard. "Go upstairs and give this to Sid. Tell her I want the usual and have our friends stateside move it into heavy rotation. Tell her I need a clone as well." Hubbard left and Rapp turned his focus back to Zahir. "We're going to be listening to everything you say, and if at any time I'm not satisfied with your efforts, our deal is off."

"Off?"

"Off means you broke the deal and you're dead."

"And what if I don't like this deal?"

Rapp raised his pistol and pointed it at the man's face. "It's pretty simple. I blow your brains all over the floor right now and you end up like those four guys over there." Rapp motioned toward the four bodyguards.

"You're not giving me much of a choice."

"And when you kidnap villagers and hold them for ransom, do you give them a choice?"

Zahir stubbornly refused to respond.

"I know you don't like this, Abdul, and the reason's pretty simple. You're a bully. You're used to pushing people around. Threatening them and their families with violence to get what you want. Now you're the one being bullied and you don't like it and I don't give a shit. The only thing that's important is that you understand and accept our deal. Do you?"

With the barrel of a gun in his face, Zahir knew he had only one option—to acquiesce. Later, when he was away from this madman, he could figure out a way to go back on the deal. "You have left me with no other choice."

"Good. I'd shake your hand but I know it wouldn't mean anything since you plan on fucking me over the first chance you get, so here's what we're going to do." Rapp grabbed his phone with his right hand, tapped a few icons, and then held it out to take a photo of Zahir. "Smile. This is for the poster I'm going to send out with a fifty-thousand-dollar bounty on your head."

"But you said . . ."

"Relax, I know what I said. If you come through with what I need, you'll be fine. I might even give you the fifty grand, but if I get even the slightest whiff that you're screwing with me, you're done. You have enough enemies as it is, if I put a bounty on your head, they'll be lining up to collect. Hell, it's probably cheaper than wasting a missile on your ass."

Hubbard came back with Zahir's phone and gave it to him. He handed a plain black flip phone to Rapp. Rapp held it up and said, "This is how we're going to talk to each other. I'll be able to track you with both phones, but this is the one we'll use to communicate." Rapp gave him the phone. "I'm going to call you in two hours and if you don't answer you're dead. If you answer the phone and tell me you haven't discovered anything you're dead. Do you understand how this is going to work?"

Zahir reluctantly stuffed the phone in his pocket and nodded. "What do I call you?"

"Harry," Rapp said, giving him one of his aliases. "Now get out of here and find out what happened to Joe Rickman."

CHAPTER 4

BETHESDA, MARYLAND

JOEL Wilson impatiently tapped the fingers of his right hand on his right thigh while he was driven through the dark streets of the sleepy Maryland neighborhood. It was a few hours before dawn, and the thought of waking his boss this early was less than appealing, but Wilson had learned the hard way that the stodgy old fool needed to be kept in the loop. It was becoming an increasing source of irritation for Wilson, whose unbridled energy did not often gel with the slower pace of Samuel Hargrave, the FBI's executive assistant director for national security. To those outside the Bureau, the job title meant little, but within the FBI it was a position that had grown significantly in stature after 9/11. Hargrave was in charge of Counterterrorism, Counterintelligence and the Directorate of Intelligence and Weapons of Mass Destruction. He dutifully reported to the top man at the FBI, and beyond that he kept an extremely low profile, and demanded the same of his people—another sore spot with Wilson.

In Wilson's succinct opinion, Hargrave was a relic from the FBI's Cold War days, a man who was no longer suited to handle the multiple threats of this faster-paced world. He reminded Wilson of that bushy-eyebrowed law professor in the movie *The Paper Chase*. He was a real pain in the butt who spent his life looking to catch the tiniest of mistakes while losing sight of the big picture. The man loved to point out every flaw no matter how small. He was the most anal-retentive, crotchety jerk Wilson had ever worked for. If only the fool would drop dead of an aneurysm, Wilson could get on with saving the country from the various threats that were circling.

Wilson believed that his job was the most difficult and demanding at the Bureau. He was the deputy director of Counterintelligence, which meant that he, not the CIA, was the tip of the spear. It was simple. The biggest threats to the nation were the foreign intelligence agencies and terrorist organizations that were looking to attack and weaken America. It was Wilson's job to stop them, and those Americans who might be aiding the enemy.

Hargrave was everything a boss shouldn't be. He was an obstacle to every decision and operation that Wilson tried to launch. Wilson's frustration had grown to the point that he began to cut Hargrave out of the decision process, only to be severely reprimanded by the director of the FBI himself. It was the lowest point of Wilson's otherwise sterling twenty-one-year career with the Bureau and it couldn't have come at a worse time. Wilson's boss, the man who ran the Counterintelligence Division, had been on leave for four months after a back surgery that didn't go as planned. Wilson had been asked to step in and take over as acting director. It was one of the three most coveted jobs at the FBI, and Wilson didn't balk at the opportunity. He took over as if he'd been running the place for several years, and not long after that he ran afoul of Hargrave.

Since then Wilson had explored every conceivable avenue around the man, but he'd been stymied. As the director himself eventually told Wilson, "The Federal Bureau of Investigation is big on chain of command for a reason." Wilson disagreed with them both, but he was not so bullheaded as to irritate the director again, so he kept Hargrave informed of his every decision, no matter how small. Wilson got the sense that Hargrave knew what he was up to, but so far the man had remained unflappable. Tonight's developments, however, might be enough to undo him.

But for now, Wilson was once again forced to perform this stupid dance. That was why he was rolling along this beautiful tree-lined street in Chevy Chase when he should have been with the rest of his team boarding one of the Bureau's Gulfstream 550s for a jaunt halfway around the globe. The vehicle began to slow and Wilson noticed his driver searching for the right address.

"It's up there on the left," Wilson said. "The white Colonial with green shutters." Under his breath he added, "Boring . . . just like his personality."

"Excuse me, sir?" the young agent asked.

"Nothing," Wilson replied.

Cal Patterson was in his third year with the Bureau and he considered himself a lucky man to be one of the youngest agents in the Counterintelligence Division. He liked his job, but his boss made him nervous. Patterson casually turned the wheel of the Ford Taurus and edged the sedan into the narrow drive. "Anything you'd like me to take care of while you're briefing the EAD, boss?"

Wilson grabbed the handle and said, "Check in with the Go Team. I want everyone on that plane and their gear stowed when we arrive. We should have been in the air an hour ago."

"I'll let them know, sir."

Wilson closed the car door and proceeded up the brick-lined walkway. He glanced through what looked like the dining room window and could see the faint glow of a light in what he presumed was the kitchen. The front stoop was small—enough for two people. Wilson reached out to press the doorbell and then caught himself. Probably better to knock at this hour. He held his left hand up to the door and rapped his knuckles twice on the green door. He waited a long moment and then heard the locking mechanism turn. The door cracked to reveal the high forehead of Samuel Hargrave. Without so much as a nod, Hargrave opened the door and motioned for Wilson to enter.

The senior man closed the door and started down the center hallway to the back of the house. Wilson took in the black leather slippers, the Black Watch plaid pajama bottoms, and the navy blue robe. The man looked as if he'd stepped off the set of a Cary Grant movie. Wilson started to ponder what it was like to be born fifty years too late, but before he got too far Hargrave asked him if he'd like a cup of coffee.

"No, thank you. I've already had my fill and I have a long flight ahead of me."

Hargrave stared at him for a moment, dissecting the words, trying to decode the shaded message. He poured himself a cup of black coffee and sat at the small four-person kitchen table. After a sip, he asked, "Long flight . . . where are you headed?"

"Afghanistan." Wilson offered nothing more.

"Afghanistan is a big country. Any place in particular?"

"Jalalabad."

"Jalalabad," Hargrave mused. "I think this is a first."

"A first?" Wilson frowned. "I don't understand, sir."

Hargrave had told him to call him Sam a hundred times, but Wilson still refused. It was a control thing, he knew, but Hargrave wasn't willing to make a big deal out of something so petty. Still, it was one more reason to worry that his acting director of Counterintelligence was someone who needed close monitoring. If he played these kinds of games with him, what must he be like with his colleagues and subordinates? How were his convictions when it came to following the law? Hargrave had learned long ago that these little things could eventually spell big problems for the Bureau.

"In all the years I've been doing this, I've been pulled out of bed for a lot of reasons, but no one has ever told me they're flying to Jalalabad." Hargrave set his cup down and rubbed his eyes. "We really have become a global law enforcement agency."

No shit, you moron, Wilson thought. *Where the hell have you been for the last decade?*

"So why Jalalabad?"

"Joe Rickman." Wilson had a bigger target in mind, but Rickman would do for now.

Hargrave was familiar with the name. He'd heard some rumblings that the covert officer had become a bit of an obsession with Wilson. He could tell the temperamental Wilson was on edge so he chose his words carefully. "What has Mr. Rickman done now?"

"I received a tip three hours ago that he was kidnapped from a safe house in Jalalabad."

Hargrave did not speak for several moments. His mind was occupied with all of the ramifications of someone like Joe Rickman's falling into the hands of America's enemies. To say that the men and women at Langley would be distraught would be an understatement. "Do you know who took him?"

"No, but I find the timing suspicious."

"Suspicious?" Hargrave asked with a curious tone.

"I have been investigating him for the past two months." Rickman as well as a few others, but Hargrave didn't need to know that.

"Excuse me?" Hargrave asked, not quite sure he'd heard right.

"Starting almost a year ago I began to receive some disturbing information about Mr. Rickman. Accusations that he was siphoning off large amounts of money from his covert fund and that he was getting a little too close to some nefarious individuals."

Hargrave closed his eyes and then held up his right hand. "You've known about this for almost a year and didn't bring it to my attention?"

Wilson's back stiffened. "It didn't *warrant* your attention, sir. It was nothing more than rumors to begin with. If I passed along every rumor that came into my office, I'd be running upstairs to meet with you eight times a day."

Hargrave could feel the pressure building and reminded himself that his doctors had warned him against getting too upset. "Mr. Rickman," he said slowly, "is a unique individual. Anything concerning him and his activities automatically rises to the top of the heap, so I don't accept your premise. I am very disappointed that you decided to keep this from me." Hargrave shook his head and added, "We've been over this before. You were told by the director himself what was expected of you."

Wilson had known this was how it would play out and he was ready. "I am sorry, sir, but there are some extenuating circumstances."

"Really?"

"Yes."

"I'm listening."

Wilson intentionally fidgeted in his chair. He wanted to convey the sense that he was taking all this very seriously. "The information was originally passed on to me by a very important person who did not want their name connected to this in any way."

Hargrave had started his career at the FBI, and then at the age of forty he was appointed to the U.S. Foreign Intelligence Surveillance Court. He had spent eleven years on the bench and knew how this game was played. "And that person is?"

"I'm afraid I can't say, sir." Wilson tried to appear stoic, although inside he took great joy in the fact that Hargrave's pale face had turned suddenly red.

"That is unacceptable. We sat in the director's office less than a month ago and he specifically told you that you were to keep me involved in any investigations your office was handling. There was no gray area." Hargrave shook his head. "The director is going to be very disappointed. I'm not sure you're going to be catching that flight to Jalalabad."

Wilson had expected this and was prepared to take the right tack. "Sir, there has been no investigation, just some very troubling accusations made by a very prominent player. I didn't feel it was right to bring any of this to your attention because frankly it was beneath you. Until

I could figure out if these accusations were fact or fiction I didn't want to give the matter any more life than it deserved."

Hargrave dissected the words for a few seconds and said, "I'll ask again. Who is the power player who made the accusations?"

"I'd rather not say, sir."

"I'm sure you wouldn't, but that's not how this works. I'm your boss and if you want to fly to the other side of the world and spend taxpayer dollars investigating a fellow federal employee, you need to read me in."

Wilson crossed his legs and made a great show of looking at the round clock on the wall. He sighed and offered, "The person in question is a senator, sir, and as part of our agreement, he made me swear that his name would not be dragged into this."

"How convenient."

"I'm not making this up," Wilson said defensively.

"It doesn't matter. If you want to get on that plane you are going to tell me the name of this mystery senator."

"Sir, I gave my word."

"I'm losing my patience, Joel. I'm your boss. This isn't the Cub Scouts, it's the FBI, and we have rules and laws that we are duty bound to follow. A personal promise you made to a politician holds no water with us. You are going to tell me everything you know right now, or I will call Dulles and pull your flight plan and then in about four hours I'll be having breakfast with the director and I will brief him on your most recent activities. When I'm done, he will ask me for my recommendation as to your future as acting director of Counterintelligence." Hargrave paused and stared at Wilson for an uncomfortably long moment. "Based on your refusal to follow the most simple of orders I'm fairly certain my recommendation will be less than stellar."

Wilson had been fairly certain this was how this little drama would play out, but in order to make it convincing he had needed to follow his script. He blurted out the name. "Carl Ferris."

 Hargrave nearly choked. "You mean to tell me you launched an investigation based on innuendo from one of the biggest partisan hacks to ever serve in the United States Senate?"

Wilson played dumb. "I have no opinion on the man, sir. When a sitting U.S. senator asks for a private meeting I take it very seriously."

"Good God, you fool," Hargrave said haltingly. "I don't believe for a second that you are that naïve." Hargrave was on his feet pacing now—his brain struggling for a way to unwind this potential mess before it saw the light of day. Carl Ferris was a master manipulator of the media and the supposed facts they reported.

Wilson offered an additional piece of information. "He told me you had it in for him."

"Excuse me?"

"Senator Ferris told me that you didn't like him. He wouldn't get into specifics, but he said it had something to do with your days on the FISA bench."

Hargrave turned to Wilson and said, "The issue he is alluding to is sealed and not up for discussion, but I can tell you that the senator did not comport himself well."

"I don't want to get in the middle of a pissing match between you two. What happened is none of my business."

"There is no pissing match." Hargrave didn't like the way Wilson had turned this into a personal matter. "What's at issue here is that you have once again failed to keep me informed of what you are up to and now you are about to get on a plane with one of my Go Teams and insert yourself into an extremely delicate situation." Hargrave grabbed the back of one of the chairs and said, "Let me ask you something. Have you bothered to think of how our friends at the CIA are going to react when you show up and start sticking your nose in the middle of this mess?"

"Personally, I couldn't care less what those Neanderthals at Langley think."

Hargrave had encountered this type of behavior in others before and he knew how destructive it could be. "We are on the same team," he said flatly.

"And my job is to make sure we stay on the same team."

"What is that supposed to mean?"

"In my department no one is above suspicion. My job is to stop the enemy from penetrating our national security apparatus, and the easiest way for the enemy to do that is to get one of our people to turn on us."

"What are you implying?"

"I'm implying nothing. The facts are that Joe Rickman is one of the darkest spooks this country has. He's a walking, breathing encyclopedia of things that are so wrong it's ridiculous. If he has been kidnapped it is our duty to offer Langley our capable assistance if for no other reason than that we need to get a handle on the breadth of the damage. We should be the coordinating agency, because God knows Langley will want to admit only a fraction of the possible damage. We need a full accounting of our exposure."

Hargrave didn't want to but he had to concede the point. Six months from now it might look very bad if he forced Counterespionage to sit this out. "I see where you're coming from, but I want you to play nice."

"I will be there to offer assistance in finding Rickman, and if along the way I see that any laws have been broken I will consult you before I move my investigation in a new direction."

"That's what I wanted to hear."

Wilson smiled. There was no need to report his other concerns at this point. As Senator Ferris had already warned him, Hargrave wouldn't believe them anyway. Wilson stood, saying, "Thank you, sir. Now if you'll excuse me, I need to get moving."

"One more thing, Joel. I want you to check in with me every day. I need to know what you're up to."

"I was planning on it, sir."

Hargrave walked Wilson to the door and watched him leave. He didn't believe for a second that Wilson was planning on keeping him informed, and he found it even less believable that Wilson was planning on simply aiding the CIA in finding Rickman. All things considered, though, he had to let him go. Rickman was a valuable asset and the FBI needed to make sure the broader national security interests were being looked after. Still, he couldn't shake the feeling that there was something else going on here. Something that Wilson was keeping from him.

CHAPTER 5

JALALABAD, AFGHANISTAN

HUBBARD was clearly agitated. He'd gone over to the window to watch Zahir and his men leave. Rapp ignored him and took a moment to discuss something he wanted Coleman to follow up on. Rapp was just finishing his point when Hubbard approached them.

Hubbard blinked several times and asked Rapp, "Do you have any idea what you've just done?"

"I think so," Rapp replied calmly.

"I'm not sure you do. That man is crazy." Hubbard pointed toward the door as if Zahir was still there. "I have to work with him. What in the hell were you thinking?"

Rapp remained cool and said, "You can't bribe a guy like that. He'll screw you over in the end. Every time. The only way to deal with a guy like Zahir is to make him fear for his life."

Hubbard was incredulous. "Darren is going to flip when he finds out. He's worked nearly a year to bring Zahir back into the fold."

At the mention of Sickles's first name Rapp began to lose his grip. "Darren is an idiot."

"Idiot or not, he's my boss and the Agency's top guy here in Afghanistan."

"Are you done?" It was more of a warning than a question.

"No . . . I'm not done. I'm far from done. You're going to be here for a week or two at the most and then you'll head back to the States and I'll have to deal with him. You don't know shit about Zahir. He's a ruthless son of a bitch. He's probably going to kill me."

"Then kill him first," Rapp growled.

Hubbard looked at Rapp as if he'd lost his mind. "Darren's his handler . . . I can't kill him."

"I'll deal with Darren. In the meantime you need to grow a set of balls. The way you let him walk in here and talk to you. What the hell is wrong with you? You work for the damn Agency, Hub, not the State Department. Start acting like it, or find another job. Shit . . . you've got mercenaries, former Taliban, Northern Alliance, former coalition Special Forces . . . they're all hanging out looking to make a buck. You could have gone to Rick, given him ten or twenty grand, and found fifteen guys that'd be willing to shoot the prick in the head when he left his house in the morning."

"It's not that easy."

"Really?" Rapp asked, his jaw clenched with anger. "Well, then I must be frickin' Superman, because I've lost track of how many scumbags like Zahir I've plugged over the years. It's not fuckin' rocket science," Rapp said, poking Hubbard in the chest.

"Darren would lose his mind," Hubbard said in his own defense.

"I just told you, I'll deal with Darren." Rapp couldn't wait to get his hands on the pencil-pushing prick. "Right now I need you to work every source you have. Start shaking the trees and find out what happened to Rick, and if you run into Zahir and he so much as looks at you the wrong way I want you to call me. Do you understand?"

Hubbard slowly nodded, knowing it was unwise to continue to push the point with Rapp. "Yeah, I'll get on it."

"Good, and remember, we need to move fast." Rapp heard his

name called from upstairs. He looked at the staircase and then back at Hubbard. He slapped the taller man on the shoulder and said, "Remember who we are, Hub. Don't take any crap . . . especially for the next forty-eight hours. If we don't get Rick back, Zahir is going to be the least of our problems."

Hubbard moved toward the door. Coleman stood at Rapp's side, his .45 caliber H&K hanging loosely at his side. When the junior operative was gone, Coleman said, "I'm not sure he's cut out for this job."

Rapp wasn't sure either, but he couldn't be mad at Hubbard. "If Darren Sickles had been my boss God only knows how I would have turned out."

Coleman kept his blue eyes focused on the door and said, "If Darren Sickles had been your boss, you would have killed him. Hell, Stan was your boss and you almost killed him, and he's one tough bastard. Sickles is a pussy."

Rapp thought of Stan Hurley, the man who had trained him. Pound for pound, Hurley was the toughest man Rapp had ever known—one mean son of a bitch. That was more than twenty years ago, though. More recently, Hurley had begun to show his age. His mind was still sharp as hell, but he was looking frail. "They don't make 'em like Stan anymore."

Coleman cracked a smile. "They sure don't, but you're not too far off."

Rapp feigned insult. "Are you trying to say I'm some crotchety, set-in-his-ways old man who drinks and smokes too much and still chases women like I'm in my twenties?"

"You're more like him than you'll ever admit. If he was here the two of you would have gotten in a fight over who got to stick a gun in that terrorist's face."

Rapp laughed. "Yeah, and he would have won and then he would have flown up to Kabul and done the same thing to Sickles."

"Well, the day's far from over. I'd say there's a better than fifty-fifty chance you and Sickles will have it out."

Rapp cursed under his breath. *One more thing to deal with*, he thought to himself. He heard his name called again and walked to the bottom of the stairs, stepping around the dead bodyguards. He looked up the flight of stairs and said, "What's up?"

A brunette poked her head around the corner and said, "I think you should come up here. There's something you need to see."

Rapp started up the stairs, keeping his feet near the wall so as to not step in the trail of smeared blood. Sydney Hayek was the newest member of Rapp's team, and it had been Kennedy's idea to have Hayek fill a vacant spot. Rapp had been less than enthused for several reasons. The first was pretty straightforward—his line of work didn't lend itself toward trusting people. The room for error was thin and the stakes were so high that Rapp preferred running an op with an understaffed team over risking a new recruit who might get the entire team killed. The second reason for his apprehension was obvious—Hayek had come to them from the FBI.

Rapp hit the top landing and asked, "What's up?"

Like the rest of the team, Hayek was wearing an olive drab field jacket, the pockets stuffed with the various tools of the trade. As directed by Rapp, she wore her flak jacket under her field jacket to draw less attention. She was also wearing a pair of jeans, a pair of Merrell hiking boots, and a blue Detroit Tigers baseball cap with a light and a small fiberoptic camera clipped to each side of the visor. She looked at Rapp with her almond eyes and asked, "Scott told you about the safe?"

"Yeah. Any sign of forced entry?"

"No. I'm afraid it looks like it was opened by Mr. Rickman."

Rapp frowned. "Let's not jump to any unfounded conclusions."

Hayek shrugged. "I never met the man, but I assume he was the only person within a couple thousand miles who had the code."

It was more like seven thousand miles, but Rapp didn't bother to correct her. Hayek had grown up in Detroit, the only daughter of Armenians who had emigrated from Lebanon. She was fluent in Arabic and, most important, she could walk down the streets of nearly any

Middle Eastern city without anyone giving her a second glance. In response to her accusation, Rapp said, "He was the only one with the code."

"Well, the safe was opened using the code. There was no tampering with the locking mechanism and as best I can tell it wasn't hacked."

"You're sure."

"As sure as I can be after being here less than an hour."

Rapp tried to picture how it had gone down. "So he was forced to open the safe at gunpoint."

"I didn't know the man, so I can't say."

After working with her for seven months Rapp was starting to get a sense of how Hayek operated. It was more what she didn't say than what she said. "You have some concerns."

"I always have concerns."

"Share them."

"Some things don't make sense."

"Such as?"

She hesitated and then said, "Come here and I'll show you." They started down the hall. "Careful where you step."

Rapp looked down and stepped around a sizable pool of blood. That was when he noticed the splatter on the wall. "What's this?"

Hayek looked over her shoulder. "One thing at a time. I want to show you the office first." She entered the room and walked behind the desk. There were no windows, the walls and ceiling were covered with acoustic foam, and the floor was covered with a series of rubber squares. Behind the desk, a narrow door covered in foam was open. Behind it was the open safe.

"What am I looking for?" Rapp asked.

"Nothing." Hayek turned off the lamp on the desk and then hit the UV light on her visor. She looked down at the floor in front of the safe and then expanded the area, sweeping the light back and forth. "No blood. Not a drop."

"I still don't get it."

"Come here." She walked across the room and stepped into the hallway. She hit the light switch and extinguished the hallway lights. The UV light on her visor lit up splotches and splatters of blood. "Lots of blood out here, but none in there. Now, I don't know Rickman, but I've heard he was a pretty serious man."

"Your point?"

"I've been around you long enough to guess that someone would have to beat you to a bloody pulp before you'd even think of opening that safe."

Rapp nodded.

"There's no blood in the office."

"The rough stuff could have started anywhere . . . down in the kitchen."

Hayek shook her head. "And there would be blood in that office . . . even if it were just small traces, but there isn't any."

Hayek's theory was slowly sinking in. "What else do you have?"

"This mess." Hayek pointed at the blood on the wall. "Best guess is it belongs to one of the bodyguards downstairs."

"The one missing half his face?"

"Yeah." Hayek edged closer to the wall. She pointed at a gooey chunk. "I have samples of everything and I'll be able to test them for verification when we get back stateside, but I'm 99 percent sure this is brain matter with a little bit of bone and blood. Consistent with the gunshot wound received by John Doe number four downstairs."

"And this should interest me how?"

"Look at the pattern of the splatter." Hayek acted as if she was holding a gun. "The bodyguard would have been facing this way toward the stairs. The person came up and shot him from behind. The bullet tore through his head, exited, leaving this large splatter on the wall, and then the bodyguard fell facedown here. That's why there's the big pool of blood."

Rapp studied the blood splatter on the wall. It all lined up. "I agree. So what's your point?"

"Three of the four guards were shot in the face . . . makes sense. They were reacting to the intrusion. Going to meet the threat. This one, though, is shot in the back of the head. Doesn't make sense. He should have been shot over there at the top of the stairs, by the perps coming up the stairs."

Rapp ignored her police talk. He was a little irritated with himself for not seeing it sooner. "How closely did you look at the bodies downstairs?"

"Close enough."

"Did you take measurements of the entrance wounds?"

"Not exact, but I'm pretty confident that the first three men were shot by a nine-millimeter."

"And you know that how?"

Hayek held up a Ziploc bag with three brass shell casings. "I found these on the floor."

"And the fourth man?"

Hayek shook her head. "I've looked all over this hallway and the stairs and I can't find the casing."

"Best guess on the caliber?"

"Best guess . . . a .45 . . . hollow point. Definitely not the same caliber that took out the other guys."

Rapp ran all the information through his head, knew where it was taking him, but didn't want to go there even though he knew he had to. He looked back in the office. There was no sign of struggle. Not a thing out of place. The hallway was a bloody mess. Rapp's eyes focused on the Rorschachlike splatter. "I suppose the slug is buried in that wall."

"Yeah . . . I was going to dig it out but I wanted to ask you first. I don't know this team coming in from Langley . . . don't want to step on their toes."

It would be a problem but Rapp could deal with it. "Dig it out as quick as you can. Anything else you need to tell me about?"

Hayek hesitated and then said, "No."

"What is it?"

"Nothing." She shook her head. "I'll know more when I start matching up the blood samples with the bodies. I think we'll be able to get a pretty clear picture of where everyone was when this thing went down."

"Nice work, Sid. Do me a favor and keep this between the two of us. Until we know for certain, I don't want anyone running around pedaling half-baked ideas. Anyone leans on you, send them to me. Understood?"

Kennedy had asked her to relay as much information as possible as quickly as possible. Hayek could see that she was caught between her two bosses, but Rapp was just starting to trust her, so she said, "Understood."

"Good. Wrap things up and be ready to pull out in ten."

"What's the rush?"

"There's a meeting back in Kabul. The whole alphabet soup."

"You hate those kinds of meetings."

"I hate any meeting, but especially this kind." Rapp thought of Sickles running the meeting without him. Why the man worked for the Company was beyond Rapp's ability to comprehend. "I need to make sure a certain idiot doesn't make this shit show any worse than it already is."

CHAPTER 6

U.S. EMBASSY, KABUL, AFGHANISTAN

"I'VE never even heard of this man," the woman said with obvious frustration. "Who the hell does he think he is?"

Colonel Hunter Poole took a final drag from his cigarette, then tossed it to the gravel and crushed it with the heel of his black jump boot. "I don't know much about him."

"But you've heard of him?"

Poole knew he needed to be careful. Arianna Vinter was a passionate woman whose one glaring weakness was that she thought she could bully her way to any victory, and from what he'd heard about this Rapp fellow, it was probably not wise to attack him in a direct fashion. Poole shrugged and said, "He's a spook. They don't exactly advertise their resumes."

Vinter regarded her military man with a skeptical squint of her hazel eyes. "You're holding back."

Poole played it cool. "I've heard a few things . . . the kind of stuff that doesn't make it into official reports." He lit another cigarette and said, "He's notorious in certain circles."

"Notorious how?" Vinter asked, taking a deep pull off her thin menthol cigarette.

Their liaisons had become increasingly common. The embassy was a crowded, cramped place, and smoking indoors by Americans was strictly forbidden, even in a country where virtually everyone smoked. And then there was the simple fact that they needed to be careful about their relationship. So they came to this corner of the compound where the multicolored shipping containers were stacked. It was the hinterlands, where the workers and the occasional jarhead came to replenish supplies, but never the higher-ups from the embassy, and Poole and Vinter were definitely higher-ups.

Poole placed a hand against a rust-colored Conex container and thought about the various rumors regarding Mitch Rapp. The man, like Poole, was in his midforties. Unlike Rapp, however, Poole had a sterling record. He'd graduated in the top 5 percent of his class from West Point, completed Ranger School, and then blazed a trail through the big Green Machine with stops at the U.S. Army Command and General Staff College and the John F. Kennedy School of Government at Harvard University. He was a platoon leader in the first Gulf War, and by the time the Iraq campaign started he was the company commander of Alpha Company, Second Ranger Battalion. He completed three combat tours with the Rangers, two in Afghanistan and one in Iraq. During his second tour in Afghanistan he was serving as an intelligence officer on the Joint Special Operations Command staff when he heard his commanding officer tell a story about a CIA covert officer who had bluffed his way into a detention facility at the Bagram Air Base by impersonating a U.S. Air Force colonel from the Office of Special Investigations.

A week earlier two high-value Taliban commanders had been caught on the battlefield and thus far had refused to talk. In less than an hour Rapp managed to get one of the men to spill the beans on an impending terrorist operation set to target the United States. The rumors about how he pulled this off were varied, but they all circled around some very Orwellian tactics that created a mix of awe and fear among the men at JSOC. There were other stories out there about Rapp, most of them from second- or third-hand accounts of his exploits in Indian country. If they were to be believed, Rapp was a person capable of extreme violence, with little concern for his own mortality and an absolute disregard for the political and legal issues that the men and women in uniform had to wrestle with.

Poole had followed the rules as any smart West Pointer would, and he was now on the doorstep of receiving his first star—a lifelong dream, but that wasn't where it was going to end. Poole felt he had the right stuff. Shooting for the chairmanship of the Joint Chiefs was his ultimate goal, and if that worked out, who knew, maybe even the Oval Office was a possibility. Up until recently Poole would have found it difficult to understand a man like Rapp. Poole had been a rule follower, but Vinter had opened his eyes to the reality of Washington. She had shown him that there were times where rules were senseless obstacles. Rapp appeared to have built his entire career and reputation on the same philosophy. As enticing as it was to cut corners, Poole knew he needed to be careful. The U.S. Army was an entirely different playground. One misstep in the eyes of the wrong general and your career was over.

It was the fear of just that kind of misstep that caused Poole to temper what he knew about Rapp. "It's not easy to separate fact from fiction where he's concerned, but if you believe even half of what is said about him, he's an extremely reckless individual." *The kind of man that could sink my career*, Poole thought to himself.

"Dammit!" Vinter flicked her cigarette into the side of the container, sparks cascading to the ground. "The last thing we need right now is some brute from the CIA screwing this up. I've worked way too hard." Vinter thought of her career at the State Department and all of the sacrifices she'd made to climb the ladder alongside all of the other scheming and plotting diplomats. She'd taken this god-awful posting in Afghanistan for multiple, complicated reasons and one very simple one—because it would further her career. Vinter hated Afghanistan. It was a country filled with people who were stuck in some ancient misogynistic culture that should have died a century ago. The place was filled with hocus-pocus religious fanatics, who had less respect for women than most men had for their dogs.

As much as it bothered Vinter that a bunch of bearded freaks could terrorize women with impunity while the U.S. government stood by, her boss had made it clear that there were other priorities. The orders had come from the White House that with the election bearing down on the administration they needed to accelerate the military withdrawal. The administration was looking for an excuse, any excuse that would satisfy the independent voters. For several years, Vinter had been pushing reintegration as a solution. The original term had been amnesty, but it didn't poll well, so she came up with something more benign. After multiple focus groups and $125,000 to one of K Street's top PR firms, they landed on reintegration. The word had a more clinical sound to it, but more important, it would pave the way for exit and victory.

It was one of those rare moments in Vinter's career when her genius had led to something that she didn't want. It had been nearly a year ago when the secretary of state's assistant told her to come on up to the palatial office for a very important meeting. It started out well enough. The secretary told her the president loved her idea. Vinter had beamed with pride, like a child finally receiving due recognition from a distant parent, and then came the bad part. The president wanted her to take the lead, run with her idea, and make sure it got implemented. Her boss told her, "The president wants you on the ground in Kabul supervising the entire operation. You'll report directly to me. We're putting a lot of power in your hands. The ambassador will be told to aid you in any way you need and the White House is prepared to lean very heavily on the Pentagon and the CIA to make sure they support you. For all intents and purposes you will be running the show in Afghanistan."

Vinter didn't really hear the rest of it; her mind hung up on the part about living in Kabul, as if it were some bone-jarring pothole in an otherwise smooth road. Vinter had traveled to Afghanistan on multiple occasions, and she had long ago decided that she detested the place, but this was a career maker. She knew almost immediately that if she did her year or two in hell she could demand any post she wanted afterward. Her husband was not thrilled that she had failed to consult him on the decision, but she knew he wouldn't have the balls to really stand up to her. And besides, her teenage son was driving her nuts. There was too much testosterone in the house for her liking. She rationalized that it might be the best thing for her to take a break from the two men in her life, and if it caused her marriage to fall apart, that was something she could deal with. After seventeen years, change might not be the worst thing.

"He's a small cog in an extremely big wheel," Poole said, trying to calm her down.

Vinter was an extremely intelligent and passionate woman, but she could handle only one passion at a time, and Poole was more interested in getting her to hike up her skirt at the moment. He reached out and placed his right hand on her shoulder. "One call to the secretary and you can have him shipped off to Antarctica." He started rubbing her shoulder.

Vinter turned that possibility over in her mind until she figured out that her little Army boy was a bit too earnest in his physical contact. "What in the hell are you doing?"

"I'm trying to help you relax. You don't think clearly when you get like this."

"And you don't think clearly when you let your dick do your thinking. I've seen that look in your eye before. You're not worried about me thinking clearly, you're focused on having sex." Vinter saw the playful grin on Poole's face. "It's only been, what . . . six weeks and I already have you figured out. There will be no screwing back here between the storage containers like a couple of dogs in heat. It happened once. It was a moment of weakness, and it will never happen again."

"Come on," Poole half moaned. He pulled her close, adding, "I need you."

"You had me two days ago. I don't think you need it that bad."

"Normally I'm not like this, but you make me crazy." He kissed her lips while his hands found her backside.

Vinter pushed him away. "We have a meeting in ten minutes. Snap out of it. Zahir is threatening to take his men and go back to the mountains. If that happens it could create a domino effect and all of the progress I've achieved over the past year will vanish. All because some spook got kidnapped." She thought about the strange turn of events. "I hear this mercenary who is trying to undo all of our hard work is going to show his face at the meeting."

Poole pulled Vinter's hand toward his crotch. "Speaking of hard."

Vinter almost slapped him. "Stop it. We need to focus. Darren is absolutely beside himself. He says this Rapp has serious mental issues. Do you know what Washington will do if they hear we screwed this up?"

Poole had finally got it through his head that they weren't going to have sex. He took a deep sigh. "You're making way too big of a deal out of this. We didn't screw anything up. We're on schedule with reintegration. If this thing goes off the tracks at this point we blame it on Rapp. We lay it at the feet of the CIA and get out of the way."

"That doesn't work for me. I don't fail." Vinter stabbed herself in the chest with her index finger, attempting to add some unneeded emphasis to her position. Her hazel eyes wild with fury, she added. "I'm not going back to D.C. a fucking disaster."

Poole sighed. It appeared that a confrontation was unavoidable. He wondered if there was any way to minimize the oncoming clash. Vinter would expect 100 percent support from him, but Poole had already decided it would be foolish to confront Rapp in such an open way. Poole had learned that when going into battle against an unknown enemy you must set your ego aside and have a contingency in place for a tactical withdrawal. That was the careful course he would have to navigate. Vinter would scream at him later, but even with the great sex, he was growing tired of her browbeatings. Maybe this would present an opportunity to balance the scales and make her more compliant.

"I'm going to support you, but I'm warning you he might not be the kind of guy you want to pick a fight with."

"Well, I'm not the kind of woman you want to pick a fight with. And it's not going to be a fight. I'm going to tear his balls off and send him packing and that's going to be the end of it."

As much as Poole wanted to believe her, he shared none of her confidence. "Arianna, I know I'm not going to be able to change your mind, but don't tell me I didn't warn you." Having no desire to hear her response, Poole turned and began making his way toward the main building.

CHAPTER 7

INTER-SERVICES INTELLIGENCE HQ, ISLAMABAD, PAKISTAN

N ADEEM Ashan walked down the broad hallway with a sense of dread. After twenty-nine years of working for Pakistani intelligence, one would think Ashan would be used to these bumps in the road, but this particular bump concerned him for reasons that he was extremely reluctant to share with anyone else in the building. Ashan was an expert navigator when it came to the turbulent waters of the ISI, and that historical knowledge only added to his growing concern. The place was not some monolithic bureaucracy where like-minded men shaped the intelligence-gathering and covert activities of Pakistan. The ISI was a deeply divided, sectarian institution composed of intelligence professionals and military personnel who had vastly different ideas about what was best for their country.

The main fault line lay between the secularists and the religious fanatics, with various groups within each camp. The secularists typically pushed for modernity and stability. They had warned for years that the intelligence agency's support of the Taliban in Afghanistan and Lashkar-e-Taiba in Kashmir, India, would eventually bite them in their proverbial behind. The religious fanatics saw the Taliban as an ally that could be used to keep neighboring Afghanistan weak, and the fiercely nationalistic element of the group refused to waver in their support for the terrorists in Kashmir. Their hatred for India ran so deep that they blindly supported the savages who intentionally killed civilians in an effort to make Kashmir a free state.

The hard-liners were exposed as reckless fools in the aftermath of the Mumbai terrorist attacks that left 195 dead and the world-famous Taj Hotel a smoldering ruin. The international outcry was deafening. As the deputy general for Analysis and Foreign Relations, Ashan heard it the loudest. Even before the attacks on New York and Washington, Ashan had had a very close relationship with the CIA and MI-5. After those attacks, Ashan began to see just how dangerous it was to support the mongrel dogs of jihad. Even President Musharraf began to see the light, and when he moved to support the United States in the War on Terror, those dogs turned on him and tried unsuccessfully to take his life seven times during his tenure as Pakistan's head of state. Only five of those incidents had been reported. Ashan and his colleagues at ISI helped cover up the other two due to the conspirators' ties to certain intelligence officials.

All of these incidents were embarrassing for the ISI, but none of them compared to what was uncovered when the Americans sent in one of their elite commando units to kill the world's most notorious terrorist. Bin Laden, it turned out, had been hiding in Pakistan for years. Ashan instantly knew that factions within the ISI had been harboring him. Money would have changed hands, to be sure, but the primary motivation was undoubtedly ideological symmetry. No matter how Pakistan tried to deny it, there were a significant number of men in the Pakistani military and ISI who supported and applauded the actions of the Taliban and al Qaeda.

Ashan was on his way to see just such an individual. Lieutenant General Akhtar Durrani was the deputy general of the ISI's External Wing. Durrani and Ashan ran two of the ISI's three main groups. Their influence was vast, and they both reported directly to the ISI's director

general. Ashan managed to move back and forth between the secularists and the hard-liners depending on the situation, while Durrani was
firmly in the camp of the hard-liners. Ashan's pragmatism was driven
by an obvious fact—Pakistan was overwhelmingly a Muslim country.

Ashan moved past the handpicked military bodyguards and his
colleague's male personal assistant with nothing more than a nod. ISI
Headquarters was a sprawling compound and the Foreign Relations
Wing was a healthy distance from the offices of the External Wing,
but even so, the two deputy generals were very close. Almost every
day Ashan made the lengthy walk from his office to Durrani's. Unlike most of the Pakistani men his age, Ashan was very focused on his
health. Neither of his parents had made it to sixty. His father died of a
heart attack brought on by years of smoking cigarettes, and his mother
died of lung cancer brought on by years of smoking. Ashan abhorred
smoking and made every effort to eat right and walk every day. He was
intent on living well into his eighties.

The heavy door to Durrani's office was closed. Ashan glanced over
his shoulder at the assistant, who checked the lights on his phone.

"He's alone."

Ashan knocked on the door and turned the knob. He stepped into
the large rectangular office and was enveloped in a haze of gray smoke.
Ashan didn't hesitate. He flipped a switch on the wall and the hum of
an exhaust fan kicked in. He had had the unit installed nearly four
years ago, because he could no longer tolerate sitting in the smoke-
filled office. He considered chastising his friend for not having it on,
but thought better of it. The man was breathing the carcinogens directly into his lungs. The exhaust fan would make little difference.

"Nadeem," Durrani said, leaning back in his high-back black
leather chair, "what a pleasure." Durrani was dressed in his Army uniform, lest anyone forget the duality of his importance.

Ashan, having served only four years in the Air Force, was dressed
in a blue suit and yellow tie. "I was in the neighborhood and I decided
to stop by."

"Exercising again." Durrani smiled and held out his cigarette. "I've warned you, if you keep that up it will kill you."

"Yes, I know. If only I smoked like you and the rest of the country I would be much healthier."

"You might have more fun," Durrani said with a broad grin forming under the ample black mustache that seemed to be a prerequisite for being an officer in the Pakistan military.

"I have plenty of fun." Ashan continued past the two chairs in front of his friend's large desk and sat in the chair by the window that looked out onto one of the many inner courtyards of the compound. The armchair was something else he had ordered on his own. The two chairs in front of Durrani's desk were stubby little things that forced the occupants to look up at Durrani as if he sat high atop K2. Ashan couldn't be certain, but he suspected that the seating arrangement was a holdover from the old colonial days when British officers ran their country.

"So what brings you to my little enclave this morning? Do you need the dirty tricks of the External Wing to save your rear end once again?"

More serious than kidding, Ashan said, "Your dirty tricks are usually what puts my posterior into the hot water."

"Oh, come now," Durrani said with a deep laugh. "We all have our roles to play."

Ashan was not in such a playful mood. He knew his friend too well. Knew his capabilities and his weaknesses, and if he had been stupid enough to lend any of his people or expertise to facilitate the lunacy in Jalalabad, then they were all in a great deal of trouble. "Let us just pray for a moment that no one in the External Wing had anything to do with what happened across the border last night."

"Which border are you referring to?"

Ashan ran a hand across his clean-shaven face and tried to gauge whether his old friend's ignorance was real or feigned. The man had become so adept at playing this game that Ashan could no longer tell the difference. He decided to play it straight. "The border to our north."

"Ah . . . Mr. Rickman. Very unfortunate. I'm surprised you have heard."

Ashan was used to the constant shots at the capabilities of his department. "Foreign relations is our specialty."

"How did you learn of it?"

"The embassy. They sent a cable this morning." Ashan told only half the truth. He'd also spoken with the CIA directly. "The Americans are very upset."

"I would imagine they are. Mr. Rickman is not someone I would want to lose."

Ashan turned and glanced out the window. He sensed his friend was playing some kind of game, but he could no longer be sure. They had met thirty-five years ago while he was studying at Oxford and Durrani was at the Royal Military Academy at Sandhurst. Back then Durrani was an open book—transparent about his passions and plans. Ashan had always appreciated his honesty and forthright manner. The ISI had slowly turned him into a duplicitous spymaster, however, and Ashan feared there was an ever-deepening divide between them. "Akhtar, I have to ask you something."

Durrani gave a welcoming smile, signaling for his friend to proceed.

"You will not like this question."

"People ask me questions every day that I do not like. It is part of my job."

Ashan watched him light another cigarette and then casually asked, "Do you or any of your people have any information about the kidnapping of Rickman?"

Durrani didn't answer right away, as he was taking in a deep breath of smoke to make sure the cigarette stayed lit. Only fools had to relight a cigarette. He shook his head and exhaled, saying, "That is a pretty broad question. Could you be more specific?"

"Did you have any knowledge that he was a target?"

"Personally, I had no knowledge."

"And your people?"

Durrani scoffed. "Why would my people be involved in something so reckless?"

Ashan could come up with a half dozen reasons that would make his point. He was going to let it go, and then something pushed him further than he had gone with his friend in some time. "Maybe you should tell me, since we both know some of your people decided it was a good idea to hide bin Laden from the world. In our own backyard, I should add."

Durrani's easy expression hardened. "It has been decided that we are not to discuss that matter."

Yes, it had been decided. In the embarrassing aftermath of the SEAL team raid, the president and the director general had asked Ashan to investigate any potential involvement by the ISI in aiding bin Laden. A two-star Army general had been ordered to investigate the potential involvement of the armed forces as well. The general had come back with a pathetic report that cleared the military of all involvement. Ashan's investigation was an entirely different matter. Six intelligence officers were implicated as well as five Army officers and a handful of subordinates, and there were more. Before Ashan could finish his investigation, the director general stepped in and seized all evidence and had it destroyed.

Ashan had been furious, but he was told it was for the good of Pakistan. The director general told him the Americans had penetrated his investigation and were now in possession of information that they could use to blackmail Pakistan into doing their bidding. Ashan knew the answer was a complete fabrication. His investigation was taking him to the doorsteps of some very influential people. He was on the brink of exposing to the world that senior Pakistani officials had harbored the world's most notorious terrorist. Rather than clean house and admit their mistakes, the president and his senior cabinet members decided to bury the entire matter. Not a single person was punished, and since firing those involved might bring about more speculation, they were allowed to stay in their positions. Ashan found the entire thing infuriating but was left with no recourse except one. He very quietly and carefully passed what he knew on to the Americans.

"Yes, it has been decided that we are not to discuss the matter, but we have always prided ourselves on being realists, and since we are in your office, which we both know to be secure, I see no harm in pointing out that we know for a fact that some of your people are indeed reckless."

"Don't be so smug. Your department was implicated as well."

"Yes." Ashan nodded. "One reckless moron, and I have done my best to make his life miserable. I have him stuffed down in one of the sublevels digitizing old files. And the five men in your department, how are they faring?"

"How I run my department is my business."

Ashan took the defensive answer for what it was—an admission that the duplicitous scum still held their old positions. "So now that we've established that we have people in our fine organization who would indeed participate in a plan as reckless as kidnapping someone like Joe Rickman, how do you suggest we make sure that none of our people had anything to do with this?"

"I would suggest doing nothing."

"Nothing?"

"Even investigating such a thing will draw the attention of the Americans. I see no reason to open my wing up to more of their accusations when I am confident that my people had nothing to do with this. Afghanistan is a rough place, as the Americans have found out. They should have gone home a long time ago."

Ashan made no attempted to conceal his exasperation. "Why must you continue to treat the Americans as if they are our enemy?"

Durrani stabbed out his cigarette in the large copper ashtray and folded his hands across his tight green uniform shirt. "Afghanistan is our toy. The British thought it was their toy for a long time, and then the Russians thought they could take it, and then the Americans in their arrogance thought they could do what neither the British nor the Russians could accomplish. They thought they could tame the savages and take what is ours."

Ashan shook his head. He had heard all of this before. "Again, you have conveniently left out the part where al Qaeda attacked them."

"We could have handled al Qaeda for them. All they had to do was ask. They didn't need to invade our neighbor. Look at all the damage they have caused."

Ashan started to speak and then stopped. It was all a waste of his time. They had been over all of this before. Durrani loved to feign ignorance and spout his dislike for the Americans, all while gladly taking their money. It was rumored that he'd pocketed millions over the course of the war, some of it undoubtedly coming directly from Rickman. Ashan had been on the verge of leveling the accusation on multiple occasions but had always maintained just enough control to avoid suicide. Durrani wasn't the only one who took money. Most of the leadership at the ISI received some form of payment from the Americans, including Ashan himself. The problem with Durrani was that he took the money and then worked feverishly to undermine the legitimate goals of their ally.

"The damage they have caused? And I suppose you think we've had no hand in this mess . . . training and funding the mujahideen and then the Taliban and even some members of al Qaeda."

"Afghanistan is a mess, but it is our mess. It is time for the Americans to leave."

"And what do you think they're trying to do? This reintegration program that I've been helping them with is so they can pull out."

"And maintain a network of paid spies to continue to manipulate the affairs of this region." Durrani shook his head. "It is unacceptable."

"It is understandable considering everything they've been through."

"Would they allow us to meddle in the affairs of countries in their geographical sphere of influence?" Durrani didn't wait for an answer. "They most certainly wouldn't. They have worn out their welcome. It is time for them to go home."

Increasingly, this was how their conversations played out. To push further would be a waste of time and energy. "And what about Rickman?"

The general shrugged. "Another casualty of war. Everyone involved in this mess has lost thousands. Rickman is just another body."

Ashan shook his head in genuine disbelief. "That's where you're wrong. Joe Rickman is not just another body. He is one of the CIA's most important assets, and they are not just going to sit back while he's tortured. The man has too many secrets . . . extremely valuable secrets."

"You are overstating his importance, and even if you weren't, good luck finding him."

"Overstating his importance." Ashan stood and walked to the other side of the large desk. He faced his friend and said, "Do you know who the Americans have dispatched to find Rickman?"

"I have no idea."

Ashan placed both hands on the desk and said, "Your old friend Mitch Rapp."

Durrani looked away and swallowed hard. After a moment of silence he said, "We will offer him any assistance he needs." The words were flat, with no real commitment behind them.

"Akhtar, we have been friends for a long time. I don't want you to react . . . I don't want you to say a word. For once, please listen to me. Mitch Rapp is an extremely dangerous man. The fact that they have sent him over here is proof of how serious the Americans are about getting Rickman back. Rapp doesn't care about diplomacy or politics. He is the last man you want to cross. He will kill anyone who has anything to do with this. I'm going to leave now, but I suggest you follow through on your words. Offer him any assistance he needs, and if you find out that any of your people have aided the Taliban in—"

"We have no idea who did this," Durrani said, with more than a tinge of irritation in his voice.

"You are correct," Ashan said in a soothing voice, "but we can make some educated guesses, and if the usual suspects are involved, we can almost guarantee that somewhere, someone has a connection to the ISI. We need to put our people to work. They need to tell us what they find out and we need to hand it over to the Americans. I know this is painful for you, but you need to act like a true ally."

Durrani looked as if he'd taken a bite out of a sour lemon. "I am sick of the Americans and their arrogance. This is not my problem. They can find Rickman on their own."

Ashan stepped back. "Fine, you stubborn fool. Rapp has already warned you what he would do to you if you stabbed him in the back again." He retreated toward the door and asked, "Does he strike you as a man who doesn't follow through on his threats?"

"I am not afraid of Mitch Rapp."

Ashan placed his hand on the doorknob, a genuine feeling of sadness in his heart. His friend had turned into a stubborn old fool who thought the Americans lacked the resolve to play this nasty game at his ruthless level. For the average American he had a point, but Mitch Rapp was in no way average. Ashan opened the door and over his shoulder said, "If you aren't afraid of Mr. Rapp then you need to have your head examined."

CHAPTER 8

KABUL, AFGHANISTAN

RAPP looked out the porthole of the enormous MRAP Cougar. The drive from the airport to the embassy was short, just under two miles. The Army Corp of Engineers had done a nice job widening the Great Massoud Road to relieve as many choke points as possible. Cameras had been installed and fresh blacktop prevented insurgents from trying to bury roadside bombs. No parking was permitted on the street, and the sidewalks were kept clear of garbage, vendors, and pretty much anything that could conceal a roadside bomb. Despite all of these precautions, Rapp was filled with anxiety.

While most people found comfort in the Mine Resistant Ambush Protected vehicles, Rapp thought of them as big rolling coffins. You might as well paint a sign on the hulking side that said Infidels. Rapp preferred a more low-profile form of transportation. The Clandestine Service at Langley bought older-model vehicles and had private contractors make sure the cars were in top mechanical shape. Occasionally they would add bulletproof glass and some armor, but in Afghanistan, Rapp felt the key was to change vehicles often and blend in.

As they hit the big turnaround at the corner of the embassy, Rapp felt his chest tighten. They were close to the gate and this was where the crazies liked to attack. The vehicle came to a sudden stop. They were the third in a three-vehicle convoy. Rapp looked up at Coleman with irritation washed across his face and asked, "Why are we stopping?"

Coleman gave him an easy shrug. "Probably checking our creds."

"You mean to tell me those dumbasses didn't pre-clear us?"

"No idea." Coleman smiled, amused at Rapp's nervousness.

Rapp punched the button to lower the back hatch. "Well, I'm not going to be a sitting duck." As the stairs lowered, Rapp nimbly navigated them before they were all the way down.

Coleman laughed at him and popped the button to close the hatch. The Air Force security guys driving the vehicle were grumbling up front, wanting to know who the moron was who had just compromised their secure vehicle. Coleman waved them off and apologized.

Outside, Rapp came face-to-face with a U.S. Marine who couldn't have been older than twenty. The corporal gave Rapp a knowing nod and said, "I don't like those things either."

Rapp took a quick look around and realized the Marine was part of a security team that had been pushed out one hundred feet from the main gate. They were in a semicircle spaced every thirty feet; a loose cordon designed to create a secure pocket while credentials were verified and vehicles checked. The embassy's perimeter blast walls, ballistic glass, and Kevlar-reinforced walls were impervious to car bombs, but visitors were vulnerable during this brief window when they were at the embassy's doorstep. Two four-man fire teams composed the extended security.

What a shitty job, Rapp thought to himself. They were a thin tripwire out here to slow down any crazy bastards who were barreling down on the gate in an explosives-laden vehicle. Their early shots with their M-4s were not likely to stop the vehicle, nor were the rounds of the M249 SAW. It was the job of the big .50 caliber guns back at the gate to punch a hole in the engine of any unauthorized vehicle.

"How'd you end up with this powder-puff job?" Rapp asked, as his eyes continued to sweep the area.

The Marine tapped the two chevrons on his sleeve. "Shit rolls downhill and, as my gunny likes to remind me, the Corps is not a democracy. So I do what I'm told."

Rapp nodded—understood it was the way it had to be. "Good luck." Rapp turned and headed for the door next to the big steel gate. A sergeant in his tan combat utility uniform and decked out in body armor intercepted him. Rapp pulled out a set of fake State Department credentials.

The sergeant took the credentials and said, "Wait here." He walked over to the closest guard booth and slid the identification through the metal box. A few moments later he returned with Rapp's fake creds and a badge. "Are you armed, Mr. Cox?"

Rapp shook his head and said, "Nope," even though he was carrying two pistols and a knife. He followed the sergeant to the small door and stepped through. On the other side a familiar face was waiting for him. Rapp was neither pleased nor bothered to see Mike Nash. "Irene decided to send over reinforcements."

Nash had been attached to Rapp's team for almost five years and had recently been promoted to deputy director of the Counterterrorism Center at Langley. "I'm only the first wave. She's pulling in clandestine boys from all over the place."

Rapp grimaced. He didn't have the time or the patience to manage all of these people. It quickly dawned on him that he wouldn't have to. That was why Nash was here. Still, he needed to have a say in what these people would be doing or they'd end up falling all over each other. "And what are we going to do with everyone?"

Nash shrugged. "They're gonna beat the bushes until we find something more specific."

Normally Rapp would have been drastically against drawing too much attention to what they were doing, but this little disaster was a unique problem. Beating the bushes was as a good a start as any for the moment. "Any orders?" Rapp asked, knowing there would be.

"Yeah," Nash said as he jerked his head toward a tree-lined walkway, signaling Rapp to follow him. The two men looked enough alike to be confused as brothers. Rapp was five years older and an inch taller. His hair was black with a touch of gray where Nash's was dark brown. The main similarities were in their square jaws and overall demeanor. When they were a good distance away from the gate Nash found a spot under a towering cypress tree. "What'd you find out in Jalalabad?"

"Four dead bodyguards, safe's empty, his laptop is gone, and God only knows what else. It's a fucking disaster."

"Any leads?"

"Not really." Rapp shook his head. "Although I met some asshole named Zahir. He used to be a terrorist, but now he's supposedly our friend." Rapp's tone made it obvious that he didn't buy the last part.

"Abdul Siraj Zahir. I'm familiar with his work. I warned both Rick and Sickles that we didn't want to get in bed with him, but they ignored me."

"Well, the asshole showed up at the safe house and tried to throw his weight around."

"And I'm sure you employed all of your diplomatic skill to defuse the situation."

"You're a smart man. He took a shit all over Hubbard, and when I couldn't take it anymore I stuck a gun in his face and threatened to blow his head off."

Nash laughed. He thought briefly about telling Rapp how dangerous Zahir could be, but he'd be wasting his breath. Mitch knew his type all too well. "Not the most subtle approach."

"Listen . . . I'd love to be all sneaky and clever about this, but we don't have the time. We either get him back in the next few days or all hell is going to break loose."

Nash concurred. "Irene agrees. We all know the score and know what has to be done."

Rapp was suspicious that the higher-ups in D.C. were of a single mind. "Listen, I've seen this movie before. They say all kinds of shit, talk tough, and demand results, and then we run off and start kicking in doors and knocking heads and then a year from now, if things start to leak, they'll act all shocked and demand we swing from the mast."

"I don't disagree, but at least this time, Irene says DOD, State, and the White House are all on board."

Rapp still wasn't buying it. "That's what they say now, but I'm telling you . . . down the road they'll bail on our asses so fast it'll make your head spin."

"You're probably right, but what in the hell are we going to do about it? We either play by the book and watch it all fall apart or we get rough and hope we get him back before he spills the family jewels."

"I know what we have to do, and I'm willing to do it, but you're not going to convince me that those clowns in D.C. will support us for a second."

Nash didn't have much faith in his fellow bureaucrats and even less in the politicians who ran the city, but they had more leverage than Rapp was giving them credit for. "Did you know Rick became the de facto paymaster for this reintegration program?"

Rapp was surprised by the news. "I thought State was running that cluster fuck."

"They were the lead agency, but they didn't have the wherewithal, or I suspect the guts to actually shake hands with this collection of misfits, so the president asked Irene if we could help out."

"And she said yes."

"That's correct, so Irene has a little more leverage on all of them this time around since they all signed on. Maybe they'll be more cooperative."

"I won't hold my breath."

"None of us expect you to, which is what we need to talk about. This meeting that's about to take place . . . Irene wants you to keep a low profile."

"Why?"

"She's working directly with the Sec Def and the Sec State to keep their people in line. The White House is helping out and she thinks she can get all of them to basically close their eyes and cover their ears for the next seventy-two hours."

"Fine by me."

Nash pressed. "She doesn't want you to pick any fights."

Rapp scoffed and shook his head. "With who?"

"With anyone."

"What about that Sickles dumbass?"

"She wants me to handle him."

"Really," Rapp said with a raised brow, "then you'd better keep him away from me."

Nash knew this wouldn't be easy and dancing around the issue would only make it worse. "Listen . . . everyone knows you're point on this, but you have a history of not playing nice on the playground with the other kids."

Rapp heard the first MRAP roll through the gate, shook his head in frustration, and said, "Spit it out. I'm not in the most patient mood this morning."

"You're never in a patient mood, so I need you to slow down for a second . . . hear me out. There's going to be a woman in this meeting . . . Arianna Vinter . . . have you heard of her?"

"No."

"She's from State . . . she's the one who came up with this whole reintegration business. Apparently she's a real ball buster . . . very connected and she's not afraid to chew ass."

"Wonderful."

"Yeah . . . well, Irene thinks you two are going to have a problem."

"Why would you guys want to put me in a room with this woman?"

"Believe me, Irene thought long and hard about it."

"Then why don't I just skip it?"

"We thought about that, but Irene wants them to understand how serious this is, and she wants them to all know that we are running the show until the White House says different."

"Then I don't see a problem."

"Irene's not so sure. She doesn't want you getting distracted and she thinks this Vinter will do exactly that."

This was the type of stuff that drove Rapp nuts. In the best of times he couldn't give a rat's ass about the feelings of some State Department bureaucrat, but now, in the midst of one of the worst debacles the Agency had seen in decades, his fuse was so short, he was ready to explode. He pointed his finger at Nash and was about to unleash a torrent of expletives when Coleman rolled up and interrupted him.

"Mike, how was your flight?" Coleman extended his hand.

"Fine." Nash shook his hand and then pointed at Rapp with his thumb. "I'm just trying to calm down our friend."

"Don't waste your time. Where's Stan? I need to talk to him."

For no apparent reason, Nash's demeanor melted into a mask of concern at the mention of the man who had trained both him and Rapp.

Rapp picked up on it immediately. "What's wrong?"

"He's not going to be making the trip."

"Why?"

Nash looked at the ground for a few seconds and then said, "He got some bad news while you guys were in the air."

"What kind of bad news?" Rapp asked.

"Cancer."

"Shit," Rapp said under his breath. "His lungs?" Stan Hurley had smoked for more than forty years.

Nash nodded. "Stage four. They're giving him six months. Maybe a little more . . . maybe a little less."

It was as if all of Rapp's energy had left him. Just melted away from his head down to his feet and onto the pavement. His relationship with Hurley was a complicated one that couldn't have started off on a worse footing, but over the last two decades the irascible old cuss had become an extremely valuable mentor. Often he was the only person that Rapp could really confide in. Hurley was the only man who had truly walked in his shoes. Rapp turned away from Coleman and Nash and began to walk. He had no destination in mind, only a feeling that he needed to be alone so he could get a handle on the sadness that was beginning to wash over him.

CHAPTER 9

THE assassin's attention was focused on the fifteen-inch screen of his laptop. A Do Not Disturb sign was hung on his hotel room door to make sure housekeeping didn't accidentally wander in and catch him doing something nefarious. Even so, if they did, there wouldn't be much for them to see. Gone were the days of all the bulky surveillance equipment: tripods for big cameras with even bigger lenses, video recorders and big dish parabolic microphones and the big suitcase packed with monitors for video and audio. All of that now fit into a wireless device no bigger than a tissue box. He had helped design it in his ample spare time for just such a reason. The Americans would love to get their hands on something so portable and effective.

The act of surveillance was far more complicated than one would think. Static targets, like embassies, often conducted countersurveillance. Standing in the window of a hotel room across the street from a major embassy with a pair of binoculars to your eyes and a set of cameras on each side was a near sure ticket to getting your door kicked in and a bag put over your head. What would follow after that was sure to be very unpleasant. The assassin had been on the receiving end just once, and he had spent years trying to erase his unpleasant week as a guest of the Russian Foreign Intelligence Service. He had no desire to be the subject of such barbarity again, and while the Americans were not quite as ruthless as the Russians, they had shown that they could be brutally efficient in the face of an enemy who refused to put on a uniform.

The new surveillance equipment consisted of two cameras and a directional microphone. Both cameras were capable of extreme magnification, but for the assassin's purpose he kept one on the wide-angle setting so he didn't lose sight of the big picture. The two cameras and microphone were combined in the tissue-sized gray box. It was mounted on a small, lightweight tripod with a motor that allowed him to remotely turn and focus the device. The functions were controlled with a joystick and the laptop's mouse. Instead of standing in the window and risking exposure, he sat on the bed with the lightweight computer on his lap.

It felt good to be back in the game. The assassin had never fully retired, but he had significantly cut back on the number and type of contracts he would take. He still traveled a great deal—most of it to handle his far-flung finances, but he had also created a job that gave him the perfect cover to travel. He was now a security consultant. Having spent so many years trying to figure out how to kill someone, it was an easy transition. He basically stalked his client and then instead of killing him, he would debrief him by pointing out his vulnerabilities and the precautions he should take. The pay was okay and the work was somewhat fulfilling, although ultimately disappointing. Hunting a fellow human being without killing him was a little bit like getting half a blow job—thrilling yet ultimately disappointing.

This contract, however, had been a little unusual from the start. He had been contacted through his legitimate consulting firm for a job in Abu Dhabi. He did a lot of business in the United Arab Emirates so he thought nothing of it. A week later the assassin checked into his room at the Jumeirah at Etihad Towers. An hour later a package was delivered to his suite containing a smartphone, a very vague explanation of the job that was being offered to him, and how he would be paid. His client was exceptionally cautious, which the assassin liked. He also liked that the client was offering a large sum of money. His finances were still in decent shape, but $3 million would go a long way. The only thing that he didn't like was that the target was described only in vague terms. But even though he didn't like it, it wasn't that unusual. The most serious clients usually made you jump through a few hoops to gauge if they could trust you, and then they would reveal the full identity of the target.

The size of the contract, combined with the challenge of assassinating an American official in Afghanistan, was too much to resist. So, as per the instructions, he turned on the smartphone, tapped the texting icon, and punched his answer into the dialogue box. That had been two weeks ago. Since then, the assassin had flown more than twenty thousand miles and received $1 million in three separate wire transfers. As per his orders, he had checked into the Kabul Grand Hotel the previous day and patiently awaited further instructions.

Five minutes earlier a text had informed him that the target was headed his way in a military convoy consisting of three vehicles. The first tan MRAP came into view and the assassin's anticipation grew that he would finally learn the identity of the target. He'd spent much of the last two weeks wondering who it could be. He liked a challenge, so part of him was hoping it would be the ambassador or a four-star general, and based on the fee his wishes were likely to come true. He'd done some checking, however, and the ambassador was already at the embassy, so he could rule him out.

The trucks came to a stop outside the main gate of the embassy, as was to be expected. A few seconds later, he watched as the back hatch of the last vehicle opened. A head popped out into the bright sunlight and the assassin squinted as he watched a man hurry down the steps. His fingers quickly adjusted the camera and brought the picture in tight on the man. The hair on the back of the assassin's neck bristled with a combination of excitement and fear. His job had just gone from complicated to dangerous.

Most of his targets over the years had been businessmen or government officials who were either too corrupt or too pious. Usually men in their fifties or sixties who were out of shape, their senses almost completely dulled by women, drugs, booze, and a life of luxury. They were often surrounded by bodyguards who were well past their prime. The man he was now staring at on his screen was far from past his prime, and even if had lost a step he was perhaps one of the most dangerous animals on the planet. It had been a few years since the assassin had last seen the CIA operative, but the details of that near-death experience were forever seared into his psyche. He still moved with that rare mix of athleticism, grace, and menace. He stopped next to a soldier and spoke a few words. The assassin watched as Rapp's head turned from side to side, surveying the landscape for any threats.

His first encounter with Rapp had been eerily similar. Even back then there was a part of his deeply embedded survival instinct that told him this wasn't someone to be messed with. The challenge, however, proved too great to resist, and the assassin was lucky to be alive. Reason would dictate that Rapp was here to protect the prospective target. The assassin ran through a quick list of possibilities. A mid-level CIA official would not garner a $3 million payday, and it was unlikely that Rapp would be wasting his time riding shotgun for such a person. It was possible that it could be an Afghan official, but again the price was too high. The image of the woman popped into his mind almost without effort. Irene Kennedy was the director of the CIA, and she and Rapp were very close. That would make perfect sense.

It had to be Irene Kennedy, the director of the CIA. The assassin suddenly got the feeling that he had made a huge mistake. As a general rule the CIA was not an organization you wanted to cross swords with, precisely because they had men like Rapp who would hunt you to the end of the world to settle the score. The price also seemed a little low for someone like Kennedy.

For a long moment the assassin considered his options. If the target was Kennedy, the smartest course would be to pack up his gear and catch the next flight out of Kabul. It wouldn't matter where, just so long as it was as far away from here as possible. If it came to it he would return all of the money and eat his expenses. He needed the money but it wasn't worth it. The odds for success with Rapp involved decreased by at least half, and there were other issues that complicated the matter. It would take no longer than five minutes to pack his gear. He picked up the HTC One phone that his employer had left him. With one simple text he would find the identity of the target. The agreement had been such that once the identity was revealed the assassin could not back out. He was tempted to run but he was more curious to find out the identity of the target. The assassin tapped out his message: *The convoy has arrived. I am in position.*

He hit Send and then sat back and watched Rapp enter the embassy grounds through a gate. So far the client had been good about getting back to him. It had been a strange dance up to this point, but one that had a certain logic to it. The contract had rolled out in a graduated manner. The basic terms were agreed on, but the target was not to be revealed until he was in-country and in a position to act.

Five minutes passed, and then ten, and the assassin was growing uncharacteristically anxious. He went to the bathroom and heard the phone beep as he was washing his hands. When he came back into the bedroom he opened the text and stared at the icon for an encrypted file and then tapped it. A split second later a photo of Mitch Rapp engulfed his screen. The assassin dropped the phone on the bed and almost opened the shades, before he caught himself.

"How in the hell . . ." he blurted out as he began to sweat. He told himself to calm down and think this through very carefully. There had to be a way out of this. $3 million was not enough money to take on someone like Rapp. $10 million wasn't enough, and even if it was, there were other factors to consider. The assassin ran his fingers through his dark brown hair and walked into the bathroom. He stared at himself in the mirror and asked himself how he had gotten into such a ludicrous situation. It was the money, of course, and the thrill of the hunt. Domestic life had become extremely boring, but it was better than being dead.

"What are the odds?" he asked aloud. The question steered his mind in a mystical direction and he now focused on a powerful word that was thousands of years old. It was karma, of course. It was the only thing that could explain the odds. What he had done years ago had almost certainly led him to this place. He owed a debt and it was time to repay it in full. With absolute conviction, the assassin knew what he must do. He went back into the bedroom and forwarded the encrypted file to his laptop, where he began to review Rapp's dossier. It was incredibly detailed. So detailed, it caused the assassin to worry about who had hired him. There were very few organizations that could put something like this together.

He flipped back to the surveillance screen and found Rapp talking to another man inside the embassy compound. The odds were staggering, but the payoff would be far better than just the $3 million. A smile of anticipation spread across the assassin's face. This would be perhaps the most fulfilling contract of his career. The trick, of course, would be to get close enough to Rapp without alerting him first. If Rapp detected him, he would be dead before he had a chance to collect on his debt.

CHAPTER 10

THE conference room was located off one of the interior corridors on the sixth floor of the embassy. It was State Department turf, which Nash didn't like, but Kennedy wanted him to make this one effort to play nice and get these people to understand what was at stake. If they didn't get in line after that, he was supposed to turn Rapp loose. The idea that Nash could control Rapp in the first place was ludicrous. He made that exact point to Kennedy, but she remained obstinate on the matter. She wouldn't go into detail about why they had to go through this little dance, but as director of the CIA, Kennedy did not always feel that she had to explain every order she gave. She operated on a level that was way beyond Nash's understanding, influenced by people and organizations that he fortunately didn't have to answer to. Add to that the fact that she was the smartest person he'd ever worked for, and he decided to simply carry out her orders.

That was all back in Washington. Over here in Afghanistan, however, he was once again questioning the wisdom of her strategy. To say that Rapp wasn't suited for this kind of thing wasn't entirely fair.

A more accurate description would be to say that these other people weren't suited for the War on Terror. Rapp was more driven than any person he'd ever encountered, and that took a lot of getting used to. His lack of patience was a by-product of that drive and his intimate knowledge of the enemy. While others debated a problem from every conceivable angle, often arguing over degrees, Rapp analyzed the same problem with a rapidity that was astounding and then chose a course of action or decided not to act. His default setting more often than not, however, was to act. Rapp understood that kinetic energy was more apt to bring about a desired result than sitting around waiting for the enemy to move first. If they got through this meeting without Rapp punching Sickles, Nash would consider it a major accomplishment.

Darren Sickles, the station chief, had assured Nash that the room was secure. Nash received the information as if he was satisfied and then followed his own protocols and quietly had a member of his team sweep the room for devices. Sickles found out about it shortly before the meeting was to commence and told Nash that he was offended. With Kennedy's orders paramount, he offered Sickles a halfhearted apology and said something to the effect that you can never be too careful. There was a very good chance Nash would put Sickles's reaction in a report when this saga was over. Kennedy preached vigilance when it came to making sure lines of communication were secure. No one in the community had a right to be offended by someone taking extra care to make sure a room was clean. That Sickles felt the need to let Nash know he was offended was juvenile.

Nash was growing used to it, however. When he was called on to run the CIA's Counterterrorism Center at the relatively young age of thirty-nine, it had pissed off a whole bevy of professionals who had more experience than he did. Nash gave it all as little thought as possible, but there were certain individuals whom he had to act more guarded around, and Sickles had just added his name to that list.

Nash stepped off the elevator and was surprised to see Rapp standing in the hallway by himself. "I just lost a hundred dollars."

"Why?"

"I didn't think you'd show."

Rapp ignored his friend's attempt at humor. "Let's go. The sooner we get this thing over, the sooner I can get back to what's important." Rapp turned and started down the hall.

"Have you seen Darren?" Nash asked.

Rapp shook his head.

"You know he's upset . . . right?"

Rapp stopped, turned abruptly, gave the appearance that he was going to blow his lid, and then restrained himself.

"I just wanted to make sure you knew the lay of the land," Nash said, a bit defensively.

"Trust me, I know the lay of the land and I don't give a shit about Darren Sickles and whether or not he's offended."

"Mitch, this is coming from Irene. I'd prefer it if you skipped this meeting, but she insisted that you be here. Why, I have no idea. So if you don't think you can keep your temper in check, then I think you should take off."

Enough anger flashed across Rapp's face that Nash took a step back. Rapp said, "Let's be clear about something. I know you have a fancy new title and a nice office at Langley, but you are not in my chain of command. You're Irene's message boy, and I personally couldn't give a fuck what you think. If Irene wants me here then I'll act like a good soldier. I'll follow her orders, but I don't need your personal input or Darren Sickles or anyone else's, for that matter."

Nash was used to Rapp's rough edges, but there was something more to this. The two men had been in plenty of heated arguments over the years, but there seemed to be some genuine animosity this time— as if Rapp now thought they were on opposite sides.

Nash took a long breath and said, "You've never been one to follow orders and I sure as hell don't see why you'd start now."

"Very funny, big man. I'm really not in the mood for your shit. I'll play your game, but I'm warning you, that idiot Sickles better watch himself or I'm coming across the table."

"Don't let Darren get to you. He's freaking out because all of this went down on his watch. He's probably scared to death that this will be a career ender."

"Yeah . . . well, I'm freaking out too. Joe Rickman is missing, and if we don't get him back the bodies are going to start piling up from here to Islamabad and Tehran and God only knows where else. Good people who have put their asses on the line for us are going to die, and on top of that I just found out the man who trained me, who I've spent the last twenty-plus years working with, has terminal cancer. So excuse me if I'm not exactly in the mood to deal with these people and their petty turf wars."

"That's fine. I'm not looking forward to it either, but we need to work with these people. You said it yourself . . . Rick's files are gone. These people are our only hope. We need what they have. We need to know who Rick's been meeting with. Somebody got on the inside and helped pull this thing off."

Rapp slowly nodded. "I know we need their shit, but that doesn't mean we have to kiss their asses."

"Yes, it does. At least to start with."

Rapp mumbled something to himself and then walked away. Nash followed a few steps behind, wondering if perhaps Hurley's diagnosis had affected Rapp more harshly than he would have guessed. True, they'd worked closely together for a long time, but both men had an emotional side that was about as soft as granite. Nash followed Rapp into the conference room, closing the door behind him. Standing to his left, in the far corner, were Sickles, Arianna Vinter, and a man who he assumed was the DOD's military attaché. Nash had skimmed his jacket on the flight over. He couldn't remember his name offhand, but recalled that he was a West Pointer. The room was standard government decorating. The carpet was a dark mix of gray and black that would serve to hide any stains, and a large brown table with a fake wood grain top dominated the room. In the center of the table was a tray with a coffeepot, cream, sweetener, sugar, some straws, a half dozen mugs and as many bottles of water. There were ten black swivel chairs arranged four on each side and one on each end.

Vinter held up her hand in a gesture to silence Sickles, then smiled at the two men who had just entered the room. "Good morning. I assume you are Mr. Rapp and Mr. Nash."

Rapp didn't speak, so Nash answered for them. "That's right. And I assume you are Arianna Vinter."

"Yes, please have a seat."

Nash noted that she was much prettier than in the photograph on her government-issue ID. He looked at the man to Vinter's left and noted the eagle on the patch in the center of his chest and the name on the right side of his chest. Reaching across the table, Nash extended his hand and said, "Mike Nash, Colonel. Nice to meet you."

Poole took his hand. "Counterterrorism, right?"

"That's correct."

Poole looked at Rapp and stuck out his hand. "Colonel Poole, military attaché. Mr. Rapp?"

Nodding, Rapp took the man's hand but didn't say anything. After a firm handshake, Rapp sat down.

"May I offer either of you anything to drink?" Vinter asked.

Rapp kept his mouth shut and offered only a slight shake of his head. Nash said, "Coffee would be great."

Vinter grabbed the carafe and poured a cup. "You strike me as the kind of man who takes it black."

"That's right." Nash smiled. "Thank you." He took the mug and set it in front of him.

Vinter told Poole and Sickles to sit and then she grabbed a seat across from Rapp and Nash. Sickles was on her right and Poole on her left. She directed her gaze at Rapp and in a sweet voice said, "Mr. Rapp, we've never met before. What exactly is it that you do for the CIA?"

"I'm in the Clandestine Service."

"Do you have a title?"

Rapp shook his head. "I report directly to DCI Kennedy."

"I see," Vinter said, placing her hands flat on the table. She examined her fingers for a long moment and then in a casual voice asked, "Do you think I'm stupid, Mr. Rapp?"

Rapp didn't take the bait. He instead turned to Nash and gave him a look that said, This is your show . . . feel free to jump in.

Nash cleared his throat. "Arianna, I'm not sure we understand the question."

Her expression flared briefly as she turned her attention to Nash. "I wasn't addressing you. I was speaking to your colleague Mr. Rapp. Now, Mr. Rapp, I asked you a straightforward question. Do you think I'm stupid?"

"I don't know you."

"You don't know me. That's all you have to say."

"I've never met you before and I haven't heard anything about you until this morning, so I'm not really in a position to answer your question. You could be a genius or an imbecile. As of right now I can't answer that question, but keep talking and I should be able to give you an answer in a few minutes."

Vinter took in a long breath. "Do you think the president is a smart man?"

Rapp thought about that for a moment. The man had his strengths and weaknesses, but, all in all, he was no dummy. "Yes, I think the president is a smart man."

"Well, the president put me in charge of this little hellhole because he thought I was the best person for the job. My team and I have worked extremely hard to implement the president's plan and things were going very smoothly until you showed up this morning and shoved a gun in the face of one of our allies." Vinter's agreeable façade was slowly melting away, revealing her angry side. "I know you think you're some hotshot, but you need to understand something. I'm in charge around here and if I don't like you and what you're up to, you're going to find your ass on the next flight out of here. Do you understand me?"

Instead of answering the question, Rapp again turned to Nash and said, "I think you'd better field this one."

"Arianna, we are in a unique situation. None of us are questioning what you have accomplished, but you need to understand—"

"I don't need to understand a thing," Vinter said, slicing her hand through the air like a karate chop. "I live here. I know what's going on. You two don't." She wagged her finger at Nash and then Rapp. "I'm not going to have you come in here and screw up a year's worth of work because you're upset that one of your black-bag guys got kidnapped. No fucking way that's going to happen. So let's be real clear about this. I don't want you two going to the bathroom without asking me for permission first. You don't talk to anyone who's involved in reintegration unless I clear it. Do you understand me?"

Rapp raised his hand as if he was waiting to be called on by his teacher.

"What?" Vinter asked.

"I have the answer to your question . . . I think you're an imbecile. There could be some underlying psychological issues as well but I'd need to spend more time with you, which isn't going to happen. Beyond that, I'm pretty sure you're stupid."

Vinter's even complexion became blotchy with anger. "Don't fuck with me. I'm not going to warn you again. You two are not in charge. I'm running the show. I make one phone call and your lame ass is on the next military transport out . . . in fact I'll make sure it's one of those big ones with all the props that makes you feel like you've been in a blender."

"A C-130," Rapp said, "the vibration helps me sleep."

"I don't give a shit if the vibration gives you a hard-on. One wrong move and you two are gone."

"Listen," Nash said, "we're all on the same team."

"I'm not on your team," Vinter said with absolute conviction.

Rapp turned his attention to the CIA station chief. The fact that he had decided to sit on the other side of the table spoke volumes about him. "Did you bother to brief her on who we are?"

Sickles cleared his throat. "I gave her some basic background."

"That's it?"

"More or less."

Nash dropped his head into his hands and waited for what was about to happen. There could be no blaming Rapp this time. This woman had clearly picked the fight.

Rapp knew Sickles was holding back. They'd revisit all of this later when they could keep it within the family and Rapp would remind Sickles in a very persuasive way where his loyalties were supposed to lie. But for now Vinter was the problem. He looked across the table with his near black eyes and said, "Do you like your job?"

"Let me guess . . . this is the part where you're going to ask me a bunch of questions and then threaten me. Well, I'll save you the time. You can't threaten me. I'm untouchable. I'm the president's point person in Afghanistan. I'm in charge."

"There's a few generals and an ambassador who might disagree with you, but I don't have the time to argue the point. If you're in charge, all the better. We need you to hand over everything that you were working on with Joe Rickman."

"That's not going to happen. It's highly classified information."

Rapp shook his head in semidisbelief. "You do realize we're the CIA? Our *job* is classified information."

"Not my classified information."

After nodding a few times, Rapp stood. "So there's not going to be any cooperation?"

"I told you the deal. You two don't move without talking to me first. We'll see how you behave and then we'll revisit the cooperation."

Looking at Sickles, Rapp asked, "Have you briefed her on how serious this is?"

"She understands the situation and she also knows about your reputation. We've worked long and hard on reintegration and none of us are too happy to see you barge in here and begin destroying everything we've accomplished."

Rapp stared at Sickles for a long moment. He could scarcely believe what he was hearing. He pointed at the station chief, snapped his fingers, and then hooked his thumb toward the door. "You're done. Get the hell out of here. I'll come find you in your office when I'm done."

"You have no right to—"

"Darren," Rapp yelled, "shut your mouth. I have every right. I have the DCI's full backing on this and I swear to God, if you're not out of this room in the next five seconds you can kiss your pension good-bye. As it is, your ass is in hot water. Joe Fuckin' Rickman got snatched on your watch. Do you have any idea how bad this is?"

"I . . ."

"Never mind. Just get the hell out of here. We'll talk about this in your office. Go . . . now . . . move it."

Sickles had tried to call Kennedy three times this morning and Kennedy had not taken any of his calls. Maybe Rapp was telling the truth. The station chief got up and left the room without saying another word.

When the door was closed again, Rapp looked at Poole and said, "If you'd prefer to leave as well you won't hear me complain."

"I'll stay."

"Fine." Turning his attention back to Vinter, Rapp said, "You might think you're connected . . . you might even think you're important and in certain circles that might be true, but not this time around."

"Oh, really?"

"Yeah . . . Let me explain how this works. We're the guys they call in when the shit hits the fan. Go ahead and call your boss when we're done. She'll tell you the same thing. In fact I'm pretty sure she'll tell you to do what we ask and then get the hell out of our way."

Vinter shook her head. "The secretary of state has complete confidence in me. After I tell her what you did to Commander Zahir this morning, you're the one who's going to be praying they let you keep your pension."

"You go ahead and make that call, but just remember, I warned you. This reintegration crap is a circle jerk and everyone who's anyone in D.C. knows it. It's a gimmick so we can declare victory and get the hell out of here. Joe Rickman getting snatched is serious shit and they all know it. You see, his head is full of a lot of nasty secrets that will embarrass your boss and a lot of other heavy hitters back in D.C. They don't like being embarrassed, so your little circle jerk is going to take a backseat to my problem for a while. I don't really care if the papers print nasty stuff about your boss or anyone else, but I do care about all the agents that work for us who will more than likely end up dead if we don't find Rick and find him quick."

"You have no idea who you're screwing with, Mr. Rapp."

"Actually, I have a really good idea. You're some spoiled brat who's gotten her way her entire life." He pointed at her wedding ring and added, "Your husband is miserable. Some poor browbeaten son of a bitch. You probably keep his balls in a little box on your desk, and based on your selfish attitude this morning I'd say there's a pretty good chance you've been having an affair with the colonel here. The point is I don't give a shit who you are, but you'd better care who I am and understand that I'm the meanest son of a bitch you will ever meet. That's why the president sent me over here. Because he wants results and he knows I won't put up with people like you. So you go ahead and call your boss and anyone else you need to and after they've all told you what I've just told you, you will hand over every shred of information you have regarding Joe Rickman and the scumbags you had him making deals with. And if you don't, I can guarantee you will be the one on the next flight out of here."

CHAPTER 11

JALALABAD, AFGHANISTAN

H E lay on the floor wearing only a pair of U.S. Army–issue boxer shorts, curled up in the fetal position, his face and body battered to a pulp. Joe Rickman tried to open his eyes, but they were either too swollen or too caked with dry blood to yield. He had never felt such pain. Never even imagined that it could be so bad. His trainers back at the Farm had warned him, and he had nodded as if he understood everything they were saying at the time, but they said he didn't. Anyone who hadn't been through it could never really understand just how bad it was. Now Rickman understood. He'd kept it together so far, but just barely. There had been a few moments when he was on the verge of calling it quits. He told himself that they would know when to stop. After all, Rickman had always known when to call his people off.

He had sat through countless interrogations and had never lost a single subject. Rickman's methods, and those of his colleagues, were a bit more clinical, though. Before an interrogation started they met and put a script in place. What questions were to be asked and what methods they would use to inflict pain. Rickman was never one to get his hands dirty, of course. He didn't even like his people getting *their* hands dirty. That was why he was such a big fan of electricity. It was nice and clean. No blood to mop up when everything was done. His team appreciated it as well, as they were the ones who had to clean up the room. It wasn't as if you could grab a janitor and bring him to the secure detention facility to clean up the blood from a rough session that in the eyes of some of his fellow countrymen was blatantly illegal.

Rickman's captors were obviously less concerned about the mess. The people in this part of the world were far more accepting of torture. In a sense, these animals had followed their version of a script. They had spared his feet and genitals and, for the most part, had slapped rather than punched him in the head. Most of the beating had been inflicted with a rubber hose and open palms, methods that were designed to elicit pain without causing life-threatening injury. At least that's what he kept telling himself as each blow landed. Even during the height of the beating, Rickman had kept a careful inventory of where and how they were hitting him. Fortunately, they had restrained themselves from striking him in the head too many times. Other than a heart attack, the easiest way to lose a subject during interrogation was to create hemorrhaging in the brain.

Rickman tried his eyes again and got one of them partially open. The eyelid fluttered to life to reveal his dank surroundings. He was in a cellar of some sort with a dirt floor. White sheets were draped along the walls. His hosts had spray-painted the word *Infidel* in black across one of the sheets. They had made sure to follow their script while filming his beating and kept the word *Infidel* in the frame just behind him.

The place reeked of urine. That was the first thing Rickman thought of when they'd brought him here, and he was repulsed by it. He was a neat freak and the idea of being held captive in such a foul place gave him almost as much anxiety as the impending session. After the beating started, however, the smell quickly became the least of his problems. And now he cared even less, since he was pretty sure he'd added to the potpourri during his beating.

Rickman tried to lift his head, but it hurt too much, so he lay there and tried to take an inventory of his pain. Nearly every inch of his body was aching, but there were a few areas that stood out. Chief among them were his ribs. He was pretty sure a few of them were broken or at a bare minimum bruised. The majority of the session had been conducted with Rickman's arms strung above his head to some contraption on the ceiling—his flanks exposed to the brutal blows. Even when they weren't beating him, his shoulders screamed with pain as if they were going to be ripped from their sockets.

Rickman gathered the strength to roll from his side onto his back. He winced as shards of pain shot through his rib cage. Slowly he turned his head toward the door. The video camera was mounted on a tripod. The red light under the lens told him it was still recording. That was good. Record all of it, for all he cared. He heard movement and voices outside the door. Rickman tensed with the anticipation that the beating would begin again. The door opened, throwing more light into the room. The man turned off the camera and stood over Rickman. He was wearing a gray knee-length shirt with gray baggy trousers that the locals called Perahan Tunban. He squatted and held a bottle of water to Rickman's swollen lips.

"It will go much easier if you tell them what they want to know. It doesn't have to be like this."

"I guess I'm into pain. What can I tell you?"

The man frowned and shook his head in a sad manner. After a long moment he fished a bottle of pills from his pocket and took off the cap. He tapped out two pills into the palm of his hand and then shoved them one by one into Rickman's mouth. "These will help."

Rickman tried to spit them out, but the man covered his mouth with his hand and said, "Don't be a fool."

A little bit of water and the pills slid right down. The man stood and walked back to the door. He opened it and waved another man in. The new man was carrying a small black bag.

It occurred to Rickman that he was a doctor. That was a good sign. His captors were taking this seriously. The man dropped to one knee next to Rickman and placed a stethoscope against his chest. After that he slapped on a blood pressure cuff and then dilated both eyes with a penlight. After no more than two minutes the doctor announced that he was strong enough to resume the interrogation.

The doctor left, two new men entered the room, masks pulled on to conceal their faces. The camera was turned back on and the man in the baggy gray pants nodded for the two men to continue. A rope ran through a pulley on the ceiling and was tied to Rickman's wrists. The two men yanked on the rope and pulled Rickman into a standing position.

"This time you will answer my questions . . . yes."

Rickman looked at the man through his one good eye and spat a glob of blood into his face. The beating commenced immediately. Strangely, the blows didn't hurt as much this time. He told himself to stay strong. It wouldn't be much longer. It couldn't be, or he might die, and he doubted these men would want that. Discipline was paramount.

CHAPTER 12

KABUL, AFGHANISTAN

EVERYONE made mistakes. It was how you handled them that counted. Own up to them, make a few adjustments, and move on. At least that was the way Rapp had been taught. Anything short of that was counterproductive, self-serving, and typically dishonest. Rapp didn't like having his time wasted under normal circumstances, but in a crisis like this it unnerved him when people couldn't at least set aside their issues, grab a bucket of water, and help put the damn fire out. Act like Sickles and deny that a mistake had been made and that little pressure cooker inside Rapp's head got so hot he became explosive.

There was a distinct possibility that Rapp might break the station chief's jaw and Nash knew it. He also couldn't blame him, but at this point it might or might not solve their problems. There were certain guys at Langley who were old-school and would be more than willing to take a beating if it saved them from being dragged back to Langley, but Sickles wasn't one of them. He would love nothing more at this point than to claim victimhood, and Nash couldn't allow that to happen.

Rapp stopped outside the secure door that led to the CIA's suite of embassy offices. He looked at Nash and said, "Tell me again why you think we need him."

"He knows these people. He's worked with Rick for the last two years. He has to have some info we could use. We ship him back to Langley and he's going to become significantly less cooperative."

"I don't give a shit. We ship him back to Langley and he'll realize real quick I'm not the only who's pissed at him. His career is over unless he gets some religion real quick, and even then I'd stuff him in some cubicle."

Before Nash could respond, Coleman approached and said, "Hubbard called. He talked to that veterinarian in J-Bad."

"And?"

"The vet says he never put the dog down. Told Hub he couldn't figure out what was wrong with it, so he referred Rick to another vet here in Kabul. Better animal hospital."

"So was Hub wrong or misinformed?"

"I'm not sure I understand."

"He told us the dog was put down by a vet in Jalalabad. Did Rick tell him that or did he just assume?"

"I don't know."

"Get him on the phone. I want to talk to him." Rapp pivoted and faced Nash. "You've got about a minute to convince me. We need to be out there, not in here. We need to be kicking down the door of every scumbag we can find and maybe if we get a whiff that Iran is behind this, we need to return the favor."

"I'm as pissed at him as you are. He broke our first rule. He forgot who he works for. It's not State . . . it's us. But you said it yourself. The clock is ticking. This trail is going colder by the second and let's face it . . . Rick's got the brains, not the brawn. If he hasn't already broken it won't take much longer. We need Darren to give us everything now. Not two or three days from now when he's back at Langley and Irene finally makes him see what a jackass he's been."

Rapp didn't like it, but Nash was right. "Then put all the cards on the table and give him two clear choices: He either gets his shit together and remembers which team he plays for or he's done. This is his last chance."

Nash nodded and said, "I think you should be the one to deliver that message."

Before Rapp could reply, Coleman handed him the phone. "Hub . . . did Rick tell you that he had Ajax put down by the vet down there in Jalalabad or did you just assume he did?" Rapp listened as Hubbard relayed his answer and then said, "Text me the info on the vet here in Kabul. I'm going to have a talk with him." Rapp handed the phone back to Coleman and before he could return to the problem of Darren Sickles, Nash asked a question of his own.

"What was that all about?"

Rapp wasn't about to go into his suspicions. Not until he had more information. "I'm just trying to run down a few leads. Darren is all yours. I need to get out of this building or I'm going to commit some serious violence."

"Give me five minutes," Nash begged, holding up the fingers on his right hand.

"No. I'm sick of talking. I need to get back out there."

"A vet . . . what in the hell is he going to tell you?"

"Don't worry about me. Focus on Darren and those other idiots. We've got more people coming in," Rapp checked his watch, "about three hours from now. They need to hit the ground running and that means you have to put a game plan together for them."

Nash's face soured. "Who said I was the office manager?"

"It goes along with your fancy new title. You're the senior man on the ground, so you get to stay here and babysit everyone while we go kick down some doors and knock a few heads."

"This is bullshit."

Rapp smiled. "You're a national hero. We can't afford to lose you."

"More bullshit," Nash barked. "You were there, too. In fact, you were the crazy son of a bitch who rushed those guys with nothing more than a pistol."

"Shhhhh," Rapp said with a finger over his mouth. "That's classified information." He laughed and then said to Coleman, "Get the boys saddled up."

"You want to travel light or in force?"

"Light . . . just you, me, Joe, and Reavers. And none of that MRAP shit." Rapp started to walk with Coleman at his side. "Find us an old beat-up sedan."

Nash was genuinely conflicted as he watched Rapp and Coleman walk down the long hallway. It pained him to not be included in stuff like this. He had officially become a paper pusher and it killed him. It made his wife a great deal happier, and in light of the fact that he had four kids, one of whom was still in diapers, it was probably a good idea to hang up his spurs, but God, he missed it.

CHAPTER 13

THE assassin had killed eighty-seven of his fellow human beings. At least that was how many he had specifically tallied. There were likely a few more, bodyguards and such, who died later from injuries suffered at his hands. So he reasoned the number could be as high as one hundred, but the official tally stood at eighty-seven. Many of those kills he was proud of, nasty people who were creating pain and destruction in their lust for power or profit. There were also more than a few that he knew he'd answer to his maker for. Most of those came early in his career before he'd honed his skills and become more selective. Some were mistakes, and some were a simple lack of experience. He'd used his hands, wires, knives, and poison, but most often he used a gun or a rifle. There were a few regrettable times when he'd employed explosives, which were extremely effective, but unruly in the sense that the odds for collateral damage increased dramatically.

He was good at killing. Too good, really, and that was what brought about his near downfall. You didn't get good in this line of work from a lack of confidence, but you could definitely end up dead from an overabundance of belief in your abilities. After thirteen years in the business he learned that there were certain times when you needed to say no—sometimes for no reason other than the fact that you'd said yes too many times. The challenge to test your abilities and the money were incredible motivators, and he'd found himself competing to be the best. Increasingly, he needed to take the most difficult jobs, so he could prove to himself that he had no peer. It was stupid, really, as if there would one day be an awards ceremony for the greatest assassin of the last decade.

Eventually his ego and an extremely big payday put him on a collision course with mortality. That one job had changed everything. It had made him wiser. He was still confident, but he was also keenly aware of his weaknesses and the fact there were others out there who were every bit as talented as he was, and even a few who were better. The last and final piece was perhaps the most difficult to judge. By necessity, he never met his employers. He didn't want them to know what he looked like, and if they had any brains they knew it was best not to reveal themselves to a world-class killer. This type of arrangement necessitated a middleman who was able to negotiate contracts and make sure that payments were made on time. He had used three such individuals over the years. The first two were dead—one of natural causes, the other from a bullet to the back of the head while he was taking a leisurely stroll through El Retiro Park in Madrid. The Spaniard, it turned out, didn't fully embrace the confidential aspect of their work, and it didn't help that he was stealing money from him.

His agent for the last two-plus years had been a Russian, and up until this point things had gone smoothly. This current contract was beginning to take on the stench of a job that he should have declined. Separate the most obvious problem, which was the target, and he was left with a bevy of red flags. Chief among them, his employer was showing himself to be a control freak. Just in the last few hours the anonymous employer had provided information that left him to wonder who he might be. It was natural to wonder such things in this line of work, but more often than not, there was a simple motivation. This one was beginning to feel different. The mystery man was feeding him with information that could be provided only by someone on the inside. In the assassin's mind, that distinctly raised the possibility that he was being watched. The anonymous employer was now calling the shots at a level the assassin did not like. This employer was a puppet master who thought he needed to pull the assassin's strings, as if the assassin was an amateur. After revealing that the target was none other than Mitch Rapp, a bellman delivered a large manila envelope that contained an address, a map, a key, and specific instructions on when and how he was to take the shot. The assassin was at first offended. He was the professional, after all. If this employer was so good at this, he should come and take the shot himself.

The assassin checked his ego, however, and for the moment was willing to explore what was increasingly feeling like a contract that fell outside his normal risk parameters. One voice inside his head, the one that was ruled by common sense, was telling him to go to the airport and leave the country immediately. If he was being watched, though, this could cause a problem. The other voice inside his head, the one that could sometimes get him to overextend himself, was telling him this was far too exciting to walk away from. For the moment, curiosity and the large payday got the best of him.

He retrieved his alias passport from the hotel safe with a matching credit card and cash as well as other worn forms of ID that any seasoned customs agent would expect to find in a fortyish man's wallet. He donned a pair of cargo pants, hiking boots, field shirt, and light gray North Face vest. Into the left cargo pocket of his pants he slid a Kershaw Black Blur folding knife in the event that he needed to discreetly kill someone.

Next came what he considered his lifeline, should things go drastically bad. He laid his specially designed backpack down on the bed and went over his gear. Inside was an FNH 5.7 single-action, auto-loading pistol. He'd fired virtually every handgun known to man, and in the hands of a trained marksman there was no better pistol to carry into a gunfight, for three reasons: The first was the low recoil of the weapon, the second was the twenty-round magazine capacity, and the third was its unique 5.7x28mm round, which was capable of defeating all but the best body armor. The pistol had a short suppressor attached to the end and three extra magazines. The pack also contained two M84 stun grenades with timers, which he'd learned could come in very handy should he need a distraction to complete his job.

The backpack itself was the most impressive piece of equipment. It was made out of ballistic fabric and with the quick pull of a zipper and the yank of a handle he could pull half of the backpack over his head, where it would rest on his chest. With a few swift moves that took no longer than two seconds, the backpack became a bulletproof tactical vest with his pistol and his other much-needed tools readily available on his chest. He hooked a fanny pack around his waist. Inside was a second lens for his digital camera and a subcompact 9mm Beretta with a two-inch suppressor on the end.

The rest of his gear was thrown into a generic black carry-on bag. He was always careful about what he touched, so it didn't take more than five minutes to wipe down the room. The hotel was filled with security cameras, and he wouldn't be surprised if the embassy had real-time access to those cameras. There was absolutely no doubt that his image would be captured, and as much as he didn't like it, there wasn't a thing he could do to prevent it from happening.

So he slung his Canon EOS 5D Mark II camera around his neck to complete his cover as a freelance photographer and headed for the lobby. He kept the two key cards, one in his backpack and the other in his wallet, in case he needed to return to the hotel, but past experience told him he would not be coming back. In fact it was extremely likely he would be making a hasty exit from the country. He smiled for all of the digital cameras in the lobby and then asked the doorman for a taxi. The man asked him if he was checking out and he told him no even though it was likely he was doing just that.

The assassin had been to virtually every major city on every continent with the exception of Antarctica. He had a very good grasp of how standards of living fluctuated from one country to another. Even with all of the money that the Americans and their coalition partners had used to build up the city's infrastructure, Kabul was still basically a hellhole. Garbage was plastered against the curbs of virtually every pothole-strewn street, and if the city owned a street sweeper there was no evidence of it. The relative high altitude and lack of rain helped cover everything with a film of dirt. Beyond that, the city's inhabitants seemed to embrace throwing their garbage wherever they liked, almost as if it were a national pastime.

The driver was a talkative fellow, which the assassin didn't like, but things were coming to a head so quickly that there was no time to be picky. Normally he would have changed cabs at least three times, but he was more interested in checking out the location where he had been told to kill Rapp. That was the part that was grating on his nerves more than anything else. He was a professional and was used to picking a time and place of his own choosing. This entire thing was becoming a little too orchestrated.

The office building was a half block off the Kabul River, a muddy morass of refuse that in the late spring and early summer was bursting at the banks from all the snowmelt from the mountains, but in the fall it slowed to a trickle and again revealed that the inhabitants of Kabul thought of the river as a garbage dump. Even though the office was only a few miles from the hotel the drive took nearly fifteen minutes. The lack of traffic lights and the heavy noontime traffic made the going slow. His Arabic was basic enough to find out that the driver spoke English, which made things much easier. After some haggling they agreed on what it would cost to hire him for the next few hours. The assassin directed him to the location where he wanted him to wait and then tore a hundred-dollar bill in half. The driver didn't like that one bit. After some cursing, the assassin explained to him that he'd get the other half when he came back and a fresh hundred-dollar bill as well. This seemed to calm the man a bit. The two exchanged mobile numbers and then the assassin left the taxi along with the roller bag in the trunk.

He circled the block, snapping photos as he went, but in reality he was taking a digital recording of everything. It was a mixed business-residential district with a good number of two- and three-story buildings. By European standards the place was a dump, but here in Kabul it was considered upper class. Vendors lined both sides of the streets selling everything from the popular vests that most men wore to brightly colored plastic chairs and tables to tea, with a surprisingly varied selection. There were fruit and produce vendors of almost all imaginable kinds. These merchants, the assassin knew, would have their finger on the pulse of this street where they lived six days a week from sunrise to sundown. Anything out of the ordinary and they would seem a bit agitated.

He was careful to not appear to be taking any direct shots of any particular people, as it could make them jumpy. Rather he made it look as if he was taking long-distance shots of faraway objects. The veterinary hospital was near the end of the block with a park next door that was adjacent to the side door of the hospital. The office building he was supposed to take his shot from was across the street and about 80 meters down the block. At first glance the location was perfect.

The assassin took a final casual look around and then entered the building. There really wasn't a lobby, just a small landing for the stairs that led to the second floor. He did a quick walk-through of the first floor and was alarmed to see that there was no secondary exit. That was reason enough to pull the plug on the assignment, but he had some time to spare, and curiosity drove him to take the steps to the second floor. It took his eyes a moment to adjust to the poor lighting. He walked past the office that was in his instructions and went to the end of the hall, where he was relieved to find a ladder that led to the roof. Going back to the office, he unzipped the fanny pack and slid his right hand around the grip of the Beretta should he need it. The key slid into the lock easily enough.

The assassin stayed behind the doorframe and pushed the door open. The office was a simple fifteen-by-fifteen-foot space with dirty, cracked walls and carpeting that was worn in the places where the previous tenant's desk had sat. Underneath the window someone had set up a folding table and chair. On top of the table sat a rectangular tan nylon bag that he had seen many times. He closed and locked the door and approached the bag as if it might bite him. After hesitating for a moment, he retrieved a pair of latex gloves from his fanny pack and snapped them on each hand. He ran the zipper all the way along the perimeter and carefully folded the top over to reveal a shiny new Heckler & Koch HK 416. A soft whistle of admiration rolled past the assassin's lips. The H&K 416 was the most advanced M-4 carbine available. The weapon was outfitted with the top-of-the-line optics that in the hands of the assassin would make it lethal out to six hundred meters. At eighty meters a headshot would be a snap. The short-stroke, gas-piston operating system delivered the round with incredible accuracy, and more important, the weapon rarely jammed.

He lifted the weapon from its case and turned it over in his hands. The suppressor was tucked in a separate compartment. The carbine was a fine piece of craftsmanship. His thumb pressed the magazine release and he inspected the rounds. As per his request the magazine was loaded with Remington's revolutionary 300BLK subsonic round, which had significantly more punch than the standard 5.56. He seated the magazine back into the weapon, turned on the EOTech sight, and brought the weapon up to his right shoulder. Standing five feet back from the window he sighted in the front door of the clinic. With both eyes open, the red dot balanced perfectly on the door handle. At this short distance there would be no need for a tripod or shooting stick. At this distance he wouldn't need the 3x magnifier, but he flipped it into place nonetheless. He wanted to see if there was anyone out there watching him. He started to his left and searched for a likely sniper position.

After five minutes of carefully probing he was left with no evidence that he was being watched, but he knew the absence of such evidence meant nothing. If the person was good, it was a simple thing to conceal a position that was one thousand meters away. After placing the H&K 416 back in the case he picked up a manila envelope and dumped the contents on the table. There was a handmade map that showed the location of the rooftop access and a line of exfiltration across several rooftops to a ladder that would lead to the street. He set it off to the side and picked up a photo of Rapp. This caused him to frown. His employer had already provided the same photo via text. He grabbed his lighter and burned both map and photo, dropping them to the floor and stamping them into the carpet when they were nothing more than a few fragments.

He grabbed his digital camera and began going through the footage he'd taken. He was roughly three minutes in and had picked out two interesting individuals who seemed to pay him a little too much attention. They were also conveniently located at each end of the block.

The assassin was about to explore this further when a text arrived informing him that Mr. Rapp was on the way. Estimated time of arrival was six minutes. He felt his heart begin to quicken—something that hadn't happened in a long time. The assassin took in several deep breaths and then shook his arms loose to try to let out some of the tension. Why put two watchers on the street if they already had eyes on the target? The answer was unfortunately obvious. They were not here to keep an eye on Rapp. They were standing at their posts doing one of two things. The first was simple enough. His success or failure would be reported in near real time to his employer. No real harm, but another sign that his employer had some serious assets at his disposal. The second possibility was more ominous—his employer planned on killing him as soon as Rapp had been taken care of.

CHAPTER 14

THE silver Toyota 4Runner hadn't been washed in over a month. The windshield had a divot from a rock and a crack that crawled its way along the bottom, dying in the right corner. The front bumper had seen some use but not as much as the rear. Both sides had enough scrapes and dents so that the vehicle fit right in on the wild streets of Kabul. This all made Rapp happy, as he greatly preferred anonymity to large steel-plated vehicles that screamed U.S.A.

Rapp was in back looking out the dirty rear-passenger window at nothing in particular. His mind was revisiting what he'd seen at the safe house that morning. Sydney Hayek didn't think she'd get the preliminary ballistics back for another twenty-four hours, and Rapp was already starting to think he didn't need them. The way the bodies were strewn about the house, the big .45 caliber hole in the back of the one guy's head, and the security system being defeated without the slightest warning, it all looked bad. Throw the dog on top of that and he cringed at the possible outcomes. The real question was why?

Rickman was a strange bird, there was no doubt about that, but it was a big jump from being a little different to being a traitor. Rapp knew he was getting a bit ahead of himself, though. The dog could have been an honest mistake. Hubbard could have easily misheard Rickman or just assumed that he'd put the dog down at the local clinic, but when Rapp got these kinds of feelings, more often than not they turned out to be right. The difference this time around was that he was hoping he was wrong.

Maslick was driving and big Reavers riding shotgun with his bushy dark beard, a pair of wraparound Oakleys, and his standard fuck-off expression on his face. Like a pit bull, he was not the friendliest creature when it came to new faces, but immensely loyal to those whom he knew. Coleman had been his CO when the two men were SEALs and then after they had continued to work together as private contractors for the CIA. Maslick was former Delta Force and had been attached to Rapp's team on and off for three years. Both men had a cool detachment that had been honed by killing enemies who had desperately tried to kill them first. They never looked nervous, but they never stopped surveying the landscape for threats.

Rapp pulled out his phone and checked to see if there were any new emails from Langley that might shed some light on Rickman's location. Kennedy had told him that Rickman was the top priority for the National Security Agency until the president said otherwise. Every conversation, email, tweet, and text within a thousand miles was being translated and crunched by the NSA's Cray supercomputers. They were bound to pick up something. Rapp just hoped it was enough for him to get a solid lead.

"So are you going to tell me why you've got a hard-on for some vet?"

Rapp looked up from his phone and wondered how much he should share with Coleman. It wasn't that he didn't trust him. Next to Kennedy and maybe Hurley there was no one he trusted more, it was just that a gut feeling like this could poison what they were trying to do.

Coleman waited a few seconds for Rapp to answer and then said, "You're not the only one who thinks this thing doesn't smell right."

Rapp made no attempt to hide his surprise. "What are you talking about?"

"Please . . . I've been in enough shootouts to know how things go down. You're hung up on the bodyguard . . . the one missing half his face."

Rapp confirmed his suspicions with a simple nod.

"It jumped out at me, too. The rest were all shot with nine millimeters and then there's this guy who was obviously tapped by a .45 and we both know Rick loves his big Kimber."

"And the guy was shot in the back of the head while he was moving down the hall away from Rick's office and bedroom," Rapp added.

"I noticed the same thing, but then I started thinking, what if Rick found out this bodyguard had set him up? Maybe he had some suspicions and then the guy went and took the security system off-line. Hell, Rick could have been sleeping. He hears the commotion downstairs and as a last act of desperation, he shoots this guy in the back of the head."

Rapp turned Coleman's scenario over in his mind, hoping that it would explain away his fears. "I hadn't thought of that." Rapp tried to imagine Rickman being roused from his bed and springing into action. Joe Rickman was anything but a foot soldier. Officially, he was a mid-level case officer in the CIA's Clandestine Service. Unofficially, he'd spent the last eight years running the Clandestine Service's black ops in the Islamic Republic. He didn't show up on the flow charts that were given to Congress. There was no important title before his name. He wasn't a station chief or a deputy director. He was a black hole that happened to be a repository of a mountain of dirty, nasty secrets. So far no one knew the exact number, but the best guess was that more than a quarter of a billion dollars in cash had passed through Rickman's hands while he'd played this dangerous game. There was no oversight, no accounting, no one back in Washington asking for receipts and riding his ass to fill out expense forms. The suits didn't want to know the details of what Rickman was up to, and because of his big brain he was able to keep it all straight without writing anything down. He continued to pass his twice-a-year lie detector test, and that was good enough for the people in charge. Rapp had worried for some time that it was a recipe for disaster.

Yes, Rick loved his Kimber, but there could be an absolute chasm between spending time on the range in a controlled environment and getting yanked from a deep sleep and not shooting yourself in the foot. The more Rapp contemplated the mess, the more he thought the biggest red flag was the security system. If Coleman was right, and the one bodyguard had been the inside man, he would need to see proof that this guy had the ability to defeat an extremely complicated security system. Rapp was no dummy, and he'd been stymied plenty of times by the technological aspect of his job. That was why he normally traveled with experts like Marcus Dumond, who was a hacker extraordinaire.

"Rick was no shooter," Rapp said. "I'm not saying it's not possible, but I have a hard time seeing Rick plugging a guy in the back of the head in the middle of the night. Especially one of these hardened guards we chose for him."

"We'll find out. If the bodyguard was bad, there'll be something. Now, what about this vet?"

Rapp sighed. "Rick had a dog."

"I remember. Rottweiler . . . slobbered all over the place. Thing never left his side . . . he treated it like it was his kid." Coleman shook his head with disapproval. "No way to train a dog like that."

"I asked Hub about the dog. He said it'd been sick. Only six years old or something like that. Rick brought it to the vet down in J-bad and had it put down. I told Hub to talk to the vet and make sure the dog was put down."

"The vet didn't put it down."

"Nope. In fact he couldn't figure out what was wrong with it so he told Rick to bring it to the big-city vet up here in Kabul."

Coleman looked skeptical. "Sounds like a bit of a reach."

Maslick announced that they were two blocks away from the clinic.

Rapp looked out a window as they passed a green Ford Ranger pickup that was the local police department's main form of transportation. Four men were sitting in back decked out in full combat gear. More to himself than Coleman, he said, "Yeah . . . well, we're about to find out."

CHAPTER 15

THE office window consisted of two laterally sliding pieces of glass with an aluminum frame. There was no screen and the channel was filled with so much debris that it was difficult to open the window. It was neither a warm nor a cold October day, and the way people smoked in this city a cracked window would not stand out as a possible threat, even to someone as aware as Rapp. The assassin decided four inches would give him enough range to cover the twenty or so feet in front of the clinic's main door. He checked his sight line once again and then returned to the question that was chewing on his nerves.

It was possible that his employer was cheap and simply wanted to save himself $1.5 million, but considering the lengths that he'd gone to that was unlikely. The more plausible explanation was that this control freak on the other end of the text messages and envelopes didn't like loose ends, and the assassin was about to become a loose end. He prided himself on his instincts, and when a hunter realizes he might soon become the hunted it is a feeling that is impossible to ignore. His mind was speeding to calculate his avenues of escape, when a truly frightening thought hit him square in the cerebral cortex. What if his employer had somehow discovered his past with Rapp? Surely there were a handful of people in the U.S. government who knew the details of that catastrophe. The scales in his mind that were trying to weigh his employer's honesty against the possibility that he was being set up suddenly jerked in favor of the latter as if an anvil had been dropped on that side. There was no longer any doubt in the assassin's mind. He was being set up.

The front door did not seem like a great option, as both ends of the street were being watched, but the roof gave him even greater concern. It was obviously the avenue of escape that the employer preferred him to take, which likely meant there was a trap waiting for him. He looked down at the phone that had been his link to the employer and had the ominous feeling that it was being used to track his every move. Even worse, the thing could have a small bomb in it. Not enough to kill him unless it was placed next to his ear. Intelligence agencies had used cell phones to assassinate enemies for more than a decade. He decided he wouldn't be answering any calls.

As if on cue the phone bleeped and the screen lit up. The assassin flinched slightly and was embarrassed. Control of his nerves would be the difference between life and death. The screen told him his target was less than a minute away. It also gave him the make and model of the vehicle. As if by reflex, he picked up the M-4 and snapped the suppressor onto the end of the barrel. His eyes looked over the case, taking a quick inventory. The magazine in the rifle was the only one provided. No spares in the event of a shootout. He let out a deep sigh and the thought occurred to him that the room itself could be wired for sound and image, or worse yet, booby-trapped to explode after he'd completed his mission. That idea more than anything caused him to go through the motions. He placed the tactical sling over his head and stepped a few feet back so that no one on the street could see him. He brought the rifle up and tested the sling as if he was trying to find the right amount of tension. He eased his eye in behind the viewfinder and placed the red dot on the front door of the clinic. His mind was already counting down the seconds to Rapp's arrival. Everything at this point was natural, pounded into his brain through repetition. Physically he was doing everything that he would normally do, and if he was being watched there would be no reason for his employer to think he was onto him. He lowered the rifle and kept his breathing easy. The shot would happen during a brief window—maybe five seconds as Rapp left the vehicle and made his way to the door.

While all looked normal physically, his mind was behaving quite differently. It was churning through every available option over and over, trying to calculate which avenue would lead to his best chance for survival. Suddenly the money didn't mean very much. Oh, he'd keep the $1.5 million, and if he made it out of this hellhole alive, he'd do his best to track down this asshole who was setting him up. He wondered if Yuri was in on it. His agent, a former Russian SVR intelligence officer, was more than capable of doing what was best for himself. That was why the assassin had never met him face-to-face and communicated with him almost entirely through email. All of this would have to be dealt with later. For now, he needed to stay focused on saving his own hide.

The Toyota SUV rolled into sight beneath him and stopped at the curb directly in front of the clinic. The assassin brought the rifle up and thanks to the modern technology of his EOTech sight was able to keep both eyes open. He timed his next move perfectly. All four doors of the SUV opened and men piled out, all of them wearing baseball hats. Even though he couldn't see Rapp's face, he knew which one he was within a split second. He slid the red dot in the center of the viewfinder onto the middle of Rapp's back and moved his finger from the trigger guard to the trigger. He watched Rapp cover the ground between the car and the front door, smoothly following him with the weapon.

Suddenly, the assassin's head jerked toward the door as if he'd heard a noise in the hallway. His finger slid off the trigger and straightened. He moved quickly to the door and listened for any other sound. After a few seconds he returned to the window only to see that Rapp was already in the building. Two of his men were standing on the sidewalk, keeping an eye on the car. He did his best to look disappointed. The assassin picked up the camera, popped out the memory card, and slid it in his pocket. He didn't want to lug the camera around.

Not knowing what he would find in the hallway, he unslung the M-4 and then pulled the cord on the backpack that converted it into a tactical vest. He wanted quick access to one of his stun grenades if anyone was waiting for him in the hall. After grabbing the M-4, he moved to the door and did not hesitate. He yanked it open and took a quick look. The hallway was empty, so he moved with speed to the stairs and down one flight. As he pushed through the main door onto the sidewalk he was fully committed. The M-4 was slung with the butt just under his right armpit and the suppressor down by his left thigh. His right hand gripped the handle but his finger was clearly visible and off the trigger. As he moved onto the street he looked to his left and then his right and all his fears were validated. Parked at the end of each block were police trucks filled with officers in full combat gear. When he looked across the street at Rapp's men he saw that they had also noticed the men. The one with the beard noticed him first. He casually changed his stance and brought his rifle into a position where he could quickly dispatch this potential threat.

The assassin let his weapon hang from his neck, raising both hands to shoulder height, his palms out. When he was twenty feet away, he kept moving and said, "I need to speak to Mitch." The familiarity in his voice seemed to relax the two watchdogs a bit. The assassin closed the distance to within six feet and then stopped. He looked to his right and then to his left. One of the men whom he had seen earlier was talking on a cell phone and began yelling and motioning at the police officers to get out of the truck. A second truck with six more men raced to a stop behind the first. The assassin resisted the urge to raise his rifle and shoot the spotter with the cell phone.

Instead, he turned to the two big Americans and in near flawless English said, "I think you guys better call for some backup."

CHAPTER 16

THE sparse waiting area held four people, a dog, three cats, and a bird. The bird was in a cage behind the receptionist's counter as well as the two cats that were sleeping in wicker baskets. A little boy not more than eight held the leash of a small pooch while his mother sat protectively next to him. An elderly man with a cigarette dangling from his mouth cradled a sickly-looking black cat that was missing large clumps of hair. The old man looked depressed. Neither adult made eye contact, but the little boy gave Rapp a friendly smile. Rapp returned the gesture with a nod of thanks. Most of the people in Kabul tried to ignore foreigners, and Rapp didn't blame them one bit. Their country had been at near constant war for thirty years. There were others who stared you down as if they wanted to kill you, and a small minority who would smile and maybe even say hello.

Rapp approached the blue Formica reception desk. A nice young woman in a black hijab looked up at him and asked in English, "How may I help you?"

"Do I look that American?" Rapp asked, trying to seem offended.

"No, but he does." She pointed over Rapp's shoulder at Coleman.

Rapp turned around and looked at his friend's blond hair and blue eyes. Coleman's Northern European ethnicity made it nearly impossible for him to blend in on ops like this. "Yeah," Rapp said, "he works for the United Nations. I think he's Swedish or something like that. I can't understand a thing he says. At any rate, we were hoping to speak with Dr. Amin."

"I'm sorry, but he's at the university right now."

"Do you expect him back this afternoon?"

"Normally not, but if we're busy he stops by on his way home. May I ask what you need to discuss with him?"

Rapp hesitated. He was not used to sharing information, but this woman seemed nice enough, and she might be able to save him a step. "It's a rather important matter." Rapp retrieved his Joe Cox credentials emblazoned in gold with the seal of the United States and the all-important, somewhat vague words *Federal Officer,* raised and embossed. "We're trying to track down a missing person. We were told that he brought his dog to your clinic about a month ago. He was an American and his dog was a Rottweiler. Do you remember anyone like that?"

She shook her head. "No, but I'm only here part-time. Do you have a name?"

Rickman had more than a few aliases as well. Rapp had no idea if he had used one, so he started with Rickman's real name. The receptionist spun her chair around and crab-walked the chair over to a row of file cabinets. Rapp looked over his shoulder to find Coleman with his arms folded across his chest and shaking his head.

"Swedish? What in the hell is wrong with you?"

Rapp started to laugh, and then his eyes caught something beyond the glass doors. His left hand slid between the folds of his jacket and around the grip of his 9mm Glock. The change in Rapp's demeanor didn't go unnoticed by Coleman, who did a casual 180-degree turn to see what was going on. Rapp could scarcely believe his eyes. It was as if a ghost had walked out of his not-so-distant past. Nearly four years ago, to be exact. He watched the man walk past Reavers and Maslick, stopping briefly to point at something down the street. In Rapp's mind it was a move to distract them, but Rapp could not be distracted. Not by this man. He drew his gun and lined the sights up on the head of the man who had killed his wife.

The receptionist said something, but Rapp didn't hear her. He was too intent on the man coming through the door. The only thing that prevented Rapp from shooting him on the spot was that he had his hands in the air in what seemed to be a genuine posture of surrender.

Coleman said, "Is that who I think it is?"

"Yes."

One of the glass doors opened and the assassin stepped slowly into the lobby. He glanced at Coleman and then focused on Rapp. "We need to talk and we must do it quickly."

"Give me one good reason why I shouldn't shoot you."

Louie Gould kept his hands in the air and gave a slight shrug. "I can give you several, but since time is of the essence, let's start with the fact that I didn't shoot you in the head when you got out of your truck a minute ago. Even more important, I think you're going to need my help in the very near future. Possibly the next thirty seconds."

Despite the anger that was coursing through his veins, Rapp's pistol was extremely steady. "What in the hell are you talking about?"

Gould took a quick look around the waiting room. He would have preferred to have this discussion in a more intimate setting, but there was no time for that, so before he got into the details he looked at Rapp's blond-haired friend and said, "I told your guys outside that they should call for backup but I don't think they took my advice. Trust me, you are going to want to make that call and do it quickly." The assassin then said to Rapp, "I still take the occasional contract."

Rapp shook his head. "That wasn't part of the deal."

"I know," he said sheepishly, "but we needed money and I have been very selective." He shook his head, showing the first sign of frustration. "We can discuss this all later. The important thing is that I took a contract from an anonymous employer. My instructions were to fly into Kabul yesterday. About ninety minutes ago I received instructions to come to an office building on this street. When I arrived, this rifle was waiting for me along with a photograph of my target." Gould pointed at Rapp. "You."

"You're full of shit."

"I wish I was, but that's not the real problem." Gould kept his hands up while he took a step back to see if he could see what was going on at the one end of the block. As he did so, one of Rapp's men came through the door.

It was Maslick. "There's something going on out here. Both ends of the street are blocked by the police and they've got about ten guys at each end that look like they're planning some kind of an assault."

Gould confirmed with his own eyes what the man had said. "They're here to kill you. And me, too, I suppose."

A single rifle shot cracked the relative calm of the afternoon. The four men in the lobby were all combat veterans and none of them flinched. They all looked at Reavers, who was standing on the sidewalk. Before any of them could react, a fusillade of bullets rang out. The glass doors shattered and when they looked up, Reavers was falling to the ground.

Coleman shouted above the roar of the rifle shots, "Suppressive fire? I'll grab him."

Rapp moved to his left and pushed his back against the wall while Maslick moved to his right and did the same. Both men began squeezing off well-aimed shots at the officers at the opposite end of the street. Coleman holstered his gun, yanked open the door, and grabbed Reavers by the tactical vest. The big man didn't budge on the first try so Coleman put all of his muscle into it. Bullets were zipping past his head in both directions. He backpedaled into the reception area and immediately noticed the streak of red blood on the white tile floor. Out of the line of direct fire he knelt and tried to find where he'd been shot. His hands slid over Reavers's body, checking for blood. Within seconds he found two fatal wounds. The first was in his hairline on the top right side of his head and the second was in the groin. Reavers's brain was gone, but his heart was still pumping, and from the looks of the pool of blood on the floor, his femoral artery had been hit.

In battle, the passage of time slowed for Coleman. In a brief instant he acknowledged that his friend was gone and that now was not the time to deal with it. That would come later—anger, frustration, genuine sadness, and some laughs, to be sure, but right now was about survival.

"Reavers is dead," Coleman announced above the roar of fire. He grabbed his friend's M-4 rifle and started stuffing the extra magazines into his vest and cargo pockets.

Rapp stole a quick glance at Reavers's lifeless body, and then he noticed the frightened look on the little boy's face. He yelled to Coleman. "Get these people back into one of the exam rooms!"

Gould showed up at Rapp's side and dropped to one knee. He began firing well-aimed single shots. In less than five seconds he counted three kills with as many shots. "We need to put someone on the roof." After a couple more shots he yelled, "And you might want to see if you can get someone to come help us!"

"Scott," Rapp barked without taking his eyes off the street, "call Mike and tell him what we're up against. Tell him we need a Quick Reaction Force ASAP or we're all dead." Rapp stepped back, ejected an empty magazine, and popped in a fresh one. Yelling back to Coleman he added, "A gunship would be nice!" Rapp popped off a couple of rounds and saw a man go down. Then, looking down at Gould, he said, "Get up on the roof and see what you can do. I'll join you as soon as I can. How much ammo do you have?"

Gould shook his head. "Just this one thirty-round magazine, and then I'm down to my pistol."

Rapp noted the make and model of the pistol in Gould's vest. "At these distances I bet you're pretty good with that thing."

Gould nodded. "The best."

"We'll see about that. Grab one extra magazine for the M-4 from the blond guy, and then get your ass up on the roof before we're all dead."

CHAPTER 17

COLEMAN had stashed the old man, the mother and son, their animals, and the receptionist in one of the exam rooms down the hall. Rapp assumed there were some nurses and at least one vet somewhere in the building, but there wasn't a lot he could do about their safety other than keep the local police at bay until the cavalry arrived. As best he could tell, three more pickups filled with combat-clad cops had arrived. It begged the question, could that many Kabul police officers be corrupt?

The front entrance to the clinic was a tangled mess of broken glass and chipped stone. The door, and the two side windows, were completely blown out, and the metal frame was twisted and punctured from bullet strikes. Rapp was about five feet from the edge with his back pressed against the wall. Maslick was standing directly across from him. They were alternating darting out and taking a few shots to keep the cops from rushing the door. So far they were succeeding, but just barely. Rapp watched Maslick eject a spent magazine and insert a fresh one. Their advantage in this fight was their ability to hit targets with consistent, frightening accuracy. Coleman, Maslick, and

Rapp had all fired thousands of practice rounds a month with pistols, carbines, and long rifles. Rapp had no idea how much Gould practiced, but his fee was likely a good predictor of his ability. Even though they were outgunned, this was all going to come down to ammunition.

Rapp knew a little about how these men were selected and trained. Most of them were simply trying to make a living and were extremely brave, as the Taliban often targeted them and their families. He found the idea that they were all corrupt to be a bit of a stretch. It was more plausible that it was someone in their chain of command who was corrupt. Rapp thought of Commander Zahir down in Jalalabad. Until recently the man had been a terrorist and had a bounty on his head, courtesy of the U.S. government. Not only was the bounty gone, but the man was now on our payroll. How many assholes like Zahir were now wearing the uniform of the Afghan Police? Innocent or not, these cops were trying to kill Rapp and his men, so he was left with no alternative if he wanted to survive.

A fresh barrage of bullets slammed into the front wall of the building, peppering Rapp with tiny pebbles. He darted out, fired two well-aimed shots, and ducked back into the lobby as a dozen-plus bullets raked the spot where he'd been standing less than a second ago. Rapp shook his head with anger. That had been closer than he would have liked. He looked across at Maslick again and noticed a splotch of blood on his right shoulder. This position was quickly becoming too hot to defend. Sooner or later one of them was going to pop out and take a bullet in the head. Rapp made a snap decision and ordered Maslick to the roof.

Maslick tried to argue, but Rapp made it clear there was no time for debate. As Rapp began his retreat from the lobby he passed Reavers's body. He noted the Sig P226 pistol still in the man's thigh holster. Kneeling, Rapp grabbed the gun and the three spare magazines. The anger came boiling to the surface and Rapp said to himself, "I swear to God I'm going to kill these idiots who came up with this reintegration crap." The image of Sickles popped into Rapp's mind and it suddenly occurred to Rapp that Sickles had probably recruited the man who was now trying to kill him. Rapp popped in his earpiece and looked up Sickles's mobile number. He tapped the number and listened as began to ring. Rapp left the lobby and entered the hallway that bisected the building. Down at the far end Coleman was stacking and shoving equipment against a side exit.

Taking up position against the doorframe so he could cover the front entrance, Rapp began to wonder if the wall he was behind was thick enough to stop a .223 round. The answer was likely no, so as Darren Sickles' voice came on the line, Rapp walked back into the lobby. "Hey, dickhead," Rapp barked above the roar of gunfire, "did Mike tell you the shitstorm we're in?"

Rapp holstered his gun, stepped behind the reception desk, and began yanking up on the heavy Formica countertop.

"He just told me. I have no—"

"Shut up and listen to me." Rapp gave the top one more shove and it broke free. "This is your fault. You recruited these scumbags, and you were dumb enough to think you could trust them." Rapp grabbed the top and lugged it back into the hallway. "You are going to get on the fucking phone, and you are going to call every last one of them, and you are going to tell them that I'm going to place a million-dollar bounty on every one of their fucking heads, and I'm going to be the one collecting it."

Rapp tossed the heavy top up against the doorframe and leaned against it. He drew his weapon again, feeling a lot better about his position, but not so good about Sickles, who was yammering about how he didn't understand any of this. That it simply didn't make sense. With more important things to do than listen to Sickles' senseless speculation, Rapp yelled, "Darren, I don't give a shit what you think! Just get on the damn phone and make it clear to these assholes that I'm going to hunt them down and kill them." Rapp was tempted to tell Sickles that he was going to kill him as well, but it was likely to be an extremely counterproductive threat, so he bit his tongue and hung up.

Rapp knew what their next move would be, and it likely wouldn't take long. The U.S. had outfitted the Afghan Police with takedown gear that included battering rams, breaching shotguns, ribbon charges, and bulletproof riot shields. It was the bulletproof riot shields that worried Rapp the most. All a thoughtful commander needed to do was grab a couple of shields and do the old Roman tortoise. The first man in the line would hold the shield directly in front of him and the second man would hold the shield above them, protecting them from the men on the roof. They'd rush the front door with one or two lines of men. If that happened, Rapp knew they would overpower him and his little 9mm pistol in a matter of seconds. The thought of dying like that got Rapp thinking, and he yelled down the hall, "Scott?"

Coleman shoved a big metal exam table against his pile and turned to look at Rapp. "What?"

"You come across any oxygen tanks?"

"Yeah." Coleman didn't have to be told what to do. He ducked into one of the rooms and came out with two green tanks. He dragged them down the hall by the necks and dropped them at Rapp's feet.

Rapp kept his eyes and his pistol on the door and asked, "Any more?"

"Yeah."

"Put 'em in front of your pile down there and get your ass up on the roof."

Coleman shook his head. "You get up on the roof. I've got this handled."

"Stop wasting time. Drop the tanks down there and get moving. They're probably running low on ammunition."

Coleman reluctantly dropped two more tanks by the side door and then stopped to offer Rapp Reavers's M-4 rifle.

"Nope . . . no need for that down here. This is all close quarters. Get your ass up on the roof and buy us some time." Coleman started to leave, but Rapp grabbed him by the arm. "What did Mike say?"

"He said he'll get some shooters here as soon as is humanly possible."

"Call him back and tell him we'll take anything. Get a Little Bird to give us an ammo drop and maybe a SAW or two." Rapp glanced back at the front door. "Maybe some grenades, too."

"I'm on it." Coleman had his phone out and was calling Nash again. "Call if you need help."

Rapp knew he'd be making no such call. He'd hold them off as long as he could and then, if he was still alive, he'd limp his way up to the roof. *What a shitty way to die*, Rapp thought to himself. All of the close calls he'd had and it was going to come down to being killed by men who were supposed to be his allies. He heard Stan Hurley's gruff voice telling him to suck it up. Now was not the time to think about death unless it was the other guy's mortality that you were focused on. Hurley was fond of saying that no matter how bad things got there was always a way out. Rapp clung to that idea, as there was an ebb in the volume of shots being fired—just a pop here and there instead of the sustained blister of rounds smacking into the building.

Unfortunately, Rapp knew what that really meant. It was too soon for Nash or Sickles to have been able to call off the dogs, so it was more likely that someone in a command position with half a brain had showed up and was now getting the men ready for an organized assault. Rapp holstered his gun and dragged the two oxygen tanks into the lobby. He stopped about six feet short of the front door, laid the tanks on their sides, and then drew his gun. Lest they think no one was guarding the front door, he slid along the wall until he had an angle to shoot from. He squeezed off two shots and then two more and ducked back into the lobby. He was pretty certain the first two shots had hit one man, but the second two had bounced harmlessly off a clear Plexiglas riot shield. Rapp went back to his position in the hallway with the foreboding feeling that this might be one situation he wasn't going to be able to get out of.

CHAPTER 18

GOULD popped the hatch and had to will himself onto the flat roof. Somewhere out there, he feared, a sniper was still lurking. He rolled onto his side, the M-4 cradled protectively in both hands, and then crawled his way to the parapet of the roof. There was a two-foot stone parapet that provided sufficient cover. He carefully brought his head above the lip and scanned the buildings across the street. With no shooters in sight, he got up on his right knee and brought the butt of the rifle up to his right shoulder. Gould swung the muzzle over the edge of the roof, sweeping it from left to right with both eyes open, the big square EOTech aperture bringing his targets clearly into view.

The spotter in civilian clothes was standing behind one of the police trucks with his cell phone held to his left ear.

"There you are, you little prick," the assassin said with a smile creasing his lips. Gould placed the red dot right over the cell phone, let loose an even exhalation, and then casually squeezed the trigger. The rifle jumped a quarter inch, but Gould never lost sight of the target. The heavy bullet shattered the cell phone and then exploded through the man's head, spraying blood, bone, and brain matter in a mini mushroom cloud onto the men and street just past him.

Three police officers were left standing in shock, gaping at the man who had just been urging them into action, and then three seconds after that they were all lying on the street dead. Gould worked his targets methodically, keeping the rifle in single-shot mode. It took the police approximately ten seconds to realize there was a new threat on the roof, but it had cost them dearly. Seven officers had been dispatched. Gould was about to swing his rifle around so he could go to work on the cops at the other end of the street when the air around him exploded with the sharp snaps of bullets. He dropped flat behind the lip as bullets began to thump into the stone like a jackhammer. It took a second to sink in, but Gould realized that his position had been discovered and that the men at the other end of street had something more to bring to the fight than the relatively light M-4 rifle. Since everything they had was provided by the Americans it was likely that it was the heavier-caliber M249 Squad Automatic Weapon or SAW. The machine gun fired the heavier 5.56x45mm NATO round and was effective out to one thousand yards. Gould guessed that they were firing from no farther than one hundred yards.

The machine gun continued to rake the edge of the roof, raining down shards of stone on Gould. For the moment all Gould could do was take cover beneath the edge of the roof and try to move to a different position. On his own, this was pure suicide. Gould began to wonder why he was sticking around. He had done his job and warned Rapp. True, the act had not been entirely selfless, as it had gotten him out of his own hot corner, but now he was in an even less desirable situation.

He glanced across the roof, wondering what lay on the other side. He couldn't tell if there was a small gap between the two buildings or if they shared a wall. Worst case, he'd have to jump a gap. He could then scurry across that roof and find access to the street. The police would be so focused on this gunfight that he was sure to go unnoticed. Gould made up his mind. He'd done enough, and martyrdom really didn't suit him, so better to bolt before another hundred cops showed up and brought this building down around them.

It was time to save his own ass, so without further internal debate Gould rolled onto his stomach and began to crawl toward the far side. He was halfway across when one of Rapp's men popped out of the hatch and asked, "Where you going?"

Gould ignored the question and said, "They're raking the parapet with machine-gun fire."

The man nodded, looked over at the parapet and asked, "Which direction is it coming from?"

Gould pointed to their left.

"All right, you get back over there near the middle, and when I give you the signal, stick your rifle over the parapet. Don't bother firing any shots until I've taken care of the machine gun. Go." Maslick watched the man crawl away and then scrambled over to the corner on all fours. Once in position, he checked his weapon and visualized what he was about to do. He then whistled and signaled for the man to make his move. Maslick watched as the black barrel went over the parapet. A split second later the position was hammered with incoming fire. Maslick shouldered his weapon and popped over the parapet. Below him, no more than fifty yards away, six green police pickups were blocking the intersection. Men were huddled behind each, but in the bed of one of the vehicles, a man was crouched down with an M249 in his hands and the bipod resting on the roof of the cab. Maslick brought the man into the center of his sights just as the machine gun ran out of ammunition. The police officer had turned to reach for another canvas ammunition drum, when Maslick shot him in the head.

The fact that Maslick had just killed someone who was more than likely on his side was irrelevant to the former Delta Force operator. The only thing on his mind, as he began shooting one man after another, was his friend Mick Reavers.

CHAPTER 19

THE ebb in the relative number of shots fired at the front entrance was bringing on a bit of an adrenaline hangover for Rapp. This wasn't the first time he'd experienced the physiological problem. It had happened many times before. It started with a dry throat and sour stomach. For most people it eventually led to a headache, sometimes one that was debilitating, but Rapp got only the dryness and the upset stomach. His hands used to get a little shaky and his vision would blur at the far edges, but he'd mastered those two crucial problems. Either through willpower or through repetition, his body was no longer as shocked by these near-death experiences.

Rapp's left ear was ringing from all of the shots that had been fired. Whenever possible, he operated with a suppressor. He did so for multiple reasons that included stealth, increased accuracy, and the fact that he didn't want to be deaf by the time he was fifty. Because of the loud reports from all of the gunshots, he almost missed the beeping tone in his right ear that was coming out of his Bose Bluetooth earpiece.

Reaching into his pocket to look at the caller ID seemed like too much effort, so he tapped the button on top of the device and said, "Rapp."

"It's Mike. I just spoke to Scott. We haven't been able to get anyone at the Afghan Police to cooperate, but I'm on my way with some boys from JSOC."

"I hope by chopper."

"Yeah . . . We've got two Black Hawks and two Little Birds."

"ETA?"

There was a long pause, and then, "They're firing up the birds right now. We hope to be airborne in the next sixty seconds. Pilot told me we should be on station two minutes after that. You're not far."

Rapp pushed back from the wall and took a deep breath. He didn't like the silence and suddenly felt the need to see what was going on out on the street. As he moved slowly across the lobby he asked, "Have you guys discussed your ROEs?" Rapp knew this was going to catch Nash off guard. ROEs, or rules of engagement, within the military, and especially Special Operations, were very specific. They outlined who could be engaged and how, and Rapp very much doubted the brass was going to let their shooters come in and open fire on the Afghan Police no matter how fucked up the situation was.

"No, we haven't."

"Let me save you guys the headache of trying to sort this mess out. We have police at both ends of the street. My guess is when you guys show up they're going to think you're here to help them. Hopefully they'll stop shooting. Put the Black Hawks over them and hit 'em with the rotor wash and then bring the Little Birds in to pick us up on the roof. I don't think they'll shoot at you, but I can't make any promises."

"I'll pass it along. Anything else?"

"Yeah. If I don't make it out of here, there's something you need to know. Does the name Louie Gould ring a bell?"

There was a moment of silence followed by, "The man who killed your wife?"

"That's him. Somebody hired him a few weeks ago to fulfill a contract in Kabul. He says he didn't know it was me until this morning. He was set up in an office building across the street and was supposed to shoot me when I showed up to see the vet."

"How the hell . . ."

"Exactly . . . do you want to tell me how the fuck somebody knew two weeks ago that I would be in Kabul talking to this vet when I didn't even know I'd fucking be here?"

"I have no idea, but no more of this bullshit about not making it. We'll be there in minutes, and after I pull your ass out of the fire again, we'll figure out what in the hell is going on."

"I'll tell you what in the hell is going on. Somebody set my ass up. Rick was the first domino and they knew how we would react. We're being played." Rapp carefully moved along the wall until he was just a few feet from the blown-out entrance.

"Is Gould still with you?"

"Yeah, he's on the roof." The only police that Rapp could see were taking cover behind their vehicles. "Did Scott tell you we lost Reavers?"

"Yeah. I'm sorry about that."

Rapp flexed his knees and then stuck his head out so he could see down the length of the front of the building. He ducked back just as a flurry of shots rang out. What he saw scared him more than the shots. "Mike," Rapp yelled as he hustled across the lobby, "they're getting ready to rush the building with riot shields. You guys better haul ass or there's going to be no one left to save."

"We're getting in the birds right now. Hold on for a few more minutes."

Rapp didn't bother to answer. He moved in behind his piece of Formica and switched his pistol to his right hand. He counted the seconds in his head, figured it would take the cops another eight seconds to shuffle down the sidewalk in their tight formation. He extended his arm, sighted the Glock in on one of the tanks, and then decided it would be better to pull the gun in close and cradle the grip with his left hand. The first shield came into view, the man behind it clasping the shield with his left arm and holding a pistol in his right hand. Three men followed, all with shields, two protecting their flanks and the fourth holding his shield above their heads. When they reached the front door, Rapp slid his head back behind the Formica, closed his eyes and squeezed the trigger. The 9mm round punctured the first tank and the explosion was instantaneous.

Rapp attempted to pull the gun back behind his relative cover, but there wasn't enough time. The energy from the shock wave hit him like a massive hammer. It slammed into the countertop and shot Rapp across the hall and into the far wall. He bounced off the wall and slid to the floor with the countertop and a good portion of the wall falling on top of him. His hearing was completely gone. He tried to open his eyes but felt himself slipping away, falling into a deep hole, and then everything went black.

CHAPTER 20

COLEMAN joined Maslick and Gould on the roof just as things were settling down. The sun was starting to slide out from the cloud-filled sky and the wind was picking up a bit. Coleman ran across the roof in a low crouch as sporadic bullets zipped overhead. He did a quick ammunition check with the other two and then handed each of them a thirty-round magazine, leaving himself two. Coleman then surveyed the situation at both ends of the block. It appeared Maslick and Gould had taken the fight out of the police.

Coleman had seen it many times before. Put a group of Special Operators in an all-out gunfight with a force superior in size and they would balance the scales quicker than you could imagine. The simple fact was that at these distances they hit what they were shooting at. It was demoralizing for the opposing force as they watched one friend after another get shot in the head. The ones who managed to stay alive got the message real quick that it was a good idea to keep their heads down. And when you decided to keep your head down you ceased to become an effective fighter for the simple reason that you couldn't hit a target if you weren't willing to expose yourself and aim your weapon properly.

Having been in combat many times, Coleman knew how to recognize the ebb and flow of a battle. The frantic adrenaline rush of the initial engagement was almost always followed by a lull as each side took stock of its losses and either retrenched or prepared for another assault. The dynamics of this battle dictated who would do what. They were in no position to launch an assault, so it would be the other side that would have to make the next move.

Coleman moved to the roof's edge a few feet away and dropped to one knee. "Any movement on the roofs across the street?"

Gould glanced across the street. He'd been worried about the same thing. Crossways from them was a three-story building that was the high ground on the block. Gould pointed his rifle at the building and said, "If they put a few decent shooters up there they could make our lives miserable."

"Yeah . . . keep your eye on it."

Gould looked behind them. There were multiple elevated rooftop positions within five hundred yards. "If they get behind us we're done for."

Coleman checked his watch. "We'll be out of here before they figure that out."

Off in the distance he heard the dull thumping of rotor blades. Coleman looked to the east, toward the airport. At first he couldn't find a sign of the helicopters, as they were flying so low, and then he saw the shimmer of movement as they skimmed the rooftops almost two miles out.

"Scott!"

Coleman turned his head and looked at Maslick, who was pointing over the edge of the building.

"We've got trouble."

Coleman looked down and saw the men with the clear bulletproof shields forming up along the edge of the building. He looked to his right and saw the same thing. He grabbed Gould and said, "Get over there and help him."

A bullet slammed into the top of the stone parapet, just a few inches from Gould's face. He almost immediately realized from the trajectory that it had to have come from above. Lunging forward from his knees, he shoved Coleman to the ground as a barrage of bullets hit their position. Gould rolled off Coleman and said, "I'll deal with the men across the street." He handed Coleman one of the canisters from his vest. "It's only a flash-bang but it might help."

Coleman grabbed it from him. "I'll try to draw their fire in a second." On all fours he stayed near the edge and began crawling to the far corner. He looked back at Gould, counted down with his fingers, and rose onto one knee. He was surprised to see four gun barrels pointed in his general direction from an elevated position. He was expecting just one or two. Coleman's right index finger began rapidly squeezing off rounds. His aim was far from exact, as he was trying to draw the attention of these men so Gould get a few good shots.

Gould came up a second later and quickly moved his aperture into position. He placed the red dot on the closest man's head and fired. At the exact same instant he saw a muzzle flash from the man he was trying to kill. Before Gould had a chance to seek out a second target, he was knocked on his ass. He knew immediately it was his left shoulder. He looked over and saw the near-perfect circle of blood slowly growing. His shoulder was screaming with pain, but Gould knew the injury was not fatal. At least it wasn't if he got medical care in the not-so-distant future. His best hope for that was if he got off his ass and back in the fight. With a grunt and more effort than he should have needed he got back on his knees and took aim at the men across the street. Gould's left hand was still functional, so his aim was as steady as ever, although he knew that might not last. Only two heads were visible. Gould lined up the first one, took the shot, and saw the man go down. He was moving the rifle into position for the second shot when there was a large explosion beneath him. The building shook for a second and then all was quiet.

"Dammit," Coleman yelled. "Cover me." He tore off across the roof for the hatch.

Gould shouldered his weapon and began firing on the rooftop position across the street. More barrels suddenly appeared and he had to seek cover beneath the stone parapet. When he looked back the blond-haired guy was gone. Gould lay on his back for a moment trying to survey the damage to his shoulder, and then he suddenly became aware of the growing noise of helicopter rotors slicing through the air.

Coleman found his way down the ladder as quickly as you'd expect from a guy who had spent a good portion of his life on ships. By the time he reached the staircase he had Reavers's M-4 up and ready to engage. He flew down the stairs and into a cloud of floating debris in the first-floor hallway. He didn't care how many men there were, he was going to rush them head-on. Moving down the hallway at a steady pace, he saw the pile of debris near where he had last seen Rapp. Coleman's heart sank as he stepped on the pile and swung his weapon to the left to engage the men who would be coming through the front door.

He was shocked to find not a person standing. On the sidewalk just outside the front entrance there was a tangle of bodies. Coleman saw some movement and almost fired. One of the cops was trying to roll onto his side. Coleman's conscience got the better of him and he took his finger off the trigger. Two sounds suddenly filled the relative silence. The first was a low moan, which seemed to be fading, and the second one was the roar of U.S. Special Operations helicopters, which was definitely growing in volume.

Coleman turned and looked down at the pile of debris that he had just walked over. He began yanking ceiling tiles and pieces of wood and Sheetrock from the heap, and then he saw the blue countertop that Rapp had used to fortify his position. Next he spotted a hand and an arm. Coleman released the rifle, letting it hang from the sling around his neck. Taking both hands, he lifted the large piece of Formica up, revealing a dusty and pale Rapp. He chucked the large board off to the side, dropped down to one knee, and stared at Rapp's lifeless face. Coleman placed a finger on Rapp's neck to search for a pulse and then slapped him a couple times on each cheek.

Rapp gasped, his eyes shot open wide, and his left hand shot up and grabbed Coleman by the throat.

Coleman removed Rapp's hand from his throat by applying just the right amount of pressure to his wrist. "It's me, you idiot. Do you think you can stand?" The former Navy SEAL could tell by the way Rapp's eyes were darting around that he still wasn't entirely with it. He ran his hands up and down Rapp's body looking for any injuries. The thump-thump signature of the helicopters was growing louder by the second. The thought of missing their ride, or worse, getting one of the birds blown out of the sky because they weren't up on the LZ, made Coleman skip the rest of the medical assessment. He stood and grabbed Rapp by his tactical vest, yanking him to his feet. Rapp wobbled and almost fell to his left, but Coleman steadied him.

"Come on . . . this way. Our ride is waiting for us."

"What the fuck are you talking about?"

"We have a hot double date." Coleman squatted, threw Rapp's right arm around his neck, and then moved the two of them down the hallway. "Don't want to be late. Come on, we need to hustle."

"Where the hell are we?" Rapp wobbled again and his legs gave out.

Coleman struggled to keep him upright and then decided he needed to change tactics. He spun Rapp toward him, bent over, and threw Rapp over his shoulder. Coleman hefted him in a fireman's carry and started up the steps. "Damn, you're getting fat."

"Put me down, you idiot. What are you doing?"

"Saving your fat ass, dumb shit." Coleman reached the second floor and stopped at the ladder that led to the roof. The rotor wash from one of the helicopters was blowing through the opening. Coleman didn't think he could climb the ladder with Rapp over his shoulder, so he set him down.

Rapp's pupils were as big as saucers.

"Shit," Coleman muttered. He turned Rapp toward the ladder and placed his hands on the rung just above his head. "Come on, climb. Let's go."

Rapp turned his head and gave him a blank stare.

Coleman screamed at him, "We're going to die if you don't get moving. Snap out of it!" Coleman grabbed him by the waist and started pushing him up the ladder.

Rapp seemed to finally come out of his stupor, his hands grasping at the rungs above him.

"That's right," Coleman prodded him on as they made painfully slow progress. Fortunately, Maslick appeared in the hatch opening. He grabbed one of the shoulders on Rapp's vest and practically yanked him onto the roof. By the time Coleman cleared the ladder, the big former Delta Force Operator had Rapp on his feet and was dragging him toward one of the waiting Little Birds.

Coleman watched as bullets began impacting the ground around Rapp and Maslick. He snapped his M-4 up to his shoulder, flipped the selector to full automatic, and began raking the roofline across the street with fire. Coleman marched steadily forward, and when his weapon locked out he ejected the spent magazine and inserted a fresh one, charging the weapon and then releasing another volley.

Ducking under the Little Bird's rotors, Coleman kept up the suppressive fire and jumped onto the portside external bench. He looked inside the back compartment and saw Rapp and Gould in a pile on the floor. Maslick was sitting on the starboard side bench laying down suppressive fire. Coleman took his finger off the trigger and reached forward, slapping the pilot on the shoulder. Coleman gave the man the thumbs-up signal and the bird immediately lifted into the air.

They banked to the right, which gave Coleman a good vantage point to fire at the building with the men on the roof. No one, however, was getting up to shoot at the helicopter. They were either all dead or had finally taken the hint that it was a good idea to stay down. As they gained elevation and distance Coleman released his rifle and strapped himself in. That was when he noticed that Rapp was out again. He reached in and slapped him on the cheek. Coleman had seen a lot of concussions, and this was not the norm. Gould was lying next to Rapp with a bullet hole in his shoulder, his face tight with pain. Coleman seemed to remember seeing some blood on Maslick as well. A hospital was more important than getting back to the embassy. Plus, the CIA had its detention facility at the Bagram Air Base.

Leaning forward, he shouted above the roar of the rotors and engine, "We need to go to Bagram. Straight to the base hospital."

The pilot nodded and began speaking into his lip mike. About five seconds later the Little Bird and one of the Black Hawks broke formation and headed to the northeast for the fifteen-minute flight to the main U.S. air base and its level-one trauma center. The Black Hawk pulled alongside, and Coleman could see Mike Nash sitting in the back of the much larger Black Hawk, talking on a headset. The fallout from what had just happened was going to be huge. Nash was probably already dealing with it. Coleman checked on Rapp again. He was still unconscious, which from a medical standpoint was a concern, but there was a silver lining. If Rapp were awake right now, he'd probably have them on their way to assault the police headquarters in Kabul.

No Afghani politician or State Department official would be able to calm Rapp down. Even Kennedy would have a hard time convincing him to stand down. The only thing that could stop him would be a hospital bed. Once Rapp started, Coleman knew there would be no stopping him. He'd kill every last corrupt official he could get his hands on.

CHAPTER 21

JALALABAD, AFGHANISTAN

RICKMAN no longer wondered if his ribs were broken—he was convinced. Three of them, he was pretty sure. Both eyes were now firmly closed, the skin so swollen and tight that he probably looked like he was morphing into an insect. His tongue told him that two of his teeth were knocked out and a third was chipped. He had finally broken. He'd heard the maxim many times before—everyone broke. He was no different, of course, and no one would expect him to hold out for very long. He had lived a life insulated from physical pain. He'd been hired for his intellect, not, like Mitch Rapp, for his predatory instincts. Emotional agony Rickman could write the book on, but this physical stuff was an entirely different game. He had prepared himself. In a broad conceptual sense, he understood what it would be like and that it would not last forever, that the physical scars would heal.

Nothing, however, no amount of meditation and careful consideration could prepare him for the absolute brutality, the hair-splitting agony that would result from his nerve endings being so assaulted. There was some embarrassment that he couldn't even last two days. Barely twenty-four hours after the torture started, Rickman caved. The secrets came flowing out in a torrent. He babbled from one subject to another like a crack addict who could not keep a train of thought. It would take multiple experts to decipher what he had really said, and that was intentional on Rickman's part. There was just enough truth in his words to make them believe him, but there were also traps and deceptions that would give the CIA the time they would need to maneuver and possibly save a few people. There were also a few scores to be settled, some enemies who would now have to answer to the Taliban and defend what he'd said they'd done. The words would be a waste, as they always were with groups like the Taliban. The group was all that mattered. Individual needs were not important. The more the person tried to deny something that couldn't be proven, the more it looked to these obtuse fools as if that person was putting himself before the needs of the group. Unable to decipher what had really happened, the Taliban would act predictably. They would kill the perceived traitor. It was a complex mix of facts, outright lies, half-truths, and complicated misinformation that was possible only with Rickman's genius.

They thought they were in control, but they weren't. By the time he was done with them, Rickman would have these fools killing each other. Terrorist would be pitted against terrorist. Unfortunately, a few allies would be killed, but his side was not without fault. Soldiers died every week in this war. A few intelligence assets weren't worth getting too spun up about.

Rickman heard the door open, and he didn't bother to try to open his eyes. He'd stopped trying hours ago. They were too puffy to work properly. He felt a certain sense of calm. The end was near, and then the pain would stop.

"It is time," a steady, soft voice announced.

Rickman sighed. He so much preferred this one to the others. He was smart and actually knew what questions to ask. "But I'm having so much fun." Rickman tried to smile through his swollen lips.

"I know you are, but we all have our orders to follow."

"Yes," Rickman said, "we all must be good soldiers."

The man squatted next to Rickman, keeping his back to the camera. Deftly, he slid an unseen syringe into the crook of Rickman's left arm while pretending to take the man's pulse. He depressed the plunger. He doubted Rickman noticed the prick. The man's body was so overwhelmed with pain that this little stab wouldn't even register.

"So now that I've begun talking it would be nice if we could conduct the follow-up questions in a more civilized setting."

"Hmm . . ." The man seemed to be pondering Rickman's request. "There's only one problem."

"What's that?"

"You lied to us."

"I did not lie to you. I told you what you wanted to know."

"Ahh . . . I find it interesting how you phrased that. You told me what I 'wanted to know.' That is not what I wanted. I wanted the truth."

"I gave you the truth."

"You did not," the man said in a voice bereft of emotion.

Rickman grew nervous and began coughing up blood. "I've told you everything," he managed to blurt out in his defense.

"You are a devious man." His tone had shifted to that of a disappointed father. "We all know this. So the beatings will have to continue, but don't worry. You will learn very quickly that your games are not worth the effort."

"Please." Rickman blindly reached out, clutching for the man's arm. "I am doing everything you have asked of me."

The man stood and took a step back. "Not everything. You have told us a few of your secrets, but you have also told us many lies. That means we will have to do this the hard way."

"Please!" Rickman started crying. "I will tell you what you want to know."

The man was wearing a mask over his face and shook his head sadly. "You will tell me the truth . . . not what I want to know. The truth is the only thing that will save you."

"I will tell you the truth, then," Rickman pleaded.

"Yes, you will." The man turned and walked past the camera, its red light glowing. In the hallway he took off his hood and tossed it on a wooden table. The two men were waiting like obedient dogs for instructions on what do next. Vazir Kassar was apprehensive about how to proceed. He didn't have much confidence in these men. One of them started to speak, but Kassar held up a hand. The men had at least learned that much. Kassar despised people who talked too much and had explained to the two halfwits that there was nothing they could say that he hadn't already thought of.

After fishing out a cigarette and lighting it, Kassar exhaled a cloud of smoke and said, "It is time to increase the pain."

Both men nodded eagerly. The taller of the two said, "The genitals . . . can we hit him in the genitals now?"

"Yes, you may hit him in the genitals." Kassar took no joy in this. It was simply part of the job. "I have given you the area I want you to focus on. Where I know he has lied. You will increase the pain until he tells us the truth. Yes?"

"Yes," both men answered.

Kassar waved for them to proceed. He took another puff of his cigarette while the two simpletons put their masks on. Kassar couldn't shake the feeling that these two fools might somehow mess this up. There were no guarantees in life, and definitely none in the dangerous waters where they were swimming. Kassar settled into a wooden chair and watched the single monitor. He checked the time on his watch and made a quick calculation. "This shouldn't take long," he said to himself.

Rickman was strung up once again by his wrists. They had yet to lay a hand on him, but he was already sniffling. The men began taking turns slapping him in the head and heaving insult after insult at him. Kassar could tell that the CIA man was losing control of his legendary wits. He'd been awake for a day and a half and he'd been beaten so severely that he could barely stand. He was exhausted and on the verge of a complete collapse.

The men paused for a moment and then without warning one of them took a rubber hose and swung it up between Rickman's legs, striking him in the groin. A glob of blood exited Rickman's mouth as his entire body convulsed forward. His sniffles turned into sobs and his chin was coated with spit, tears, and blood. Rickman was begging for them to stop, but the men paid him no heed. They were literally kicking the crap out of him as Rickman defecated in his boxers. This only upset the men more. The slaps were now replaced with punches.

Kassar watched Rickman slump suddenly, his legs completely giving out. The Pakistani moved closer to the screen and tried to see what was wrong. It was not unheard-of for a subject to lose consciousness during an interrogation. Kassar checked his watch again and frowned as the two men continued to beat their unconscious prisoner.

It took them another minute to realize that something was wrong, and by then it was too late.

CHAPTER 22

BAGRAM AIR BASE, AFGHANISTAN

RAPP heard voices. He opened his eyes and looked up at a ceiling he was pretty sure he'd never seen before. His brain didn't seem to be working quite right as the only thing he could figure out was that he was in a bed and his head hurt. The voices were coming from somewhere down by his feet. Moving his eyes caused discomfort, but he caught a glimpse of two men and a woman talking. None of their faces were familiar, but one of the men and the woman were wearing white coats. The other man was in what looked like light-blue pajamas. Rapp didn't know why, but their clothes had some meaning to him that he couldn't grasp.

He closed his eyes and let out a long sigh. Suddenly the three people were standing over him, two on his right and one on his left. He opened his eyes and could see their lips moving, but it was all scrambled. Suddenly the woman shined a bright light in his eyes. Rapp didn't like it one bit, but his limbs felt as if they were encased in concrete, so all he could do was lie there. Thinking of moving them hurt his head, so he gave up on the idea and let the woman move the light from one eye to the other. When she finally clicked the light off he was so relieved he fell back asleep.

Rapp had no idea how long he'd been out, but sometime later he woke to find a familiar face. His head rolled to his right, and there in a chair next to his bed was someone who he knew was very important to him. He couldn't come up with her name, or how he knew her, but he knew he should have known. In a moment of panic he asked himself if he knew his own name. He came up with that one pretty quickly, but when he asked himself where he was, a half dozen cities popped into his head, which got him wondering what he did for a living. Then things got really murky.

"You're awake," the woman said with a warm smile.

Rapp noted the familiar brown eyes, the glasses, and the auburn hair pulled back in a tight ponytail, and then something clicked. "Boss."

Irene Kennedy said, "You had us a bit worried."

"Where am I?"

"Heath Craig Joint Theater Hospital . . . Bagram Air Base."

Rapp frowned and another link popped into his head. "Afghanistan?"

Kennedy looked at him with appraising eyes. "Mitch, what is your last memory?"

Rapp looked past her at the far wall. Some part of his brain was telling him to bluff his way through this, but another part was telling him he needed to tell her the truth. He couldn't remember everything about her, but he knew she was someone he could trust—perhaps the only person he could truly trust.

"Is there any water around here?"

Kennedy grabbed a covered plastic glass with a pink straw sticking out of a round hole in the center of the lid. She raised the elevation on Rapp's bed about six inches and then held the straw to his lips. After he'd had a good gulp, she repeated the question. "So . . . what is the last thing you remember?"

Rapp tried to recall, but nothing was coming to him. He gave a slight shrug and said, "I don't know."

"But you remember who I am? Where you work? Things like that?"

"It took me a moment to remember you . . . it didn't come right away."

"And where you work?"

"Ahh . . . I think it's in Washington, but I'm not sure exactly where."

"My title?"

"You're my boss."

Kennedy nodded. The doctors had warned her that things could be patchy. "I'm the director of the Central Intelligence Agency."

"Oh," Rapp said as something fell into place. "It's coming back to me now."

"Good. Do you remember my son?"

Rapp started to shake his head and then stopped because of the pain. "Sorry."

"That's all right. His name is Tommy. The two of you are rather close."

"What happened to me?" Rapp reached a hand to his head and winced.

"There was an explosion. You hit your head. You have swelling on the brain. They call it a subdural hematoma."

"Explosion?"

She shook her head. "I don't think we want to get into that right now. The fact that you're awake and fairly lucid is a good sign. The doctors tell me all of this is normal and with time you should regain most if not all of your memory." Kennedy smiled and put on a brave face. Rapp was her top operative. Even at 90 percent he could be exceptional, but that depended on which 10 percent was lost.

"How long have I been out?"

"A little over a day."

"A day?" Rapp asked in surprise.

"Yes." And a stressful day at that. Twenty-one dead police officers, all killed by her men and an assassin, which further complicated the entire affair. She was sitting on that particular piece of information for the moment. The facts, as she'd gathered them, showed that Rapp and his men were left with no choice but to defend themselves. Those facts, however, didn't matter to the Afghani people and their political leaders—at least not in the immediate aftermath of the slaughter. The president had ordered Kennedy to Afghanistan to see if she could straighten out the mess before the damage was irreversible. By the time she landed she was in possession of the information she needed. Her people had already identified the corrupt Afghani Police commander who had ordered the attack. The man had simply vanished, his government-sponsored house cleaned out of anything of value. Contacts within the Afghan National Police confirmed that most of the police officers who were killed were former Taliban members whom the corrupt commander had brought onto the force. They were all part of the State Department's vaunted reintegration program. Kennedy gave the go-ahead for her assets to begin sharing this information far and wide.

By the time she landed, the Afghans were firmly split. One camp of hard-liners refused to blame anyone other than America for the catastrophe. It was no shock to anyone who followed Afghan politics that these men were the ones who had pushed reintegration in the first place. The second camp was made up of the various groups that had fought the Taliban for more than a decade and had warned the first group that their scheme of bringing them into the fold was short-sighted and naïve.

Kennedy arrived at the U.S. Embassy, and after giving Darren Sickles a very cool reception, she kicked him out of his office and called the president and his national security team. In her typical analytical manner, she relayed the information regarding the corrupt Afghan Police commander. The president asked just two questions. Did we suspect that this commander was a bad egg, and did Kennedy think this was linked to the abduction of Rickman?

The first question was easy to answer. The CIA had a file as thick as a phone book on Lieutenant General Abdul Rauf Qayem. They had warned the State Department that the man was hard-core Taliban and should not be included in the reintegration program. Kennedy relayed this as dispassionately as possible. The secretary of state would get beat up over this, and Kennedy didn't need to pile on. They had a good working relationship and she wanted to keep it that way. The answer to the president's second question was less clear. Kennedy wasn't ready to share the information surrounding Louie Gould until she knew more. It was looking as if the abduction of Rickman and the attack on Rapp were part of a coordinated effort to damage the CIA's ability to operate in Afghanistan. Until she had more information, though, she simply told the president that they were proceeding under the premise that the two events were linked.

CHAPTER 23

K ENNEDY spent another ten minutes with Rapp, both answering and evading his questions and gently probing to gauge the depth of his memory loss. His inability to recall information stretched across all aspects of his life. One pattern did emerge, though—his mind was blank when it came to anything that involved the last three days. Before that things were spotty, but Rapp's recall seemed to get better as each memory fell into place. Not wanting to overwhelm him, she didn't bother to tell him that in the middle of the night, the doctors had been on the verge of drilling into his head to drain the clotted blood that was creating pressure on the brain. The prognosis was very iffy at the moment.

The military doctors had ample experience with head trauma caused by explosions. Every case was different. Some patients progressed to a full recovery with nothing more than a week's bed rest, while others never fully recovered despite the best effort and medical care. Kennedy would not allow herself to think the worst. Over the years Rapp had proven that he had an extremely strong ability to survive what would kill most people. His refusal to be deterred, despite overwhelming odds, while it often put him in harm's way, was the very thing that drove him to never quit. Dying simply wasn't an option.

His recovery right now depended on rest and relaxation—two things that were as foreign to Rapp as not barking at a stranger was to a dog. This put Kennedy in a unique quandary. She needed Rapp to find Rickman. There was no other asset up to the task. There were others who could help, but she needed Rapp's fearless, ruthless behavior to deal with the miscreants who orbited their interests in this part of the world. Unfortunately, he was sidelined until the doctors told her otherwise. So far they were being vague, telling her he would likely be kept in bed for a week and then there would be another week of rehabilitation. A variety of symptoms could persist, including lethargy, slurred speech, difficulty in walking, blurred vision, numbness, headaches, amnesia, dizziness, and pain. The last part didn't concern Kennedy. Rapp's pain threshold was off the charts. She was betting that he would recover way ahead of the curve, but she couldn't count on that, so she told him she had some things to attend to, but that she'd be back to see him in a bit.

Kennedy then found one of the doctors in the hall, an Air Force major, and told him that Rapp was awake. She filled him in on their conversation, and the doctor said this was a very positive development. He then excused himself and went to personally check on his patient.

Kennedy found Coleman in the small lounge with two of her bodyguards. She asked her men for a bit of privacy and sat down next to Coleman.

Kennedy grabbed Coleman's hand. "You know you saved his life."

Coleman was embarrassed. "Let's not get all melodramatic."

An uncharacteristically big smile spread across Kennedy's face. "I don't think you understand. You'll be able to hold this over his head for years."

Coleman joined in with a big grin. "Good point. The only problem is that I think he's saved my life at least twice. I'm still behind."

"His memory is a little shaky at the moment. Maybe he'll forget he's ahead. I'll never tell him."

"He's awake?"

Kennedy nodded.

Coleman breathed a sigh of relief. "Thank God. How's he doing?"

"He seems to be okay, but he doesn't remember much."

"What does that mean?"

"I'm not sure he knew who I was when he woke up. He recognized me, but he had to struggle to come up with my name. He remembered his own name, but he couldn't tell me where he worked . . . at least not at first. As we talked, more and more things seemed to fall into place."

"Rick?"

"No idea. In fact I don't think he can remember a single detail over the past seventy-two hours."

"Shit." Coleman dropped his face into his hands. "So he's out of commission."

"I'd say for at least the next week."

"What are we going to do?"

"I'm not sure at this point. Do you have it in you to take the lead?" Kennedy thought she knew the answer, but she needed to ask the question.

Coleman thought about it for a moment and then said, "I have the drive, but Mitch and I are very different. You know that. I'm not afraid to break a few rules and even a few noses, but I'm an amateur, compared to him. The only other person I know who could do it is Stan, and from what I heard yesterday, he's not exactly up to the challenge."

"What about Mike?" Kennedy asked, referring to Mike Nash, her counterterrorism director.

After inhaling sharply, Coleman shook his head. "I like Mike, but I'm not sure he's cut out for this rough stuff. I don't blame him. He's got a wife and kids and you gave him an important job with a nice title. He'll do well, and if he had his back to the wall, he'd do whatever it would take to survive, but that's not what this is."

"What is this?"

"You want Rick back, you need to find someone who's willing to throw out the rule book. You need someone like Mitch who doesn't give a shit about the politics . . . someone who's fearless. Someone who will make these dirt bags fear for their lives."

Kennedy agreed. The only problem was that she had no such man available. "Louie Gould . . . have you had a chance to talk to him?"

"Only briefly."

"Do you buy his story?"

Coleman let out a small laugh that said what he thought of the question. "I'm not sure I believe a thing that comes out of that guy's mouth. What does Mike say?" Nash and another CIA interrogator had been tag-teaming Gould since the night before, trying to sort through his lies.

"He says progress is slow. I'm going over there in a minute. Gould doesn't know it but I have some leverage on him. He'll tell us what we need to know and then some."

"If we can find out who hired him . . . everything might fall into place."

"It would be nice if it were that easy, but I'm guessing there are some firewalls in place that are going to make that very difficult."

"Probably, but he might be able to point us in the right direction."

"I'm counting on it." Kennedy closed her eyes briefly and then said, "You lost a man?"

Coleman wore the fateful memory on his face. "Yeah . . . one of my best."

"Mick Reavers."

"That's right."

Kennedy could tell Coleman had some emotions that he hadn't yet begun to deal with. She looked away and said, "Through back channels I've made it very clear that I want his body back by the end of the day."

"I appreciate that." Coleman looked across the room for a second and stared at a poster of an A-10 Warthog. "He never had a chance. They shot him before he even got his weapon up."

It wasn't often that Kennedy allowed herself to get pissed off, and it was even more rare for her to show it. She supposed she was filling the void left by both Rapp and Hurley. "Scott, I want to make something clear. We are not going to allow this crap to go unchallenged. I've got more shooters on the way over and within twenty-four hours I am going to have some targets for you. We're going to find General Qayem. It might not be this week or the following, but you are going to find him and you are going to kill him. Do you understand me?"

Coleman nodded. "That's what I was hoping you were going to say."

"And by the time we're done, my guess is there's going to be a few more names added to our list."

CHAPTER 24

INTER-SERVICES INTELLIGENCE HQ, ISLAMABAD, PAKISTAN

ASHAN had been summoned to the director general's office, and he thought he knew why. His people had informed him of the developments across the border. Not only was Rickman gone, but another operative in Jalalabad had gone missing and there had been an attempt on Mitch Rapp's life. As the deputy general of the Foreign Relations Wing, the only thing that surprised Ashan was that he hadn't heard directly from the Americans. Even so, he had directed his people in both Jalalabad and Kabul to aid their counterparts from the CIA.

The ISI was an extremely controversial yet influential part of the Pakistani government. In recent years there had been pressure to make the intelligence agency more accountable. Parliament had decided that the best way to avoid future scandal would be to make sure the head of the spy agency wasn't anyone too special. In other words, they wanted someone they could control. They found just the person in Air Force General Ahmed Taj. Taj's career in the Air Force had been spent almost entirely in supply and logistics. He had both a fondness and an aptitude for moving men and equipment from point A to point B.

Ashan had noticed this some time ago, as it seemed that nearly every time he was called to Taj's office he was ordered to get on a plane and go somewhere. When he'd been informed of the meeting, he called his wife and asked her to pack a bag for him just in case. The office of the director general was decadent. The space was nearly as big as a tennis court. The walls and ceiling were covered in a deep brown rosewood paneling and there were three granite fireplaces. Most of the walls were covered with bookcases, but there had been updates that included several large flat-screen monitors tastefully concealed behind tapestries.

Ashan was five minutes early and was irritated to find his friend General Durrani seated and sharing tea with their boss. It was just like Durrani to arrive early in an attempt to reform and dictate the agenda. The room was divided into three parts. To the far left was the director general's mammoth desk, a map table, and four chairs. The middle of the room was dominated by a conference table for sixteen. The most Ashan had ever seen at the table were six people. To the right was a sitting area. A massive leather couch that could seat six was centered on the fireplace. Two more couches framed the area around a large glass coffee table.

Taj greeted Ashan and asked him if he'd like some tea. Ashan graciously accepted and sat by himself on one of the shorter couches. He accepted his tea and saucer with both hands and placed it on the glass tabletop. He would very much like to know what the two men had been discussing, but would never want to seem so desperate. Besides, there was a good chance it would be revealed during the course of their conversation.

"How are things in Foreign Relations?" Taj asked.

Ashan was pleased to see that in a break from his predecessors, Taj was dressed in a light gray suit as opposed to his military uniform. "We're getting along."

"Good. So," said Taj, picking up his cup of tea and taking a sip, "I assume you've been following the recent developments in Afghanistan."

"I have."

"Any thoughts?" Taj was less than average in height, and sitting by himself in the middle of the massive couch gave him kind of a childlike appearance.

Ashan hated such open-ended questions. Especially when there was likely an agenda or at least a formed opinion behind it. His job was to offer his insights to the director general, so he took in a short breath and pushed ahead. "It appears, at least from a timing standpoint, that someone has decided to launch an operation against our American friends."

"Any idea who?"

This was where it always got tricky. Ashan decided to start out cautiously. "Beyond the usual suspects, no, sir."

"As for the usual suspects . . . I'd like to hear your list."

"The Taliban is the obvious choice, although I doubt that they have the organization to be able to conduct such a complicated operation."

"Explain, please."

"Two different targets, all individuals, which means it's very hard to predict where they will be in advance. From everything we know, the Taliban by themselves don't have the assets to pull something like this off."

"By themselves?"

"They are," Ashan started, and then stopped. There was a safer way to go about this. "All we need to do, sir, is look at a map. Afghanistan is landlocked." Ashan ticked off the neighbors. "Iran, Turkmenistan, Uzbekistan, Tajikistan, China, and us."

"Don't leave out the Americans," Durrani interjected.

Ashan was struck by the stupidity of the statement. "You think the CIA is doing this to itself?"

"I don't pretend to know the American mind. I'm simply saying they are highly invested in maintaining their influence over the region."

Ashan decided to let the stupidity of his colleague's statement stand on its own. "Historically, the Stans have had no relationship with the Taliban. If anything, they have been pulled into America's orbit. It is, however, possible that Russia could be involved."

"Do you have any evidence?"

"No," Ashan said with a quick shake of his head. "Although they seem to be taking great joy in poking the Americans as of late, so we should at least consider them. Iran is growing in influence, and we all know they have ample hatred to attempt something so brazen. China, so far, has shown almost no interest in the region. As to why, that is fairly obvious. There are no natural resources other than the opium trade. As we've discussed, if Afghanistan had oil, China would be very interested."

The director general rubbed his fingers along his mustache while he considered the analysis. "So we think it is likely that it is either the Iranians or the Russians."

"There is one more possibility, sir. You forgot about us." It was immediately obvious that Durrani had been waiting for this.

"I told you he would try to pull us into this sordid mess."

"I am trying to do no such thing," Ashan answered in a voice bereft of tension. "The director general asked for my analysis and I gave it to him."

Durrani ignored his old friend and looked directly at Taj. "I warned you. This is dangerous. He has absolutely no evidence, yet he is willing to implicate us. How long do you think it will take until the Americans get word of this? They have spies all over this building." Shifting his butt so he could face Ashan directly, he asked, "How many people have you told of this?"

Ashan would have burst out laughing if the entire thing wasn't so serious. "Akhtar, you must not be listening. Let me phrase this a different way. If you were the Americans, where would you start looking?"

"I don't give a damn about the Americans. This is not our problem. It is theirs, and we should keep it that way. Not help them try to implicate us."

Ashan sat back and threw up his hands. "Director General, I do not understand his animosity. There is no place for it here."

Taj looked as if he wished the entire matter would simply go away, but with these two strong-willed subordinates the chances of that were remote. "I think you both have valid points." Looking meekly at Durrani, he added, "You really should take a less aggressive approach when it comes to the Americans."

"I assume that when we are in your office you would like us to speak freely." Durrani acted hurt by his boss's admonition.

"Unless," Ashan added quickly, "the subject involves your department's unseemly relationship with the Taliban. Then we're not allowed to speak freely."

Durrani realized he had set himself up for the rebuttal and could see that his anger was pushing the director general toward Ashan's position. Rather than speak and risk alienating the director further, he clamped his mouth shut and began a lengthy internal indictment of his friend.

Taj took a last sip of his tea, placed it on the saucer, and pushed it a few inches away. After leaning back and throwing his arm over the back of the couch, he announced, "I think we need to show the Americans our support. Nadeem, I spoke with Director Kennedy earlier. She's at the Bagram Air Base. I'd like you to fly up there and offer our assistance."

Durrani practically leaped to his feet. "Surely you can't be serious. I don't trust him. Not at all. How do you know he won't say to her what he just said to us?"

The last time Ashan had seen his friend this upset was after the bin Laden raid. "You've met Director Kennedy before." The woman's intellect within the intelligence community was well known. "You don't think she's already thought of this herself? You don't think the entire bin Laden fiasco isn't seared into her brain?"

"Why do you keep bringing that up?"

"Because it's relevant." Ashan couldn't believe he had to keep pointing out something so obvious. "The more I think about it, if I were them, the first place I'd look is the External Wing."

Durrani was on his feet this time, stabbing the air with his finger, threating Ashan that his career was over. "There is no room for Anglo lovers in our world anymore. We are a sovereign nation. Not their trained dogs. If I were—"

"You are not me, and I must tell you, Akhtar, you are behaving like a man who has something to hide."

"I will not stand here and take this," Durrani proclaimed, looking at the director for support.

Taj made a calming motion with his hands. "Sit. Everyone needs to calm down."

Ashan felt like pointing out that only one person needed to calm himself, but Taj was smart enough to know that. Bringing it up would only serve to irritate Durrani.

"Akhtar, if you do not trust Nadeem, then I think you should accompany him to Bagram." Taj paused for a long beat and then held up a cautionary finger. "Your lack of emotional control, however, worries me. If you cannot conduct yourself in a civil, helpful way with our American friends, then I do not want you to go anywhere near them. Are we clear?"

Durrani looked like someone had just force-fed him a shit sandwich. He didn't want to leave, especially not now. He needed to keep an eye on things, but at the same time it pained him to think of Ashan licking the boots of the Americans. Ultimately, the only rational choice was to stay in Islamabad. If Ashan was right, and he usually was about these things, the Americans would already have his department under their watchful eye. Ashan could go play nice with the Americans. Durrani would stay where he was and make sure there was nothing to raise their ire.

CHAPTER 25

BAGRAM AIR BASE, AFGHANISTAN

THE CIA's offices were off the main drag from the airport in an area that housed the Intel Fusion Center and the snake eaters from the Joint Special Operations Command. Langley also had another piece of real estate at the far end of the flight line where they housed their planes and a few other things. It was their own little domain within the sprawling air base. Out of necessity the spooks had to share information with the various military branches, but there were times when it was unwise for the CIA to be too open with its military brethren. Necessity was, after all, the mother of invention, and the CIA had a real need to keep much of what they did secret. Louie Gould was a perfect example. Bagram had a brand-new shiny detention center replete with prayer rooms, prayer mats, video games, flat-screen TVs, and a Koran on every bed. Putting a man like Gould under the care of the military was an inherently bad idea, for the simple reason that once they had their hands on him there would be an official record.

Kennedy made it clear to Nash in the aftermath of the disaster with the Afghan Police that Gould's identity was to be kept secret from everyone outside their immediate circle. She went so far as to put Darren Sickles and anyone else at the embassy on an exclusion list. Until they knew more, Gould was nothing more than another one of Rapp's hired guns who was shot during the conflict. Kennedy wanted him kept under wraps until she could question him herself. The two had a shared history that she was certain Gould was not entirely aware of. Early reports were that he had been evasive and uncooperative when questioned by Nash. Kennedy had a piece of leverage that she was almost certain Nash didn't.

Kennedy left the hospital and asked her security team to bring her back to the hangar where her plane was parked.

Clark Jones, the head of her security detail, gave her a concerned look. "Are we leaving?"

"No . . . just some business I need to take care of."

They rolled down the base's smooth asphalt streets in the black Suburban that had been provided by the base chief. They passed the post office, a Burger King, a fitness center, and bunch of other non-descript buildings. The place was a little slice of America. The hangar was at the far end of the flight line, far away from prying eyes. It looked like all the other hangars. The helicopters parked on the tarmac were no different than the U.S. Army Black Hawks all up and down the flight line. The black SUV pulled into the hangar and two beautiful Gulfstream G550s came into view—noticeably absent were any U.S. Air Force markings. Three twin turboprop MC-12 surveillance planes were clustered in the other corner, and a smattering of other smaller planes and helicopters were spread about the cavernous space.

Kennedy's vehicle came to a stop near the glass offices. Her security team jumped out of the vehicle before she could put her hand on the door. Bill Schneeman, the base chief, was waiting for Kennedy by the office door. The bodyguards dismounted and formed their protective bubble around the director. She found the entire thing a bit much, but Jones had given her a firm lecture on the flight over. Jones had been in charge of her detail for just under two years. This was the first time he had "laid down the law," as he called it. He was rarely briefed on the intricacies of what was going on, but because of his proximity he often picked up bits and pieces of information.

In this case he'd heard about the abduction of Rickman, one of her most senior people in Afghanistan, and the attempt on the life of Mitch Rapp, her most trusted advisor and top counterterrorism operative. There was one other piece of information that he was not privy to. John Hubbard, the Jalalabad base chief, had gone missing and local assets were frantically searching for him. Even without the knowledge of Hubbard, Jones and his men hovered like overly protective mothers of a first child. It was all very stifling.

Schneeman started to approach Kennedy but stopped on the other side of the security team. "Boss," Schneeman called out with his typical smartass grin, "do you think you could get your guys to relax a little? We own this site. All the jihadists are on the other side of the wire."

Kennedy gave Jones a sideways glance. "Clark, while we're on base, do you think you guys could relax your posture just a bit?" Kennedy put her words in the form of a question, but her tone made it was obvious that it was an order.

Jones didn't flinch. His dark eyes and tight black skin gave him a no-nonsense intensity that was perfect for his job. He might as well have had "Don't mess with me" on his forehead. For a moment it looked as they were going to have at least a standoff, if not a confrontation. Jones looked around the hangar as if he was making one last check for threats and then motioned for his men to give the director some room.

Schneeman moved past the big men with all the weapons and extended his hand. "Welcome to Spa Bagram."

Kennedy grinned at the reference. Back at HQ, people liked to joke that the Bagram assignment was a cakewalk. Most of the people posted to Bagram came back thin, fit, and in the best shape of their careers. Kennedy knew the real toll of the posting, however. Marriages had fallen apart due to distance and, in more than a few cases, infidelity. The bigger problem, though, was stress—long hours and big demands for results had burned out a good number of her people.

"Sorry I didn't stop by sooner, but I was at the hospital," Kennedy offered.

"Don't worry about it. How's he doing?"

"Better. He's awake, but it looks like he's going to be out of commission for a while."

"That's not what I wanted to hear . . . I mean the part about him being out of commission."

"I knew what you meant." Very few people knew that Kennedy had increasingly turned to Schneeman to get a handle on what was going on in-country. She had lost confidence in Sickles months ago as she began to receive reports of his unabashed enthusiasm for reintegration. How one of the top people in the Clandestine Service could think the plan was a good idea was beyond Kennedy's ability to comprehend. The blame, she knew, rested squarely on her, as she had been the one who made him station chief in Kabul, and then the fool had gotten too cozy with the State Department contingent, that awful woman Arianna Vinter in particular.

"What have you found out about Hubbard?"

"Nothing so far. His phone doesn't even show up on the satellites, which we both know is a really bad sign." Schneeman shrugged and added, "I hate to give you more bad news, but it is what it is."

"Keep looking. We can't keep losing people like this." She was about to add the fact that it was embarrassing, but she knew it would sound self-serving. These were the people that she sent into harm's way. Her number-one priority was to get them back alive.

"I'm not going to lie to you. A lot of our people are spooked. They think this has to be part of bigger plan by the Taliban to cripple us in-country."

"They might be right."

After staring at his shoes for a second, Schneeman said, "No one's turned me down yet, but I almost had to make them draw straws to see who would go down to J-bad to search for Hubbard."

Kennedy did not take this information well. This was another reason she needed Rapp. His unabashed, fearless attitude was contagious. The last thing she needed right now were operatives who were afraid to leave the base. If this problem got worse she would have to lean on JSOC for muscle. The Special Operators shared Rapp's bold manner.

Schneeman motioned toward a doorway next to the glass-walled offices. "Can I get you a cup of coffee?"

"Tea, please."

Schneeman led and she followed. "I apologize, but things are pretty hectic around here. Including the nine people in your entourage, we have fifty-six additional people who've been brought in over the last two days."

"You need to push them out. How many people did you send down to J-bad?"

"I'm keeping all the analysts up here. I sent six operatives and twelve SOG guys. I told them I don't want anyone going anywhere by themselves. I assigned two SOG guys to each operative and they need to check in every hour."

They entered a small break room with a microwave and refrigerator. Schneeman started rifling through cupboards until he found a box of assorted teas. He handed the box to Kennedy and then poured himself a cup of coffee and Kennedy a cup of hot water.

"When was the last time this room was swept?" Kennedy asked.

Schneeman knew Kennedy's expectations. "Less than thirty minutes ago."

She gave a nod of satisfaction and asked, "How closely was Rick working with Darren?"

"The short answer is, I'm not sure. I mean, I'm out here most of the time. Darren runs the show from Kabul. Don't ask me how, but I think he got the sense that I'm his replacement. He's been a real prick the last five months. The good news is I'm lucky if I see him once a month. The bad news is he hasn't been managing his people. I have no idea what he and Rick were up to."

Kennedy gave him a small, disbelieving frown. Their business was to collect facts, but intermixed with the facts was often a lot of gossip and innuendo. "Brian, you can't honestly expect me to believe that you haven't heard a thing."

"The guy's my immediate boss, Irene, and he's a real prick. Not to you, of course, but to most of the people who work for him, he's insufferable."

"I understand there's a chain of command, but how do you people expect me to make good decisions when you keep me in the dark on this stuff?" Rapp had warned her that he thought Sickles was in over his head, but no one else had bothered to make so much as a peep.

"I don't know what to say. We're thousands of miles away. We deal with what we have as best we can. These are all decisions that get made way above my pay grade."

Kennedy wasn't going to push the point. Schneeman was right, of course. Going behind your boss's back to say that he was incompetent without any real proof was a great way to torpedo your career. "This stays between the two of us. Darren is not going to be the station chief much longer."

Schneeman wasn't totally surprised. "How much longer?"

"I'm not sure he's going to make it to the end of the day, but I need to get a few things out of him first, so we'll have to see."

Schneeman almost asked who was going to be his replacement, but thought it would sound too self-serving. Instead, he moved back to the earlier topic. "There were a few things that didn't exactly pass the smell test."

Kennedy folded her arms across her chest and asked, "Like what?"

"Over the last few months they seemed to really kick this program into high gear. They were handing out bags of cash to every asshole in the country. Most of them guys we've spent the last ten years trying to kill." Schneeman shook his head in disgust and added in an acid tone, "Fucking Abdul Rauf Qayem . . . I told Darren I'd put a bullet in the guy's head, and he could pocket the cash. Do you know what Darren did?"

"No," Kennedy responded.

"He freaked out, and not about the bullet in the head. He gave me this big lecture about the inspector general's office and how they were all over him. How they had controls in place to make sure every penny was accounted for."

Kennedy was surprised, as this was all news to her. "The inspector general?"

"That's right."

For obvious reasons, Langley's inspector general had a certain amount of autonomy; that was the idea, after all, an in-house group tasked with making sure the spooks were playing by the rules. The idea was almost laughable and had of course been foisted on the Agency by the politicians on Capitol Hill. The fact that they thought it would work was interesting in itself. If the CIA could penetrate the world's top governments, how difficult would it be to recruit a few people who worked in the inspector general's office? The answer was simple—it wasn't. Kennedy had people in the office who kept her informed of anything of consequence. If they had been looking into Rickman and this reintegration business, Kennedy would have known. As a precaution, though, she would need to do a little double-checking.

"What about Hubbard?" Kennedy asked.

He gave a shrug. "He's competent enough."

"I've heard he became Rick's go-to guy."

"Yeah. If he needed any heavy lifting done he usually arranged it through Hubbard, although . . ." Schneeman's voice trailed off. He was thinking about something he'd heard.

"What?" Kennedy asked.

"Rick was involved with a lot of bad characters. Always has been, but when this reintegration thing got going, he really started hanging out with a rough crowd. I picked something up from one of the SOG guys. More of a complaint, really."

SOG stood for Special Operations Group. They were the paramilitary arm of the National Clandestine Service and were the men and women whom Kennedy used to conduct covert operations. "What did you hear?"

"Guy told me Rick's security was dog shit. Couldn't understand why he'd turned everything over to the natives. Said a guy like Rick should always have some American shooters with him. He had too big a target on his back to trust everything to a bunch of local mercenaries."

"You passed this concern on to Darren?"

"Yep."

This was the first Kennedy had heard of any of this. "So Rick's normal detail . . ."

"They stayed at the air base and he used them from time to time when he needed to make a show of force."

Kennedy considered the new information for a moment. In the aftermath of stuff like this, certain bits of information could take on oversized importance. She told herself not to get hung up on it. If it were important, she would revisit it later. "So we have no idea where Hubbard may be?"

"None, and we've talked to a ton of sources."

"Okay." She looked back toward the door. "Our number-one priority right now is to find Rick. Number two is Hubbard. Number three is Qayem."

"Understood."

"Good. Now tell me what you and Mike have learned from our guest."

CHAPTER 26

Nash had followed Kennedy's orders to the letter. She wanted Gould treated with respect until she said otherwise. The injury to his shoulder wasn't too bad. The bullet had gone clean through and left a dime-sized pucker on entry and a quarter-sized one on the back end. It was easy to pass Gould off as one of the CIA's hired guns that they used for security. The medical officials at the base hospital had worked on people from every NATO country multiple times, and the CIA had a reputation for outsourcing. The doctors had learned to not probe too deeply with men who wouldn't even admit they worked for the CIA, and instead threw out the generic acronym OGA, which stood for Other Government Agency.

The doctor cleaned and patched up Gould's wound, gave him some blood, put him on some antibiotics, and at the urging of Nash sent him on his way. After leaving the hospital the previous evening, Nash and Schneeman brought Gould to the air hangar where they had a suite of rooms that doubled as an interrogation facility. It was nothing more than two soundproof rooms, one of them wired for sound and video and the other to receive and monitor.

The initial interrogation produced nothing more than the same story Gould had told from the beginning. He'd taken a contract and was instructed to fly to Kabul and await further instructions. He spent one night at the Grand Marriott and then received a text and was told to go to the office building across the street from the veterinary clinic. While waiting to take the shot, he received for the first time the photo of the man he was supposed to kill. That was when he discovered it was Mitch Rapp.

"Do you understand our history?" Gould asked Nash.

Nash was tired and his nerves were frayed. He probably should have played dumb, but Gould was giving him so little to work with he said, "You mean the fact that you killed his pregnant wife? Yeah, I'm well aware that next to child rapists, you're probably the biggest piece of shit on the planet. So you'll have to excuse me if I don't believe a single word that comes out of your mouth."

Gould sighed as if this man was so predictable and said, "I am telling you the truth."

"Do you want to hear the actual truth?" Nash said, leaning across the table, his jaw rip tight with anger. "The truth is I don't understand why Mitch spared your life. I get why he couldn't kill your wife and your kid, but you . . ." Nash shook his head. "It makes no sense, and I'm beyond trying to figure it out. He's my friend, you caused him a shit-load of pain, so I figure I should do him a favor and toss you in a Black Hawk, fly up to one of the remote ranges, and toss your ass out the door. No one would even know you're gone. Your wife and kid would probably thank me."

It was the only time Gould showed any emotion, but it lasted for only a split second. "You don't want to do that," Gould said, regaining his composure.

"And why not?"

"Because I can help you."

Nash laughed at him. "We've been talking half the night and you haven't said a single thing that has helped me."

"I told you, I need to talk to Mitch."

"He doesn't want to talk to you, so you're going to have to deal with me."

And so it went round and round for most of the night, with Nash and Schneeman taking turns, neither of them getting any useful information out of the assassin. At four in the morning Nash called Kennedy midair and gave her a vague report covering what they had learned, which was pretty much nothing. Kennedy told Nash that she wanted all of them to get some sleep, and that included Gould. Despite his anger at the man, Nash didn't stop Schneeman from giving Gould a bedroll, pillow, and blanket. The door locked from the outside and they put one guard in the hallway and another one in the observation room to keep an eye on the prisoner.

They let Gould sleep until almost noon and then fed him and started again. Again Nash failed to learn anything of value. Gould refused to speak to anyone other than Rapp. With everything this clown had done, Nash could not understand why they weren't taking off the gloves and slapping him around. He was thinking about what kind of rough stuff he'd like to try, when the door opened.

"Time for a break," Schneeman announced.

"This is not personal," Gould said to Nash. "I need to speak to Mr. Rapp."

Nash pushed his chair back and stood. Schneeman closed the door and led Nash into the observation room, where Kennedy was waiting.

"How's it going?" Kennedy asked the question even though she knew they hadn't learned a thing.

"Horseshit."

Kennedy digested his coarse answer with a nod, then looked at the surveillance monitors. "So we've learned nothing of value."

"That about sums it up," Schneeman said.

"Erase everything."

"Excuse me?"

"Erase everything you have of Gould. I don't want a shred of proof that he was here." When she noticed that they were hesitating, she said, "It's of no value. Erase all the recordings and then turn off all the equipment."

"What's your plan?" Nash asked.

"I'm going to go in there and he's going to tell me what I want to know."

"Really." Nash flashed a crooked grin. "You're just going to ask him."

"That's right," she said without undue confidence. "Now, if you'd please open the door for me I'd like to talk to him."

Kennedy followed Nash back to the interrogation room, where he punched in the four-digit code on the cipher lock. Nash held the door open for his boss and then tried to follow her in.

Kennedy held up a hand. "I've got this." Leaving a stunned Nash in the hallway she closed the door and turned to face Louie Gould. Kennedy took a seat and studied the man she had spent more time thinking of than even she realized. He had a nice face. Nothing too sharp, and his mouth had an almost perpetual soft smile. He was an interesting contrast to Rapp, whose face was composed of sharp lines. Rapp knew how to blend in and hide the fact that he was a killer, but he had to put some effort into it. Gould was a natural. His soft eyes had a sadness in them that she was sure he'd used to get past more than a few bodyguards.

"You know who I am?" Kennedy asked.

Gould shook his head.

"You sure?" Kennedy said as she offered him a faint smile.

"Sorry."

"Mr. Gould, I know more about you than you could possibly imagine."

"I need to speak to Mr. Rapp."

"I'm afraid that's not going to happen."

"Why?"

"Because if I let him in here I'm pretty sure he'll kill you."

Gould let out a deep sigh and let his sad eyes drop to the tabletop. "I want to try to help him. I know I owe him."

"Then why don't you stop lying?"

"I am not lying." Gould looked exasperated. "Why won't anyone believe me?"

"You can't be serious?" Kennedy asked, more amused than upset. "I ask you a simple question . . . do you know who I am, and you can't even answer that?"

"I did. I told you I didn't know who you were."

"And you are lying. As I said, Mr. Gould, I know everything there is to know about you. Where you grew up, the units you served in when you were with the French Foreign Legion, and a good number of the people you have killed over the last fifteen-odd years."

Gould shrugged. "I'm not impressed."

Kennedy flashed one of those confident smiles that only a person who is holding all the cards can carry off. "I'm not trying to impress you, Mr. Gould. I'm simply trying to speed along this process and get you to drop your charade."

Showing a hint of anger, Gould leaned forward and said, "If it wasn't for me, Rapp and the rest of your men would be dead. Is there anyone around here who knows how to show some gratitude?"

"And if you don't know who I am, how is it that you know they are my men?"

Gould shook off her question. "It was a lucky guess."

"No, it wasn't," Kennedy said with absolute confidence. "We both know that you know who I am. What I'm trying to figure out is why you think denying that you know me will somehow help your cause."

"This is a waste of time. Get Rapp in here. Until you do that, I'm not saying a word. I have done nothing wrong. I've helped you guys," Gould said while poking himself in the chest.

"Maybe we could get your wife on the phone and you could try to explain to her what you were doing in Kabul?"

"Nice try."

"Claudia and I spoke yesterday."

"You're full of shit. You think because you have a name you can scare me into thinking you've got something on me."

Kennedy paused. She wasn't sure if she admired the way he was sticking to his story or thought him a fool. She would have her answer in the next few minutes.

CHAPTER 27

RAPP awoke from another slumber to find a new woman sitting at his bedside. There was a similar feeling of recognition, as if they had a common past, a collection of faint memories that he couldn't access but nonetheless were there, just beyond his grasp. There was also something different. With Kennedy the sentiment had been one of safety and familiarity, almost as if they were relatives. With this woman there was an emotion that told him their history was very different from that of being siblings.

Rapp tried to come up with her name. She was in her early to mid thirties, with raven-black hair pulled back in a low, loose ponytail. She had beautiful, dark almond-shaped eyes set atop high cheekbones and a strong jawline. She was all the more stunning because she wasn't wearing any makeup. If Rapp was in love with her or lusted for her it was easy to see why.

His memory had been coming back in chunks, and even though he could not place this woman, he was confident that she meant something more to him than just a casual friend. He feigned familiarity, smiled, and asked, "How are you?"

Sydney Hayek returned the smile and said, "I'm fine. You're the one we're all worried about."

Rapp played it off like it was no big deal. "I'm a little sore, that's all."

"I heard you have some memory issues."

Rapp didn't notice an accent. Her diction was flat, like all the TV anchors. She was probably from the Midwest but she looked as if she'd been born in Amman or Beirut. Michigan popped into his head, giving him the first clue to her identity. "That's what they tell me."

"Well?" she asked in a nonprodding manner.

"Well, what?"

"How's your memory?"

Rapp held up his hand and let it wobble back and forth. "It's a little iffy."

Hayek gave him a suspicious look. "What's my name?"

Rapp smiled. "I know you're from Michigan."

"That's correct."

For reasons that he didn't know at the time and couldn't explain later, he reached out and grabbed her hand. "I'm sorry. I feel like you're important to me. That we've shared something that could be important."

It wasn't easy to see Hayek blush with her smooth olive skin, but she was. Her lips formed a smile that was one part shock and the other part excitement. "We work with each other."

"And I get the feeling there's a little something more to our relationship than just work."

Hayek cleared her throat and laughed. She had sensed the tension between them, but her history of work relationships was so bad that she had ignored it to the best of her ability. That didn't mean, however, that she wasn't attracted to him. She was very much so. To the point where she was worried that it had begun to affect her work. She had even allowed her mind to wonder what it would be like. Rapp was such a dynamic force, volatile but in a very predictable way, that he actually scared her at first. The man across from her now, however, was a new version of Rapp, where all of those walls had been stripped away. For a split second she was tempted to tell him that they were in a committed relationship and then she decided against it.

Instead her juvenile streak took over and she said, "We've been sleeping with each other for the last six months."

Rapp's eyes opened wide. "Really?"

Hayek burst out laughing and, unable to talk because she couldn't stop laughing, she managed to shake her head. Finally after about ten seconds she said, "No, I'm sorry. I shouldn't have said that. We're coworkers . . . you're my boss."

Rapp looked bummed out. "That sucks."

"I'm sorry." She giggled some more, placed her other hand over Rapp's, and said, "That wasn't very nice of me."

Rapp cracked a smile and asked, "Do you think there's a chance we might be able to?"

Hayek laughed even harder this time and had to cover her mouth. This was so unlike Rapp, she wished she had taped it to show everyone. No, that would be mean, she thought, but it would be fun to show him. "Do they have you on any painkillers?"

Rapp smiled, and his smile gave her the answer to her question. Now it was his turn to clasp her hand in both of his. "Are you sure we never slept together?"

CHAPTER 28

KENNEDY had maneuvered Gould to the exact spot where she wanted him. The intelligence business was many things, but stripped down to its basic elements, it was about people. How they interacted with other people in normal day-to-day activities and how they might change their behavior in a stressful situation. It was easy to lose sight of this and get hung up on all the satellite imagery, signal intercepts, and endless reports from analysts, but it all came back to human interaction. Kennedy was fairly certain Gould was a misogynist. It was observable in the way he treated his wife. For a misogynist, it was almost impossible to underestimate a woman.

"So," she said, "you think you are the only one who keeps secrets?"

"Everyone has secrets."

"Claudia . . . your wife, does she have secrets?"

Kennedy saw a crack in his detached demeanor. The mention of his wife in such a personal way had its desired effect. "In case you've forgotten, she was the one who contacted me after you screwed up and killed Mitch's wife. You see, she knew that she couldn't bring a baby into this world with that kind of dark cloud hanging over her head.

Unlike you, she gets it. She understands that you can't take innocent life and expect to create life."

"Save your psychobabble for someone who cares. I can only imagine how many people you've killed over the years."

Some people in Kennedy's position would try to argue the fine point with Gould and claim that they had killed no one, but Kennedy had never deluded herself that she was uninvolved because someone else pulled the trigger. She understood fully the responsibilities of her job. Kennedy did not want to get sidetracked from the point at hand, but she needed to clear something up first. "You'll have to excuse me, but I'm not naïve enough to buy your postmodern relativism. I have killed people, more people than you have, but there are several rather distinct differences between us. I have received no fees, bounties, or contract payments for the people I have ordered killed, and I most certainly don't find some perverse thrill in it, as you do. I kill bad people in an effort to keep innocent people safe. You, on the other hand . . . it doesn't matter to you if you kill good people or bad people just so long as someone is willing to pay your fee."

"Please," Gould scoffed.

"I'm not sure why you think this game is helpful, but we both know the truth. You are not a good man. You are a selfish, narcissistic ass who, despite being given a second chance in life, could not walk away from an extremely dangerous profession. A profession that will likely get you, your wife, and your daughter killed."

"Please stop lecturing me, and go get Mr. Rapp."

Kennedy was ready to drop the bomb. "Claudia and I have been in contact for the last four years. She usually calls when you've left her and Anna to go on one of your trips where you claim you need to see your bankers." Kennedy caught the change in his eyes and she knew she had him. "I've even had you followed a few times."

Gould shook his head. "I don't know what you're talking about."

"You're not very good at this."

"Neither are you."

"My people were following you when you killed your old business partner Gaspar Navarro, in that park in Spain." This information should have been enough to get him to fold, but it was obvious he had a rather severe obstinate streak. "You thought he was taking money from you, yes?"

Gould shook his head. "None of this matters. Rapp is the only person I will talk to."

"That's not going to happen, Mr. Gould."

"Why?"

"I already told you . . . I'm fairly certain if I put the two of you in a room together he is going to kill you, and to be honest, I'd like to keep you alive for a little while."

"Why?"

"Why do you think?"

He shrugged as if he didn't have the foggiest idea.

"You possess information that I require. Information that you will give me sometime in the next minute or two is my guess."

Gould laughed in her face. "Oh, are we going to start the CIA's vaunted enhanced interrogation process now? Please, if you think those techniques will work on me you are a fool."

"This doesn't happen very often, but I'm tempted to test you just to see your arrogance stripped away."

"Torture will not work, and you have yet to convince me why I would want to tell you a thing."

Kennedy smiled. "Because I hold the key to your future, and I'm actually fond of your wife. I think she's a good person who fell in love with the wrong man. I wouldn't want to hold that against her . . . the fact that you're a serial liar and a murderer, amongst other things."

"You don't know a thing about me."

"You couldn't be more wrong. Mr. Gould. In fact, I think I care more about your wife than you do. You have gotten into bed with some bad people. I think it's safe to say they wanted you dead yesterday after you completed their work for them. People like that won't stop until they get what they want. They are running now, trying to tie up all their loose ends to make sure there is nothing left to connect them to you. So while you sit here and refuse to talk, your wife and child are vulnerable. The men who hired you don't know you're here." Kennedy stood. "They will start looking for you, and they will eventually find your wife and child."

"You don't really expect me to fall for this, do you?"

"Oh, I do, Mr. Gould, because if I could find them I'm guessing that your employer can as well."

"You're bluffing."

Kennedy spoke each word in a staccato rhythm. "Nelson, New Zealand . . . 4102 Vickerman Street." She saw the panic in the way his right cheek twitched. At least he cared about them. "Would you like me to describe the house to you?"

The façade melted away at the mention of the city, let alone his address. He shook his head.

"I had Claudia and Anna placed into protective custody last night." Kennedy turned for the door. "And just so we're clear on this, I did it because I don't think they should die because of your greed and stupidity."

Gould felt the walls closing in around him. He watched Kennedy reach for the buzzer next to the door and he blurted out, "How did you find us?"

Kennedy made a half turn and looked down at Gould. "This is your last chance, Mr. Gould. You either tell me everything I want to know, or I will tell Claudia how you have continued with your little hobby despite promising her you were done. I will tell her about the type of people you've been working with and how you have put her and Anna in harm's way, all for your own selfish gratification. And then you can spend the rest of your life in a cell, agonizing over your stupidity and wondering what your daughter looks like with each passing birthday. So what's it going to be, Mr. Gould, are you ready to talk or do want to continue with these stupid games?"

His head hung in defeat, Gould said, "I'm ready to talk."

"What is my name, and what do I do for a living?"

"You're Dr. Irene Kennedy. Director of the Central Intelligence Agency."

Kennedy nodded and pressed the buzzer. The door opened a second later to reveal Nash. She told him, "I need a pen and a pad of paper. Mr. Gould is about to give us a good deal of information."

Nash looked more than a little surprised that his boss had been able to accomplish what he couldn't, and in only a few minutes. He nodded and turned to get what she'd asked for.

"And you can turn everything back on." Kennedy let the door close and surveyed the strange man sitting across from her. "You might not understand this, but I care about what happens to you."

Gould looked up at her with disbelieving eyes.

"I know that's hard for someone like you to believe, but it's true. Mitch spared your life for reasons that I don't entirely understand, which leaves me to wonder if there isn't a bigger reason that none of us understood, and still don't understand." Kennedy watched for a sign that the man was capable of feeling either guilt or gratitude. She saw neither, but she wasn't displeased, for his expression was one of fear, and Kennedy knew from personal experience that fear could be a great motivator. "You have a role to play here, Mr. Gould. I don't know what it is yet, but I think we're about to find out."

CHAPTER 29

JOEL Wilson was used to getting his way. So much so that when people didn't bow to his whims, he became such an insufferable bastard that his opponents' only option was to surrender. At least that's the way it usually worked, but every once in a while Wilson ran up against someone who was more than willing to match him toe-to-toe in his little game of threats, wild conjecture, and pure bluster.

It had started off well enough. Wilson had landed at the Kabul International Airport without alerting the CIA, or anyone from the FBI, for that matter, that he and his team had arrived. He then placed a call to the FBI liaison at the embassy and explained to him that they needed to talk. "No," Wilson explained to the man, "you are not in any trouble—at least none that I know of, so I suggest you follow my orders to the tee." Wilson went on to explain that no one, including the ambassador, was to know that he and his people were in the country. The liaison went along with Wilson's requests and within the hour his team was inside the embassy and ready to descend upon the CIA personnel.

That was when things started to get a little bumpy. Wilson, primed for his first confrontation, was extremely disappointed when he discovered that Darren Sickles, the CIA's station chief, was not in the building. Wilson badgered Sickles's secretary for a good ten minutes. The only thing he managed to get out of her was that Sickles was at the Ministry of the Interior on important business. When he asked for Sickles's second in command he was told he was in Jalalabad. When he inquired as to the whereabouts of Mitch Rapp, the woman completely shut down. It didn't matter how many threats he leveled at her, she refused to answer his questions.

In the end it was the liaison that came through, a pasty little man with too much hair. Wilson thought he looked like a foreigner. Apparently there had been a gunfight with the local police and Rapp. It was causing an uproar in the capital. Early reports had it that Rapp and his men had killed more than twenty police officers and Rapp had been injured in the battle. The liaison discovered that Rapp had been taken to the Cure International Hospital, so Wilson loaded up his team and went to see what they could find out.

The decision proved to be a colossal mistake. Angry relatives and locals had congregated at the hospital, where many of the dead and wounded police officers had been taken. Wilson and his people were pelted with rocks and garbage as they entered the hospital, only to find out that Rapp wasn't there. They wasted two additional hours at the hospital, waiting for a military escort to take them back to the embassy. By then Wilson had heard bits and pieces of what had happened to Rapp and his men. Apparently a corrupt police commander had ordered the attack. Wilson had his own priorities to deal with but this also sounded like an area he might have to look into.

After returning to the embassy, Wilson learned that Director Kennedy was in the country. Wilson became irate over their squandered opportunity. Kennedy could easily insert herself between Wilson and her people, making his investigation nearly impossible. The liaison came to Wilson for a second time claiming to know where Rapp was. Wilson told him if was wrong this time, he would find the worst posting the FBI had and he would make sure he was sent there. The team went back to the Kabul airport, and was ferried by helicopter up to the Bagram Air Base.

Landing at the base was uneventful, as they were met by another contingent of FBI special agents who were assigned to the base. Wilson was pleased to see the stress that his visit had induced. They were transported to the base hospital. And that was where the real problems started. The nearly insurmountable obstacle came in the form of a short Latino Air Force sergeant, who for reasons that Wilson could not grasp, had decided to become his archenemy.

It started out simply enough, the fuzzy liaison from the embassy inquiring at the main desk about a patient named Mitch Rapp. The young man sitting behind the desk had two chevrons and a star. Wilson had no idea what rank that was, but he assumed it was very low because the enlisted person in question had bad acne. The airman first class was a law-abiding, extremely patriotic twenty-one-year-old from Kansas who didn't have it in him to challenge authority, so he simply gave them directions to the ward where Rapp could be found.

It was at that second desk where Wilson ran into immovable Air Force Command Master Sergeant Sheila Sanchez—all four feet eleven inches of her. In hindsight, Wilson realized that his tactics had been wrong, something not easy for him to admit. His five-person entourage had grown to nine special agents by the time they'd arrived at the hospital. These wards were filled with young men and women who'd had their bodies mangled in the most awful ways, typically from explosions. That meant that the people who cared for them conducted themselves almost as if they were cloistered nuns who had taken a vow of silence.

So the mob of agents stumbled upon the ward that among other things handled head trauma. The badges came out and Wilson was both too loud and too firm about what he wanted. The women behind the desk grew horrified as the male agents began looking in open doors to see if they could identify Rapp. Upon hearing the disturbance, Sheila Sanchez quickly removed her reading glasses, spun her chair

away from her computer, and waddled at double pace out of her office
and into the hallway.

Sanchez ran her ward with an iron fist. The patients came first and
the patients on this particular floor needed a great deal of rest, which
required peace and quiet. As she was the highest-ranking noncommis-
sioned officer on the floor, even the doctors gave her a wide berth. It
wasn't that they feared Sanchez so much as that the woman knew what
she was doing, so the officers let her call the shots, everywhere except
the operating room.

Sanchez had seen it all in her time on the base. Presidents, vice
presidents, cabinet members, generals from every service, admirals,
rock stars, movie stars, and comedians. They all came with their en-
tourages and even though they meant well, they were all a pain in the
ass. Sanchez had made it very clear to the people down at the front desk
that when these groups came through, they were not to be sent to her
floor. Send them to see the patients with broken bones and bullet holes,
but leave her head trauma patients the hell alone.

The first thing she did was draw the index finger of her left hand
up in front of her mouth and shush the entire group of men. Having
silenced the crowd, she headed for a man who had made it around the
desk and had pushed his head into one of the rooms. The agent, caught
in no-man's-land, didn't know what to do, so he stood there frozen in
the doorway. Sanchez swatted him in the ass as if he were a three-year-
old boy who had just run out in the street. When the agent turned to
protest, Sanchez grabbed him by the tie and yanked him down the hall
and back to the area on the other side of the desk.

Keeping her voice down but her intensity extremely high, Sanchez
hissed, "Do you people think you're at the zoo? My patients are just
animals . . . you can just walk in here, loud as hell, and start poking
around?"

Wilson stepped forward with a scowl on his face and his credentials in his left hand. "Listen here, lady. We're here on official FBI busi-

ness. I need to speak to one of your patients, and I need to speak to him right now."

"Lady?" The word flew out of Sanchez's round little mouth like a counterpunch. "You see this here?" She swung her left shoulder around so Wilson had a clear view. "It's not 'lady,' it's Command Master Sergeant Sanchez."

Wilson still didn't get it. He rolled his eyes and said, "I don't have time for this. I am running a very important investigation. Get out of my way or—"

"Or you'll what?" Sanchez stepped forward and poked Wilson at the base of his sternum, right above his solar plexus.

Wilson retreated two quick steps and brought his hand up in case she tried again. "You just assaulted a federal agent."

"Then arrest me, you big pussy."

"I'm not going to warn you again."

Without turning, Sanchez called to one of the nurses, "Amanda, get base security up here right now."

"Listen, la—" Wilson almost said "lady," but stopped himself and then noticed the name tag on this crazy woman's ample breast. "Ms. Sanchez, this is a federal facility. We work for the FBI. We have jurisdiction over this base."

"The hell you do," Sanchez laughed in his face, "and it's Command Master Sergeant Sanchez, Special Agent Dumbass, or whatever your name is. I have been in this man's United States Air Force for thirty years and I know every regulation from top to bottom. Did you check in with USAF Security Forces when you came on base?" She paused a beat to see if he could muster an answer, which he couldn't. "Of course you didn't. Are you working with the USAF Office of Special Investigations?"

Wilson knew he was in trouble and managed to look at one of the special agents who was assigned to the base to see if he could offer a little assistance. The man shrugged and shook his head. "Command

Master Sergeant Sanchez, I run the Counterintelligence Division at the FBI. This is a national security issue and if you don't step aside, I'm going to have to have you arrested."

Sanchez raised her fist again as if she might strike him. "I can't seem to get it through your thick head—you are not in charge here. I am."

"I am a federal—"

"I don't give a rat's ass who you are. You are not authorized to be on my floor."

"But—"

"But nothing. You've got two strikes and that means you only have one more chance. Here comes the third pitch, and my guess is you're gonna whiff on this one just like the first two." Sanchez held up the stubby index finger on her right hand, started with the first man on her left and then continued around to her right, saying, "Do any of you have a warrant issued from a federal judge that specifically states that you can bully your way into an intensive care unit on this particular United States air base?" She continued her sweep, looking each man in the eye for a second time. When she made it back to Wilson, she said, "I didn't think so." She stepped forward, shooing the herd of men toward the staircase. "So get the hell off my floor right now, and don't you dare come back until you have that warrant."

CHAPTER 30

JALALABAD, AFGHANISTAN

KASSAR attempted to remain calm as he studied the twenty-three-inch color monitor. The hostage was limp, his arms stretched above his head, his knees buckled, the two dimwitted interrogators trying to figure out what to do. Kassar looked calm, but inside his stomach was turning flips. If he botched this in any way he might as well put a bullet in his own head and save himself from the misguided hope that they might let him live. After calming himself with a few deep breaths, he pushed himself away from the table and grabbed his mask. Before entering the room he pulled it down to make sure none of his face was showing.

The door opened to reveal the two fools checking Rickman for a pulse. They had pulled their masks up so they fit like winter caps. They looked like a couple of common criminals in a Hollywood movie. Kassar filed past the camera and went straight to the extremely valuable Rickman. He shooed the other two men away and checked Rickman's neck. He spent almost a minute searching for a pulse. Two separate times he thought he felt a weak pulse but then he lost it. Next he tried the wrist and there was nothing.

His anxiety growing with each passing second, Kassar finally placed his ear over Rickman's heart. Again there was nothing. Kassar stepped away from the lifeless Rickman and looked at his men.

The two simpletons couldn't have looked more ashamed. "He was doing fine. The doctor said he could take more."

"We didn't hit him that hard," the shorter one said.

Kassar was more nervous than angry. "I forbade you two to kill him, yet that's exactly what you did."

"We are sorry."

"Not as sorry as I am." Kassar turned to leave and while facing the camera he drew his pistol from under his tunic. A long silencer was attached to the end. Kassar stepped to the side and spun around, facing the men. "I told you I would kill you if anything happened to him."

"I'm sorry," the bigger one said in a pleading tone.

Kassar squeezed the trigger five times in quick succession and then turned the weapon on the other man, who was cowering with his hands over his face. Kassar was amused that this idiot thought covering his face could somehow stop a bullet. Kassar placed the tip of the silencer against the man's palms and started pulling the trigger. He didn't bother to count this time. He let his rage flow.

When the pistol was empty, Kassar turned to face the camera. They could still make it look as if Rickman was alive, at least for a while. All they had to do was release some propaganda on the Internet showing Rickman when he started to break. The Americans would fear the worst. Kassar kept telling himself that it would work. He'd been telling himself the same thing for days, even though he had his doubts.

He would have to move quickly, though, or all would be lost. Kassar swung his empty pistol at the camera, knocking it to the floor. The camera broke into several pieces, the red light blinking several times and then going out. Kassar stuffed his pistol back in his waistband and yanked off the stifling black hood. He walked from one wall to the other and back, going over what had to be done. With his nerves calmed just enough to allow him to carry on, he approached Rickman and with a knife cut the rope that was holding him up.

Kassar caught the body over his left shoulder, and after moving him around a bit he had him balanced just right. The stench of urine and feces was awful. Kassar almost retched twice before he even got him out of the room. He stopped in the next room and closed and unhooked the laptop that had recorded all the sessions. He then started up the stairs and again almost vomited.

Kassar was about to lay Rickman on the floor and then he thought of the long drive ahead. There was no way he could stand the smell, and if he was stopped by the police or border agents the smell alone might cause them to search the vehicle. So, instead of tossing him on the floor, Kassar carried him down the hall to the back of the house and laid the body in the bathtub.

He checked his watch and wondered how much time he could spare. He decided ten minutes wouldn't make a difference. Kassar turned on the water and used his knife to cut Rickman's foul-smelling boxers from his body. Once the underwear was disposed of it was relatively easy. A little bit of soap and a washcloth and the body was clean enough for the journey. Kassar dried Rickman as best he could and then carried him to the bedroom, where he dressed him in some loose-fitting clothes. The only problem they had now was the bloody and battered face. Kassar would lay him in the backseat and cover him with a blanket. If he were stopped he would tell them that he was bringing his brother home to be buried. In the West it might have seemed strange, but here in Afghanistan, morticians were not so common.

Kassar had to take care of one more thing. He sat down on the edge of the bed and opened the laptop. His fingers glided over the track pad until he had what he wanted. He had edited the video earlier in the day. Rickman had spoken a few lies, but he had also given up some valuable secrets. The Americans would lose their minds when they saw this. Kassar was smiling as he posted the video on a popular jihadist website. Like a pebble in a lake, the video would ripple across the World Wide Web. There was no way the Americans could hope to contain it.

CHAPTER 31

BAGRAM AIR BASE, AFGHANISTAN

WILSON was back down in front of the main desk, and the pimple-faced airman was trying to figure out how some uneducated Latino woman could deter nine special agents of the Federal Bureau of Investigation from doing their job. The only reason he wasn't yelling at his overpaid, overqualified entourage was that he'd been unable to get past her as well, and he was in charge.

Wilson hadn't gotten to where he was in this world by simply quitting every time an obstacle was placed in front of him. No, Joel Wilson was better than that. If this Air Force bitch thought she could defy his authority, she was in for a rude lesson. Tapping the reception counter with his knuckles, he demanded, "Who's in charge of this place?"

"I'm sorry, sir, you'll have to be more specific."

"This place," Wilson repeated, and waved his arms around. This further cemented Wilson's belief that the military had become the great dumping ground for America's dim-witted masses.

"Brigadier General Earl Kreitzer, sir."

Wilson filed that one away. "What about this hospital?"

"Overall is Colonel Wyman, sir. He's the task force medical commander, but Lieutenant Colonel Brunkhorst is the medical chief of staff."

"Are either of them here right now?"

"Lieutenant Colonel Brunkhorst is, sir. May I ask what this is about?" The man snatched the handset out of the cradle. "She's going to want to know."

"It's about that rude woman you have in ICU . . . Something, something Sergeant Sanchez."

The eyes on the young man from Kansas grew large with recognition and he placed the handset back in its cradle. "Command Master Sergeant Sanchez."

"That's right."

The Kansan looked over both shoulders. "Technically, sir, Lieutenant Colonel Brunkhorst is senior in the chain of command, but truth be told, Command Master Sergeant Sanchez runs this place."

"Shit." Wilson slapped his hand on countertop.

"I hope you didn't do anything to upset her, sir." Then he leaned forward and whispered, "She's not someone you want to get on the wrong side of."

"No shit, Sherlock." Wilson was on the verge of really losing it, when the most surprising sight caught his eye. Coming down the hall toward him was one of his former FBI special agents, Sydney Hayek. They had once had a deeply complicated relationship that Hayek had ruined. According to Wilson's very credible information, she was now working for the CIA. Wilson stepped away from the desk. "Sydney," he shouted with a friendly wave. "You're the last person I expected to find here."

Hayek, normally good at masking her emotions, was incapable of doing so. Joel Wilson was the sole reason she had decided to leave the FBI. "Why are you here?"

Wilson flashed the boyish grin that he was so proud of. "I'm the one asking the questions around here." He reached out to touch her shoulder, but she took a quick step back. Wilson tried to cover and said, "You look good."

Hayek crossed her arms, her eyes glancing at the men behind Wilson. "Why are you here?"

"Well, it's good to see you as well, Sydney," Wilson said in an easy tone. "It's too bad I had to fly to the other side of the planet to run into you. Do you have time to grab a cup of coffee?"

There was no answer. Hayek couldn't process what she was hearing. Standing before her was a man who had tried to destroy her life. A man who had sexually harassed her and made her actually contemplate suicide. He knew all these things, yet here he was, standing in front of her, acting as if they were old friends.

"We're not going to have coffee," Hayek said, remembering how her therapist had told her she needed to be firm and unambiguous.

"That's too bad, because I could really use your help on something. I hear you're out at Langley these days."

"What I do is classified. None of your business."

Wilson laughed heartily. "You must not be aware of my new job at the Bureau. I'm running the Counterintelligence Division. You know . . . who watches the watchers, and all that stuff."

Hayek shrugged in an effort to convey what she was thinking, which was: *I don't give a shit what you do.*

Wilson leaned forward and with a suave smile said, "So your business actually *is* my business."

Hayek wanted to crawl out of her skin. She took a step to the side and said, "I need to be someplace right now." Two steps later he grabbed her arm.

"Slow down there, missy."

Hayek pivoted and came back at Wilson with her left fist cocked. "Take your damn hands off me!"

Wilson let go and put his hands up in the air. "You need to calm down. Striking a federal agent will land your pretty little ass in jail."

"How about sexually harassing a federal agent and stalking her?" After having kept it pent up for years, and thinking she was free from this imbalanced egomaniac, she could no longer keep her feelings bottled up.

Wilson had handled her before and he could handle her now. "I see that Arab temper of yours hasn't gotten any better."

"I'm half Lebanese, half American, you arrogant WASP."

Under his breath, but loud enough for several of them to hear, he said, "Hell hath no fury like a spurned woman."

"Is that what you tell yourself? You think stalking your subordinate and making up fake excuses to be alone with me and me shutting down your perverted attempts at getting me into bed somehow adds up to me wanting you?" Hayek had been over and over all of this in therapy with Dr. Lewis, the CIA's resident shrink. Hayek had been raised in a culture in which she was a disappointment. Her father, a Lebanese immigrant, had wanted her to be nothing more than a nurse. Women had their place in this world and it didn't involve a gun, a badge, and chasing down bad guys. He wanted to marry off his beautiful daughter at eighteen to one of his friend's sons. It was all arranged. She was supposed to begin providing grandchildren immediately. Without her knowledge a date had already been set at St. Maron's Church. Hayek, a gifted student, had caught the eye of her high school's guidance counselor. By the time her father announced his grand plans, Hayek had already been notified that she had not only been accepted to the University of Chicago, but she was going on a full ride.

Her entire world fell apart in just a few days. She defied her father and he in turn threw her out on the street. In a classic I-will-show-you showdown, neither Hayek nor her father backed down. The years ticked by and the distance grew and Hayek found out she could survive without her family. Her classmates at the University of Chicago became her new family and the FBI became her life. Hayek became a force of independence, promising herself that she would never be a victim. That she would never allow a man to dictate her life. She had done just fine until the deceitful and manipulative Joel Wilson came along.

During the seemingly never-ending therapy sessions, Dr. Lewis helped her see that she had built up some very unhealthy coping mechanisms. The most obvious was that she rarely let her feelings be known. She simply put her head down, kept her complaints to herself, and moved forward. When Wilson began twisting her into knots, her silence only made things worse.

Well, there's not going to be any more silence, she told herself.

"I'd hoped you got some help after you washed out of the Bureau. But it doesn't look like it."

"You asshole. No one can manipulate the facts like you." Hayek turned back toward the other men, some dressed in dark suits, others in more casual base attire. "Do any of you actually like working with this jerk?" They all stared at her stone-faced. "Well, don't trust him. Never . . . not for a second, because you don't mean a thing to him. You see, he's the only honorable man in all of D.C. That means all of you are expendable."

"That's enough," a red-faced Wilson snapped. "Your psychological issues aside, I'm here in an official capacity and you are going to answer some questions."

"Pound sand, asshole. You want to talk to me, you call my lawyer and set it up."

Wilson grinned. "You already have a lawyer. You must have something to hide."

Hayek had said her piece. She was shaking from the release of all the things that she should have said years ago. "Let's hear it," Hayek said forcefully, for all to hear. "Ask your questions. Let's go."

Wilson wasn't quite ready for this level of vitriol. In his mind he had been nothing but supportive of Hayek's career. They were two extremely attractive people, and it seemed natural for them to indulge in a physical relationship. In his mind at least, he was in an open marriage. "Nice try. This is a highly classified investigation. Why don't you take a ride with us and we'll discuss."

"What in the hell is going on here?" The icy voice cut through the air. It wasn't loud or forceful, but it had a tone of absolute authority.

Wilson watched his sea of agents part to reveal CIA Director Irene Kennedy and a group of men who made his gaggle of FBI agents look like a bunch of pussies. Her security detail looked like a collection of mixed martial arts fighters carrying machine guns and lots of ammunition. "Director," Wilson said, trying to sound calm, "you're just the person I wanted to talk to."

Kennedy stood her ground, like a predator trying to decide if this was worth the physical exertion. After an uncomfortable silence, she said, "I find that hard to believe."

"What's that?" Wilson said casually.

"That you wanted to talk to me."

"Come now, Director, I always enjoy catching up with you."

"How could I be just the person you wanted to talk to when you didn't even know I was here?"

Wilson smiled awkwardly while he tried to come up with an answer. Kennedy was no fool. "It's not every day the director of the CIA lands in Bagram. Word travels quickly on these bases."

Kennedy appraised him with cautious eyes. She didn't believe him for a second. "I think it's far more rare to have the FBI's acting head of Counterintelligence so far from home."

"We go where we must."

Normally Kennedy would have been more diplomatic, but with one of her men dead, two missing, a fourth in the hospital, and the entire Afghani government screaming for blood, she was in no mood for whatever Wilson was up to, so she cut to the heart of the matter. "What did you want to question Agent Hayek about?"

Wilson hesitated for a second. "I'm sorry, but I'm not at liberty to discuss matters pertaining to an ongoing investigation."

"You think so?" Kennedy said, taking two steps forward. "I want you to think long and hard about how you answer this next question. Are you aware of the protocols you are to follow if you want to question one of my people?"

"Of course I am."

"So you went through all the proper channels?"

"Agent Hayek and I go way back," Wilson said, as if the entire thing was being blown out of proportion. "It was going to be a simple off-the-record discussion."

Kennedy nodded slowly and then walked across the lobby until she was just two feet from Wilson. She gestured with her finger for him to come closer so they could speak in confidence. Wilson bent forward at the waist and offered Kennedy his left ear.

"I am well aware of your history with Agent Hayek. Stay the hell away from her, or I will make your life miserable in ways you can't even begin to imagine." Kennedy took a step back and in a voice loud enough for everyone to hear said, "Now, in the future, Special Agent Wilson, if you would like to conduct an interview with any of my people you will contact my office to coordinate. Are we clear?"

Before Wilson could answer, a shrill voice carried down the hallway like a Klaxon. "What in the hell is going on here?"

Wilson looked over his shoulder to see the ball-busting Latino waddling her way toward them. His face went slack.

Shaking her finger at Wilson, she said, "You better have that warrant we talked about or I swear to God I'm not just going to have you thrown out of this hospital, I'm going to have you thrown off this base."

Wilson had had enough altercations for the day, and he really didn't want to stick around and answer more of Kennedy's questions. "Sorry about the miscommunication, Director. I'll be in contact with your office." Not waiting for a reply, he brushed past Kennedy and out the door.

Kennedy watched with more than a bit of confusion. The blustering Joel Wilson was known for seeking out confrontation, not running from it. She looked back to a very upset Command Master Sergeant

Sanchez, who was still making her way down the hall. Kennedy had spoken with Sanchez earlier, and the woman had been very helpful in regard to Rapp's care. "Command Master Sergeant Sanchez, what was that you said about a warrant?"

Sanchez was out of breath and flushed. She held a finger up to Kennedy and said, "Excuse me one second." She turned to the young airman behind the desk and said, "Get base security on the horn. I want to speak to Colonel DePuglio ASAP, and if he's not available get me Major Callahan. You'd think we were running a damn zoo here." Turning back to Kennedy, Sanchez took a heavy breath and said, "I'm sorry, Director. What did you want?"

"That man who just left. Did you say something about a warrant?"

She nodded vigorously, "He was trying to bully his way in to see your man Mr. Cox, although he was calling him Mr. Rapp. Part of some official investigation, he said, all full of himself."

Sanchez was still talking, but Kennedy was only half listening. She had the ominous feeling that someone out there, or more likely an organization, had gone to great lengths to cripple the Clandestine Service. Too many seemingly random things were beginning to pile up—far too many to be a coincidence. Wilson would be easy enough to play. The man had an infatuation with himself, and by extension a need to validate himself, by tearing down those who were not part of the Counterintelligence Division. Unfortunately the CIA was the perfect target for him. And Wilson had a reputation for tenacity. He would dig until he got what he wanted, and he wouldn't play fair. Kennedy decided then and there that she was going to need to get proactive.

CHAPTER 32

KENNEDY asked Sanchez if Wilson had gotten in to see Rapp, and if so, what he wanted. Sanchez retold the events in her colorful, clipped military diction and made it very clear that she wasn't going to let that clown get anywhere near any of her patients. Mr. Cox was safe, Sanchez assured Kennedy. Kennedy wondered if she should suggest placing a guard outside Rapp's door, but thought better of it. Sanchez was likely to take that as an indictment that she couldn't do her job. A better angle was to bring Sanchez into her confidence.

Asking her for a word in private, Kennedy followed Sanchez down the hall about twenty feet and then said, "I need to be very careful about what I say, since this is all very classified material, but I get the sense I can trust you."

Sanchez nodded as if to say "you're damn right."

"Mr. Cox is one of my top covert operatives. He was working on something very sensitive. Another one of my people has gone missing and we need to find him ASAP. I think Mr. Cox might have some information that could help us, but unfortunately his memory is very spotty at the moment."

Sanchez nodded. "Doctors told me they don't expect that to last. Every day he'll remember more and more."

Kennedy smiled, "And when he does, I need someone there. With your permission I would like to have one of my people at his bedside."

"Twenty-four-seven." Sanchez frowned. It was obvious she didn't like the sound of this.

"If at any point you think someone is misbehaving, by all means you can throw them off your floor, but I can assure you, Command Master Sergeant, like you, I run a tight ship. My people will be as quiet as church mice."

After considerable thought, Sanchez relented. Kennedy thanked her for all of her help and handed her a card. "That's my mobile number. I always have it. If you need me for anything, please call. And if that man from the FBI shows up again, please call. I will have him dealt with."

When Sanchez was gone, Kennedy turned to her assistant. "Eugene, please get Samuel Hargrave on the line and tell him it is extremely urgent."

Paranoia was part of her business. Sometimes it was a big part and other times not so much. As discomfiting as it was, you were a fool to ignore it. The key was to make sure it didn't paralyze you. After nearly three decades in the intelligence business Kennedy had learned to recognize the natural rhythms of the job. The pace, usually glacial, was often interrupted by moments of extreme action—like right now. This one felt different, though. It was too orchestrated.

Her mentor, Thomas Stansfield, had taught her to think in broad strategic terms—like a battlefield commander. Your flanks must always be protected and your center must be anchored with reinforcements. Supplies needed to be secured from raids and scouts needed to be deployed as aggressively as possible to discern the strength and position of the enemy.

The problem right now was that Kennedy was flying blind. Someone was maneuvering against her and she had no idea who they were or what their next move would be. Rickman, Hubbard, the attack on Rapp, and now Wilson showing up: She had an unnerving suspicion that they were all part of a concerted effort to weaken her Clandestine Service. She and her people could draw up a list of who would benefit most from this type of action, but it would only be a list. Kennedy wanted something more concrete, and she thought she knew where to start.

"Mike," Kennedy said to Nash. She motioned for him to follow her, and the two walked to the far corner of the lobby. "Where is Marcus?"

"Virginia, as far as I know." Nash thought about their extremely quirky computer hacker. Despite all of the protocols they put in place, the man could be unnervingly difficult to track down.

"Find him and bring in your best people. I want to know what Joel Wilson is up to."

Nash's face turned pensive. "Are you sure this is a good idea? If anything goes wrong . . ." Nash shuddered at the thought of the FBI finding out they were spying on them.

Kennedy remained stoic. Nash was one of her top people, but he was increasingly becoming the type of person who was followed by dark storm clouds. In other words, he spent too much time worrying about the downside of everything. This had been Rapp's chief complaint of late. "Mike," Kennedy said in a firm tone, "we're flying blind, and it looks like someone has launched an operation aimed at crippling the Clandestine Service. Sitting around is not an option. Get your people spun up. In two hours I want to hear how you are going to penetrate Joel Wilson's group, and I want to start seeing results in the next twenty-four hours."

"What about Hargrave? He's Wilson's boss. You two have a good relationship. Maybe he can tell us what's going on."

Kennedy exhaled sharply and gave Nash a look that said her patience was gone. "Do you honestly think that I haven't already thought of that?"

"No . . . I just . . . I'm trying to make sure we don't make a mistake we'll regret."

Kennedy had heard enough. "Mitch is laid up and I don't know when I'm going to get him back, and Stan has just been told he has a few months to live. You're the next guy on my bench. I need you to execute for me, not question my orders."

Nash didn't like being shut down like this and his face showed it.

The fact that he couldn't simply suck it up and follow an order was the breaking point for Kennedy. "Forget it," she said, "I'll find someone else to handle it." Not waiting for a response, she left him in the corner and motioned for Scott Coleman to follow her.

She repeated the orders to Coleman, who received them without protest. After Kennedy was done explaining what she wanted, Coleman had a better idea.

"The guy's right here . . . on base. I'll put him under surveillance starting now and see what I can find out."

"And call Marcus."

"First thing I'll do. Anything else?"

Kennedy thought about it for a second while she looked back down the hall at Mike Nash, who seemed to be pouting. For the first time, she understood Hurley and Rapp's recent frustrations with the man. When this was over, she was going to have to reassess his role moving forward. Turning back to Coleman she said, "That's all for now. Let me know the second you find anything."

CHAPTER 33

THE image of a bloodied and battered Joe Rickman was all over the Internet. Thanks to an alert analyst in the CIA's Ops Center, Kennedy was spared having to learn the information from Al Jazeera. The analyst who was working the night shift was surfing her way through a series of hard-core jihadist websites when she stumbled across the video. Ten minutes later she had a voice match on Rickman and the alert went out. For reasons Kennedy could never quite understand, Bagram and Kabul were eight hours and thirty minutes ahead of D.C., not eight hours or nine hours. The thirty minutes threw her off, so when Eugene told her that it was 10:13 in D.C. it took her a second to run the calculation—it was 6:43 a.m. in Bagram.

Eugene handed Kennedy the secure phone and she sat up in bed.

"It's Brad," he informed her.

Kennedy rubbed the sleep from her eyes and said, "I'm here, Brad, what's up?"

"Irene, it's not good."

Kennedy was billeted in one of the base's VIP trailers. She motioned for Eugene to turn on the TV. "I'm listening."

"It's Rick. It's all over the Internet."

Kennedy felt a lump in her throat as she assumed the worst. "Is he alive?"

"Barely. His face is unrecognizable. We had to do a voice analysis to make sure it was him."

"But you're sure it's him?"

"One hundred percent."

Kennedy heard the stress in her deputy director's voice. Brad Stofer had been in his new job for just eight months, but he had been at Langley for twenty-six years. He was a pro, and if he was bothered by what he had seen, it meant it wasn't good. Kennedy also knew that voiceprints rarely came back with a 100 percent match. She feared the worst. "Describe it to me."

"It's four minutes and thirty-seven seconds long. It's heavily edited. His arms are tied above his head. Looks like he's hanging from the ceiling. They were smart enough to cover the walls with sheets. Two men handle the interrogation. It starts out with a lot of head slaps and then they bring out the rubber hoses. He's a bloody mess by the end of it." There was a long pause and then Stofer added, "It's fucking horrible."

Kennedy started to think about what Rickman was going through, and then she got a grip on her emotions. Now was not the time to lose it. "What does he say?"

"The audio isn't great, but our people say they can clean it up. We should have a good copy in the next thirty minutes. I'll get it to you as soon as it's ready."

"Brad," Kennedy said in a slightly impatient voice, "how bad is the damage?"

"Bad . . . some names are thrown around."

"Which ones?"

"Five of our people in Afghanistan . . . the two cabinet members, the general, the head of intel, and the president."

The Afghanistan assets were the least of her concerns. The accusations were already out there. The people expected it. "What else?"

"He mentions how much we're paying them, and we're pretty sure he names the bank in Switzerland where we keep their money for them. We'll know more when the audio gets cleaned up."

"What else?" She knew there had to be more.

"He mentions Nawaz."

"Gillani."

"Yep."

Kennedy thought of the Pakistani foreign minister who had been their best window in the decision-making process of their hot-and-cold ally. Trying to pull him out would be impossible. "Does he know?"

"Yes. He's going to sit it out. I think he's betting on indefinite house arrest."

Kennedy wasn't so sure, but there wasn't much she could do about it. "What else?"

"There's a spot on the tape where it sounds like he says 'Sitting Bull.' "

Kennedy threw off the covers and stood. Sitting Bull was the code name for their highly placed mole in Russia's Foreign Intelligence Service. "Does he say anything other than the name?"

"No. He blurts it out in the middle of one of the beatings."

"Send me the current version. I need to see this for myself."

"It's on its way. What do you want to do about Sitting Bull?"

Kennedy was holding a fistful of her hair. She had on a modest pair of gray pajama pants with a matching long-sleeved top. Eugene was in a pair of boxers and a T-shirt. He wasn't doing any good standing there, so she covered the phone and said, "Wake everybody up. Get the coffee going and tell them we have a meeting in twenty minutes." She watched Eugene leave and looked at Al Jazeera on the TV. So far there was nothing, but that wouldn't last. A CIA Clandestine Service operative being tortured was their bread and butter. "Give me a second," she told Stofer.

The damage assessment in the immediate aftermath of Rickman's abduction hadn't come anywhere near Sitting Bull. "Get our people to take a fresh look at this. I want to know how in the hell Rick even knew about Sitting Bull. As far as I know, he wasn't read in on him. Get his handlers in tonight and find out if one of them happened to casually mention it to Rick, and if no one fesses up, hook 'em all up and polly them."

"So we leave him where he is?"

"I need to think about that." Sitting Bull was their best source in the Russian government by a long shot. She needed to be certain before she gave the order to bring him in. "Put an extraction team on standby. Find out if he has any reason to travel in the next twenty-four hours. If we can meet him on neutral ground we can have a sit-down and he can decide, but I don't want anyone telling him until we know for certain. Am I clear?"

"Yes."

"Anything else?"

"Those are the major points. He mentions Hubbard and Sickles and a few other people, but other than Hubbard everyone is secure."

"All right." Kennedy let out a huge sigh as she tried to digest the scope of the problem. "Give me twenty minutes and I'll call you back." Kennedy ended the call and turned on her laptop. She used the bathroom and brushed her teeth while she waited for the encrypted file to download. When she came back out, she sat on the edge of the bed and hit Play. Her job required a good deal of detachment, but there was no way to remain detached from this. She winced with each blow, felt Rickman's pain, wanted to scream along with him, but knew she had to keep it together. By the end of the tape she was on the verge of throwing the laptop against the wall. Instead, she bit her fist and let loose a silent scream. Tears streaming down her cheeks, she closed the laptop and went back into the bathroom to collect herself. In a matter of minutes she would be watching this in a room with as many as eight of her people. She needed to keep it together. Emotions would only cloud her judgment. She was going to have to make some very difficult decisions, and her people needed to see that they were coming from a spy boss, not some blubbering mother.

CHAPTER 34

C AL Patterson was about to shit a brick. He'd busted his ass at Holy Cross, playing football and graduating with honors and an accounting degree. Three years later he had a law degree from the University of Virginia and a job with the FBI. He'd made all the right moves. Done everything his uncle had told him to do. His uncle had put in thirty-five years with the FBI and Patterson idolized him. During Patterson's first two years he worked seventy-hour weeks and volunteered for everything that was dangled in front of him and then some. His bosses loved him and he was rewarded with an assignment to the Counterintelligence Division. Even his uncle was impressed.

Now after just twenty-nine days in his new job, his entire career was hanging in the lurch. Patterson was all screwed up from the time change and couldn't sleep, so he rose early, put on his workout gear, and headed to the base's fitness center. Patterson was pleased to find out that the facility was nicer than anything the Bureau had. He was in the middle of a five-mile run on the treadmill when he saw the screen on his phone light up with the words *Private Number*. Patterson smacked the Pause button and yanked out his earbuds. Private Number usually meant Wilson or someone in their group.

"Hello," he said, a little out of breath.

"Special Agent Patterson."

"Speaking."

"This is Executive Assistant Director Hargrave. Would you like to tell me just where in the hell Agent Wilson is?"

"Ah . . . I assume he's sleeping, sir." Patterson knew exactly who Hargrave was, as he had just brought Wilson by his house before they left for Afghanistan.

"Any idea why he's not answering his phone?"

"Probably because he's sleeping, sir." Patterson regretted the answer immediately.

"Agent Patterson, who do you work for?"

"The FBI, sir."

"That's correct, and who does Special Agent Wilson work for?"

"The FBI, sir."

"That's correct. We don't turn our phones off . . . ever. Do you understand me, young man?"

"I do, sir."

"Do you like your job?"

"Ahhhh . . . yes, I do, sir. Very much, sir."

"Well, let me give you a little advice. If you want to keep working for the FBI, you are going to follow my instructions to the letter. Do you know where Agent Wilson is right now?"

"I think he's in his quarters, sir."

"And where are you?"

"I'm at the gym."

"Well, you are going to go wake his insubordinate ass up and you are going to call me back and put him on the phone. Have I made myself clear?"

Patterson stepped off the treadmill. "Crystal clear, sir."

"If I don't hear back from you in ten minutes, your career is over."

"Sir?"

"What?"

"I need your number."

"I'll text it to you. Call me back in ten minutes."

Patterson was about to respond but the line went dead. He noted the time on his watch and stuffed his phone and his earbuds in the zippered pockets of his running shorts. He grabbed his sweatshirt and started running. The trailer where Wilson was sleeping was only two minutes from where he was, but Patterson wasn't about to take any chances. It was getting light outside as he broke into a near sprint.

People were already out doing their morning PT, and Patterson got more than a few strange looks as he blew down the street as if he was running for his life, which he basically was. There was a moment of near panic when he couldn't locate the specific trailer. They all looked alike. On his second try he found the right place and as he burst through the door he found one of his fellow agents drinking coffee and staring at his iPad.

"Where's Wilson?"

The agent pointed with his coffee mug toward the back of the trailer. "Sleeping."

Patterson pulled out his phone and was relieved to see the text from Hargrave. He tapped the number as he moved down the hallway, passing the smaller bedrooms on his left and right. He was tempted to knock on the door, but when he heard Hargrave answer, he decided not to stop. He flung the door open and marched right to the bedside. Wilson looked up, dazed and confused by the light spilling in from the hallway.

"Here he is, sir." Patterson placed the phone in front of Wilson's face and said, "It's an emergency."

Wilson took the phone and said, "Hello?"

"I have been trying to call you for the past sixteen hours."

Shit, Wilson said to himself. Hargrave was the last person he wanted to talk to. "Ah . . . sorry, but I've been a little preoccupied."

Wilson rolled onto his side and looked at his watch. "What do you need?"

"I need you to follow through on your promises. Remember a few days ago when you woke me up in the middle of the night to get permission to go on this little excursion of yours? Do you remember what you promised me?"

"Not really," Wilson yawned. "You're going to have to cut me some slack. This time change has me a little off. You woke me up."

"Have you been asleep for sixteen hours? Because that's how long I've been trying to get hold of you."

"No, it's just that things have been kind of complicated since we landed. Listen, why don't I call you back in thirty minutes and give you a briefing."

"You'll do no such thing. Before you left, we agreed that you would call me every day and give me a progress report. You have not called me once. I received a call from Director Kennedy. She wanted to know why, in the midst of the extremely serious problems she's trying to deal with, you decide to show up and start questioning her people."

"Sir, there's a reason for that."

"Stop talking. I get the feeling every time I hear your voice you're lying to me. I need you to listen and listen carefully. Because you decided not to return my calls I was not able to return Director Kennedy's calls. She is so incensed by your poor timing and self-important behavior that she decided to go over my head and call our boss. The director of the FBI, remember him? As the old saying in this town goes, shit rolls downhill. I was attempting to enjoy a nice evening with my wife when the director called me and asked me if I'd lost my mind. I had a sneaky suspicion it involved you and your asinine behavior and the director confirmed those suspicions. Director Kennedy told him about some stunt you pulled at the base hospital . . . trying to bully your way onto the ICU so you could interrogate one of her people who had barely escaped an assassination attempt."

Wilson was standing now. "I did not try to bully my way—"

"Don't speak. I'm not done talking. Before you left I told you how I expected you to behave. I explained to the director the scope of your investigation. That you told me that you were going to be there to offer assistance in finding Rickman, and if along the way you saw that any laws had been broken you would consult me before moving the investigation in a new direction. You lied to me."

"I did not."

"You sure as hell did, and that's how the director sees it as well. What I can't figure out is how you thought you were going to get away with this. You already have a reputation as a duplicitous bastard. People are watching you. And your timing is awful, by the way. The CIA is in the middle of a shitstorm and you show up and start poking them with a stick. Do have any idea the respect that Irene Kennedy garners in this town?"

"I think a better word is *fear*."

"You're a fool, and I'm wasting my time trying to help you. The director wants you back here immediately, and just so you have something to think about on your long flight, it looks like he's going to order an official inquiry into just what in the hell you've been up to."

Wilson had already been through one of those and it had almost killed his career. He doubted he would survive a second one. "Sir, you're making a big mistake."

"The only mistake I made was letting you go in the first place."

"That's not true, sir. There are some things you don't know."

"By all means, please enlighten me, and keep in mind, I've learned my lesson with you. This call is being recorded, so don't think you can sell me another pile of lies and then feign ignorance later."

Wilson was thinking as fast as he could, trying to find a way to give Hargrave as little information as possible and still convince him that he should be allowed to not only stay in Afghanistan, but also increase the scope of the investigation. "I have reason to believe that Joe Rickman and Mitch Rapp have been stealing millions of dollars from the U.S. government."

Hargrave laughed at him. "Reason to believe . . . that's the best you can do, Joel?"

"Sir, you're going to have to trust me on this."

"I am going to have to do no such thing. You have burned your way through all the trust I have. You have precisely one minute to convince me that you deserve the latitude to go digging around one of our country's most secretive institutions."

Wilson saw no other choice. "I have the account numbers, the amounts, when the transfers were made, and a sworn affidavit from the banker who says Mitch Rapp came into his bank and set up the account."

"Where's the bank?"

"Zurich."

"And how long have you had this information?"

In truth Wilson had possessed the information for eighteen days, but telling Hargrave that in his present state of mind would do him no good. "About two weeks."

There was a long silence and then, "You've had this information for two weeks and you didn't bring it to me."

"I wanted to make sure it was real first."

"And just how did you come to possess this information?"

Wilson knew how this was going to sound, but he also knew that sooner rather than later he would have to present a chain of evidence. If there were any inconsistencies the former judge would eat him alive. "The information was provided by an anonymous source."

"Good God," Hargrave yelled. "How long have you worked in Counterintelligence? Do you have any idea how many times the Russians alone have tried to turn us against ourselves with this little trick?"

"I am well aware, sir. That's why I followed up and met with the banker."

"And you've fully vetted this banker? You know for a fact that he's not a foreign asset?"

"I'm in the process of doing that right now, sir."

"You don't think you should have done that first?"

"The abduction of Rickman forced me to move up my timetable."

"So you thought you should lie to me and then jet off to Afghanistan so you could ambush Rapp. Do you understand that he was almost killed? He's in ICU . . . he can barely remember his name."

"How convenient."

"Do you have any common sense? Do you understand that the CIA is our sister agency? That we are supposed to work together?"

"I thought we were supposed to keep them honest, Sam."

"When the evidence dictates . . . yes, but that doesn't mean running off half cocked because of an anonymous tip, and by the way, how did you receive this anonymous tip?"

"I received a package."

"Where . . . your house or the office?"

"What does it matter?"

"Answer my question."

"The office."

"Postmark?"

"Zurich."

"And let me guess . . . the lab didn't find any fingerprints, or DNA, or anything that could help us find this anonymous source."

"That doesn't prove anything."

There was a long sigh of frustration and then, "You're done. Pack up your team. You have precisely two hours and that jet is going to be in the air, and during those two hours you are not to speak to anyone from the CIA. Am I clear?"

"Oh, I'm reading you loud and clear." Wilson was sick of being kicked around by this old fool. "Are you still recording our conversation, because I want to make sure you get this part. I didn't tell you any of this because I can't trust you. Because the entire Counterintelligence Division knows that you're too close to Director Kennedy, and based on what I've experienced the last few days I'm inclined to believe those rumors. So you better get ready for your own board of inquiry." Wilson spun around and whipped Patterson's phone against the wall. "Fuck."

He collapsed on the edge of the bed, his head in his hands, trying to figure out how everything had gotten all twisted around. Hargrave was an idiot. The Clandestine Service was filled with crooks—Rickman, Rapp, and probably dozens of other officers. Senator Ferris had shown him the numbers; almost a billion dollars in cash had passed through the Clandestine Service and into the hands of all of those corrupt warlords, drug dealers, and politicians. The system was rife with corruption and Wilson had the evidence to prove it. There was only one reason why Hargrave would do this, and it was to protect Kennedy.

Wilson had no choice but to return to D.C., but he wasn't going to do it quietly. Senator Ferris was no slouch. They shared a belief that the CIA had been given too much power and not enough oversight after 9/11. That was going to change. Once the people found out that these crooks were stealing taxpayer dollars, Hargrave, Director Miller, and all the other assholes would get dragged up to Capitol Hill and have to explain how they interfered with his investigation, and then the Senate would clean house. After that, Wilson could write his own ticket and they could all kiss his ass.

CHAPTER 35

KENNEDY caught Rapp's doctor just as he was about to start his morning rounds. Major Nathan was a thirty-five-year-old neurosurgeon who spent two weeks of every month at Bagram and the other two at Sloan-Kettering in New York. He had a surprisingly affable bedside manner, for a brain surgeon. "Good morning, Major. Do you have a second to chat?"

"I was just heading to see Mr. Cox." The major smiled. "I don't suppose that's his real name?"

In a rare moment of honesty, Kennedy shook her head. "I was wondering if you could tell me how he's doing?"

"Much better. According to his recent scan, there's been a drastic reduction in swelling."

"Do you think he's ready to fly?"

Major Nathan winced and shook his head. "These head cases are tricky, they're all unique. Some patients bounce back after a few days, some people never bounce back."

"So he could fly if he had to?"

The major sighed. "If he absolutely has to, yes, but I'd like to give it a few more days."

Kennedy frowned.

"What's the problem?"

"I can't really talk about it, but let's just say Mr. Cox is extremely good at his job and we need him." Kennedy wanted him back, but she also wanted to put Rapp somewhere where Joel Wilson couldn't get his hands on him.

The major had immediately recognized Kennedy when one of the nurses had brought her into his office the day before. She explained politely that his newest patient was one of her top operatives. Nathan had already guessed that Mr. Cox was no mere analyst. It was standard procedure for the staff to cut the clothes off emergency patients, since they only got in the way. Mr. Cox had no open wounds, but Nathan counted three bullet holes and a scar that looked like it had come from a knife. Even the nurses commented. His battle scars, combined with his rock-hard physique, made the deduction simple. Nathan had rotated in and out of Bagram for nine straight months. He had pretty much seen it all. Or at least he thought he had. Mr. Cox was something of an anomaly.

Nathan understood that Kennedy held a unique position. If he could, he would try to help her. "Why don't we go see how he's doing, and then we can reassess."

They found Rapp sitting up in his bed with a tray of food in front of him, watching an episode of *Justified*. After some brief pleasantries the doctor looked at his chart and asked, "How do you feel this morning, Mr. Cox?"

"Better," Rapp said, moving his head around. "No headache, and I've got my appetite back."

The doctor scribbled a few notes on the chart. "That's good. How's your memory?"

"Pretty good." Rapp pointed at the TV. "I know that I've seen this episode before and I remember most of the characters . . . Dewey Crowe, Boyd Crowder, Raylan Givens, Art Mullen, and Dickie Bennett."

"Good show?" Nathan asked, without looking up.

"I think I'm the wrong guy to ask, Doc. I really don't have much to compare it to."

Nathan laughed. "And your recall in general?"

"Seems like it's getting a lot better."

"All right, where'd you go to college?"

"Syracuse."

Nathan rattled off the same questions he'd given Rapp late yesterday. Mother's maiden name, grade school, high school, childhood best friend, and on and on. Unlike yesterday, he got them all correct today. Nathan decided to expand the list. "First job out of college?"

Rapp gave Kennedy a strange look and then told Nathan he didn't know.

"Current job?"

"I think I'm an assassin." Rapp watched his doctor look up with wide eyes. "I'm just kidding, Doc. I work for the CIA and if I tell you any more than that, I'll have to . . ."

"Kill me," Nathan finished the sentence for him.

"Exactly."

Nathan glanced sideways at Kennedy. "Is he always this funny?"

Kennedy was relieved that he was coming back. She smiled and shook her head. "He's never had much of a sense of humor."

Before Rapp could comment, Nathan asked, "Favorite color?"

"Blue . . . I think."

"Wife . . . kids?"

The smile fell from Rapp's face and his entire bearing changed. He didn't answer for a long time and then he looked at Kennedy for help.

Kennedy had been dreading this. It was hard enough to live through it once. It couldn't be easy learning it for a second time. It was obvious from the pained expression on his face that he remembered something about the tragedy. "Your wife," Kennedy started, and then stopped.

Nathan picked up on the mood and nodded for Kennedy to continue. "All memories are important . . . the good ones and the bad ones."

"I remember," Rapp said, his voice almost disembodied. "Her name was Anna and she was pregnant."

Kennedy nodded slowly.

Caught up in the story, Nathan asked, "How did she die?"

"I don't think we want to talk about this right now."

Rapp looked up and said, "She was murdered."

"I'm sorry," Nathan answered softly.

There was a long silence and then Rapp began to frown as if something was occurring to him for the first time.

"What is it?" Nathan asked.

Kennedy thought she knew what it was and she stepped forward. "I think this is enough for now."

Rapp shook his head as if trying to free a jumbled thought. "There's a face. A man I know, but I can't remember his name. He has something to do with my wife, but I can't make it connect."

Kennedy chastised herself for not consulting with Dr. Lewis. Thomas Lewis was their in-house psychologist. He had worked very closely with Rapp over the years, and it was likely that he could offer insight about how they should handle this unique situation. Between Rickman, Hubbard, and Wilson showing up, she'd simply forgotten to call Lewis. Her fear that Rapp would kill Gould was not unfounded, and she wasn't even sure she would object to it, but Major Nathan had warned them that Rapp didn't need any undue stress until his condition was stabilized.

There was a knock on the doorframe and she turned to see Coleman with a welcome expression. The retired SEAL had blond hair, blue eyes, and dimples, which gave him a boyish look at times. This morning, however, his sharp jaw was set in a way that she had seen many times before. He had news that she was waiting for.

"Please excuse me for a second." Kennedy left the room and stepped into the hallway with Coleman. "Wilson?"

"Yep. We had both his phones dialed in but he wasn't using them. We found out which trailer he was staying in and bugged it while he was at dinner last night. I'm still trying to get my hands on his laptop, but no luck so far. About thirty minutes ago one of his agents wakes him up and hands him a phone. It was Hargrave on the line, and although it's a one-sided conversation, it's pretty obvious Wilson is getting his ass handed to him." Coleman held up his iPhone. "I've got it all right here for you. Would you like the highlights first?"

"Please."

"Wilson claims to have received an anonymous package at work that contained evidence that Rick and Mitch were siphoning off cash and putting it into personal accounts in Zurich."

Kennedy frowned. With Rickman it was a possibility, but not with Mitch. No way. The man had his own money. He didn't need to steal cash from Langley.

"It sounded like Hargrave pressed Wilson pretty hard. Wilson claims to have account numbers, dates of transfers, and a sworn affidavit from the banker, who says Mitch came into his bank and set up the account."

"Do we know who this banker is?"

"Not yet, but we'll keep digging. There's one more thing. Wilson's been recalled, and he didn't take it well. He told Hargrave that everyone knows he's too close to you and when he's done proving that Rick and Mitch were stealing funds, he's going to make sure Hargrave goes down."

Kennedy was thinking about Hargrave. Sam was a good man. Trying to manage an ego like Wilson was going to drive him to an early grave. "When is he leaving?"

"About two hours, from the way they're talking. He's really throwing Hargrave under the bus to his people. I mean the type of shit that could land his ass in some serious hot water."

"Maybe we'll send an anonymous package of our own."

"I was thinking the same thing."

"Any chance you can get your hands on his computer before he leaves?"

Coleman thought about it for a second. "I'll try, but it's unlikely. I'm not worried, though. Marcus can do this shit in his sleep."

Kennedy nodded. "Have Marcus start poking around their database. See what he can find out."

"Will do."

Both Kennedy and Coleman looked up to see Hayek coming down the hall. She was moving at a good clip, and as she drew to within a few steps she shook her head and said, "I screwed up."

CHAPTER 36

OPERATING in the field always presented a unique set of problems, but a good number of them were predictable. There was a mark that they were all aware of, or at least were supposed to be aware of—seventy-two hours into any crisis, the effectiveness of the team dropped off considerably. The Agency wasn't the only group that had studied the issue. Every branch of the military looked into the issue with a need to understand combat effectiveness. Battlefield commanders needed to know how long they could keep a unit in the fight without sleep, with food and water and *without* food and water. The FBI, CIA, and any other federal agencies that dealt with crisis or catastrophe all conducted their own studies and they all pretty much found the same thing—seventy-two hours was the limit. After that, your people became almost worthless. Cognitive skills were drastically reduced, hallucination set in, and the body began to shut down. As with everything, of course, there were a few exceptions.

Elite warriors, like the ones produced by Delta Force and the SEAL teams, could push beyond the seventy-two-hour mark in extreme circumstances, but not much further. They taught their men to grab an hour or two of sleep whenever they could—even during a prolonged firefight. If the manpower was available, it was crucial to rotate teams. Three teams were ideal, each one working an eight-hour shift, but Kennedy didn't have that luxury. As it was, the Go Team that had been assembled was barely sufficient to operate in two twelve-hour shifts, and that was to handle the Rickman crisis. That team was weakened when she pulled people off it to start looking for Hubbard. Then she had to deal with the aftermath of the police shooting and now with the release of Rickman's interrogation, more of her attention was put into damage control. It was no longer just about Joe Rickman.

Even though it felt like it, Kennedy knew from the start that it had always been about more than just Rickman. Rickman's brain possessed hundreds of names, and those names represented real people who were assets of the CIA. Some of them were Americans, deep-cover operatives who were operating in foreign countries without the aid of diplomatic cover. If these people were exposed, the likelihood was that they'd be killed. And then there were the agents—the men and women who worked for foreign governments. They came in every stripe from politicians to bureaucrats, to scientists, to financiers, to military personnel, to intelligence operatives and janitors and secretaries.

More than any satellite or listening device, these men and women were the eyes and ears of the CIA. They offered snippets of information that when pieced together aided Kennedy and her people in understanding the intent of their foes and sometimes, when needed, the ability to predict their next move. These assets were the lifeblood of the CIA. Without them, the Agency would cease to become an effective intelligence agency. If Rickman continued to crack, Kennedy would have no choice but to begin pulling out her network of spies. It would take at least a decade to rebuild the network, possibly longer.

Despite the urgency Kennedy knew what had to be done. Hayek looked tired. They all looked tired. They understood what was at stake, so they were all eager to prove the doctors wrong and push past the seventy-two-hour mark. Kennedy held up her palm and stopped Hayek's rambling apology. "When was the last time you slept?"

The question caught her off guard and she took an unfocused look at nothing and tried to recall the last time she'd closed her eyes for more than a few seconds. "I think I got an hour or two last night."

Kennedy looked at Coleman and asked the same question.

"As much as possible, I've stuck to a schedule. Ten on and two off."

Kennedy thought of Coleman's six-man team. "Starting when?"

"From the very beginning. I made sure everyone grabbed at least four hours on the flight over." He shrugged. "There wasn't much for us to do until we landed."

Leave it up to the retired SEAL to maintain discipline in the midst of chaos. He'd done this countless times. Kennedy was embarrassed that she hadn't maintained better discipline over the schedules.

"I'll be honest," Coleman said, "I could use some sleep. I've been up for thirty-plus hours straight. With everything that went down two days ago and losing Reavers, that put me down one man, and I didn't bother to reshuffle the schedule."

Kennedy placed a hand on his arm but looked at Hayek. "Don't be so hard on yourself. We were understaffed to start with and then the shootout with the police threw us all for a loop. We have another twenty-six people due to land in about three hours. Once they're in position, I don't want anyone working more than a sixteen-hour shift. Scott, keep an eye on Wilson until he's in the air and then stand down your whole team. Don't set any alarms, just sleep. We're going to need you at some point and you guys need to be fresh."

Kennedy considered her own schedule for a second. She'd been able to grab four hours of sleep overnight, and all things considered, she felt pretty good. She had a staff meeting in fifteen minutes, and then after that, the working group back at Langley was to give her a full report on the potential extent of the damage that could be caused by the Rickman affair. Then she had a meeting with Nadeem Ashan from the Pakistani Intelligence Service. She liked Ashan and hoped that he was here to offer some information and assistance, but knowing the ISI, his motives lay more in self-preservation.

"This police officer," Kennedy said to Hayek, "I'm not sure I understand his relevance."

Coleman answered for Hayek. "We ran into him at the safe house. He's one of Darren's reintegration projects. Abdul Siraj Zahir . . . a real piece of shit. Long story short, he barges into the safe house and starts making threats, Mitch pulls on him." Coleman looked quickly over both shoulders to make sure no one else could hear him and then added, "Mitch tells the guy he's going to blow his head off."

Kennedy shook her head ever so slightly and frowned.

"I know it doesn't sound good but when it happened it didn't seem so bad. At any rate there's some back and forth and then Mitch decides he'll let this guy live if he works for us and finds out what happened to Rick." Despite not wanting to, Coleman decided he needed to give her the full context. "Mitch gave the guy forty-eight hours to come through with some information or he was going to put a five-hundred-thousand-dollar bounty on the guy's head."

"And Mitch asked me to put a trace on his phone," Hayek quickly added. "Langley has been recording his calls and following his moves for the past two days. Only, I forgot about it until about fifteen minutes ago."

"And?" Kennedy asked.

"He's been trying to get hold of Mitch. He's left him five messages since last night."

"Saying?"

"Basically, 'Don't kill me. I have some information for you.' The guy sounds scared."

"Well, if the guy has information, call him."

Hayek shook her head. "I think Mitch needs to make the call. If I or anyone else calls, he's going to want to renegotiate."

"I agree."

"Does Mitch even remember the guy?"

"I don't know," Coleman said, "but I could probably talk him through it."

Kennedy thought about her other problems. "And Wilson?"

"I have two people on him."

"All right. Brief Mitch and make the call. If anything important comes out of it, call me."

Rapp didn't remember Zahir at first. But after Coleman described the man's shoe-polish-black beard and his snug gray-blue police uniform, he got the visual. The context of their meeting was a little more complicated. The previous night Coleman had explained to Rapp why they were in Afghanistan. Rapp had only a vague recollection of Rickman. When Coleman explained to Rapp how he had threatened the local police commander, Rapp's eyes got big. "I said that?"

Coleman laughed. "You sure did."

"Do I speak this way to people very often?"

"When they happen to be," Coleman said, "scumbags like Zahir, the answer is yes."

It seemed as if each hour Rapp was learning more about his past, and by association, himself. He had a basic overview of who he was but the details were always a little shocking. It was eerie coming to grips with the stark reality that he had murdered people. There were no oh-my-god-I'm-a-monster type moments. It was more or less, *that's who I am, I need to keep filling in this puzzle and when it's done I can sit back and judge my actions in their totality, or not.* That was the other abnormal thing about this process of getting to know himself again: The second time around you saw things that you might have missed on the first go-round.

"So I threatened to put a five-hundred-K bounty on this guy's head."

"Yes . . . and you threatened to stick a Tomahawk missile up his ass as well." Grinning, Coleman added, "I know it sounds harsh, but it couldn't happen to a nicer guy. He's a real piece of shit. I think you made that pretty clear to him as well."

"So I call him back and find out what he has."

"Yes, but you're probably going to have to be a bit of a prick. Do you think you're up to it?"

"I don't see why not."

"All right. We have him marked in Jalalabad." Coleman looked over Hayek's shoulder at the blinking red light. "Hmm . . ."

"What?" Rapp asked.

"It looks like he's just a block away from the safe house." He tapped Hayek on the shoulder. "Everything ready to go?"

"In a second." All of Rapp's clothes had been cut off him when he arrived at the hospital, and his personal possessions, such as his phones and fake IDs and credit cards, had been placed in a bag and kept in a storage room. It was just another thing that was overlooked in the chaos. Hayek was now syncing Rapp's phone via Bluetooth to her laptop, so they could record and monitor the call. When it was ready to go, she plugged in two sets of headphones, handing one to Coleman and keeping the other for herself.

"The number's already punched in," she said as she handed Rapp the phone, "just hit Send."

"You said we have people back at Langley monitoring all of his calls."

"That's right."

"And if they record me threatening to kill him on the phone?"

Coleman jumped in. "We're not the FBI. We're supposed to threaten people like Zahir. When we're done, we'll make sure all the recordings are erased."

"Fine." Rapp hit Send and tried to put himself in the proper mind-set.

CHAPTER 37

JALALABAD, AFGHANISTAN

ZAHIR had no formal police training, but he was no fool. He stroked his thick black beard and looked at the bodies. The big man he thought he recognized. He was hard-core Taliban. Unlike Zahir, who was whatever he needed to be to survive, this man had stayed faithful when the Americans swept in and mopped up the Taliban. That was the first time Zahir had done business with Rickman. He had shown up in his village on horseback with a dozen bearded fighters and two American warplanes circling overhead like predators. By then the news had spread. The Taliban had collapsed in the face of the American onslaught. For Zahir, an expert at predicting which way the wind would blow, the decision was easy.

As Rickman laid it out, Zahir could either take twenty-five thousand dollars in cash and contribute some fighters to the cause, or the Navy F-18 Hornets circling above would lay his village to waste. Zahir wasn't even offended. It was the easiest decision he had ever made. It was made all the more easier knowing that he would likely change sides many times as this war raged on. The Taliban had run to their haven on the other side of the Pakistani border, but they would be back.

Zahir liked Rickman and respected him. Rickman never took it personally when Zahir's loyalty wavered. He simply looked at it as a challenge to bring Zahir back to his side. That fool Hubbard, however, was another story. He lacked Rickman's cunning. He had been so easy to push around. Not like the crazy American from two days ago. Zahir had tried to find out who he was, but his resources were limited and he had a feeling that, like so many of these damn CIA men, he had been using a fake name.

For the first time in four years Sickles had refused to take his calls, which was not a good sign. Then Hubbard disappeared, which seemed strange since he was last seen at the air base and there was no record of him leaving the base. And then there was the big gunfight in Kabul. Twenty-one police officers killed in broad daylight by a group of American contractors. It had filled the airwaves for two straight days. He knew that most of it was inaccurate, as Zahir had been briefed that General Qayem and his men ambushed the Americans. The general had fled and the Afghan National Police were reeling from the treachery. It was one thing to siphon off funds for your own personal use, but to use your men to try and kill Americans was madness. Add to it that twenty-one of his own men had been killed and Zahir was willing to bet that the reckless General Qayem would be moved to the top of the Americans' most-wanted list.

It was total chaos. Why would Qayem do such a thing? Zahir could only hazard a few guesses, but it was likely a mix of large amounts of money and promises of more power when the Americans left. That was the new game—everyone was gambling on when the Americans would pull out and the Taliban would come rushing back in. Zahir wasn't so sure it was that black and white. The Taliban even at their peak couldn't control the entire country. Various local factions, including warlords and drug dealers, had consolidated power and armed themselves with the tools of war.

Zahir was a perfect example. Plans were in place to move all of his men and the American-supplied equipment back to their villages.

Ammunition and spare parts had been disappearing since the day he put on his uniform. And this time would be easier with the fleet of well-maintained trucks under his command. Zahir had never doubted that the Taliban would be back. They were like weeds, as much a part of the landscape as the rocks and the trees, but Zahir understood their power would be limited this time. The secret to Afghanistan was that anyone could wreak havoc but none could govern. The Taliban had learned that mistake just as countless others had, dating all the way back to Alexander the Great. Even with all of the brutality they employed against the people, they were struggling to maintain their hold on Kabul and other large cities where the people didn't feel like living under absolute Sharia law. Most Afghans were willing to live under a more relaxed form of the Muslim law, but when men from the mountains start beating your wife or daughters because they don't like the color of their hijab, resentment and hatred mounts quickly.

There was one very simple reason Zahir would never throw his complete support behind the Taliban: They had no airpower. It was Zahir's greatest fear. The Americans had killed countless men with their unmanned drones and their high-tech jets. What most people didn't understand was that the Americans would never truly leave. Those drones would always be overhead, listening and watching, and that was why Zahir wanted so badly to give the crazy American some information that would satisfy him. The future of Afghanistan was uncertain, as it always had been. Alliances would continue to shift, but on this particular day Zahir was sure of just one thing—he had stumbled upon something that would likely save his life. Now he just needed the American to call him back.

When his phone finally rang he was back on the street, smoking and relieved he was breathing fresh air. The house behind him was a mess. The basement so foul, he could not last more than a minute breathing the putrid smells. The small screen on his phone told him the number was blocked. He was both hopeful and nervous.

"This is Commander Zahir."

"You better have something for me."

Zahir thought he heard the menacing drone of a propeller overhead. Craning his neck skyward, he searched for the telltale speck of gray. A layer of high clouds made it impossible. He couldn't fight the ominous feeling that the American had him literally in the crosshairs. "I do," Zahir started. "Have you seen the tape of Mr. Rick? The one that is all over the Internet?"

There was a pause and then, "Yes."

"I have found something that you need to see."

"What is it?"

"I am pretty sure it is the house where Mr. Rick was being tortured."

"Why do you think that?"

Zahir turned and looked at the two-story stone house. He had one of his people looking into the utility and ownership records. "There is a room in the basement. Two of the walls are covered with sheets just like in the video."

"What else?"

"A rope attached to the ceiling, just like in the video, and there is lots of blood on the floor."

"Anything else?"

"Yes, two bodies." Zahir's pulse quickened. This, he hoped, was what would save his life. "I am certain they are the two men seen in the video who are beating Mr. Rick." There was another awkward silence. Zahir could barely make out other people talking.

"The men are wearing masks in the video. How can you be certain?"

"They are still wearing their masks. On their heads, not covering their faces."

"And they're dead?"

"Yes . . . shot many times."

"All right, Commander, you've made a big step in getting your ass out of trouble, but you're not all the way there. I need you to text me photos of the bodies and room. Do you think you can do that?"

"Yes."

"Now I'm looking at a screen that tells me you're close to Mr. Rick's safe house, is that right?"

"Yes. Very close."

"Do you have the house secure?"

"Yes. We have touched nothing."

"Good." After a long pause, the American said, "Send me those photos and then I will call you back in five minutes with instructions."

"Yes, but I can promise you it is them."

"And I can promise you, if you're lying to me or this is some kind of trap, you're as good as dead."

"I would never do such a thing."

"Really," the American said in a disbelieving voice. "You know General Qayem?"

Zahir cringed. This was the last man he wanted to be compared with. "Yes."

"You heard what happened in Kabul the other day with your fellow police officers?"

"Yes. We are all deeply ashamed."

"Spare me the bullshit, Commander. I was there. They tried to ambush us. We lost one man before we even knew we were in a fight. After that it was just four of us against all of those cops. It didn't turn out so well for them. Do you know what I mean?"

"I think I understand," Zahir said, turning away from one of his officers who was trying to get his attention.

"I'm not so sure you do. The point is, thanks to General Qayem we're a little itchy with our trigger fingers right now, and when we come to see you we'll be traveling with a lot more than four people."

"Mr. Harry," Zahir said with a sigh, "I am many things, but I am not stupid. I know you will hunt down General Qayem like a dog, and he will pay for his treachery. I do not want you as my enemy. I do not want the U.S. as my enemy."

"You're saying all the right things, Abdul, which makes me nervous. Don't fuck with me."

"I will not fuck with you, Mr. Harry."

"Send me the photos, and I'll be in contact."

The line went dead and Zahir stared down at his phone cursing the modern technology that enabled the Americans to track him. They'd known where he was. He looked skyward again in search of one of their drones. He thought he could hear a faint hum but he couldn't be sure. That was another effect of the Americans' air campaign. The psychological stress could be overwhelming. The fear that there was a drone circling above, out of sight, tracking your every move, was incredibly disruptive. Add to that the awareness that there was some man in a trailer thousands of miles away following you with targeting crosshairs, just waiting for the green light to press a button and end your life. Zahir had seen it drive men mad, and as he continued to search the sky for the Predator he understood how easily it could happen.

CHAPTER 38

BAGRAM AIR BASE, AFGHANISTAN

HEADACHES were rare for Kennedy. She'd already had two cups of coffee and popped two Excedrin but it didn't matter, the nagging buzz in her left temple persisted. Trying to diagnose why it had come on wouldn't do her any good, but it wasn't Ashan's fault. Nadeem was a pleasant man who had been a fair partner in the War on Terror. The same, unfortunately, couldn't be said of most of his colleagues at Pakistani Inter-Services Intelligence. Maybe that was the reason for this rare headache. Ashan had picked up on it immediately. Kennedy had a reputation as unflappable. In times of calm or crisis she always maintained her composure.

The steady demeanor she was known for made her pained expression all the more obvious.

"Are you sure you are okay?" Ashan asked.

Kennedy removed her hand from her forehead and, although she was wincing in pain, said, "I'll be fine." She looked around the table and was not comforted by the concerned expressions on both Nash's and Schneeman's faces. The two deputies whom Ashan had brought along seemed unfazed.

Nash leaned over and quietly offered, "Take a break. I'll handle it until you get back."

It was a nice offer, but one that Kennedy wasn't about to take. "See if you can find me a couple of Excedrin or Extra-Strength Tylenol. And a bottle of water, please." She watched Nash leave and forced herself to put on a smile. She thought Ashan might understand the monumental pressure. The Rickman problem was getting bigger every hour. After the posting of the video, she had been called by the head of every allied intelligence agency. They all wanted to know their level of exposure. It was common to share assets, especially with the British, and although the agreement might be for only one person at the Agency to know the identity of their spy, say in Budapest, it was not irrational to wonder if that person had told other colleagues at the CIA. Kennedy assured all of them that Rickman had not been read in on any of their assets. While technically correct, the statement in a more broad sense was false. God only knew what Rickman had picked up over the years.

The man's memory was well known. He forgot nothing, which was a great advantage until he ended up in the hands of the enemy. It was very possible that Rickman knew the code names and directorates where many of these spies worked. He also knew what information had been passed along. A skilled interrogation team could take that information and over a month or so reconstruct the damage that had been done and come up with a small list of potential traitors.

Beyond the intelligence heads, Stofer had called to report that their case officers were getting deluged with extraction requests from their assets, men and women from all over Europe, the Middle East, and Southeast Asia, who had seen the coverage of the CIA clandestine officer breaking under the harsh interrogation. They were part of the game in the most real way. The Pakistani foreign minister's residence was now surrounded by the Pakistani Army and it was reported that he was under house arrest. It was easy enough for these assets to imagine themselves in a similar situation, but for nearly all of them it would be much worse. They would be dragged from their houses, or more likely apartments, and thrown into a dark cell where they would be brutalized by men with gorilla-like forearms who reeked of cigarettes. It might sound a bit melodramatic, but for these lonely souls, who were on their own, the fear was well founded.

"Director Kennedy," Ashan said, "on behalf of the ISI, I would like to say how sorry we are about Mr. Rickman, and if there is anything we can do to help, please ask."

"Thank you, Nadeem. I've told you before, please call me Irene."

"Of course. My apologies. I would like to assure you that we are using all of our contacts to find out who was responsible for this."

"And how is that going?" Schneeman asked, his skepticism obvious.

Ashan had been hoping to have some piece of information to show that they were trying to cooperate. He was secretly hoping that they could lay this at the feet of the Taliban, but so far there was nothing. He did not blame the Americans. There was no denying the ISI's involvement in the Mumbai massacre. The Americans had the recordings of the terrorists calling their ISI handler in Karachi, in the midst of the attack. Ashan reflected on that extremely uncomfortable meeting. His colleagues had spent the better part of an hour denying any involvement, and then Director Kennedy put the ISI agent's photo up on a big screen while she played the audio of the phone call.

The meeting was held at the CIA headquarters in Langley, Virginia. Durrani was there as well, and had the gall to act enraged over the accusation. Kennedy let him bluster and cry foul play, and when he was done with his performance she put more images up on the screen that showed the bank transfers to fund the operation as well as preliminary plans for the operation, which included a list of primary and secondary targets. The last photo was the most dramatic. It showed the ISI agent lying in a pool of his own blood, with a single bullet hole in his head.

Kennedy calmly turned to Durrani and said, "General, I'd appreciate it if rather than lie in the face of overwhelming evidence you simply kept your mouth shut, because the more you protest, the more I'm inclined to think you were directly involved in this."

Their relationship with the CIA had been one of fits and starts. Ashan would get things moving on mutual cooperation and then Durrani and others would undermine the hard work of the Foreign Relations Wing. Over the years they had sat through innumerable meetings with their counterparts at Langley and had gotten to know them fairly well. Each side understood the other's rosters of personnel—the power structure of the other, who ran which division or department, and who outranked whom. There were others who did not attend these meetings but were known to the ISI by reputation or through surveillance. Mitch Rapp was one of those individuals.

Rapp attended the meeting after the Mumbai massacre, and although there were no formal introductions they all knew who he was. The fact that he sat immediately to Kennedy's right was, in Ashan's mind, a clear message. He spoke only once during the meeting. It was after Kennedy's admonishment of Durrani and the general's desperate gambit to deflect. Rather than heed Kennedy's advice, Durrani continued to protest his department's innocence and went so far as to say he was offended that Kennedy would dare make such accusations.

That was when they heard Rapp speak for the first and last time. "General, I don't attend these meetings because I can't deal with the bullshit. I'm not equipped to sit and listen to someone lie to my face. Especially someone who's supposed to be an ally. We're all professionals, and we all know what's at stake. To a certain degree we will keep things from each other, but as allies there are some lines that we should never cross. That man up on the screen," Rapp pointed at the photo of the dead Pakistani agent, Mawaan Rana. "We know he worked for your department and we know he helped fund and train the Islamic nut jobs that killed 164 people." At that point Durrani tried to speak, but Rapp stopped him. "General, I'm not asking for you to confirm or deny what I just said. I don't need you to, because I know it to be a fact. Not only do we have phone records and financial transactions, but your man Rana confessed to me that he worked for the External Wing and that he was following official orders."

Durrani scoffed at the accusation. "When did you speak to him?"

Rapp stared down the general and said, "Right before I put that bullet in his head."

Rapp's words were chilling. He didn't speak for the rest of the meeting but he kept his predatory gaze locked on Durrani as he was going over in his mind a list of possible ways to kill the man. Ashan had never seen his friend so upset. Upon returning to Pakistan they pieced enough information together to confirm that Rapp's claim was not false bravado. The message from the Americans was clear: if you continue to support terrorists in the mass killing of innocent civilians you, too, might end up with a bullet in your head.

Ashan half expected Rapp to be here this morning and was secretly relieved that the assassin was elsewhere. "Irene, I can assure you that we are using all of our resources to find out who was behind this brazen attack."

"I appreciate that, Nadeem. You know, of course, that the Taliban is at the top of our list." She didn't bother to share Rapp's insight that the abduction was too precise to have been pulled off by the Taliban.

"As you know, I have had no dealings with them, but I have been promised that the right people are looking into the matter."

The headache was starting a slow retreat, which came as a great relief. Kennedy considered Ashan's remarks and then said, "Nadeem, you have been a fair partner, but there are others in the ISI who, despite our alliance, continue to work against us. This has never been acceptable, but with the abduction of Joe Rickman we have now moved into a dangerous new arena. If at any point I discover that the ISI had any hand in this, or that you are protecting the Taliban, I will be forced to react in a very serious way."

Ashan digested her words and wondered if this was just another threat to cut off the billions of dollars in aid the Americans provided every year. "What type of reprisals are we talking about?"

"An eye for an eye, Nadeem. Joe Rickman was an extremely valuable asset. Someone has launched a well-coordinated attack aimed at crippling my Clandestine Service. When I find out who was behind it, I will make them pay dearly. It might not happen immediately, but eventually, people will disappear. They will pay for this little gambit with their lives, and I will make it my goal in life to penetrate that organization and steal everything that is valuable to them, and then when I'm done, I will leave behind so much disinformation that it will sow seeds of dissent for decades to come. This organization will cease to be effective. It will be an organization afraid of its own shadows, and don't doubt me for a second, Nadeem. I have the budget, the fortitude, and the talent to make this happen. So you can tell your cohorts like General Durrani that this is their last chance. I want Joe Rickman back, and I want him back in the next twenty-four hours or this is going to get extremely uncomfortable for everyone."

CHAPTER 39

JALALABAD, AFGHANISTAN

THEY weren't going to take any undue chances this time with any green-on-blue attacks. That was the term that the military used to describe Afghan military or police who murdered coalition personnel. As the drawdown and eventual pullout neared, the problem was getting worse, and they all agreed that the best way to avoid it was to move on the house with overwhelming force. The Predator drone that had been tracking the movements of Commander Zahir was used to provide real-time imagery of the location, and more important, they were able to go back and see how Zahir and his people deployed to the house nearly two hours ago. As far as the Joint Special Operation Command planners could tell, there were no surprises waiting for them.

The intel supplied by the drone made it possible for the planners to expedite the mission. They coordinated with the Quick Reaction Force from the base in Jalalabad. A platoon from the Seventy-fifth Ranger Regiment, First Battalion, mounted up in eight MRAPs and rolled out the main gate as the first two assets from Bagram lifted into the air. Two of the big mine-resistant vehicles were outfitted with Mk 19 automatic grenade launchers, two more vehicles had .50 caliber guns on the turret, and the remaining four all had remote-controlled 7.62mm miniguns.

It helped that the folks at JSOC had been running operations on a daily basis for more than a decade, many of them rapid deployments. There was a certain rhythm. The shooters and aircrews slept during the midmorning and into the afternoon while the ground crews made sure the birds were prepped for the evening's missions. And there was always another mission in the works. The planners in the Joint Fusion Center tasked and retasked ops, shuffling the deck based on the input of the DOD and agencies like the CIA. Rickman was the top priority in-country, so other ops got kicked and the shooters and aircrews were roused early from their slumbers.

The two Apache attack helicopters arrived on station over the target house, providing more live tactical imaging. Five thousand feet above the Apaches, the command and control bird moved into position, now receiving live imaging from both the Apaches. In the back of the specially equipped Black Hawk, three men from JSOC monitored a bank of consoles. After the blocking force rolled into position at each end of the long street, the green light was given to the assault force.

Two Black Hawks came in fast, nose on tail, and flared up fifty feet above the street. They had considered landing, but the air boss decided that it was a little too tight, so the big black ropes were kicked out, two on each side of each chopper. The men began to slither down the ropes, ten from each chopper, moving off with haste to their prearranged positions. It took less than thirty seconds, and then the aircrews pulled the pins and dropped the thick ropes to the ground. If all went well, they would be collected later. As the first two Black Hawks climbed into the late-morning air, a third Black Hawk began circling counterclockwise overhead at fifteen hundred feet off the ground. Two Delta Force snipers were strapped in, hanging out the portside door, providing overwatch for the operation. Each man carried an M110 7.62x51mm sniper rifle with a twenty-round magazine. In truth, the Apaches were mainly a show of force. In a neighborhood like this, the Apaches' M230 chain gun, 70mm rockets, and Hellfire missiles would likely bring about an unacceptable level of collateral damage. If anything popped up, the snipers flying overwatch would be called on first to deal with the threat.

Two Little Birds were the last part of the air element. They landed without hazard on the street in front of the house. A German shepherd and his handler jumped out of the first bird along with two bomb techs lugging their gear. Out of the second Little Bird came Coleman, Hayek, and Rapp. Rapp and Coleman were suited up in full combat gear, having learned a very hard lesson only a few days earlier. While Coleman wore a boonie hat, Rapp's head was covered with an integrated ballistic helmet at the insistence of Dr. Nathan.

They hadn't bothered to inform Kennedy, as she was tied up in a high-level meeting. Rapp didn't want to raise anyone's hopes until they were sure Zahir wasn't jerking their chains. A quick comparison of the photos Zahir had sent compared to the video posted on the Internet looked legitimate. The trick had been getting Major Nathan to agree to Rapp's release. The major ran Rapp through a series of tests, most of them involving balance. To the doctor's surprise, his patient fared very well on the tests. Nathan still thought it was too early for Rapp to be up and moving around, let alone flying off on a mission that might involve more concussive blasts. The doctor never really agreed to release Rapp, but he was forced to reluctantly admit that he had no authority to keep Rapp against his will. He did add, however, that if Rapp left and came back wounded he would do his best to make sure he ignored his medical needs.

The metal gate was open and Zahir was waiting for them in the driveway. Rapp and Coleman paid him no attention and instead approached the commander for the assault team. "Chief," Coleman said, "what's the status?"

"Perimeter is secure and the handler just sent in his dog." The senior chief looked at the local cops. "They look pretty nervous."

"Yeah, well, if twenty-one of our boys had just been greased two days ago we'd be pretty nervous, too."

"Good point."

"The dog have a camera?"

"Yep . . . handler's looking at that, as well as the brains back at JSOC. When the big brains give us the go-ahead the bomb guys are going to send in their robot."

Rapp asked, "How long is that going to take?"

"Twenty to thirty minutes."

Rapp frowned. "I don't want to wait that long." He looked over at Zahir. "I've got a better idea."

After the dog came back out they asked the handler if he had seen anything unusual. Other than the two dead bodies in the basement, everything looked pretty normal. While the bomb techs unpacked their equipment, Rapp told Hayek to stay put and approached Zahir with Coleman. "Commander, you and your men didn't happen to find any booby traps while you were in there?"

Zahir was very unhappy that the Americans were playing this game with him. He shook his head and refused to speak.

"Good," Rapp said, "so you're willing to go back in with us and show us what you've found."

Zahir nodded, waved for them to follow, and then marched past his men and into the house.

"You sure about this?" Coleman asked.

Rapp figured he could spend the rest of his life worrying that there was a bomb around every corner or he could get back on this horse. "You read the report on Zahir. Suicide isn't his deal. Too narcissistic. If he's willing to walk in there, we're safe."

"I hope you're right." Coleman looked over his shoulder, "Chief, we're going in. When JSOC starts freaking out, tell them Mr. Cox made the call." Having served in the military, Coleman didn't want the guy getting reamed for something that wasn't his fault. As he started walking, he called back, "You can still send in the robot if you want."

Zahir led them through the first floor.

"Anything worth seeing up here?" Rapp asked as they reached the stairwell.

"I'm sure you're going to want to take this house apart piece by piece, but I didn't see much." Pointing down the staircase, Zahir said, "The important stuff is down there."

Rapp had Zahir go first and followed him down the steps with his M-4 rifle pointed at Zahir's back. Halfway down the stairs the stench hit them. Zahir pulled out a handkerchief and covered his mouth. At the bottom of the stairs was a table with a computer monitor, keyboard, and mouse. Zahir led them through the open door and the stench became almost unbearable. Rapp and Coleman were both covering their noses with gloved hands as they looked around the rectangular room.

The first thing Rapp noticed were the two bodies on the floor. They looked like the men in the video. The sheets were covering the walls, and attached to one of the floor joists was a metal hook with a length of knotted rope.

"This one here," Zahir pointed at the larger of the two men, "is Shahrukh Ahmad Wazir. He's Taliban."

"You're sure?" Rapp asked.

"Yes."

"And the other one?"

"I have no idea, but we will find out. Very likely he is Taliban as well."

"God, it stinks down here," Rapp said. "What is that smell? These guys don't look like they've been dead long enough to smell like this."

Zahir pointed at a puddle between the two bodies and a little closer to where they were standing. It was a rusty brown mixture. "That is blood and I think feces and I'm sure urine as well." Zahir had seen many men shit themselves when interrogated, but he didn't think now was a good time to offer this knowledge.

"What was the big one's name, again?" Coleman asked. He had

his phone out and was about to send the name back to the Intel Fusion Center. Zahir spelled it for him and Coleman sent the message. If Zahir knew who he was, it was likely the name would pop up in one of their databases.

Rapp stepped around the putrid liquid to get a better look at the two men. They both had bruised knuckles and their hands were swollen. Just beyond the bodies were two rubber hoses, more evidence that this was the place where Rickman had been interrogated. He counted no fewer than four bullet holes in each man. The image of the dead bodyguards lined up in the safe house came back to him. This murder scene couldn't have been more different. "Look at this," Rapp said to Coleman. "Remember Rick's four guys, each one with a single bullet hole."

"Yeah," Coleman said, "this was done by someone who was pissed off." He turned around and looked at the other two walls. As far as he could tell they didn't have any pockmarks from bullets. This wasn't a gunfight, it was an execution.

Rapp noticed the video camera and tripod knocked over on the floor. They needed Hayek down here. Rapp reached up and grabbed the lip mike from the side of his helmet. He swung it down and hit the two-way button on his Motorola radio. "Sid, this is Harry, over."

"I'm here."

"Did you bring any masks? It smells pretty bad down here."

"Yeah, I have some."

"Good, grab your gear and come on in. I'll meet you on the first floor."

"Harry," the voice crackled over the radio, "our boss is out of that meeting and she's not very happy with you."

Rapp's memory was still a little spotty but he got the feeling that this wasn't the first time she'd been mad at him. "Tell her I'm ninety-nine percent sure we found the place where Rick was interrogated. That should calm her down a bit. I'll meet you by the front door." Rapp flipped the lip mike back up and started for the stairs.

"This is pretty fucking ballsy," Coleman said.

"What's that?"

"We're a block and a half from the safe house. We're looking all over the planet for him and he was here, just a couple hundred yards away. I hate to admit it, but it's a pretty fucking smart move. Who would have ever thought of looking this close?"

Coleman's words triggered something familiar in Rapp's mind. His brain was still having some issues, like it knew what it was searching for but it was stuck in that pinwheel mode that a computer went into when it couldn't get out of program.

Coleman could see he'd triggered something. "What are you thinking about?"

"I don't know. I think something you said is important, but the old noggin still isn't working quite right."

"It'll come."

Rapp stepped into the other room and Zahir followed him. "Mr. Harry, are you satisfied?"

Rapp stopped on the first step and looked back at the corrupt police officer. He sighed and reluctantly said, "Yes, Abdul, you've done a good job." Rapp climbed two more steps and then thought of something. "Abdul, how did you discover these bodies?"

Zahir wanted to tell him that it was through his contacts, but he was afraid the American would discover the truth. The man was no longer mad at him, so he said, "We received an anonymous call at the police station."

"Anonymous?"

"Yes."

That sounded funny to Rapp. They were offering thousands of dollars in cash to anyone who could help them find Rickman. You would think someone would want to collect that money. Rapp shook his head and started up the stairs again with Ashan in tow.

"Mr. Harry, I would just like to say that I am sorry we started off on the wrong foot."

"Me too, Abdul, but maybe we can start over." Rapp stopped in the front entryway, sidestepping the robot.

"I would like that."

Rapp thought of something else. "Good. Now you need to find Mr. Hubbard. Alive preferably."

Zahir hemmed and hawed and then asked, "Is there a reward?"

Rapp should have expected it. Guys like Zahir never changed. "Fifty grand . . . maybe more, depending on how hard you have to work."

Zahir smiled. This was a huge relief. He much preferred doing business this way. His joy was short-lived, however.

Rapp pointed the muzzle of his rifle at Zahir's chest and said, "But if I find out you're fucking me, or that you had a hand in any of this, you're dead."

CHAPTER 40

HAYEK had donned her white paper suit, hood, and booties. She wore her mask and kicked everyone out of the house, including the bomb techs. For more than an hour she thoroughly photographed everything, and in the room where the torture had taken place she took two samples of every fluid she could potentially identify. When she'd been with the FBI, they would have had no fewer than six agents combing over a crime scene like this. She was well aware that she was likely missing a bevy of potential evidence, but her focus here was very different from that of an agent collecting evidence that would be challenged in a courtroom. Her immediate goal was pretty straightforward—she needed to be able to tell Kennedy with near certainty if Joe Rickman had in fact been in this room.

Even as Hayek carefully collected her evidence she knew what she would recommend to Kennedy. She needed to bring in a forensic team from the Joint Expeditionary Forensic Laboratory at Bagram or have the FBI send one of their teams over. Kennedy wouldn't like the idea of bringing in someone from outside the Agency, but the truth was the CIA didn't have the capability to do this job at the level it needed to be done. Hayek's preference was the FBI, but she recognized that she was biased from having worked with them.

When she was finished collecting all of her samples, she was left with one small dilemma. On the floor, across the room from the two dead men, was a digital camera with a tripod screwed into the bottom. It appeared the camera had been knocked over, as only a small wire tethered the viewfinder. Several pieces of the camera's black plastic casing were also cracked and broken. If the FBI were going to get involved they would want her to leave the camera where it was so they could follow their own strict protocols for evidence collection. Hayek was no electronics expert, but she knew that some cameras came equipped with internal memory drives as well as slots for removable memory cards. Using her gloved hands she cradled the camera as if it were a bird with a broken wing. She carefully turned it over in her hands and saw that the slot for the memory card was empty. She was about to leave the camera when she decided that would be foolish.

Hayek chastised herself. There were times where she still thought too much like a law enforcement officer and not enough like a member of the Clandestine Service. The priority was to get Kennedy as much information as possible as quickly as possible. She could always hand the camera over to the FBI later, along with the photographs that would show where she'd found the camera. She carefully unscrewed the tripod from the bottom and placed the camera in a clear evidence bag.

When she stepped into the afternoon sun, she saw that everyone was in a far more relaxed posture.

Rapp was standing just inside the gate with Coleman, who looked like he was about to fall asleep. Rapp asked, "How did it go?"

Hayek pulled the paper hood off her head and the mask from her face. "I've got what we need to get a start, but we need to get someone in there to go over the entire house."

"Like who?" Rapp asked.

"Probably one of the FBI's forensic teams."

"I'm not sure I like that idea."

"I didn't think you would, but they're the best."

"Irene's going to have to make that call."

"I agree. In the meantime we need this place secured. I don't want anyone going in or out, including the local police."

Rapp looked to Coleman. "Any ideas?"

"Well," he said, rubbing his tired eyes, "having the JSOC boys guard an empty house is like asking a thoroughbred horse to plow a field. Besides, I'm sure they have ops they have to run tonight." Coleman was about to say he could call Hubbard and get some grunts from the air base to come over and secure the place, but then he remembered Hubbard was missing. "I'll make some calls. In the meantime, I'll see if we can get the Rangers to keep an eye on things."

Coleman got patched in to the ops boss back at Bagram and explained the situation. A solution was reached in less than sixty seconds. That was one of the nice things about JSOC. There was so much practical experience involving missions that on the surface were very similar, but in the details were unique. The two Black Hawks that had delivered the assault team were standing by on the tarmac only a few miles away at the Jalalabad Air Base. JSOC had already arranged for three MRAPs to transport the assault team and their gear back to the airfield for linkup with their Black Hawks and transport back to Bagram. The interim solution was to have the Rangers close up their position on the house and run security until another force could be found to relieve them. Coleman also arranged to have their Little Bird come back in and pick them up for the return to Bagram. Five minutes after they were airborne, Coleman was asleep and Rapp was wide awake, trying to understand what was gnawing at the edges of his memory.

At this juncture Kennedy was less concerned about maintaining absolute secrecy and more interested in getting results, so Hayek requested access to the Joint Expeditionary Forensic Facility at Bagram. Kennedy explained her situation to the base commander, a two-star from Idaho, who had been an extremely gracious host. One quick phone call from the CO and Hayek had complete access to the lab and any help that the staff could offer.

Hayek was impressed with the facility, which was run by the U.S. Army Criminal Investigative Command. As with all things to do with the Army, they had turned the name into an acronym. Rather than call it the Joint Expeditionary Forensic Facility they called it JEFF. Hayek laid her evidence bags out on a stainless-steel table and double-checked that she had a backup for each sample. She then took the extra bags, placed them in a larger evidence bag, and sealed them. If anything went wrong in the lab, she could rely on these samples and test them on familiar equipment back in the States. She had taken fingerprints and DNA samples from the two dead men. She turned those samples over to the lab's latent-print examiners and DNA analysts and told them which databases to check them against. The two women smiled and reassured her that they had done this more times than either of them could count.

The officer in charge of the lab was a Major Archer. Hayek showed him the clear evidence bag with the damaged camera. "Do you have anyone on staff who could check and see if there are any useful images on this?"

The major wasn't wearing gloves, so he made no attempt to touch the bag. "Yes, ma'am. We have an information technology analyst. This is just his kind of thing. I'll be back in a second."

When the major reappeared, he had a small black man with him who was wearing bulky black U.S. Army–issue eyeglasses. "Agent Hayek, this is Corporal Floyd. He's one of our best. If there's anything in there, he'll find it."

The corporal was wearing a white paper evidence suit. He snapped on a pair of latex gloves, and without saying a word he held out his hands. Hayek gave him the bag and watched him hold the camera up to the light and look at it from several angles.

When he finally spoke he asked, "Do you have a power cord?"

Hayek could have kicked herself. She could see the cord still sitting on the floor. The thought of bringing it with her never crossed her mind. "Sorry . . . no cord."

The corporal shrugged his small shoulders. "I should be able to find something. Canon cameras pretty much use the same power source." He looked at the bottom and then moved to open the bag asking, "Do you mind?"

"Go ahead."

He pulled the camcorder out of the bag and checked the SD card slot.

"No memory card," Hayek pointed out the obvious. "Any chance we can find something on there?"

The corporal nodded. "This is a Canon VIXIA HF R30 SDHC. Comes with an eight-gigabyte internal flash drive. Three hours of high-def recording. If the Wi-Fi is still working, it'll be a snap. If it isn't, I might have to take the flash drive out, which will take some time."

"How much?"

"Maybe a few hours."

Hayek wasn't happy. "Can't you just hook it up to a TV and play it back?"

A small grin formed on the corporal's lips. "If I had all the right cables and the thing wasn't all busted up, yes, I could hook it up to a TV, but I don't have those cables, so it might take a little while to get it running, but don't worry, if there are any images on here I'll retrieve them for you."

The images—that's what this was all about, and this young soldier, if he was able to retrieve them, was in for quite a shock. Hayek still hadn't gotten used to this double life. She hadn't bothered to give the officer in charge, or anyone else for that matter, her alias. There were times where she truly wondered whether she was cut out to be a Clandestine Service officer.

"Listen," she said to the two men in a confidential tone, "the images on that thing are likely to be extremely disturbing. One of our Clandestine officers was kidnapped a few days ago, and we think that camera might contain parts of his interrogation. No one can have access to those images. As soon as you get it working you need to stop."

"Stop . . . doing what?" Floyd asked.

"Stop watching it. If my fears are correct, I don't think I'm cleared to see and hear what's on that drive, and I trust, Corporal, you don't want to have to put yourself through a debriefing on this. It wouldn't be pretty."

"Fair enough. Let me see what I can do. The second I get it working, it's all yours."

Hayek turned her attention to the one thing she could get a fairly quick answer on. Every Clandestine Service officer serving overseas had a DNA sample on file at Langley, and Hayek was in possession of Rickman's. She looked at the six evidence bags that she had collected from the slurry of fluids underneath the hook where it was most likely that Rickman had been beaten. Blood would give her the best match. She took the cleanest sample and gave it to the DNA analyst. "Let's start with this."

CHAPTER 41

KENNEDY yawned into the back of her hand and hoped no one back at Langley noticed. They were nearly an hour into the secure videoconference. The yawn wasn't from boredom but from fatigue. They had spent the majority of the briefing talking about life and death. The crisis seemed to have no end in sight. In fact, it was expanding like some plague, hopping from population center to population center, creating a kind of minipanic among people in the business, with one side running and the other sensing blood in the water.

The Pakistani foreign minister had been literally dragged from his house by the ISI with the media recording every brutal moment. That visual alone had started a second exodus of lesser assets in Pakistan. Four midlevel spies had shown up at the embassy in Islamabad, despite being told not to do so. Three more had simply disappeared, and it was anyone's guess if they had been picked up or were trying to flee on their own. None of these individuals were mentioned in the video posted on the Internet, but it didn't matter. Once fear gripped the lonely mind of a spy, panic was already breathing down his neck.

The embassy in Islamabad reported that the ISI had stepped up their surveillance around the embassy and they were almost certain to have photographed the assets entering the embassy. It was only a matter of time before an official protest was filed and the Pakistanis started tossing Americans out of their country. On top of that, Kennedy would still have to deal with the fools who had ignored their handlers and fled to the embassy seeking asylum. The Pakistani government would demand that those individuals be turned over, and considering the current climate, Kennedy would be left with little alternative. How many of them would live was impossible to guess, but they would all be brutally tortured. And this was just Pakistan. The deputy director of the Clandestine Service and his staff had just delivered a devastating report.

Thirteen assets, not counting the five in Pakistan, had jumped the reservation. Five had landed on the doorsteps of American embassies throughout Europe, and their handlers were working feverishly to get them to return to their lives before anyone noticed, but so far none of them were willing. Of the remaining eight, they had no idea if they'd been arrested or were making a run for the nearest border and the safety of America. Kennedy's network of spies was crumbling with each tick of the clock, and they were only in the infancy of this crisis. She wondered how many of these brave individuals understood what she knew, that Rickman had only just begun telling secrets. The video was just the first installment of a plague that would cripple the CIA.

As she looked at the faces around the conference table, and the ones on the large screen relaying the image from Langley, she wondered how many of these people understood what was at stake. They were all smart, or they wouldn't have risen to such important posts, but there was a learning curve during a catastrophe. It was extremely easy to be myopic. There were specific tasks that needed to be performed and more than a few people were afraid to look up and see just how bad things could get. Kennedy couldn't afford to bury her head in a bunch of files. It was her job to steer this ship away from the shoals, and right now she was beginning to wonder if it was possible.

"You okay?"

Kennedy turned to look at Rapp, who was studying her with his dark eyes. There were times, like now, when that gaze unnerved her. She swore he could look into a person's soul and smell fear.

Proving her point, he said, "I know this looks hopeless right now, but we'll catch a break sooner or later."

"I wish I shared your confidence."

He leaned in even closer. "Right now it's all about damage control. The bleeding will eventually stop, and when it does, we're just going to have to bust our butt to get back in the game."

Right now Kennedy didn't feel like the bleeding would ever stop, and if it did, she wasn't so sure she would have a job. Looking at Rapp, it occurred to her that she still hadn't talked to him about Gould. There were obviously still some memory issues or she was pretty certain he would have brought it up. More than likely he would have demanded to see him. Maybe she could ask Coleman to go over it with him before Dr. Lewis arrived in the morning. At least Gould was cooperating. Nash was meticulously rebuilding the last four years of the man's life, with special attention paid to his financial transactions and employers. Kennedy found it hard to swallow that it had been purely coincidental that Gould had been hired for the second time in four years to kill Rapp. And then there was Wilson. The Clandestine Service was by necessity an organization staffed with people who were the opposite of Dudley Do-Right. Rapp had done plenty of business with banks specializing in secrecy, from Switzerland to Cyprus, to Gibraltar, and all the way to Singapore, all of it authorized by Kennedy. The question was, how did Wilson find out, and who had wanted him to find out?

The door to the conference room was yanked open and Sydney Hayek entered, out of breath and carrying a laptop. Kennedy's assistant, Eugene, was on her heels.

"I'm sorry to barge in like this," Hayek announced, "but I found something that I thought you'd all want to see immediately." Hayek followed Eugene to a console full of electronics at the far end of the room. She handed him the laptop and he connected several cables and then switched one of the flat-screen monitors over to the laptop feed. Eugene handed her a remote and left the room, closing the soundproof door on his way out. Even though he was Kennedy's personal assistant, he knew he didn't have the clearance to see everything.

Hayek took a brief moment to gather herself, looking around the table at Kennedy, Rapp, Schneeman, and Nash, and then at the larger gathering on the screen. "You're all aware of the house we found in Jalalabad. It turns out we have a DNA match for Joe Rickman."

"I heard that room was a mess," Nash said. "How sure are you that it's a match?"

Hayek rocked her head from side to side, not sure where she should begin, so she just started. "I'm one hundred percent sure. The DNA match is ninety-nine-point-nine percent, but we have other evidence." She looked at Kennedy. "There was a camcorder in the basement. It was smashed and the memory card was missing. This type of camera, however, also has an internal flash drive." The questions started in earnest, but she raised her voice and her hands and talked over everyone. "I want to caution everyone that this is extremely graphic. There are at least two hours of footage and we will be analyzing it for months to come, but I wanted to show you one thing that everyone needs to see before we get into the rest of it."

Hayek hit the Play button and started the video. The flat-screen showed the same image as the one that had gone viral. A bloodied, battered, and shirtless Rickman hung from the ceiling, his hands stretched above his head. His torso was covered with red welts. Both eyes were swollen shut and, from the unnatural angle of his mouth, it looked like his jaw was broken. The two men were beating him senseless, taking turns so they could conserve their energy. As the video continued, they began striking him in the groin with rubber hoses, and then Rickman's body convulsed and he coughed up a glob of blood. The hooded men continued their onslaught for another dozen seconds and then seemed to sense that something was wrong.

They stopped hitting Rickman and lifted his swollen chin. As soon as the shorter man let go of Rickman's chin his head dropped lifelessly to rest on his chest. The two men began arguing in Pashto and then they pulled their masks up to reveal their faces. It was obvious they were panicked while they started to check for a pulse. A third man entered the picture, a blur as he passed the camera. He ignored the two men and put his fingers to Rickman's neck. It seemed like an eternity as the man continued to search for a pulse, going back and forth between Rickman's neck and his wrists. Eventually the man placed an ear over Rickman's bloody chest. After what seemed like an eternity, he stepped away from Rickman and the two men began to defend themselves.

The third man began screaming at them and then pulled a pistol. There was more arguing and then the third man, who still had his mask on, started pumping rounds into the taller of the two men. When he was done with him he turned the pistol on the other man and kept firing until his pistol was empty. The man then turned, marched straight for the camera, swung at it with his pistol, and the screen went black.

There was nothing but stunned silence. Kennedy's mind was trying to process what she had just seen, torn between horror and sadness and relief and a deep personal revulsion over the fact that she was comforted by the knowledge that one of her top people was dead. In a matter of seconds her mind ran the gamut, processing the violence, the tragedy, and the calculation that while Joe Rickman's final days on this planet were as awful as one could imagine, he had been spared months of cruel, unthinkable torture. There was a rationalization at work—one man was dead, but countless others would avoid the gallows. With a wave of relief, Kennedy realized her network of spies was safe, and in the same time and space she hated herself for coming to that conclusion without mourning for Rickman.

CHAPTER 42

WASHINGTON, D.C.

JOEL Wilson didn't have the energy or the desire to take his dog for a walk, but it was part of the plan, so he slid on a pair of tennis shoes and grabbed his barn jacket from the front hall closet. His wife, a skinny little platinum blonde who was a fitness freak, walked the dog both before and after work, so when Wilson grabbed the leash the dog cocked his head to one side as if to say, Are you kidding me?

"I don't need any attitude from you. I've got enough shit going on."

"What was that, honey?"

"Nothing," Wilson called to his wife, who was down the hall working on the computer. "I'm going to take Rose for a walk."

"Really?" Sally Wilson appeared in the doorway of the study, a pair of black reading glasses perched on the end of her nose.

"I know it's not usually my thing, but I need to clear my mind."

"Is it that bad?" Sally worked at the Department of Energy and had a good sense of just how nasty office politics could get in the big bureaucracy of Washington.

I'm about to find out, Wilson thought to himself. "It's pretty bad, but it's not over by a long shot. Just because crazy old Hargrave is mad at me doesn't mean he's right."

She came down the hall and kissed him on the cheek. "You'll figure it out. You always do. You're the smartest, best man I know."

Wilson blushed. He loved her dearly. Most marriages that couldn't produce children ended up in the ditch. Theirs had grown stronger. They were a great team. "Thank you, honey. I love you."

"Love you, too."

Their two-story brownstone was in a new development sandwiched between Reagan National Airport and the Pentagon. An old industrial park had been bulldozed and the developer had created a neighborhood that was supposed to give the feel of historic George-town. This had been accomplished by building four different types of brownstones that were basically the same in terms of the foundation and mechanicals, but slightly different in floor plans and the color of shutters and front doors. It was a nice neighborhood filled with lobbyists and upper-middle government types.

Wilson let the cocker spaniel take the lead. To say that he was a little down would have been an understatement. The long flight back from Afghanistan had given him way too much time to think. Even the members of his own team avoided talking to him. It was almost as if they all realized he'd become toxic. He'd tried to come up with an excuse for why they had to pack up all their stuff after having landed two days earlier. They had been operating under the assumption that they were going to be in the country for at least a week and that then the bulk of the team would return to Washington, leaving a few agents behind to follow up on things. But in the mad dash to get everyone up and packed, there was no way for him to massage what was going on. Before the flight was off the ground the entire team had heard about Cal Patterson's alarming phone call from Executive Assistant Director Hargrave.

None of the team knew Hargrave the way Wilson did. They saw him as a serious man with an important title who could banish them to whatever post he liked. Wilson knew the man for the phony he was, but trying to convince his team would only make things worse.

Two blocks away from the house, under a streetlight, he stopped and looked for the car. The dog turned around, gave him a What are you doing? look, and then tried to get him to keep moving. "Stay put, you stupid mutt," Wilson hissed.

A block away a pair of headlights snapped on and the vehicle started moving Wilson's way. When the black Lincoln Town Car stopped, the only thing Wilson could see was his reflection in the tinted windows. A click announced that the power locks had been tripped. Wilson opened the rear passenger door and looked into the dark back seat.

"Get in."

Wilson picked up the dog and climbed into the backseat. He set Rose on his lap and closed the door. The vehicle started moving and the privacy glass between the front and back seats was raised.

"Good-looking dog. What's his name?"

"Rose, and he's a she."

Senator Carl Ferris reached out and allowed the dog to lick his liver-spotted hand. "I love dogs. Did you know that?"

"Nope." Wilson couldn't give a shit.

"I've had them my whole life. Three of them right now. Two of them stay at the big house up in Connecticut. The other one travels with us. A little cockapoo. Cutest thing you've ever seen."

Wilson watched as the senator went to work scratching Rose's neck and talking to her in that stupid baby-talk voice that his wife used when she thought she and the dog were carrying on a conversation.

"I'm really glad you're so interested in my dog, but I've got bigger problems right now."

Ferris kept scratching the dog. "Yes, you do. Very unfortunate, the way Samuel behaved. The man is extremely petulant."

"The word I would use is asshole."

Ferris pulled the dog onto his lap. "Just how serious are things?"

"Pretty bad. I'm supposed to be in the director's office at 11:00 a.m.

sharp tomorrow morning. I have no idea who is going to be there, but you can bet Hargrave has the deck stacked against me. I've kept him out of the loop, just as you advised me, and now he's going to use that against me, and trust me, it isn't going to be good. They take this shit very seriously at the FBI. I wish I had just let him in on what I was doing."

"That would have been a huge mistake." Ferris was a portly man with a slight comb-over. "He would have run to Kennedy and you would have never gotten your investigation off the ground."

"What does it matter? They're going to pull the rug out from under me tomorrow. They're going to transfer my ass to the Office of Equal Employment Opportunity or some other BS post. Shit, I'll be lucky if I have a job when they're done."

"Now . . . now," Ferris said in a caring voice. "You need to gather yourself and remember that while you may have stepped on a few toes, you're still right. You have uncovered a massive fraud. Millions of dollars in funds that have been stolen by a corrupt and out-of-control CIA."

"You don't need to convince me, it's them—my bosses."

"Hargrave, really. Director Miller would stand behind you if things weren't already so muddied."

"So you think I'm screwed."

"I didn't say that. I think you're in a tough spot, but I've seen worse." Ferris shifted the dog and said, "The key is for you to state your case tomorrow. You have the affidavit from the banker. You have the bank records. I don't know how they can ignore that kind of information."

"For starters, they're going to want to know how I came by all of this evidence, and they are not going to like my answers. This is the CIA we're talking about."

"I understand that," Ferris said with a trace of impatience. "Evidence is evidence. It will simply have to see the light of day. People will understand just how serious things are then."

Wilson cocked his head to the side and said, "Are you suggesting that I leak this information to the press, because if you are, I'll be the one to have my ass thrown in jail."

"Calm down," Ferris said sternly. "I said no such thing. I know you have certain rules you must follow. The key is for you to get them to see that by not letting you proceed, it will open the FBI up to allegations of a cover-up."

Wilson liked the sound of that. That was the kind of thing that could scare the crap out of any high-level bureaucrat. "You know if I dropped your name and mentioned that the Judiciary Committee was keeping an eye on this it might be enough to get them to back off."

The senator's expression soured. "For now you need to minimize our relationship. Trust me on this. We haven't reached the point yet where I'm ready to get involved, but I promise you, when the time is right, I will jump on them like an eight-hundred-pound gorilla."

"And until then I'm just going to get my ass kicked."

Ferris sighed. "Don't be so melodramatic. It's very unbecoming in a man who carries a badge and a gun."

CHAPTER 43

ISLAMABAD, PAKISTAN

GENERAL Durrani was sitting in the rear passenger seat of his armored Mercedes sedan. Two identical black Mercedes E350 sedans followed. The cars were indistinguishable from one another, and tinted windows made it impossible to see who was inside the vehicles. Durrani preferred that his car take the lead, as bombers more often than not assumed their target was in the middle sedan. Truth be known, however, Durrani didn't worry much about being blown up. The people who did that type of stuff, the militants, were all in his back pocket.

The motorcade pulled up to the main security post of his gated community, Bahria Town, on the outskirts of Islamabad. Durrani had helped the developer get his forty-five-thousand-acre gated community off the ground—evicting tenants and intimidating reluctant landowners into selling. In addition to making sure the right people were bribed or threatened, Durrani had also made sure that the private security force was composed of former army personnel who were entirely loyal to him. In exchange for his help, he was given his own compound, nestled on a very private palm-tree-lined lot. The compound was surrounded by ten-foot walls that protected an eight-thousand-square-foot main house, two guesthouses, a pool house, and an eight-car garage with rooms for his servants and bodyguards. Durrani was filled with a sense of bliss every time he entered the gated community. Only in his beloved Pakistan could you work this hard and be rewarded with such opulence.

The cars sped down a wide, tree-lined boulevard. Unlike the rest of Islamabad and Rawalpindi, here there wasn't a speck of garbage in sight. The gate to the compound was open, and two of Durrani's military bodyguards were standing next to the large stone columns, holding their Heckler & Koch G3 rifles. The vehicles sped past them and up the long private driveway. Durrani did not wait for his detail to take up their positions. This was his compound, after all, and there had to be at least one place in his life where he could feel free to move about on his own. He headed for the main house, where his butler was waiting at the door.

"Good evening, General," a small man in a white tunic and black pants greeted him. "Is there anything I can get you?"

Durrani walked past his butler without making eye contact and then stopped in the middle of the large marble foyer. "Is Vazir here?"

"Yes, General. He is in the Shahi house."

Durrani gave a quick nod and proceeded down the hallway to the elevator. When the doors opened, he stepped inside and pressed the button for the basement. Durrani was extremely paranoid, and his job only amplified his distrustfulness, so when he was having the house built he'd had the contractor, a very good friend and business partner, put in tunnels that linked all the structures on the property. As much as possible he did not want the Americans to know what he was doing. The tunnels allowed him to stay away from the prying eyes of their satellites. Durrani had even gone so far as to have an analyst give him the known overpass times of American satellites so he could be extra cautious. The problem was that Americans could move those satellites, and even worse, through the use of stealth drones they were finding more and more ways to spy on him.

Durrani punched in the code and opened the steel door. The corridors were nothing special, just poured eight-foot concrete walls and ceilings with caged industrial lights every twenty feet. The tunnel from the main house to the first guesthouse was 180 feet long. At the next door he took a right turn and continued down a much shorter tunnel. He punched in another code, entered the stark basement, and started up the steps. By the time he reached the main floor his breathing was labored. Durrani placed one hand on the railing and patted his chest with the other.

A voice called out from the next room, "Is that you, General?"

When he spoke, Durrani was still out of breath. "Yes." He reached for his cigarettes and lit one, before pushing off the railing and walking into the sunken living room. The theme for this particular house was clean and contemporary with lots of white. In the middle of the sunken living room were two white leather couches and two modern white leather chairs with chrome frames. The furniture rested on a large white shag rug and a white marble floor with subtle shades of gray.

Durrani did not approach the man in the dark suit. He was sitting with his legs crossed on one of the white couches, a magazine in one hand, a cigarette in the other, and a bulky black pistol next to him. Vazir Kassar was one of his most trusted officers. He was also an insolent son of a bitch at times. He knew that Durrani was dying to know how things had turned out, but he was going to make him ask.

"Well?" Durrani's eyes were wide with anticipation.

"Well, what, General?"

Durrani was suddenly irritated by the gun sitting on the couch. "Put that away. You are a guest in my house."

"I thought I was your employee," the dark, thin man answered in a voice that conveyed ambivalence.

"Don't play your games with me. How did it go?"

The man remained serious. "It wasn't easy."

"But he's alive?"

"Yes." Kassar jerked his head toward the hallway. "He's in the bedroom at the end of the hall."

Durrani clapped his hands together and stifled a scream of joy. "You will have to tell me all the details later, but first I must see him." Durrani hurried down the hallway, his black dress shoes clicking on the stone floor. He would have run if his lungs could have taken it. When he reached the door at the end of the hall he didn't bother knocking.

He threw open the door and froze in disbelief. The blackout shades were not pulled, and the bright afternoon light streamed through the gauzy, white linen curtains. There, in the middle of the king-size bed, filled with white pillows, white sheets, and a fluffy white feather comforter, lay a mass of purple and red flesh. The smile on Durrani's face vanished. "Good God. What did those fools do to you?" Durrani rushed to the bedside and looked at the swollen and bruised face. "Is it you? I can't be sure." The monstrous face slowly turned in his direction. The man was blind. His eyes, swollen tightly shut, looked like two peaches. His lips were cut, cracked, and so puffy the top one touched his broken and deformed nose. Durrani had seen the video on the Internet and assumed that they had used makeup to exaggerate the injuries. "What happened?"

When he spoke he sounded congested. "It's not easy to talk. I think they broke my jaw."

Durrani's entire being stiffened with anger. "I will kill them. I swear to you I will kill them."

There was gruff laughter from the doorway. "I think you're a little late for that."

Durrani looked over his shoulder at Kassar. "How could you have let this happen?"

"It was your idea," he said, not wanting to own any of this. "All part of your grand plan."

"This," Durrani said, pointing at Rickman, "was not my plan."

"Relax, Akhtar," Rickman said, reaching out with his left hand.

When Durrani saw the mangled and broken fingers he took a quick step back.

"I'm alive," Rickman said. "It worked. Vazir took care of your two Taliban dupes. I'm told the entire thing was quite dramatic. Fortunately, I had passed out by then."

"Are you in pain?" Durrani asked.

It was a relative question, or at least the pain was relative. He was not comfortable, but compared to his pain during the beatings he was at peace. "I'm okay."

"You are no such thing. You are a bloody mess."

"I'll survive."

"I'm not sure you will." Durrani looked to Kassar again. "How could you have let this happen?"

"He insisted," Kassar said. "You've told me many times my job is to follow orders. I wanted to stop sooner, but he said we had to make sure it was convincing."

"To follow *my* orders." Durrani hit himself in the chest repeatedly.

"Well, you weren't there, General. I was following Joe's orders."

Durrani found Kassar's unflappable behavior unnerving at times. Rather than start yelling at him, Durrani turned his attention back to Rickman. There wasn't an inch of his face that wasn't bruised, swollen, or cut. "Why did you do this to yourself?"

"I didn't . . . it was your Taliban flunkies. They were not very smart, by the way. Perfect for the job, really. I must compliment you."

Durrani cracked a small smile. He had always found Rickman humorous. "It looks like they went too far."

"It was the only way. I had to sell it."

Durrani was dumbfounded. He knew the American was smart,

but he had no idea he was so tough. "You are either the bravest man I know, or you are crazy. Which one is it?"

"A little bit of both, I suppose." Rickman started to smile, but then had to stop because it hurt too much.

Durrani considered the bigger picture. He would have preferred not to cut this so close, but he was thankful that Rickman was alive. He had pulled off one of the greatest intelligence coups in the history of the world. "This is a great day." He put his right hand on Rickman's shoulder and gave him a reassuring squeeze.

Rickman moaned and Kassar said, "I think his shoulders were dislocated while they were tied above his head. I wouldn't do that."

Durrani withdrew his hand and said, "Has the doctor seen him?"

Kassar shook his head and grabbed a pack of cigarettes from his suit coat. He tapped one free and pointed the unfiltered end at Rickman. "He won't allow it."

"What?"

"I said he won't allow it."

Durrani shot Kassar a scowl. He was the only person who worked for Durrani who even attempted to defy him. "I heard what you said. Why won't he allow it?"

"Because he doesn't trust our doctor. He thinks the fewer the people who see him the better."

"But he needs medical attention." Durrani looked at the broken man lying on the large bed. "We need to have a doctor look at you."

"And then you will kill him." Rickman shook his head slowly an inch to his left and then his right. "I will heal. Just let me rest."

"Thank you," Kassar said, "I will be the one who has to kill him, and I like Dr. Bhutani. He has stitched me up on several occasions . . . a very handy man to have around. I would prefer it if we could keep him."

Durrani turned halfway and swatted the air with his arm, telling Kassar to leave. The impudent man took a long pull from his cigarette, shrugged, and then disappeared. Hovering over Rickman, Durrani said, "Are you taking anything for the pain?"

"Yes." Rickman squirmed a bit in an effort to lift his head. "It's not as bad as it looks . . . at least not compared to the beating I had to go through."

"What can I get you?"

"Nothing. I just want to lie here."

Durrani's gaze narrowed. He had no great knowledge of medicine or the human anatomy, but he had been involved in plenty of interrogations. A good number of them had ended in death, and it wasn't always because the heart gave out. There had been plenty of cases in which the subject died from infection. The infections were no surprise considering the squalor of the cells. Add to that the way the nervous system was assaulted and the lack of sleep, and it was no wonder the immune system crashed and the patient died. Durrani decided at that exact moment that he would have his doctor here within the hour. He was former Army and was cleared to work with the ISI. He was also sympathetic to the cause of Pakistani self-determination. There was always a risk, of course, but Durrani could have him killed later if there was a problem.

Rickman stifled a cough and asked, "What about Rapp?"

This was the one part Durrani had been dreading. Everything else had worked so well. "He escaped death, but do not worry. He has other problems."

Rickman tried to sit up, but didn't make it very far before a coughing fit ensued and he was forced to lie back down. Blood began to trickle from his mouth as he said, "I can't believe this."

"Calm down. Do not upset yourself."

"I told you, Rapp absolutely had to be dealt with. It was the one part of the operation that couldn't fail."

"I know," Durrani said, prepared to deflect, "but your assassin didn't take the shot."

"What do you mean?"

"He walked across the street to the clinic and surrendered himself to Rapp."

"I don't believe you."

"Well, you'd better. I had two of my best men there, and I lost one of them. Your assassin marched right across the street and presented himself to Rapp. Your man failed, so I had to use my backup. General Qayem sent in his men and it was a bloodbath."

"Bloodbath?"

"Twenty-one men were killed."

Rickman was shell-shocked. "How many people did Rapp have with him?"

"Four." Durrani held up his nicotine-stained fingers, practically yelling. "And then your assassin joined his ranks. I'm told he personally killed a good number of Qayem's men."

Rickman was suddenly feeling every ache and pain. What was it about Rapp? Why wouldn't the man just die? A sense of foreboding weighed on Rickman's chest, and he began to worry that he wouldn't be able to breathe. At that same moment he feared for Hubbard. The plan had been for him to send Rapp to the veterinary clinic. Rickman had thought this through for more than a year. He knew Kennedy would send Rapp to head the search for him, and he knew how Rapp thought better than Rickman himself did. Rickman had carefully left those clues for Rapp, knowing his damn instincts would tell him that certain things didn't add up. If Rapp had survived the trap he had laid for him, that would mean Hubbard was either dead or running for his life. Rickman suddenly wished he could open his eyes so he could read Durrani's face.

"What about Hubbard? Where is he?"

Durrani knew this was inevitable, but the truth was not an option for him. Not if he wanted Rickman to work with him. His friend was already clearly agitated, which was a shame as there was so much to celebrate. The truth was that Durrani had never planned on getting Hubbard out of Afghanistan. Where was he supposed to hide a six-foot-five-inch, bald, pasty American in a country filled with dark-skinned men where the average height was five-seven? He'd gone along with Rickman's desire to bring Hubbard to Pakistan because it was the only way to get him to agree to the plan, but in truth he knew he would kill Hubbard from the onset.

"It pains me to tell you that your friend is dead."

Rickman swallowed hard. "Are you sure?"

"Yes."

"How did it happen?"

"We think it was Rapp, but we're not sure."

Rickman's battered body tensed and he yelled, "Did you do anything right?"

"That is not fair, Joe. We knew from the very beginning that this was going to be a very complicated operation. Your friend knew that as well."

"I can't believe Rapp is still alive and Hubbard is dead. You need to get men to Zurich. Rapp cannot get his hands on Obrecht."

"I have already taken care of it," Durrani lied. He had completely forgotten about the deception involving the Swiss banker. With Rapp dead, he was going to be a crucial witness to Rapp's corruption. It was Rickman's way of muddying the water. "You are still alive," Durrani said. "That is what's important. You are free, and you are rich beyond your dreams."

With each passing revelation Rickman was feeling less than stellar about his situation. "And Mitch Rapp is still alive and he's going to hunt my ass down and kill me."

"He will never find you. My plans are intact. Once you undergo the surgery, no one will ever know."

Rickman's thoughts returned to Hubbard. "How did Hubbard die?"

"We're not sure . . . other than the fact that Mr. Hubbard did not make it to his rendezvous point." Hubbard had in fact made it to the warehouse in Jalalabad, and that was where he was killed, but that information would only serve to upset Rickman. Durrani knew what was best for him. Things would be much smoother this way.

"So he might be alive?"

"We don't think so. There was a shootout . . . things are a little sketchy, but it sounds like Rapp killed him."

"Sounds like . . . so you're not sure." Rickman was becoming extremely agitated. "If Hubbard is still alive, you and I are as good as dead."

"Well," Durrani said, trying to think of a way to calm Rickman down, "he is most certainly dead. I'm just being cautious."

"Cautious! You should have been more cautious about making sure Rapp was killed. Fuck." The word was filled with despondency. "I told you killing Rapp was crucial. I've run all the calculations. Mitch Rapp is the last man I want looking for me. You don't know him like I do. He won't stop until he finds me, and that means you, too."

"They all think you're dead," Durrani said dismissively.

"Most of them will, because that's what they want to believe. But Rapp doesn't operate that way. It's not a matter of what he wants to believe or doesn't want to believe. He's a human bullshit detector. He's going to sniff out the cracks in our plan and he's going to start hammering away until the entire thing collapses and then he is going to hunt our asses down." Rickman moaned and then added, "I went through all of that pain for nothing."

"You exaggerate the abilities of your former colleague."

"I exaggerate nothing. I've worked with him for over twenty years. He's the fucking Energizer Bunny of covert operatives. He just keeps killing and killing, and if you want to stay alive, you'd better figure out a way to kill him, and you'd better do it quick."

Rickman was overreacting. "I want you to calm down. There is far too much to celebrate."

"I can't calm down as long as that man is above ground." Rickman started coughing, and it wasn't long before a trickle of blood began to run down the corner of his swollen mouth.

Durrani couldn't believe the doctor wasn't here. "Just one minute," Durrani said, holding up a finger and retreating from the room. He ignored Rickman's coughing and moved quickly down the hall and into the living room. "Get Dr. Bhutani here immediately. I am extremely disappointed that you ignored my orders."

Kassar looked up from his magazine and said, "He refused to let me call a doctor, and he was doing fine until you got here and upset him."

"One of these days," Durrani said, shaking his fist, "you are going to push me too far."

"You may get rid of me any time you like."

"Just get Dr. Bhutani and get him fast."

Kassar set down the magazine and stabbed out his cigarette in the large copper ashtray in the middle of the table. He stood and said, "I will get Dr. Bhutani, but as I said, I like the man. If you decide he is a liability at some point you will have to find someone else to do your dirty work."

"Fine," Durrani snapped. "Just get him."

"And I heard what you two were talking about."

"What?"

"Rapp."

Durrani was exasperated. He didn't want to talk right now, he wanted Kassar to get the doctor. "What about him."

"Put it out of your mind."

"Put what out of my mind?"

"Killing him, or at least asking me to kill him."

"I don't know when you got the idea that we were equals. I give the orders and you follow them."

Kassar gave a nod of mutual understanding. "You have made that clear. I am a contract employee. You have me on a retainer and if at any point you are not satisfied with my performance, my contract will be terminated. That goes both ways."

"Are you threatening me?"

"No," Kassar said tersely. "I'm simply trying to stop you from doing something stupid. Leave Mr. Rapp alone and hope that he never discovers your hand in this."

"Are you afraid of him?" Durrani asked mockingly.

Kassar pulled out his phone and began searching for Dr. Bhutani's number. "I respect the man and his abilities and you should as well. If you are foolish enough to try to kill him again, you're going to have to find someone other than me. Someone who is reckless enough to think he can take him."

CHAPTER 44

LANGLEY, VIRGINIA

KENNEDY reviewed the final edited version for the eighth time. The assault on her conscience was not quite as bad as it had been on the first or second viewing. The impact had lessened a degree or two, which made her wonder how many times she'd have to watch it before she was completely desensitized to the horror. She knew that would never happen, but there was a part of her brain that wished it could be that simple.

The internal drive from the camcorder provided exactly two hours of footage. Two hours of the most brutal, dehumanizing violence Kennedy had ever witnessed, and she was not unaware that things like this happened. She had in fact seen similar tapes before. Saddam Hussein had tapes like this all over his palaces. Those tapes never required more than a minute or two of viewing as analysts sifted through them to see if there was any actionable intelligence. Kennedy was then brought individual snippets to view.

This time she had forced herself to watch the entire two hours. She'd done it on the flight back from Bagram. The morning after Hayek had shown them the video they received word that Hubbard's body had been discovered in a warehouse of an industrial park on the outskirts of Jalalabad. The cause of death was a single bullet to the head. Mike Nash had approached her midmorning and told her that she needed to get back to headquarters. Kennedy was reluctant, but Nash was forceful, telling her that with Rickman and Hubbard dead, the worst of the crisis had passed. She was needed back in D.C., where there would be a lot of important people asking questions. They all knew it would get ugly, and Kennedy knew Nash was right. She needed to be in Washington, so she left Nash behind to help Schneeman manage the cleanup.

Kennedy had been trained to accept the more difficult aspects of her job, but she was still human. Watching Rickman beg his captors to stop was one of the most heart-wrenching things she'd ever experienced. The ugly specter of the outcome hung over the entire thing. There was no surprise ending, no hope that SEALs or Delta Force commandos would burst into the room and gun down the two interrogators. She'd seen the ending first, which made watching it all that much harder. All the relief she'd felt knowing that her secrets were now safe with the death of Rickman quickly transformed into a crippling guilt that she'd found solace in the death of someone she was responsible for.

Rapp, as always, had been able to look right through her and know what she was thinking. Somewhere over Europe, in the middle of the night, Kennedy looked down the fuselage of the G550 and decided that everyone was either sleeping or trying to sleep. She decided it was time to watch the interrogation in its entirety. She opened her laptop and began watching Rickman's final two hours of life. She cried for most of it. Somewhere near the end Rapp came up on her left shoulder and closed her laptop. She took off her headphones.

He sat down across from her, leaned forward, and said, "Why are you doing this to yourself?"

Kennedy tried to compose herself, wiping her tears with the sleeve of her sweater. "I had to watch it. I need to know what he gave up."

Rapp shook his head in a slow, disapproving way. "That's not true and you know it. You can't make out half of what he says in a quiet room . . . up here forty thousand feet you might be able decipher twenty percent. The audio needs to be cleaned up, and that's what they're doing at Langley right now. By the time we land you'll have a detailed transcript of everything he said. Twenty-four hours after that you'll have a damage assessment from your top people, and we'll deal with it, but there is no reason to watch that other than to beat yourself up."

"Thomas always told me I needed to understand just how rough things could get in the field."

Thomas was Thomas Stansfield, Kennedy's mentor and her predecessor. Rapp thought highly of the man, but there were times where he wondered if Kennedy didn't try a little too hard to live up to Stansfield and his legend. "Being detached has never been a problem of yours. Don't beat yourself up over this. It's not your fault. It's no one's fault. It's just part of the job."

"It's a part I don't like."

"It's a part none of us like, but we move on." Rapp grabbed her hand and said, "Someone I respect told me once to take a little time to grieve and then get my shit together and get back in the game."

"Stan?"

Rapp nodded. The tough, no-nonsense Stan Hurley was famous for telling people to suck it up.

"And if I can't?"

"Then you go see our favorite shrink."

Now, Kennedy spun her chair and looked out across the tree-laden landscape of the Potomac River Valley. She hadn't made an appointment with Dr. Lewis yet, but she would have to. She was going to need some help sorting through all of this guilt and relief. The problem would be finding the time. Her schedule was booked solid with meetings that had been rescheduled because of the emergency trip to Afghanistan and fresh meetings with allies who wanted to discuss the fallout from Rickman. And then there was Congress. They wanted a briefing this afternoon, and Kennedy had a little surprise for them. Hayek's DNA samples from the torture room had brought in a match. One of the men in the video was Wafa Zadran, who had spent three years in Guantanamo. Several members of the Joint Intelligence Committee were harsh critics of the detention center in Cuba and had made a platform out of lecturing the CIA and the Pentagon that Gitmo was a recruiting tool for terrorists. This particular group of politicians fell into the dangerous mind-set that Islamic radicals thought, acted, and behaved like anyone else, and if you were simply nice to them they would be nice to you in return. In its mildest form, this type of thinking was naïve, and in its harshest form it was extremely narcissistic. Either way, it was wrong and did nothing to help fight Islamic terrorism. Zadran was yet another example of their failed and short-sighted policy, but Kennedy knew these politicians all too well. They would never accept responsibility for what they'd done.

There was a soft knock on the door and then a woman in her mid-fifties entered. It was Betty Walner, the CIA's director of the Office of Public Affairs. "Everything is ready. Do I have your authorization to release the clip?"

The clip was their solution to the stampede of panicked agents and assets. Chuck O'Brien, the director of the National Clandestine Service, had advocated the idea. As O'Brien put it, "Dead men don't tell secrets. This will put an end to it."

Kennedy was averse to the idea at first. The CIA didn't like making sensitive things public, and this was about as sensitive as it could get. Her mind had been pretty much made up for her when the terrorists decided to release a second edited clip of Rickman's beating. It became obvious that they were going to try to milk Rickman's interrogation to make it seem as if he was still alive. O'Brien's idea became the toaster in the bathwater. Release the clip of Rickman's death and short-circuit the entire game. There was also a serious opportunity to embarrass the Taliban by showing the execution of the two interrogators by one of their own. It would make them look like rank amateurs.

"Yes, the White House signed off on it," Kennedy said, reaching for her cup of tea.

"I've already received more than a few requests for interviews with you."

"I'm too busy right now."

"I know you are, but you're going to need to make some statements. First about Rickman and Hubbard and their service to our country. You have to do that."

Kennedy nodded. "I will at some point."

"It needs to be today."

Kennedy didn't take it personally. Walner was just trying to do her job. "I'll have something prepared by the end of the day."

"And it would really help if you'd do a sit-down with a half dozen or so reporters."

"Off the record?"

Walner shook her head. "Not on this one, Irene. It's too big. Have you had time to read the papers today?"

"No."

"The hawks on the Hill are screaming bloody murder over the reintegration program in Afghanistan and all the green-on-blue violence. They're laying all the blame on the White House, and you're stuck in the middle. Five at the most and they'll have you in a committee room with cameras and they'll be asking anything they want. Your best chance is to start shaping your message right now."

Kennedy looked down the length of her office at the small hallway that connected her office to the deputy director's office. Stofer was leading a group of her top advisors her way. She didn't have the energy to deal with the media right now and she wanted to hear what her advisors had to say. "Stop back in a few hours with a plan and we'll review it," she said to Walner.

Walner left and Kennedy got up with her cup of tea and moved over to the seating area, which was composed of one long couch with its back to the window, a rectangular, glass coffee table, and four chairs, two across from the couch and one at each end of the coffee table. Kennedy took her normal seat and set her cup of tea on the table. "So where do we stand?" she asked her advisers.

The director of the Clandestine Service looked at Stofer and then Rapp and cleared his throat. "Irene, none of us are taking this well. It sucks, but all things considered, Rick dying is not a bad outcome. I know it sounds harsh, but it's the reality of our business."

"So this is your glass-is-half-full pep talk?"

O'Brien looked a bit sheepish. "I'm not proud of it, but if that's the way you want to look at, that's fine with me." He nervously twisted the gold band on his wedding-ring finger and added, "It could have been a hundred times worse."

Kennedy took off her glasses and rubbed her eyes. "Sometimes it doesn't feel that way."

"Remember Buckley?" O'Brien said in an ominous tone. Bill Buckley was the CIA's station chief in Beirut who was kidnapped by Hezbollah in 1984.

Kennedy remembered Buckley. He was a friend of her parents. After his kidnapping and subsequent torture, his interrogators beat information out of him until they'd discovered his entire network of spies and assets. One by one those people simply disappeared or were found dead. The disaster crippled the CIA for more than a decade in the region. "I imagine we've all spent a good deal of time thinking about Bill this week." She looked at her tea for a moment and admitted, "You're right, it could have been a lot worse, but somehow that doesn't make me feel very good right now."

"I hate to sound harsh," O'Brien said in his deep voice, "but Rick probably welcomed this. After what he went through . . ." O'Brien shook his head. "I wouldn't want to see my worst enemy have to endure that."

Rapp didn't know if it was his head injury or if he'd always thought like this, but he was not comfortable with all of the emotions that everyone was wearing on their sleeves. This was CIA, and more precisely, the Clandestine Service. The department was filled with bad-asses from every branch of the military. They were the risk takers, the ones who were sent in to do the dirty work. You could try to soften torture and call it enhanced interrogation measures, but Rapp had used more than enhanced interrogation measures and so had Rickman. It was the world they lived in. It sucked that Rickman had to endure that kind of abuse, but they were professionals. There was also something else bothering Rapp that he couldn't put his finger on. It was a feeling that something wasn't right, that things didn't add up.

"How's your head?"

Rapp looked up to see Kennedy studying him. He felt fine, just a little tired. "Not bad."

Her gaze narrowed and she said, "You looked like you were in pain."

"No . . . just thinking about something." Rapp leaned forward and brought his hands together, and then, deflecting Kennedy, asked, "So where are we with this idiot from the FBI?"

"You'll be interested to know that Scott saw him take a little ride with our old friend Senator Ferris last night."

"Do we have audio?"

"I'm afraid not."

"Do I need to worry about this guy?"

Kennedy shook her head. "He has a meeting this morning with Director Miller. We've already discussed the matter and Miller assures me Agent Wilson will no longer be a problem."

"Good," Rapp said, and then, changing gears, asked, "And the transcript? I heard Rick threw them a curveball or two."

Stofer opened a black leather briefing folder. "That's right. He tossed out a few names . . . the names of people who as far as I know do not work for us."

"Who?" Kennedy asked.

Stofer adjusted his reading glasses and said, "Aleksei Garin, SVR Directorate S." He whistled. "That's going to be a tough one to swallow."

"I'm not sure anyone over there has the balls to confront Aleksei. He's not afraid to put bullets in people's heads."

Everyone agreed and then Stofer said, "Shahram Jafari, head of Iran's Atomic Energy Organization. Another tough one to swallow, but they're so damn paranoid they might make Jafari's life miserable—at least for a while. They'll be turning themselves inside out trying to find out if Jafari is a traitor. The last one isn't so clean. He identified Nadeem Ashan with the ISI. He doesn't work for us per se, but we consider him a valuable ally."

"Why would Rick throw Ashan's name in the mix?" Rapp asked.

O'Brien poured himself a cup of coffee and said, "It could have been the first name that popped into his head. Anything to stop the pain. You know how it goes."

Rapp did, but Rickman was smarter than that. He would have had a prearranged list in his head. "We should look into Rick's relationship with Ashan. See if there's anything there."

"We're already on it," Stofer said.

The main door to the office opened and Stan Hurley entered. "Sorry I'm late. What did I miss?"

Rapp looked at his mentor as he moved across the large office with his smooth amble. For a seventy-plus-year-old with terminal cancer he sure didn't act like it. Hurley's gait was the only thing about him that was smooth. He was a hard man, with hard edges, a hard personality, and a craggy disposition. This was the first time Rapp had seen him since learning he had cancer. For a split second he was about to stand to greet Hurley, maybe even give him a hug, but the reaction lost steam as quickly as it had come on. Hurley wasn't a hugger. He didn't like people touching him. He called it an institutional hazard. So instead Rapp gave him a short nod of recognition.

Kennedy and Stofer quickly filled Hurley in on what he'd missed. When they were done, O'Brien filled the dead air by saying, "Irene,

Betty wants me to say some things to the press. A few comments about Rick and Hub and their sacrifice."

Kennedy nodded slowly. "That'd be nice. Thank you."

No one spoke for a long moment and eventually all eyes turned to Rapp, who was clutching and unclutching his hands as if he were doing some new-age stress reduction exercise. Stofer spoke first, "Mitch, what's wrong?"

Rapp wasn't sure this was the time, but he knew it was better to speak his mind now. "I'm sorry to spoil the party here, but something's not right."

"What's not right?" Kennedy asked.

"We're all breathing a big sigh of relief when I can't shake the feeling that we're being set up."

"I'm not sure I follow," O'Brien said. "Rick's dead."

Rapp wasn't prepared to refute that point, but neither was he convinced that Rickman was no longer of this world. "I was at the safe house," Rapp said, remembering the four dead bodyguards. "It was an extremely precise takedown. The kind of op we'd be proud of," he said, looking at Hurley. "A state-of-the-art security system taken offline without our watchers at Langley having any idea, four bullets, four dead bodyguards, and not a shot more . . . all suppressed. The safe is opened, not cracked, and Rick's laptop, files, cash, and God only knows what else goes missing. And not a witness to any of it."

"I'm not sure I follow, either," Stofer said earnestly.

Kennedy rubbed her forehead. She had known Mitch wasn't going to be able to accept this. Nothing could ever be this simple. Stofer, for his part, was too reverential toward Rapp. Having come up on the analytical side, he had seen many of his predecessors manage the clandestine side of the business with condescension. Stofer worked extra hard to make sure the operatives felt that they were being heard. "You agree," Kennedy said, "that Rick is dead?"

Rapp took a moment and then said, "I'm not sure."

O'Brien moaned, "Come on, Mitch, it's not that complicated. He dies right on the tape. You can see the panic on the faces of the two goons when they realize what they've done. The anger in the third guy's voice when he can't find a pulse."

"Yeah . . . I know," Rapp said, almost sounding as if he doubted himself.

"And then the third guy executes the other two. We know that was real because you guys found the bodies in the exact same position as they were last seen on the video."

"But we don't have Rick's body."

"Doesn't surprise me one bit," O'Brien said with total confidence. "They're trying to act like he's still alive. They're going to do a slow drip, releasing snippets of the interrogation, only they don't know we have the entire thing, because the idiots took the SD card and didn't know the camera had an internal flash drive."

Rapp wasn't so sure, but he stuck with what he knew. "Someone, or more likely several men, hit the safe house, and they were extremely precise in their shots. Rick is then taken only a few hundred yards to another house, presumably by the same guys. The interrogation begins and a few days into it Rick dies. The third guy, who is obviously in charge, gets upset and empties a fifteen-round magazine into these two goons who screwed up."

"And your point is?" O'Brien asked as if all of this made perfect sense.

"We're shooters," Rapp said, waving his thumb back and forth between Hurley and himself. "If we had hit that safe house it would have been no different. One shot in each guy's head. If we'd brought Scott along with his guys, there would have been some double taps . . . but my point is there's always a pattern. Good shooters are disciplined shooters. It doesn't matter how mad we get, we don't empty magazines into people just because we're pissed off."

All eyes moved to Hurley to assess what he thought. He ran his finger along his dry lips and nodded. "He has a point."

"I think this could be an exception," O'Brien said. "Going through

what they went through to get Rick and then having him die after they'd broken him, but had only scratched the surface." O'Brien
thought of himself in the same situation. "I might lose my focus for a
second or two."

"Let my try it this way. The people who hit the safe house were
pros. The two goons who beat up Rick were not pros. You can see it in
the way they move. The third guy," Rapp shook his head, "he's a different story. When I watch him on the video I can't help but think he's
putting on an act for the camera."

"That's a bit of a stretch, Mitch," Kennedy said.

"It might be, but have you guys heard about the ballistics from the
safe house?" They all shook their heads no, so Rapp continued. "Three
of the bodyguards were shot in the center of the forehead with nine-
millimeter rounds. All of them were on the first floor. The fourth guard
was shot in the back of the head with a .45 caliber round. He was on
the second floor moving toward the stairs, probably responding to the
commotion downstairs. Rick's personal sidearm was a Kimber .45."

"I heard some rumblings about this," O'Brien said in obvious
disagreement. "I think the fourth guard was the inside guy and Rick
found out at the last minute and shot him."

"And the security system getting bypassed?"

"The bodyguards had the codes to arm and disarm it."

"But, they didn't have the codes to take it off-line. To shut the whole
thing down, cameras and all . . . only Rick could have done something
like that, or Marcus. Not a bunch of clowns from the Taliban."

"They lived with Rick," Kennedy said. "It would be entirely plausible for one of them to pick up on the codes."

"Okay, how about the safe?" Rapp said. "It was opened without any
coercion. Sid checked it out. There was blood all over the hallway on
the second floor but not a speck on the safe. She makes a very strong
point that the safe was opened by someone who had not been injured.
At first I assumed Rick just wasn't very tough, they put a gun to his
head, and he opened the safe. Well, if you believe everything you see in

that video we find out he's pretty damn tough. They would have had to slap him silly to get him to open that safe and there would have been some blood."

"I don't know, Mitch," Stofer said, shaking his head. "It's pretty thin."

"I know it is, but you guys, come on . . . think about this for a minute. Put your covert ops hats on and think about how we plan stuff. The lengths we go to, to lay down deceptions to make something look a certain way when our main objective is something entirely different."

Kennedy was all for open discussion, but this type of thinking was what led to the old puzzle palace mentality where every other person in the building was a mole. "Are you trying to say Rick was in on this? That he orchestrated his own kidnapping and then endured that horrific beating and that he's still alive?"

Rapp knew how preposterous it sounded, but he couldn't shake the feeling that there was some piece of information that he couldn't access that would explain his suspicions. He stood and walked over to the window. "I'm not sure what I think."

"Mitch, I think you're way out on a limb here." O'Brien was shaking his head in disagreement.

Rapp turned to face the big Irishman. "Have you read Sid's preliminary report?"

"No."

"Read it. Study the photos from the safe house. Look at the precision. Put yourself in the shoes of the people that were trying to get their hands on Rick. It was perfect."

"I'm not saying it wasn't," O'Brien said, refusing to see things Rapp's way.

"Now look at the other part of this. The same group of professionals fuck up, kill Rick, and then kill each other."

"That's what we saw on the tape. It's pretty hard to argue with."

"It sure is. The same cool customers that took down our safe house go completely mental just a few days later and manage to capture it on a camcorder and leave it behind for us to find."

"Heat of the moment. Not everyone thinks as clearly as you do in pressure situations."

"And some people are devious as all hell," Rapp said. "We're seeing what we're seeing because we want to. The alternative is fucking horrible. Rick is still alive and he's spilling the family jewels." Rapp moved back to his chair and said, "Can any of you honestly tell me that you weren't relieved when you saw Rick die in that clip?"

They all shook their heads.

"Our lives got significantly easier."

"Mitch," Stofer said, "I kind of see your point, but these terrorists aren't always the sharpest tools in the shed. That they screwed up and their failure benefited our larger strategic goals doesn't mean we're being duped."

"I know," Rapp said, "but I can't shake the feeling that we're not out of the woods. We need to take a top-to-bottom look at this. We need to figure out what happened to all of the money Rick was spreading around. Where the hell is his laptop, and do we have any idea what was on it? And the whole time we're looking we'd better be asking ourselves one question."

"What's that?" Kennedy said.

"What if they wanted us to find that camcorder?"

"Oh, come on." It was O'Brien. "This is so thin."

Kennedy had her eyes on Hurley. She could tell he was taking a trip down memory lane, accessing his large database of real-life experiences. "Stan, what are you thinking?"

Hurley didn't hear the question right away. His mind was elsewhere, thinking about the way the game used to be played. "I think Mitch might have a point . . . then again he could be totally wrong, but we can't afford not to explore it."

"I'm not sure we can afford to explore it," O'Brien said. "The harsh truth is that Rick is dead and a lot of people want him to stay that way."

Hurley started to grumble the way he did when he was about to get angry. After saying a few things to himself he said, "So our new protocol on shit like this is to stick our heads in the sand? That's one of the dumbest fucking things I've ever heard."

An outsider would be left to think that O'Brien would be wounded by Hurley's harsh words, but they'd all worked with him so long they didn't take the rebukes personally.

"Take this thing back to the beginning," Hurley said, "and it looks like we were being played. I don't think the Taliban are sophisticated enough to have done this. They may have played a role . . . provided some manpower, they may have even taken down the safe house, but they sure as hell didn't hire Gould. Whoever was behind this moved pieces around the chessboard like the Soviets used to do. They knew Mitch enough that they could dangle that information in front of him about the dog and he'd jump on it. They had to have been monitoring Hubbard, because minutes after he told Mitch where the vet's office was, they put Gould into play and called in their corrupt police general to clean up the mess. That's not the Taliban. Way too complicated."

Stofer looked confused. "Are you saying the Russians are behind this?"

Hurley shrugged. He hadn't thought that specifically, but anything was possible. "I don't know who's behind it, but whoever it is, is one devious bastard. They set this thing up and played us. I'm inclined to agree with Mitch. Anyone who goes to that much trouble doesn't leave the bodies and camera for us to find unless they want us to find them."

Kennedy felt another headache coming, and it wasn't because she was mad at Hurley and Rapp, it was because she knew they were right. They had been suckered into thinking they had dodged a bullet. O'Brien started to argue with Hurley and Rapp. Kennedy stood and walked back to her desk. None of them noticed. She opened her top left drawer and grabbed a bottle of Tylenol. She tapped out two little red pills into her hand and washed them down with a drink of water.

"Gentlemen," she said. They ignored her, so she raised her voice until they all stopped talking and turned their heads in her direction. "We need his body. Until then we are going to work on the assumption that he is alive." She saw O'Brien start to open his mouth and her hand shot out like a traffic cop's. "Our official stance is that he's dead. But unofficially, we are going to start digging, if for no other reason than to find out which intelligence agency was behind this."

Rapp stood, feeling full of energy for the first time since he'd woken up in the hospital. He buttoned his suit coat and said, "And when we find out who was behind this?"

"We will send them a very personal message."

CHAPTER 45

FBI HEADQUARTERS, WASHINGTON, D.C.

JOEL Wilson didn't mind that his entire career was in the balance. At least that was the conclusion he'd come to while shaving in the morning. Rather than crumble, he took it as a challenge. Washington was a universally corrupt town and that corruption did not stop at the doors of the FBI. Wilson had been fighting it his entire career, and although there were times like this, when he felt as if he was the only noble person in the building, that he took solace in the fact that there were men like Senator Cal Ferris who understood what was at stake.

Now the big question was, When was Ferris going to jump in and save him? The senator was cautious to a point, and then he came out with both guns blazing—usually on TV. Ferris's strategy was growing on him. Director Miller had made a tactical error when he recalled the team from Afghanistan. It was now documented that he had interfered in an important investigation and had plainly come down on the side of the CIA. This was the type of toehold that Ferris could use to drag Miller before the Judicial Committee when the time was right. And Wilson would be the star witness.

Wilson didn't like playing down his relationship with Ferris. Especially this morning, when it seemed entirely possible that his career was about to suffer serious harm. Washington, in general, was sympathetic to Kennedy's plight, but that would all change when the truth came out about Rickman and Rapp. The misuse of government funds was a serious crime, but the brazenness with which Rickman and Rapp had abused the trust Congress afforded to the black side of intelligence was nothing short of a major breach in national security. Wilson speculated that they were the tip of the iceberg. Others in the Clandestine Service were likely involved. Wilson's next move if he stayed in his post was to look into John Hubbard. Was it possible that Mitch Rapp had killed Hubbard for fear that he was about to expose him? Could Rapp have been behind Rickman's abduction and execution—again to protect himself, or to take all of the money they had been ferreting away?

Anything was possible when discussing these clandestine warriors. They were a bunch of degenerates. If they weren't working for the CIA, a good number of them would be criminals. During Wilson's fitful night's sleep he considered whistle-blower status. While the idea, in a grand operatic sense, was appealing, it was also extremely risky. Martyrs in Washington were always vilified by one side of the aisle and sanctified by the other. It would be a tough slog, probably three to four years. In the end, either he would be disgraced and unemployable, with his pension gone, or he would receive a gigantic eight-figure judgment and become a mini celebrity with the antimilitary intelligence establishment. He'd probably even have a movie made about his gutsy decision to speak truth to power. The lure of Hollywood, a book deal, and publicly exposing the corruption at Langley was extremely tempting.

It wasn't that Wilson lacked confidence in his abilities. He truly believed he was better than any three people in this town, but the CIA was more than three people. It was a building filled with individuals whose job it was to lie, cheat, and steal. They couldn't be trusted to wage any kind of war in a fair, honorable way. No, Wilson feared, he might be able to use the whistle-blower statute to scare his bosses, but it wouldn't intimidate the CIA for a second. They would find a way to win in the end. If this got worse, Wilson would have to get the media involved. It was his only hope for success.

It was nice to have Ferris in his corner, but the FBI was still an organization with rules and regulations and a very strong chain of command. Wilson had wandered off into dangerous territory in order to keep Hargrave in the dark. Technically, the old coot had him, but Wilson had a few surprises in store for him. It was all going to come down to Director Miller and how much latitude he was willing to give him.

Wilson was sitting in the director's outer office trying his best to ignore the hulking bodyguards and predict how his bosses would come after him. He'd been waiting for more than an hour, which could not be a good sign. Director Miller was militant when it came to punctuality. Hargrave, with a stick up his ass, was sure to have everything documented. Wilson could see him in there right now, with his ridiculously bushy eyebrows, pompously and meticulously going over every perceived transgression. Wilson was filled with hatred for the man and was putting the final brushstrokes on his plan to take him down when Director Miller's personal assistant told him it was time to go in.

Wilson stood and picked up his briefcase. The secretary was a very attractive brunette with brown bedroom eyes. Wilson flashed her a smile and said, "So this must be what they felt like before they were led to the gallows."

The woman ignored his attempt at humor with a blank stare and then turned her attention to her computer screen. Wilson, in a rare moment of insecurity, wondered if she was privy to his transgressions and had already passed judgment. He straightened his tie and prepared for the onslaught. As he put his hand on the doorknob he told himself that there would come a day where this repugnant little woman and a lot of other people would be apologizing to him.

Wilson stepped into the office, closed the door, and tried to remain confident as he faced the people arrayed around the twenty-person conference table. Wilson had expected Director Miller and Hargrave, and maybe someone from the General Counsel's Office, but he didn't expect to see Lisa Williams, the director of the Intelligence Division, and Jason Smith, who ran the Office of Congressional Affairs. Perhaps the most ominous sign, however, was the presence of Wilson's direct boss, David Taylor, who was on medical leave after back surgery. As he took a quick glance at the five faces, he didn't find a welcoming or supportive expression among them.

Wilson fought the urge to sit at the far end of the table across from Director Miller. The distance would have made things even more awkward, so he picked his way down the right side of the long table and grabbed the seat next to David Taylor. Wilson set his briefcase on the floor and looked at Taylor, who was wearing a white plastic clamshell that encased his upper body from his neck down to his torso. The device was Velcroed into place at the shoulders and on the sides. Taylor looked extremely uncomfortable.

"How are you feeling?" Wilson asked.

Taylor looked at Wilson but made no effort to speak.

"Let's get right to it," started an impatient Director Miller. He pointed his pen at Wilson and said, "Do have anything you'd like to say in your defense before we get started?"

Wilson felt his throat tighten while he chided himself for not coming to see Miller the second he landed. It was a mistake to cede the discussion to Hargrave. It was obvious by the pissed-off look on Miller's face that the well had been poisoned. With his options limited he started with the avenue that seemed most natural.

"Director, I have no idea what EAD Hargrave has been telling you, but I can assure you that there is another side to this extremely complicated and important investigation and I have some very good reasons for not keeping EAD Hargrave up to speed on every aspect of it."

Wilson leaned back and took a deep breath, hoping Miller would slow things down and at least be open-minded.

Miller did not pause. He instead forcefully stated how things were to proceed. In light of the fact that he was a former federal judge, that shouldn't have been surprising. "I don't want to hear innuendo, I don't want to hear rumors. Do we understand each other?"

"Yes."

"Good." Miller looked at his watch and said, "Start."

"Sir, with all due respect, I think EAD Hargrave is not in the best position to judge me and the actions of my team."

Taylor, with his stiff back brace, held up a hand and didn't bother to try to look at anyone, as his neck couldn't move. "We are not here to discuss the men and women on your team. This is solely about you and your behavior."

"Fine," Wilson said, trying to sound reasonable. "EAD Hargrave is not in the best position to judge me."

"And why is that?" Director Miller asked.

"Because of his extremely close relationship with Director Kennedy."

Miller's face twisted into a look of disapproval while he leaned forward and tapped the screen of an iPad several times.

Wilson heard his voice emanate from the overhead speakers. *Oh, I'm reading you loud and clear. Are you still recording our conversation? Because I want to make sure you get this part. I didn't tell you any of this because I can't trust you. Because the entire Counterintelligence Division knows that you're too close to Director Kennedy, and based on what I've experienced the last few days I'm inclined to believe those rumors. So you better get ready for your own board of inquiry.*

Wilson remembered the words all too well. At the time he had spewed them at Hargrave it felt good. Hearing them now in this setting, they seemed foolish.

"This is a fairly serious accusation." Miller picked up a pen and

held it just above the surface of a yellow legal pad. "Which employees of the Counterintelligence Division believe that Sam is too close to
DCI Kennedy?"

"Sir, I'm here to answer for myself. I'm not comfortable involving
other people in this."

"But you're comfortable enough to throw around wild accusations?" Miller stared at Wilson, waiting for a reply.

"It's not that, sir, it's just that I'm willing to answer for my own
opinions, but I'm not going to get any of my people into trouble."

Miller turned to Taylor. "David, you ran that division for three and
a half years. At any point during that time did you hear anyone complain that Sam was too cozy with DCI Kennedy?"

"Not a single person."

"How about anyone else at the CIA?"

"Nope."

"Well," Miller said, setting down his pen, "that's a pretty short list.
Your case doesn't look very strong at the moment. We have protocols
in place for a reason, and it is not up to you to decide when you may or
may not follow them. So this is your last chance. Why did you think
you couldn't trust EAD Hargrave?"

Wilson cleared his throat and drummed his fingers on the table for
a minute. This was a card he'd hoped he wouldn't have to play, but he
really had no choice. "Senator Ferris told me that EAD Hargrave was
not to be trusted in this matter and that I should try to run my investigation without his interference."

Miller made a great show of taking notes. As he scratched away he
asked, "Tell me, Joel, I'm pretty familiar with the Bureau's organiza-
tional chart, but I must have missed something. Just where does Senator Ferris's name appear on that chart?"

"It doesn't, sir."

"Jason," Miller said, turning to the head of the FBI's Office of Congressional Affairs, "I assume Joel followed protocol and reported his
discussions with Senator Ferris to your office."

"He did not."

"Were you aware in any way that Joel was working with Senator Ferris?"

"No. We had no idea."

Wilson could see how bad this looked. His only hope was to get to the heart of the corruption. "Sir, I don't want people's animosity toward the senator to cloud their judgment."

"Careful," Miller snapped, like a judge warning a wayward attorney, "we're not talking about feelings or opinions. We're sticking to the facts right now. And so far the facts are looking an awful lot like you willfully withheld information from your superior and that you failed to inform Congressional Affairs that you were running an investigation based on information passed along to you by Senator Ferris."

"That's not true, sir. I received independent information that employees of the CIA were stealing millions of dollars in cash and placing the money in a private bank in Switzerland." Wilson grabbed the file from his briefcase and slid it toward the director. "I have the accounts and the amounts and dates of the deposits along with a sworn affidavit from the private banker who handled the accounts. In the affidavit the banker swears that both Joe Rickman and Mitch Rapp were the owners of these accounts."

"And how did you come by this information?" Miller asked.

"The first batch in the mail, and then I interviewed the banker myself. He's a very credible witness."

Miller looked at the file. "That affidavit is in this file?"

"Yes, it is, sir."

Miller flipped through the pages until he found what he was looking for. "The banker's name has been blacked out."

"For security reasons, sir."

Miller picked up his pen again. "Let's have it."

Wilson squirmed. "Sir, I would rather not reveal that name until the investigation is on firmer ground."

"You will either give me the name or you will give me your badge and your sidearm."

Wilson saw no way out. "Leo Obrecht."

"And this first batch of information you mentioned . . . let me take a wild guess . . . it was given to you by an anonymous source?"

"Because of the nature of our work, we receive a good number of anonymous tips."

"Are you familiar with Swiss banking?"

"Somewhat, sir."

Miller placed his hands on the file. "And how easy do you think it is to come by information like this?"

"I wouldn't know, sir."

"Lisa," Miller said.

The head of the Bureau's Intelligence Division said, "Extremely difficult, sir. We spend months on end trying to just find out if a person of interest has an account at an institution like this. Getting our hands on detailed account records is extremely rare."

Miller closed the file. "Did it ever occur to you that this is disinformation?"

"It did until I was able to interview the banker."

"Lisa," Miller barked, "how difficult is it to get these bankers to talk about private accounts?"

"I'm unaware of it happening without an order from a Swiss court."

"Did you have a court order?"

"No."

"Did it ever occur to you that these were legitimate accounts?"

"Legitimate . . . how?"

"You do understand that the CIA has to move money around the world?"

"Yes."

"And that because they're the CIA, they need to do a lot of it in a secretive manner."

Wilson nodded. "All the more reason we need to keep an eye on them."

Miller shook his head. "You're not getting this, are you."

"Getting what, sir?"

"That you've fucked this thing up so bad, you'll be lucky if you have a job by the time this is over."

"With all due respect—"

"Shut up," Miller barked. "Lisa, please explain to Senator Ferris's man what's going on."

"It appears that a hostile foreign intelligence agency launched an operation against the CIA's Clandestine Service. We believe that part of that operation involved sending disinformation to the FBI's Counterintelligence Division."

Wilson frowned. "Says who . . . the CIA? This is bullshit. Where did you get this information?"

"I'm afraid it's classified." Williams looked from Wilson to the director.

Wilson wasn't going to go down so easily. "My clearance is as high as yours."

"Your clearance *used* to be as high as Lisa's," Director Miller said.

"What is going on here? I don't get it. The fact that a few of you don't like Senator Ferris doesn't mean this information is false. You need to allow me to finish my investigation. Give me thirty minutes with Rapp. I'll hook him up to a polly and we'll get some answers."

Miller shook his head. "I've decided to pull your clearance until an official review can be completed."

"But . . . you have to let me take a shot at Rapp."

Lisa Williams, the only woman in the room, looked at Wilson as if he was nuts and said, "Do you have any idea who you are talking about?"

"You mean Rapp? Yeah, I know who I'm talking about. He's dirty and he's corrupt and I don't understand why everyone is so afraid of taking him on."

Miller shook his finger at Wilson and said, "Let's get something straight. First off, you could polly Mitch Rapp for the next year and you wouldn't get a thing out of him."

"I disagree, sir."

"Stop interrupting me. You have no idea what you're talking about. Rapp would eat you for lunch. Beyond that, you don't know jack shit about the man. He's a damn national hero. You've been played, Joel, and you've made the FBI look like a bunch of fools." Miller hit the intercom button and said, "Please send her in." Turning his attention back to Wilson he said, "You are on indefinite administrative leave until I say otherwise. If you are lucky enough to keep your badge, I can promise you that you will be assigned to some benign post where you can do as little damage as possible."

Wilson was reeling. In his wildest dreams he hadn't imagined it could get this bad, and then the door opened and it got worse.

Director Kennedy stopped directly across from Wilson. She placed a document on the wood surface and slid it across the table. After Wilson caught it, she said, "I assume you recognize the legal document in your hands."

Wilson scanned the heading. It was a national security nondisclosure contract.

"If you flip to the last page, you'll see your signature."

Wilson went to the last page and noted his signature. He'd signed the document when he went to work for counterintelligence. He began to slide the document back to Kennedy. "I think we should be looking at your—"

Kennedy reached out and stopped him from moving the document another inch. "That copy is for you. I suggest you read it, and then you find a really good lawyer. A private one, who will more than likely be very expensive, because the FBI will not be supplying you with counsel on this little screwup."

"What are you talking about? You don't decide what the FBI does or doesn't do." Wilson looked to Miller.

"No, I don't, but I do run the CIA, and we have a very good legal department, and we happen to have a very good working relationship with some federal judges who take national security issues quite seriously. We haven't even begun to investigate you, and we've already come across three instances in which you are in violation of your national security contract. I'm no lawyer, Agent Wilson, but they tell me if we want to press the issue we could have your ass thrown in a high-security federal facility for months. You screwed up here big-time, and if you want to avoid jail you had better start to show some serious cooperation, or at a bare minimum shut your mouth and crawl under some rock, but this is your only warning. If you run to Ferris, or try to claim victimhood, I will have your ass thrown in jail."

"You can't intimidate me."

Kennedy realized Wilson didn't get it. "I'm not trying to intimidate you. I'm telling you the facts. You have screwed up like very few people in your position can screw up. You signed that document in your hands and we happen to take it very seriously. Do yourself a favor and find a lawyer who has had some experience with this type of thing. He will tell you that if I decide to push this, you will go to jail."

"If you have everything all locked up, then why don't you do it?" Wilson asked Kennedy in an overconfident tone.

Kennedy looked to Miller and said, "I'm done with him. The man's a fool. If you can talk some sense into him by this evening, I'll call the dogs off. If not, my people will be in federal court in the morning." Kennedy turned and left without saying another word.

Wilson looked at his five colleagues and said incredulously, "Can't you see what's going on? She wants me to drop this because she knows I'm onto something." When no one reacted, Wilson looked at David Taylor, whom he'd worked closely with for the last three years. "David, don't you see what's going on?"

Taylor spun his chair to his left. With his back brace it was the only way he could look Wilson in the eye. "Do you know what your problem is, Joel? You think you're the only noble person in this town."

"Come on."

"I'm serious. The rest of us are all corrupt or greedy. Our motives are suspect, but not you. You're above all of that. You're a fucking martyr and you brought this all down on yourself because you're an arrogant know-it-all. Even in the face of all of this, you can't see that you've screwed up."

Director Miller looked at him with pure disgust. "Maybe you'd gain a little more perspective from our field office in Bismarck, North Dakota."

CHAPTER 46

VIRGINIA

THE house was forty minutes northwest of Langley, just past Dulles International Airport. A couple who had retired from the Clandestine Service after putting in thirty-plus years were listed as the owners of the sprawling property. They were now consultants for the CIA, and continued to be paid a generous salary, but they rarely made the commute to the George Bush Center for Intelligence. Their job was to manage the forty-seven-acre compound and its various buildings. The place was low-key, concealed behind rows of trees, a fence, and nothing more than a single gate. There were no guard dogs or men wandering the perimeter with machine guns.

Even to the more discerning eye there was very little to see. The perimeter security was all microwave trip wires and heat sensors and miniature cameras. The system itself was automated, with a software program that could distinguish a deer from a man to limit false alarms. The bulk of the security was in the house. All the windows were fixed, bulletproof Plexiglas, and the interior had been demolished to the studs. Because of the lessons learned from overseas embassy attacks, the walls were now reinforced with ballistic fabric and the doors were all titanium, covered in wood veneer. The basement contained two holding cells, an interrogation room, and a panic room as a last and unlikely resort, should the security on the first floor be breached.

Rapp was in the study on the main floor, sitting in a black Herman Miller lounge chair. A man in an identical chair sat six feet away on the other side of the fireplace, asking questions and taking notes. The man, Dr. Lewis, was the resident shrink for the CIA's Clandestine Service. He had known Rapp for a long time. He adjusted his glasses at the corner and said, "Your wife."

"What about her?"

"How much do you remember?"

Rapp remembered all of it, or at least he thought he did. It was a strange process to relive it all for a second time, and it wasn't all bad. The good memories came back as well as the bad ones. Rapp recognized that might be a good thing to share with Lewis. To a certain extent you had to share with the man, or he simply deemed you unfit for the field, and the only thing more unnerving to a Clandestine officer than a therapy session was being confined to a cubicle at Langley. There was also a feeling of trust with the doctor. It was similar to the way he had felt with Kennedy when he'd awakened in the hospital. There was also a feeling that he was not typically a very trusting person.

"At first it was just the pain . . . the bad memories . . . the loss . . . the feeling that I would never be able to recover. It all came flooding back."

"And how did that feel?"

Rapp laughed defensively. "Like shit . . . how do you think it felt?"

Lewis nodded and scribbled a quick note. "No, I would imagine that was not an enjoyable experience." He stopped writing. "And then what happened?"

"The good memories came back. Meeting each other, dating, falling in love . . . that didn't take long, and then the wedding. We were really happy. I was really happy." Rapp looked into the fire for a moment and said, "I don't think I was ever happier."

Lewis nodded. "I would say that's probably true."

Rapp pulled his gaze away from the fire. "Did you know her?"

"I only met her once, but I've watched you grow up in this business. I did your original psych evals twenty-some years ago. I've watched you through the good and the bad and you definitely had an extra bounce in your step during the time you just described."

Rapp's gaze fell back to the fireplace. "In a strange way I want that again."

"What exactly do you mean?"

"What Anna and I had. I want to find that again. How have I been since she was killed?"

Lewis did not like vague questions. "Could you be more specific?"

"As a person, did I change? Was I the same? What was I like?"

"I would say your grieving process was not untypical."

"You're holding something back," Rapp said, putting a hard stare on Lewis.

Lewis thought of Kennedy and the way she described how Rapp could look right through her at times. "You were understandably angry."

"Violent?"

"Yes," Lewis said with a nod, "although violence is a part of this business."

"But I was more violent than before?"

"Yes . . . you lacked patience. Not that you ever had a great deal of it to begin with, but after Anna's death you seemed to lose any tolerance for dissent."

"Did it interfere with my work?"

Lewis thought about that for a long moment and then said, "As far as I know, it did not, but I think you should ask Irene."

"You're holding back again."

"There was some concern that you were growing a bit too reckless. Taking too many chances. Always pushing ahead even when it made more sense to pause and regroup."

That sounded familiar to Rapp. He remembered the rage, he remembered killing certain people and feeling satisfaction that the person would never take another breath. It was actually gratifying. Rapp had spent some time trying to remember all of the people he'd killed. It was like a photo album of assholes. The Who's Who of terrorists, assassins, arms dealers, corrupt financiers, and intelligence operatives. The trip down memory lane was devoid of guilt.

"Back to the good memories," Lewis said in an effort to steer the conversation back to a point of interest. "How did they make you feel?"

"Good." Rapp shrugged. "That's why they call them good memories."

Lewis laughed and scratched another note.

Rapp frowned as a distant memory came back to him. "Didn't I tell you once that I don't like you taking notes?"

Looking as if he'd been caught, Lewis set his pen down and said, "Yes, you did."

"And we came to some kind of an agreement."

Lewis nodded.

"If I would be more open, then you'd stop taking notes."

Lewis coughed slightly and then said, "That's correct."

"So what gives?"

"It's a habit," Lewis said sheepishly.

"Were you trying to test my memory?"

"A little bit."

After pointing at the note pad, Rapp pointed at the fire. Lewis tore out the top three pages and tossed them into the fire. "Now," Lewis said, "back to the good memories for the third time. Tell me about them."

"I was happy." Rapp got a far-off gaze in his eyes. "I remembered how close we were. How it was hard to be apart, and when we were together, we couldn't keep our hands off each other."

"And you remember making love?"

"Jeez, Doc," Rapp said, fidgeting in his chair. "Come on. Can't I keep some of this shit to myself?"

Lewis smiled. "Yes, you may. I don't need to know everything. It's just good to know that you're no longer repressing those memories."

"I did that?"

"Yes. I tried to get you to talk about her on several occasions, but you became so enraged that I had to drop it."

"Did I threaten you?"

The question caught Lewis so off guard, he began to laugh nervously.

"What?"

"Your mere presence is a threat to many people."

"And to you?"

"No." Lewis shook his head. "I've known you a long time and you've never threatened me, but you need to understand that you are very good at what you do and you have some anger issues. After your wife was murdered, there was a bit of fear that you had become more volatile."

Rapp didn't like that sound of that. "Like I couldn't control myself?"

"Yes."

"Did I ever cross that line?"

"Mmmm . . . no."

"But I came close."

"Yes."

This didn't sound good. "I think I need a drink."

"Why?"

Rapp grimaced. "I don't like hearing this."

Lewis took this as a good sign. Progress with Rapp was rare and should be celebrated. "I could use a drink as well. Come on . . . follow me."

The two men left the study and moved down the hall to the open living room and kitchen. Rapp was surprised to find Kennedy in the kitchen, a series of files spread out on the table in front of her.

Kennedy looked up and asked, "How's it going?"

Rapp shrugged, not feeling that it was his place to judge his progress or lack thereof.

"It's going well," Lewis said.

Kennedy could tell by the tone of Lewis's voice that he was sincere, which got her wondering. "How is his memory?"

"Good. A lot of things are coming back." Lewis grabbed a bottle of cabernet and started searching through drawers. He found a corkscrew in the third drawer and opened the bottle. He grabbed two glasses and held one up for Kennedy.

"Please."

Rapp had filled a tumbler with ice and was standing in front of a bar cart in the living room, his right hand dancing over the tops of the bottles. "Would one of you please remind me what it is that I like to drink?"

A look of distress washed over Kennedy's face, and she shared a look of concern with Lewis.

"I'm just kidding," Rapp announced. "Vodka, occasionally scotch or whiskey, gin and tonic in the summer, margaritas when I eat at a Mexican restaurant, a little high-end tequila when I'm south of the border, and I think I got sick on Campari once." Rapp started pouring some Grey Goose into a glass. "That was years ago, of course. I think it was Stan's fault."

"That's more than I knew." Lewis shot Kennedy a raised eyebrow.

"I do remember hearing something about you not being able to hold your liquor."

Rapp came back to the kitchen table and pulled out a chair. "I think my problem was that I was dumb enough to think I could go drink for drink with Stan." Rapp's entire body convulsed at the thought. "Not a fun memory."

"Speaking of memories," Kennedy said as Lewis handed her a glass of wine. "Thank you. Speaking of memories, how do you feel about Switzerland?"

Rapp took a sip of vodka and said, "Switzerland . . . nice country. Could you be more specific?"

"Banking . . . bankers, actually. Do you remember doing any business with Swiss bankers over the years."

"Of course. Herr Ohlmeyer and then his sons. This isn't about his granddaughter, Greta, is it?" Rapp had had a relationship with the woman years ago.

"No . . . not that I know of. Is there something you'd like to tell me about Greta?"

"Not very professional," Rapp said, shaking his head in disappointment.

"How's that?"

"Just because I had this little knock on the head, that doesn't mean you guys get to go on a fishing expedition through my memories."

"It was worth a try," Lewis said with a shrug. "I've never found him to be this cooperative."

"I agree," Kennedy said, as if Rapp wasn't present. "Is there a chance he'll stay like this?"

Lewis made a great show of pondering the possibility and then shook his head. "I think he'll be the same old combative, ill-tempered man he always was."

"His authority issues?"

"Can't say for sure, but it stands to reason that those will reemerge as he regresses to his old ways."

"You two are hilarious. Why don't we ever spend any time talking about your issues?"

Kennedy and Lewis looked at each other and at the same time said, "Because we don't have any."

As they laughed at their own joke, Rapp looked on with a deep frown. "Bankers . . . we were talking about bankers."

"Sorry," Kennedy said as she took a sip of wine. "Bankers." She set down the wineglass, grabbed a blue folder, spun it toward Rapp, and opened it to reveal a photograph of a man who looked to be in his mid-fifties. "Does this man look familiar to you?"

Rapp shook his head. "I've never seen him."

"You're sure?"

"Yes."

"Could it be a blind spot? Maybe it'll come to you later?"

"That's not how it's worked so far. When you show me photos or tell me something it triggers something that helps me remember. This guy," Rapp waved his hand over the photo, "there's nothing. No sense that I've ever met him or know anything about him."

"Interesting." Kennedy pulled the file back and flipped through a few pages. "What about these photos?" Kennedy laid out a photo of an office building and another one of a house.

"Nothing."

"He works at a second-tier bank . . . Sparkasse Schaffhausen, located in District Five, Gewerbeschule Quarter."

"I know where that is." Why do I know that place? Rapp asked himself. His mind was filled with visions of a dark street and a gunfight. "I think I killed someone not far from there."

Kennedy gave him a blank stare for a long moment and then said, "That's correct. Two people, actually. You killed them not far from there and then fled to the Gewerbeschule Quarter."

"I remember." Rapp grabbed the file from Kennedy and held up the photo of the banker. "Tell me about him."

"A Herr Obrecht. We don't know much about him. I've made a few discreet calls, but our people don't seem to run in the same circles as he does."

"Is this the banker who claims I'm stealing money?"

"Yes."

"And Rick as well."

"That's right. Director Miller showed me the affidavit. The banker claims to have met you twice and Rick on five separate occasions. Each time the man says the two of you converted cash into bearer bonds and placed them in a safety deposit box."

"And how did this Agent Wilson come across Herr Obrecht?"

"An anonymous tip."

"Come on."

Kennedy nodded. "I know . . . it's ridiculous."

"This is bullshit." After looking into his drink for a long moment, Rapp said, "Hypothetically, if I was going to steal money from Langley, wouldn't I be a little better at covering my tracks? I mean, we have five accounts in Switzerland that we use to fund various operations. Right?" Rapp asked, not trusting his memory.

"That's correct."

"So why use some second-tier banker who I don't know and can't trust?"

"I'm afraid that's a question we're going to have to ask Herr Obrecht."

The excitement on Rapp's face was obvious. "Please tell me we have him."

"We have him under surveillance."

"And?"

"Nothing so far, other than some contacts with a few unsavory types. In the world of Swiss banking, however, that's hardly an indictment."

"How about I go have a chat with him?" Rapp raised an eyebrow in anticipation.

This was the old Rapp. Extremely results-oriented and rarely willing to sit back and let things unfold. Kennedy was torn between letting him do what he was so good at and the potential fallout if things didn't go well. The FBI was firmly behind her at the moment, but with Senator Ferris lurking about, who knew what next week would bring? "If I send you, what are you going to ask him?"

Rapp looked at her as if it were a trick question. "How about why did you lie to the FBI and say that I did business with you, you piece of shit?"

Kennedy frowned. "Not very subtle."

Rapp looked at Lewis. "Was I known for being subtle before I hit my head?"

Lewis sighed and said, "I'm afraid subtlety has never been your thing."

CHAPTER 47

ISLAMABAD, PAKISTAN

I N the upper left corner of the fifty-inch flat-screen TV a single car passed through the main gate of Bahria Town. General Durrani took in a drag from his cigarette, ignored the anchor on Al Jazeera, and focused on the smaller picture. The next part of his plan was so ingenious that he had kept it from Rickman so he could see the man's shock and then admiration as the audacity of it sank in. He couldn't wait to see the surprise on his accomplice's face when everything was revealed.

Dr. Bhutani had arrived the previous evening, and after spending an hour with the patient Bhutani informed Durrani that his decision to call him had been the right one. Rickman had a 103-degree temperature, a ruptured testicle, severely bruised kidneys, four broken ribs, and a shattered left orbital socket, and those were just the most immediate concerns. There were too many scrapes and bruises to count, and Bhutani had no idea if any other organs had been damaged. The doctor was no fool. He knew the importance of Durrani's job and he knew his comrade placed an extremely high premium on secrecy.

So after finishing his examination, Bhutani said to Durrani,

"That man needs to be in a hospital. I don't suppose you will allow that?"

"No," Durrani offered brusquely. "And he doesn't want to go to a hospital either."

"State secrets?"

"Yes."

"You may trust me, as always." Bhutani then took a long moment to consider the care of this intriguing patient, whom he had already identified as an American. "Antibiotics will go a long way to making sure we nurse him back to health, but there are some things we must keep an eye on. If we cannot get the fever down with antibiotics then I'm afraid we really will have to move him to a hospital, if you want him to survive. Would you like me to quietly explore some options?"

Durrani frowned and said, "It is imperative that you do not speak to anyone of this."

"I understand." Bhutani placed a calming hand on the general's arm. "I will speak to no one, but I will see where we can take him if we absolutely have to. I have some ideas. In the meantime you will need to come up with an official explanation . . . a cover, I think you call it."

"I have already taken care of that," Durrani said with a wink.

"May I send a nurse over? Someone we can trust?" When Durrani hesitated, the doctor said, "It is essential that we monitor his vitals every hour until we think he is out of danger." Seeing that Durrani wasn't convinced, he added, "I know who I can trust. People who believe in what you are doing . . . in what we are doing."

Durrani weighed the need for secrecy against the possibility of Rickman's dying. He could always kill the nurse if he felt the need to, but if Rickman died there was no bringing him back. The nurse might also help avoid having to bring him to a hospital, which would be a very difficult environment to control. "Fine, but just one nurse. She can train one of my men what to do when she needs to sleep. She must never speak of any of this. Never."

"I will make sure of it."

Durrani then attempted to hand the doctor an envelope filled with cash. Bhutani vehemently refused, and when Durrani insisted, the doctor was insulted, telling Durrani that everyone must do his part in the defense of Pakistan, and that this was his contribution.

The nurse had showed up within the hour. She was an ugly, fat thing, and Durrani decided almost immediately that the woman would have to die. She had spent the night at Rickman's side, taking care of his every need and giving him the appropriate drugs and fluids as needed.

Now, Durrani snatched the handset from his office phone and pressed the Page button and then a second button for the guesthouse living room. After a series of long beeps, Kassar answered in his disinterested voice.

"The nurse," Durrani said. "Send her to the other guesthouse. Tell her to take a two-hour break and that you will come get her when you need her."

"Is your friend here?"

Durrani glanced at the security feed. "Almost. I don't want the nurse to see him."

"What does it matter? You are going to kill her anyway."

"She doesn't need to see this, and stop questioning my decisions. Just do what I say." Durrani replaced the handset and wondered if it was time to get rid of Kassar. The problem would be replacing the man. He was so good at what he did, Durrani doubted he could find someone to fill his shoes any time soon.

Durrani returned his attention to the flat-screen TV in time to see the black Range Rover pull up to his private gate. His men did a quick inspection of the vehicle by running a mirror underneath and then checking the trunk cargo area. When the vehicle was cleared, Durrani stabbed out his cigarette, stood, and walked down the long hallway, stopping just short of the foyer. After fifteen months of hard work, the decisive moment was upon him.

He looked at his reflection in a full-length mirror with a thick gold frame. After adjusting the black beret on his head, he adjusted his tan tunic to make sure all the buttons were centered. His left breast was covered with four rows of ribbons, and each collar had two gold stars in a sea of red. Pleased with his impressive image, Durrani moved to the front door and opened it in time to see his guest emerging from the Range Rover.

"Larry," Durrani yelled with a wave. One of Durrani's bodyguards was waving a black magnetic wand over his guest, more for show than anything. Durrani yelled at the guard, "No need for that. He's fine. Larry, come." The general stood, beaming with anticipation, waving his right arm for his American friend to join him.

The American was wearing a khaki suit with a blue button-down shirt. He walked casually across the stone courtyard with a warm smile on his face. "General, good to see you."

"And you, too, Larry."

Larry Lee was an American expatriate from Wichita, Kansas. He was an engineer who specialized in petroleum refineries. "I can't get over how beautiful your house turned out." Lee stopped and did a 360-degree turn, taking it all in.

"And your house will be just as beautiful."

"Not quite, but it is nice of you to say."

Durrani had purchased a smaller lot next door for Lee, his business partner. Lee had started building at the same time as Durrani but was still months away from finishing. Lee complained that the contractors took advantage of him, but Durrani had talked to the builder and found out that the engineer in Lee made it very difficult because he wanted to inspect and sign off on every piece of work.

The two men shook hands and Durrani said, "How long until your house is complete?"

Lee shrugged as if to say your guess is a good as anyone's. "They tell me two months, but I'll believe it when I see it."

"I will see if I can hurry them along," Durrani said with a wink as he grabbed Lee by the elbow. Whispering in his ear, he said, "There is something that I want to show you." He led Lee by the elbow into the house.

Halfway down the hall to the study, Durrani stopped and pressed the button for the elevator. Lee looked surprised. "The basement."

"Yes."

"Did you put in a pistol range?" Lee asked hopefully.

"No . . . I did not think of that." Durrani stroked his mustache and then laughed. "That is a wonderful idea. I will have my architect look into it."

They stepped into the elevator and Lee took the opportunity to lecture Durrani about the engineering of an indoor pistol range. Durrani couldn't get off the elevator fast enough. He'd had about all he could take of this condescending American. He showed him to the secure door and punched in his code.

"I didn't know you had tunnels," Lee said as he walked along the cement floor.

"I had them installed for security." Durrani continued the small talk until they reached the door that led to the smaller of the two guesthouses.

As they started up the stairs, Lee asked, "What did you want to show me?"

"These tunnels are very convenient. I think we should think about putting another one in."

"Between our two properties?"

"Yes."

"I never thought of that."

By the time they got to the top of the stairs Durrani was out of breath. Lee continued to talk and eventually got around to asking a question. Durrani held up a hand, signaling that he was out of breath, while his other hand searched for his pack of cigarettes.

"You know those things are going to kill you, right? As your business partner, I have every right to get on you about stopping. If you die, our partnership will go up in flames."

There were so many things that Durrani wanted to say, but instead he stuffed a cigarette between his two lips and nodded in agreement. Kassar appeared, standing at the edge of the sunken living room. "Vazir," Durrani said, "you remember Larry?"

"Of course," Kassar said with a nod of recognition.

Durrani took in several deep drags, which in a strange way seemed to settle his breathing. After exhaling a big cloud of smoke, he waved for Lee to follow him. As they walked down the hallway, Durrani began talking in a quiet voice. "What I'm about to show you is a real tragedy. I have another American friend, who was savagely beaten by a group of street thugs in Rawalpindi. I have arranged for him to recover here where he will be safe. It is embarrassing the way my countrymen treat our greatest allies at times."

"Not everyone is so rude. Your behavior alone, General, helps a great deal."

"Why, thank you." Durrani stopped outside the closed door and said, "Give me a moment alone with him and then I'll call for you."

"Of course."

Durrani slid into the room and closed the door. He approached the bed, still not used to the ugly sight before him. "Are you awake?"

Rickman was lying with three pillows beneath his back. He let his head fall to his left and said, "Yes."

"Good . . . I see you can almost open one of your eyes."

"The nurse has been making me ice it every hour. It's torture."

"But that's good . . . isn't it?"

Rickman ignored the question and said, "You're going to kill her, aren't you?"

"Why must you always assume the worst in me?"

"Because you have a history of killing people when they no longer serve your plans."

"Oh, that," Durrani said with a smile, refusing to let Rickman's sour mood spoil this special moment. "And you are such an angel, my friend. We both do what we must do. That is why we work so well together."

"The nurse?"

Durrani sighed. "What about her?"

"Why do you have to kill her?"

"Stop it. We have more important things to discuss. I need to show you something."

"What?"

"You will see." Durrani was back at the door. He opened it a foot and signaled for Lee to join him. He held his finger to his lips and said, "We must speak softly."

Durrani walked back to the bed with Lee at his side.

"My God," was all Lee could manage to say.

"I know . . . it's horrible."

"Kids did this?"

"I wouldn't exactly say that. Grown men, really."

Lee's face was a combination of shock and revulsion. "Who is he? Have I met him?"

"I'm fairly certain you have never met." Durrani looked at Rickman. "Joe, have you ever met this man?"

Rickman craned his head back and through a narrow slit in his right eye, he took in a blurry image of the man. He gave his answer through his swollen, Vaseline-laden lips. "No,"

"Was he in a bad neighborhood?" the Kansan asked.

"You could say that. That is why I've warned you that you must be very careful."

"This is horrible. Have you contacted the police?"

"No." Durrani shook his head. "We don't need to get them involved. My men will handle things."

"And his family?"

A devilish smile creased Durrani's lips. "Ah . . . like you, he has no family."

"Where is he from?"

"Denver, I think. Is that right, Joe?"

Rickman sounded bored. "Yes."

"Is there anything I can do to help?" Lee asked with genuine concern.

"As a matter of fact there is," Durrani said with a huge smile. He glanced over his shoulder and gave the signal to Kassar. Looking back at Lee, he made an apologetic face and said, "If you would die, it would be a huge help."

Lee's face twisted into a confused frown.

Kassar had put on his gloves while they were talking and had casually unfolded the plastic bag. In one fell swoop he pulled the bag over Lee's head and yanked it tight around his neck. Kassar had learned this little trick many years ago. The key was to wear gloves, because the victim always scratched and clawed at your hands. One time, though, a very uncooperative victim had been smart enough to shred the plastic covering his face. It had turned out to be an ugly, less-than-professional kill, as they ended up rolling around on the floor. Kassar had used the remnants of the bag to strangle the man but had not walked away unscathed. His slightly crooked nose was a constant reminder that he needed to continue to refine his craft. The trash-bag manufacturer Glad solved his problem when they came out with their tear-proof ForceFlex bags.

This particular American was easy to handle. He was neither violent nor physical, and all Kassar had to do was keep him from breaking some of the furniture. He kept a firm grip on the bag and danced the man around in the ample space between the bed and the door. The script was nearly identical every time: the wild arms swinging, the body twisting, both hands clutching to pry his hands loose, then one hand dropping as fatigue set in, and then the other until the victim was spent and simply collapsed.

Kassar lowered Lee to the floor gently, as if he was laying him down for a long nap. He knelt beside the body and kept the bag tight for a ten count. When he was confident that Lee wasn't about to jerk back to life, he yanked on the two red strings, tied them off, and stood.

"Well done," Durrani said with respect.

"Thank you." Kassar was pleased with his steady heart rate.

"What do you think?" Durrani said, turning to Rickman.

Rickman was no stranger to murder, but this little orchestrated event seemed particularly absurd to him. He stifled a cough and said, "I have no idea what you are up to."

"He is a gift to you. He is your new identity. Look at him." Durrani pointed at the floor.

Rickman didn't bother lifting his head. "He has a bag over his head."

"Hmm." Durrani rubbed his upper lip and then said, "Never mind. He is the same height as you and he has the same hair color. I found him over a year ago and made him a business partner on several very lucrative deals. I am building him a house on the property next to this one. It is beautiful. It is where you will stay."

Rickman's head hurt and he could sense that the OxyContin he'd taken four hours ago was beginning to wear off. "So I will assume this man's identity?"

Durrani clapped his hands together. "Exactly! You will have a life and you will be hiding in plain sight. The Americans will never figure it out."

"The plastic surgeon?"

"He will be here in two days."

The scope of Durrani's new twist was starting to sink in. "You will make me look like him?"

"Yes," Durrani said excitedly. "You will study his past. I have compiled a detailed dossier for you, with photographs and every imaginable detail. His parents are dead and his only relative is a sister in Hawaii whom he has no contact with. He is, what do you call a fellow American who leaves your country?"

"An expatriate."

"Yes . . . that is it. He is an expatriate. For the few people who know him I will let them know that he was set upon by thieves in Rawal-pindi and suffered a savage beating. It will explain your surgery and the swelling for the next few months, but best of all you will now have a past."

"A legend."

"Excuse me?"

Rickman was thinking. "In the business, we call it a legend."

"Yes . . . well, whatever you call it, this will give you more freedom, and if your former employers ever dig into your new identity, they won't find anything suspicious."

Rickman had to admit that it was a very good tweak to their plan. The plan had been for him to get a new face and take on a fake name. They reasoned if he kept a low-enough profile the CIA would never notice, but this was even better. "I must applaud you, General. This is an improvement."

"You are welcome," Durrani said with a short bow. Then, directing his attention to Kassar, he said, "Take him through the tunnels to the garage and then when it's dark out, take him to the incinerator."

"Hold on a minute," Rickman said with a sinking feeling. "I thought Vazir was supposed to be handling my problem in Zurich."

"He is. He will leave first thing in the morning."

Rickman was gripped with panic and began cursing himself for taking the pain pills. "I told you the banker had to be dealt with im-mediately."

"Calm down. Vazir needed to take care of this first, and now he is going to rid you of your problem."

"But I told you it had to happen immediately. If Rapp discovers him, we are going to have some serious problems."

"I have heard that Mr. Rapp has some other problems he is dealing with." Durrani sounded very pleased. "That information you sent the FBI agent has worked. The agent is running an investigation on Rapp. Now when Vazir kills the banker it will make Rapp and the CIA look that much more guilty. I have instructed Vazir to make the murder look sensational."

"Bad idea." Rickman suddenly felt as if he was dealing with an amateur. "If you want it to look like Rapp, put a single bullet in Obrecht's head."

"Front or back?" Kassar asked.

"Doesn't matter, just so long as Obrecht is dead."

"Nine-millimeter, .40, Sig, .45?" Kassar asked, wondering what caliber gun was Rapp's preference.

"For something close like this he'd use a nine-millimeter."

Kassar nodded with confidence.

Rickman was suddenly back in operation mode, wishing he was healthy enough to go along and direct Kassar and his men. "How many people are you taking?"

"I was planning on handling it myself. Smaller footprint. Easier to move."

That was how Rapp liked to operate. "And on the off chance you run into Rapp while you are dealing with Obrecht?"

Kassar's expression remained unreadable. "It depends on where I see him, but I assume I will have the advantage, as I know what he looks like but he doesn't know me."

A small laugh passed through Rickman's battered lips. "It doesn't matter. He will sense you. He'll smell you from a mile away. I can't explain how he does it. Must be some kind of genetic survival instinct going back to when his ancestors were running from dinosaurs and shit." Rickman wished he could use his old contacts to find out what Rapp was up to.

Durrani folded his arms across his chest and flexed his knees. "I think you give this Mr. Rapp too much credit. You have built him into some mythical character."

Rickman knew where this was coming from. "General, you are allowing your ego to interfere with reality. As much as I would like to see Rapp dead, I do not want your talented friend tangling with him."

The general snorted. "Nonsense." Turning to Kassar, he ordered, "If you run into Mr. Rapp I want you to kill him."

Kassar accepted the order with a nod even though he was fairly certain he would disregard it. It was easy to kill a common fool like the one who was now lying at his feet, but a man like Mitch Rapp was an entirely different matter. A man like Rapp would be aware and he would fight back. Kassar looked at Rickman and said, "Maybe I should bring some backup."

Rickman thought about that for a moment while Durrani stewed over the fact that his man was asking Rickman how to run his operation. Rickman slowly lifted a hand and scratched his chin. "I think that's a good idea. Probably three men."

Kassar turned to Durrani. "May I choose the men?"

"Yes," Durrani said, even though he didn't want to.

"And," Rickman added, "if you see Rapp I want you to think seriously about aborting the operation. Especially if you have already taken care of Obrecht."

"Nonsense," Durrani scoffed. "If you see Rapp, I want him dead. Do you understand me? I am sick of this man. Rid me of this problem and I will reward you handsomely."

Rickman was tired of all the bravado, and being relegated to the role of cripple only made it worse. Not being able to stand and argue his point was extremely frustrating. "Kassar, all the money in the world won't mean a thing if you're dead. Use your judgment and don't underestimate Rapp. The man's at the top of the food chain. If you have a clean shot and he doesn't see you, go ahead and try your best, but if he gets even the slightest whiff of you, you need to run." Rickman looked at Kassar through his slitted eyes. "You are a smart man, Vazir. You know what I'm talking about, don't you?"

"Yes," Kassar replied in his standard dispassionate voice. He did understand. Men like Rapp were exceedingly dangerous, not just because of their talent and instincts. The most impressive thing about

Rapp was that he was still alive after everything that had been thrown at him. "What about the assassin . . . Gould?"

Rickman had been wondering how to handle that problem. He knew a great deal about the man, but Gould had no idea that Rickman had maneuvered him into the time and place where he'd been certain the former Legionnaire would settle his score with Rapp. Somewhere, Rickman thought, he'd miscalculated, or possibly he hadn't. An idea suddenly occurred to him. To Durrani he said, "You told me you had General Qayem and his men on standby in case my assassin failed."

"That is correct."

Rickman sighed. "I should have known you would meddle in my plans."

"I have no idea what you are talking about."

"Yes, you do. You are so transparent. You were going to kill Gould when he was done with Rapp, weren't you?"

Durrani sniffed and said, "I did not want any loose ends. He was a loose end."

"And?"

"What do you mean?"

Pushing with his elbows, Rickman managed to sit up against the pillows. He was thankful that the pain was muted by the drugs that were still in his system. "If our partnership is going to work, you must stop going behind my back. Do you understand what you did? Gould is a professional. Obviously, he saw your men and knew that you were going to kill him, so the only avenue of escape that was left to him was to cross over to Rapp."

Durrani scoffed at the idea. "Nonsense."

"No, General, the only thing that is nonsense is the way you keep ruining my well-laid plans. You need to stop interfering, and there should be no more killing unless we absolutely have to."

"I kill to protect us. Our secret is too valuable. We must keep our circle very tight."

"It's a bad policy. Killing is not the solution to every problem. What are you going to do about Vazir when he gets back from Switzerland? Are you going to kill him as well?"

"He is too valuable," Durrani shouted. "I would never kill someone so loyal."

Rickman knew that Durrani had killed plenty of loyal people, but he didn't verbalize it. Kassar was listening to every word and he was no fool. The man had no doubt wondered when Durrani would tire of his services. "From now on, General, we need to consult with each other, or we are doomed."

CHAPTER 48

RAPPAHANNOCK COUNTY, VIRGINIA

STAN Hurley arrived a few minutes before eight o'clock. The looming subject of his terminal diagnosis was not discussed for the simple reason that the old cuss had already told Kennedy they weren't going to make a big deal out of it. He apparently mumbled something about the fact that we're all dying, some just a little sooner than others.

Lewis made shrimp fettuccini and spinach salad for the group. Over dinner Rapp continued to press Kennedy, Hurley, and Lewis about Rickman. Rapp remembered that Rickman had an ex-wife and a daughter whom he rarely discussed. In fact Rapp remembered only one time when he'd heard Rickman mention them. It was at an old Soviet base in southern Uzbekistan just after the Taliban had had their asses handed to them by American airpower, a couple of dozen U.S. Special Operations warriors, a few Clandestine Service guys, and a ragtag army of mostly Northern Alliance types. Rickman had been key in putting the whole thing together, and it was the first time since 9/11 that they felt like they had really hit back.

So it was time to celebrate, and with the Taliban in full retreat and running for the Pakistani border, the booze began to flow. Even back then, Rapp knew Rickman as a guy with a big brain who had a knack for putting together complicated operations while never losing sight of the various pitfalls. And he did it all with a calm focus on the endgame, something that was no easy thing, with so many moving parts and an uncooperative enemy. For reasons that Rapp didn't fully understand, that night, a sloppy Rickman decided to unload his personal problems on Rapp. Rickman had a wife whom he'd never really loved, and he was pretty sure she'd never really loved him either. They had a daughter who had reached her teens and hated her father for being gone so much, yet when he was home he couldn't get her to say as much as hello. It was all going down the tubes, and Rickman vacillated between thinking he should save it and being pretty sure it wasn't worth saving. It was a classic one-person devil's advocate, argued by a single drunken man for the better part of an evening. Rapp succeeded in changing the discussion multiple times, only to have Rickman steer it right back into the muddy ditch.

The next day it was not brought up and it was never discussed again. A few months later Rapp heard that Rickman's wife had filed for divorce. It was not an unusual situation. During the best of times the Clandestine Service was hard on families. It took a unique spouse to be able to hold down the fort while you were off advancing America's policies in the gutters of the world. The divorce rate was high before 9/11. After the attacks it skyrocketed. The CIA never stopped deploying, and the deployments lasted years, families suffered, and marriages fell apart. Now Rapp wanted to know if they'd ever had any discussions with Rickman about the divorce and the stress of his job.

Kennedy looked at Lewis and said, "We did have a discussion about bringing him back."

"I remember," Lewis said.

"It wasn't the divorce so much. Remember, we were dealing with a lot of those. We woke up one day and realized he'd been over there for six straight years." Kennedy looked as if she was reliving a mistake.

"I was in Kabul on business and sat down with him to see how things were going. He never complained. Not once."

"Never?" Hurley said in a doubtful tone.

"Never. He had completely immersed himself in the job. He was a walking encyclopedia of information about who was fighting for whom. It got to the point where JSOC wouldn't launch an operation without checking with him first. They'd bring him a name, sometimes a photo and a location, and Rick would say things like, 'I think you've got the wrong Mohammad. The one you're looking for is in the next village over.' At any rate, I sat down, did a review, and then offered him a promotion to come back to Langley. He didn't even consider it. Said his skills would be wasted at Langley."

Hurley shrugged. "He wouldn't be the first guy to think that."

Kennedy took a sip of wine and agreed.

"You could have forced him to come back," Rapp said.

"I thought about it, but when I checked with JSOC and some other in-country assets they almost had heart attacks. To a person, they said they couldn't manage without him."

"So your solution," Lewis said, "was to bring him back for two weeks of briefings."

Hurley scoffed, "Let me guess . . . you made him get on the couch with Doc here."

Kennedy shrugged. "Standard procedure. I make everyone do them. Even you two."

"A lot of good it did me," Hurley said sarcastically. Turning to Lewis, he quickly added, "Sorry, Doc. Not your fault. I'm pretty fucked up."

Lewis smiled. "No offense taken, and you're not fucked up . . . just complicated."

"No," Rapp said, "I'm pretty sure he's fucked up."

Hurley roared, "Well, if that isn't the pot calling the kettle black."

"I'm not saying I don't have issues." Rapp grinned. "They're just not as bad as yours."

"Easy, Junior. Give yourself another thirty years and we'll see how you're doing."

"We all have issues." Kennedy held up her wineglass and said, "Considering what the two of you have been through I think you're coping quite well."

Hurley and Rapp took the words with a silent thanks and then Hurley, ever impatient, looked to Lewis and asked, "So what did you find out when you got Rick on the couch?"

"Not much. We had only had two sessions. Each one about two hours."

"Did you get a sense that he was holding on too tight?" Rapp asked.

Lewis shook his head. "I didn't get a sense of anything. You guys," Lewis said, pointing at Rapp and Hurley, "are two of my more difficult patients. It took me years to earn your trust and you still will only crack that door a fraction. Rickman makes you two look like ideal patients. Have any of you read his jacket?"

Kennedy nodded while Rapp and Hurley shook their heads. "His IQ," Lewis said, "is 205."

Hurley scratched his cheek and said, "That doesn't mean jack shit to me."

"The highest in the building," Kennedy said, "by a good margin."

"The two of you combined," Lewis said, pointing at Hurley and then Rapp, "might match him."

"Doc, I'm sure he's smart as shit, but my experience with guys like that is that they don't cope real well with life."

"That's a fair point. There were a few things I picked up during our session. A potential sense of isolation, difficulty in dealing with people, especially those outside his immediate circle. As you said, coping issues."

"But," Kennedy quickly added, "coping issues are not unusual for our people when they've been abroad for extended periods of time. The two of you have experienced it many times. You come back after enduring some pretty hard stuff and you have no patience for people who want to complain about the mundane."

Actually, Hurley had a very low tolerance for people in general. "Any chance he went native?"

"We don't have even close to enough information to say that, but he definitely began to withdraw over the past year." Lewis was quick to add that he wasn't passing judgment on anyone. "Looking back on things, it's much easier to see a pattern. Sickles lost all control of him. It's almost as if Rickman had become Darren's boss, or at least stopped answering to him."

"Irene," Rapp said, "I really hope you hammer Darren. He's an incompetent ass and a damn embarrassment."

Kennedy was getting a lot of advice from a wide range of people regarding what she had to do in the wake of the disaster in Afghanistan. "We're debriefing him right now. I want to make sure I know everything he knows and then I'll make the decision on his employment." She didn't want the conversation to stray from the point, so she said, "Back to Rick . . . we don't have anything definitive, and I'm not sure we will, but I've got three of my best analysts going over everything. If he made a mistake they'll find it."

Rapp shook his head, as if he wasn't buying it. "They won't find anything. He didn't make mistakes. He always covered his tracks unless he wanted anyone looking to find something."

"Like the banker," Hurley said. He took a gulp of Jack Daniel's and added, "Is that guy on your approved list, and if he is, what in the fuck is he doing talking to the FBI?"

Langley had a list of private bankers they used to handle funds for black operations. The banks were spread around between Switzerland, Cyprus, Gibraltar, the Caymans, Singapore, and a few other places. The banks and the bankers were thoroughly vetted before they were approved for business. Kennedy was the only person in the building who had possession of the complete list. She shook her head. "No . . . he's not on the list."

"What about the bank?" Rapp asked, thinking that maybe Obrecht had spied on one of his colleagues.

"No. We've never done business with this bank or anyone who works there."

"And you've seen this affidavit?" Hurley asked.

"Yes . . . this afternoon. If we can believe Agent Wilson, and I'm not sure we can, Obrecht claims he did business with both Mitch and Rick. Helped them open several accounts and received deposits of several million dollars in cash. There's also a safety deposit box."

"Contents?" Hurley asked.

Kennedy shook her head. "It doesn't say."

"And, Mitch, you swear you've never seen this guy?"

"Never. I have no idea who he is."

Hurley looked at Lewis. "Could it be the head injury?"

"It's too soon to say, but his recall seems to be pretty good. We have yet to find an instance where once he's reminded of something it doesn't trigger the recall."

"I've never seen the guy, and besides," Rapp said, looking at Kennedy, "I've disclosed all my financials. You've seen how well my brother's done for me. I don't need to steal money." Rapp's brother was a brainiac on Wall Street and had taken Rapp's savings and turned them into a very nice portfolio.

"You better not have disclosed all your financials," Hurley said in his typical gruff tone. "Have you learned nothing from me?"

"Stan," Kennedy said in a chiding tone.

"Stan, nothing," Hurley shot back. "We're out there putting our nuts on the chopping block. We don't get any hazard pay. You know the rule: if we come across some ill-gotten gains along the way they go into our rainy-day fund."

This was all old-school. Kennedy hated it when they talked this way around her. On a certain level she understood where they were coming from, but it was something she could never condone. "This is the type of talk that gets a man like Wilson all lathered up."

Hurley slapped his hand through the air, rejecting the complaint. "We're not stupid. The majority of the stuff we come across gets kicked into the various accounts we're talking about to help fund these ops, but you can't begrudge my boys' taking a little commission along the way. It's the only insurance we have if we need to run."

"Well, you shouldn't need to run."

"That's bullshit and you know it." Hurley was getting angry. "Try to tell that to this idiot Wilson and that cocksucker Ferris. Shit." Hurley set his drink down and grabbed a pack of unfiltered Camels. As he lit the cigarette he caught the look of concern on Kennedy's face. Hurley exhaled a cloud of smoke into the lights above the table and said, "Listen here, princess. I have cancer. I'm going to die. A couple more of these aren't going to matter." Hurley took another drag and then felt bad for the rebuke. Kennedy was like a niece to him. "I've had an amazing life. No regrets . . . at least none that I'm going to tell this group . . . well, maybe I'll tell Mitch before I croak, but I don't want to see any long faces. We're all dying. The fact that I've made it this long is amazing." Hurley held up his glass. "To a full life."

They all touched glasses. Kennedy wiped a single tear from her cheek and laughed. "It is pretty amazing that you made it this far. You've been smoking those things for as long as I can remember."

"Before you were born," Hurley added with a wink and a swig of Jack Daniel's. "Started at fourteen back in Bowling Green." Hurley got a faraway look on his face as he thought of his childhood, stint in the military, and then the glory years of working for the CIA behind the Iron Curtain. He had lived a blessed life. He shook his head to clear his thoughts and said, "Back to this banker. I assume we're digging deep."

"I have Marcus on it, as well as a few other things. So far nothing to go on, but we do have something that . . . ah, is a little odd." Kennedy looked almost sheepish as she turned to Rapp. "Something we need to discuss, actually." She didn't know exactly how to do this, so she just said it. "Does the name Louie Gould ring a bell?"

The glass of vodka was half full. Rapp looked into it and for a moment considered throwing the whole thing back. Instead he pushed it toward the center of the table and said, "I remember him."

"You remember what he did?"

Rapp didn't flinch. "He killed my wife."

Kennedy swallowed hard and asked, "Do you remember what happened with him in Kabul?"

"That part's a little fuzzy. I remember seeing him right before all hell broke loose and then nothing."

Kennedy had been trying to figure out the odds of this strange coincidence. "Would you care to take a guess where Gould does his banking in Switzerland?"

"Herr Obrecht."

"That's right. He is Mr. Gould's private banker."

"You're shitting me." Hurley was out of his chair. "This whole fucking thing is really starting to stink."

Kennedy was used to this kinetic behavior. Hurley, like Rapp, was not good at sitting still for very long. She likened it to sharks that never stop moving. "Gould has other bankers that he uses, but Obrecht is one of his main ones."

Hurley paced to the refrigerator, exhaled a cloud of smoke, took a drink, and then came back to the table. "You know what this is starting to look like?"

Kennedy nodded. She'd thought it through.

"A well-planned, multipronged attack. Layered like the Russians used to do. Confusing as all shit until you got rid of all the deceptions and the feints and focused on their objective."

"And what's the objective this time?" Kennedy asked.

"The hell if I know. I mean we know, in a general sense, that this was designed to cripple us, but we don't know the specifics yet."

Rapp frowned and shook his head. A memory was coming back to him. A conversation he'd had with Rickman a long time ago. It was vague because Rickman had been talking so fast and flying off on tangents and then circling back.

Kennedy noticed the look on Rapp's face and asked, "What are you thinking?"

"Something Rick said to me years ago . . . probably fifteen-plus. I don't remember all of it, but it was about clandestine operations and how they should be set up and run on multiple levels. It was about recruiting high-placed assets. That it wasn't enough to just recruit them. To increase our chances for success, secondary and tertiary operations needed to be launched that would distract the watchers . . . the guys who would be keeping an eye on our asset to make sure he wasn't spying for the other side. He was very animated when he made the point that to increase our chances of success we needed to disrupt those people." Rapp's face brightened as it started to come back to him. He snapped his fingers. "His idea was to frame the watchers, for example, by making it look like they themselves were spies . . . set up real accounts in their names and if our asset was uncovered make the information public so the watchers would be distracted defending themselves. He advocated sleeping with the person's spouse and a slew of things . . . anything that would trip the watchers up."

"So you're saying that's what another intelligence agency was doing to us by using Herr Obrecht?"

"Possibly . . . they set up this bullshit story with this banker and they spoon-fed the info to the FBI to throw us off our game. And it almost worked. If Wilson had gotten a toehold, you and I and a lot of other people would be spending a shitload of time with the Feds right now, trying to prove our innocence."

"If your theory is right," Kennedy said, "then what's their endgame? What are they trying to distract us from? And what does a theory Rickman had fifteen years ago have to do with it?"

Rapp grabbed his glass of vodka and took a drink. He thought about the last week and its roller-coaster of emotions. The "oh, shit" fear when they'd found out Rick was gone, the horror and panic over the release of the interrogation clip, and the absolute relief many of them had felt when they'd found the camera and learned that Rickman was dead and his secrets were safe. That was the feint, Rapp realized. "You're not going to want to hear this again," he finally said, looking at Kennedy. "Like I said before, Rick's really not dead. They just wanted us to think he was dead."

"You have no proof . . . it's just your gut!"

"I told you already. I didn't buy the idea that the same people who hit the safe house could have accidentally killed Rick and then conveniently left behind that camera for us to find."

For Kennedy it was a frightening proposition. "Look, you know we've been taking your theory seriously, but remember, this is still all conjecture."

"Hunches are what make or break us in this business."

She thought about that for a long time. "You're right."

"Then I'd better get my butt to Zurich ASAP."

"Are you up to it?"

"I feel fine."

Kennedy looked at Lewis for his opinion. "Just don't hit your head," the doctor warned Rapp.

"Zurich's a safe city. I'll be fine." Looking back to Kennedy he asked, "Surveillance?"

"I have a team in place."

"How aggressive?"

"Not . . . I don't want to spook him."

"Good."

Kennedy glanced at Hurley. "You up for the trip?"

"Let me see. I can either stay here and listen to my oncologist try to talk me into taking rat poison, or I can go to Switzerland and beat the shit out of some banker. Tough call."

"Stan," Kennedy said in a tone that showed she was not amused.

"Of course I'll go."

"Good." Turning her attention back to Rapp she said, "One more thing. I want you to talk to Gould before you leave."

Rapp was caught off guard. "Why?"

"He knows something about Obrecht and I think he's holding back."

"And you think he's going to open up to me?" Rapp suddenly looked agitated. "I don't have time for this. I need to get my team in the air ASAP."

"Your team is already assembled . . . well, mostly assembled. Scott is handling something for me, but he'll be there by the time you're ready to take off."

Rapp frowned. "You spun up my team without talking to me?"

"I know this is hard for you to grasp at times, but I'm in charge."

Rapp didn't want to be in the same room with Gould. "So you're ordering me to talk to him?"

"That's right." Kennedy slid a file across the table. "Read through this quickly and then go downstairs and find out what he knows about Obrecht. There's also a USB stick in there. It has some surveillance footage Gould took of the area by the veterinary clinic right before the assault. I think you will find it interesting. You and Stan should watch it together."

Rapp didn't care about the file or the footage. "How rough can I get?"

Kennedy inhaled sharply and thought about it. "Use your judgment."

"And if I decide to kill him?"

Rapp's dark eyes gave Kennedy an unsettling feeling. He was her friend and at times it was easy to forget that at his core he was a killer. She cleared her throat and said, "I don't want you to kill him."

"Why?"

"For reasons that I can't explain right now. You'll have to trust me."

"Reasons you *won't* explain, you mean."

"However you'd like to take it, but it is worth reminding you two," Kennedy said, pointing at Rapp and then Hurley, "that you're not in charge. I'm calling the shots, and for now I say he lives. Are we clear?"

Rapp wasn't even sure he wanted to kill the man. His emotions were all over the board when it came to Gould and his wife and child. There'd been only a handful of times where he'd castigated himself for not killing Gould when he had the chance. It was Anna's memory that had kept him from doing it and he had come to terms with that strange twist of fate. That decision had been made with the naïve assumption that Gould would retire and take care of his family. Learning that the reckless idiot had squandered his chance at a second life had Rapp second-guessing his decision. Kennedy might be his boss, but Gould owed Rapp his life. *When the time is right*, Rapp thought, *I'll be the one to decide if he lives or dies.*

Rapp leaned back and crossed his legs. "For now, I'll do it your way."

"Good. Something that's not in the file . . . I placed Claudia and Anna in protective custody."

Rapp got that faraway look in his eyes. "Where were they?"

"New Zealand."

"How'd you find them?"

"She and I have stayed in touch."

Rapp was surprised and then he realized he shouldn't have been. Kennedy was thorough. "How old is the girl?"

"Anna is three."

The fact that the mother had named her after Rapp's deceased wife had screwed up Rapp's thinking in ways he could have never predicted. He had spent months tracking Gould and his wife down, with the absolute conviction that when he found them he would kill both of them without hesitation, and then when the moment finally came, and he confronted the mother and the baby girl, it all fell apart. It was as if his wife's soul had seized him and told him killing them would serve no purpose other than to orphan the baby girl. For a man who had spent more than fifteen years killing people it was the most foreign sensation imaginable.

"Gould had been hiding from Claudia the fact that he was still in the game," Kennedy said. "He's trying to act like he doesn't care, but deep down he's scared to death that she's going to leave him once she finds out. It will be your best source of leverage with him."

Rapp nodded but was thinking of his own ways to exert leverage. A gun to the fool's head just might be the simplest course of action. The only problem with that tactic, Rapp knew, was that once he got started he might not be able to control himself.

CHAPTER 49

AURORA HIGHLANDS, VIRGINIA

WILSON wasn't wondering if he was depressed; he knew he was depressed beyond any reasonable doubt. For the first time in his career he actually thought about sticking his service pistol in his mouth and ending his misery. It was a short-lived thought, as Wilson couldn't bear to think of the mess it would leave behind. And if he somehow screwed it up, which based on his current run of bad luck he would, there was a better than ever chance that he'd end up crippled in an institution for the rest of his life watching the world go by and not be able to communicate a single thought. No, Wilson decided, if he was going to commit suicide, he would take pills.

Ferris must have sensed his desperation, because he had one of his aides call to tell him that he'd meet him on their street corner at 10:00 p.m. sharp. Now Wilson found himself in the front hall of his house for the second night in a row, getting ready to do something he didn't like with a dog he didn't particularly care for.

He poked his head into the office and said, "I'm going to take Rose out for a walk."

Sally turned away from the computer screen. "Are you sure? I'd be more than happy to do it."

Wilson hadn't told her about his monumentally horseshit day. He couldn't bear the thought of her judging him. There would be so many questions. She had told him once not long ago that she loved him very much, but that he couldn't be right all the time. Any conversation about today's events would eventually lead to that place, and she would look right through him and ask how it was that Director Miller, who had a reputation as a fair and honest person, could be so wrong. And then she would dig deeper and he'd have to tell her that not a single person had stood up for him. She would seize on that as proof that the majority had ruled and he was wrong. Wilson could not take having that conversation, not tonight and probably never.

"No," he told her, "I need to clear my head."

"You've been awfully quiet. You don't want to talk about the meeting?"

"No . . . I need to sort a few things out."

"I'm always here if you want to talk." She stood, walked over, and gave him a kiss on the cheek. "You're a good man, Joel."

"Thank you. I'm lucky to have you."

"Yes, you are." She brushed his cheek with the back of her hand and then walked him to the door.

Moving down the front walk took great effort. It was if his feet were carrying him to a place he did not want to go. As they turned up the block, a gust of wind hit him the face and Wilson shivered, clutching at his jacket and turning his collar up. He felt cold and vulnerable, and he didn't like it. Rose led the way and Wilson followed at a sluggish pace. When he reached his corner he didn't even notice the Lincoln Town Car until the driver flashed his lights. Joel sighed and braced himself for what he assumed was going to be a lame pep talk from the blowhard senior senator from Connecticut. After opening the rear door, he picked up Rose under her belly and tossed her into the backseat. She and Ferris were welcome to have their little love affair.

Ferris grabbed the dog and pulled her onto his lap. He scratched her neck while saying, "I heard today didn't go so well."

Wilson tugged at his jacket. "It was a complete fucking disaster."

"Must you be so vulgar?"

"You have to be shitting me. You expect me to believe that you don't swear when you're angry?"

Ferris shook his head in a slow, disapproving manner. "There was a time, but I've learned it does no good."

"Well, *you* have a day like I had today and then you can fucking lecture me about swearing." Wilson looked out the window at the passing brownstones. "Do you know exactly how bad it was?"

"I don't have any details other than the fact that you've been placed on administrative leave."

"Do you know what that means?"

"It typically means that you continue to get paid while an independent panel decides if you've committed enough wrongdoing to be fired."

"Maybe in your normal government job, but not at the FBI. Administrative leave is a mark so black you can kiss your entire career good-bye."

"That's one way to look at it."

"It's the only way to look at it. Three of my direct bosses were in that meeting, and in their eyes I'm done."

"Well, they're not the only people who matter in this town."

Wilson balled his fists in frustration. "You don't get it. They've already determined that this bullshit with the Swiss banker is an attempt by a hostile foreign intelligence agency to destabilize the CIA."

"I don't believe that," Ferris scoffed.

"They sounded pretty convinced, and to really make sure I understood, they brought Kennedy into the meeting. Do you know what she did?"

"No."

"She pulled out a copy of my national security nondisclosure document and threw it in my face. Told me if I so much as talked to anyone about any of this she'd make sure I went to jail."

"She's bluffing. They're all bluffing because they're scared."

"Miller doesn't get scared. He's been running the FBI for four years, and he might be a lot of things, but a shrinking violet is not one of them. If he thought this stuff on Rapp and Rickman was legit, he would go after them until they were behind bars. He's seen something. Somebody showed him something that convinced him all of this information is bullshit."

"Probably falsified by Kennedy. She's not afraid to operate that way. How do you think she holds on to power?"

A thought slapped Wilson in the face, and he turned to Ferris and asked, "Where did you get your information about Rapp and Rickman?"

"From a very well-placed source."

"Sure you did. Who's the source?"

"I don't like your tone," Ferris said with a steely stare.

A crazy laugh rumbled up from Wilson's bowels. "That's the best you can do? You get me all worked up and I jump on this for you and now my career is in the toilet and the best you can do is tell me you don't like my tone? Well, fuck you very much, Senator."

The senator's face flushed with anger. He was clearly not used to anyone speaking to him in this way, let alone a public servant. "Joel, I can help you, but you need to trust me and you need to keep your calm. Good God, man! I thought you were a professional. This is the first quarter of this little game and you're acting like it's over."

"Well, from where I'm sitting, it pretty much *is* over."

"It is not, and get hold of yourself." Ferris tossed the dog back onto Wilson's lap. "I have yet to hold a single hearing. When I do, Kennedy is going to have to answer a lot of questions, and you will be my star witness. She will regret the day she threw that document in your face."

Wilson wrestled with the dog. "How can you be so sure?"

"As I've told you, I have my sources. You need to trust me."

Wilson shook his head. "You're going to have to do better than that. I'm the one drowning here, while you're sitting on the Lido deck sucking down some fruity drink. I need some reassurances. Part of my review is going to be a lot of questions about how I was pointed in this direction . . . questions that will eventually lead to you. At this point, if you want me to play ball I need some confidence that I will be proven right."

Ferris rubbed his index finger along his lips while he thought about it. After a few seconds he said, "I cannot tell you who my source is, but he is a very high-ranking government official of one our staunchest allies. Someone of impeccable character."

"Will this person testify if called on?"

"God, no. Don't be a fool. That's not how this works."

"So I'm the only person who's putting his career on the line? This other person gets to make accusations and play it safe?"

"Don't be naïve. This person would lose everything. He brought the information to me as a favor."

"That's not going to do me any good." Wilson was feeling more and more isolated. Rapp and Rickman and who knew how many other scumbags, and that bitch Kennedy, were all guilty as hell, but Ferris and this mystery informant weren't exactly exuding courage. "This is bullshit."

"Joel, I feel bad for you." Ferris recognized that he was in danger of losing Wilson. The same characteristics that had made him the right man to sic on Langley were now isolating him from Ferris. "But you need to hang in there. Very soon I will be in a position to put a great deal of pressure on Ms. Kennedy. Until then, though, I need you to do something."

"Why does it always involve me doing something for you? When are you going to do something for me?"

Ferris had had enough. He stared angrily at Wilson and said, "You need to snap out of it, buddy. You're acting like a baby. Stop feeling sorry for yourself. This is Washington. It's a tough place. What did you expect . . . that people like Kennedy and Rapp would quake at the sight of your badge and roll over?"

"No," Wilson said defensively.

"Then get your head in the game. I told you, this is early days and you are on the team that is going to win, and when we do, Director Miller and an awful lot of other people are going to have to kiss your ass and apologize."

Wilson liked the sound of that. "Okay, okay. What is it that you need me to do next?"

"You've heard of Darren Sickles?"

"CIA station chief, Kabul . . . I just met him."

"Well, apparently he's been recalled and Kennedy and Rapp are making his life miserable."

"And why should I care?"

"Because, apparently, Mr. Rapp made certain threats against Mr. Sickles's life."

Wilson was suspicious. "Where did you hear this?"

"Arianna Vinter from the State Department."

"I met her as well."

"Well, you should interview her. She said that Mr. Rapp was extremely threatening."

A scowl washed over Wilson's face. "Stuff like that is not easy to prove in court."

"I'm not talking about court. I'm talking about a public hearing on Capitol Hill, in my committee room with cameras and lots of press. You need to stop thinking like an agent all the time. We need to crucify Rapp in public. Paint a picture of an out-of-control sociopath who threatens, lies, and cheats to get what he wants. Once we do that, your legal case will fall into place."

Two blocks away Scott Coleman was sitting in the back of a black Honda Odyssey minivan. The bug had been easy to plant. A cable company uniform and a few dog treats were all it took. The little pooch was

not a guard dog. Even so, Coleman laced the treats with a mild seda-
tive, parked the van in the alley, dropped the treats over the fence, and
pretended to check the cable lines. After five minutes he entered the
backyard and greeted the dog with a few more treats of the nonmedi-
cated variety. He dropped to a knee, and while petting the dog, fixed
the bug to the collar.

A quick sound check with the men in the van verified that it was
working. Coleman and his men then left the area, knowing that Wilson was at FBI headquarters. When Wilson left the building shortly
after noon, a second team followed him home and was able to listen in
on the bug. Nothing of real interest was reported other than the fact
that the team thought they heard Wilson crying at one point. Having
lost men in battle, Coleman had no respect for a man who cried over
his own fuckups.

As the former SEAL listened to the dialogue between the senator
and Wilson, he nodded with the confidence that he was going to be
able to give Kennedy some actionable intelligence. If the senator was in
fact getting his intel from a foreign intelligence asset, he had recklessly
placed himself in a very precarious position. On top of that, they now
had his game plan. The man wanted to hold public hearings.

Coleman transferred the audio file of the conversation onto his
smartphone and placed it in an email marked Urgent and sent it to
Kennedy. He then asked the driver to pull over.

"Guys," Coleman said to his two men, "stay with them and email
me any updates."

"Where are you going?" the wiry tech asked him.

"Zurich. Keep sending me stuff. I should be back in a few days."
Coleman closed the door and jogged off in the direction of his car.

CHAPTER 50

ISLAMABAD, PAKISTAN

NADEEM Ashan had endured difficulties before, but none of them compared to what he was now going through. In the middle of dinner last night there had been a knock on the door. He had feared such an event all day, ever since a second video of Joe Rickman had been released. In it he had clearly implied that Ashan was an American agent. Ashan knew he needed to confront the lies, so he had gone directly to the director general's office to state his innocence and to offer his assistance in any way that would help disprove what was an obvious attempt at disinformation. Ashan could tell by Taj's tepid response that this was not a problem that would go away easily.

The rest of the day was businesslike. His counterparts both stopped by his office to lend their support. Durrani was confident that the accusations would be proven baseless. Lieutenant General Mahmud Nassir, the deputy director of the Internal Wing, offered his apologies that an investigation was necessary. Ashan and Nassir had never had a warm relationship, so the chilly meeting did not seem out of character.

At the sound of the knock, Ashan's heart sank. His wife had already spent much of the night crying, as she was friends with the foreign secretary's wife and had seen how he was dragged from his house. It was not a big leap to think that the same thing could happen to her husband. When he opened the door he was not surprised to see Lieutenant General Nassir, but he was surprised to see his friend Durrani.

Before Nassir could speak, Durrani stepped forward and said, "I'm here to make sure you are treated with the respect that you deserve."

Nassir remained as impassive as ever and motioned for his men to proceed. Ashan and his wife were put in separate rooms, and fortunately, Durrani went with Ashan's wife to comfort her, as she was not prepared for a lengthy interrogation. Three men plus Nassir accompanied Ashan into his study and proceeded to interrogate him for six straight hours. Despite being asked multiple times to not smoke in his house, the men ignored him. Ashan made a mental note that when this was all over he would make sure these three were punished for their brazen disrespect of his rank. Nassir, on the other hand, was hopeless.

If it weren't for Durrani, Ashan would have been a mess worrying about his wife. Shortly after ten o'clock his friend informed him that his wife had been allowed to go to bed. Ashan felt a bit of relief that they were being civilized with her, but that relief was short-lived. Durrani then informed him that Ashan's son and daughter had both been picked up for questioning. His son was a doctor in Karachi and his daughter an engineer in Islamabad. His son would be fine, but his daughter was an extremely attractive young woman, and the ISI was not known for its restraint.

Ashan looked daggers at Nassir and said, "I am innocent of these charges, and will be cleared. If my daughter or son are harmed in any way, I will make sure that your children experience the same degradation."

The threat probably had a fifty-fifty chance of working on its own, but then Durrani made sure it stuck. After unleashing a string of obscenities, he screamed a more vivid account of what he would do to Nassir's children and then threw a few threats at his three men for good measure. Of the three deputy generals, Ashan was by far the most civilized and Durrani was the least. Fearless in his attacks against Pakistan's enemies, he had a reputation for being ruthless that was well-known by the men of the Internal Wing.

Nassir promptly excused himself so he could go in the other room and make it very clear to his men that he would execute anyone who did not treat Ashan's children with absolute respect. A little less than an hour later, Nassir and his men called it a night. After Durrani's graphic description of how he would have each of them sodomized, repeatedly, the men seemed to have lost their zeal.

Ashan thanked his friend profusely for his support. Durrani stated that if things were reversed, he knew that Ashan would do the same for him. Ashan went to bed wondering if that was true. He held his wife and nervously waited for his children to call. His daughter called first and wanted to know what was going on. He told her it was all a misunderstanding and was keenly aware that the conversation was being recorded. It took almost two and a half hours for his son to call, and neither Ashan nor his wife slept while they waited. Finally, after reassuring his son that everything would be fine, Ashan fell asleep with his wife in his arms at four-twenty in the morning.

Two hours later he woke, shaved, and dressed for work. When he left the house he noted the cordon of military vehicles and wondered if he would be allowed to leave. An Army colonel approached and informed him that he would be escorting him to ISI headquarters. Ashan was gripped with an ominous feeling as he climbed into the back of the unfamiliar vehicle. In Pakistan it was a national pastime to assassinate government officials in their cars.

The drive to the office was fortunately uneventful, but the morning was not. Ashan arrived to find out that all three of his secretaries and two of his deputies had been arrested during the night. His office was crawling with Internal Wing types who were pilfering confidential files. This was more than the intelligence professional could take. He left immediately for the director general's office. Three assistants tried to stop him from entering, but Ashan pushed past. He opened the door to find Director General Taj, Durrani, and Nassir. The look on Durrani's face was not comforting.

"What's wrong?" Ashan asked.

"Please sit." Taj pointed to a spot on the couch next to Durrani.

Ashan remained standing. "There are men in my office. Men who are looking at classified files."

"I am aware of that. You need to sit." Taj pointed at the couch with his cigarette.

"Those men are not cleared to see those files," Ashan said as he sat. "It is a major breach of protocol." He looked at the other three men for some sign that they understood the enormity of the problem.

Taj looked at Nassir and gave him a sign to proceed. Nassir opened a gold file and held up a sheaf of documents. "Do you recognize these?"

"No."

"Are you sure?"

"Give them to him so he can read them," Taj ordered.

Ashan took the pages and felt his world slipping from him. He had never seen these pages before, but he was smart enough to recognize what they were. "These are not mine."

"Then why did my men find them taped to the underside of one of your desk drawers last night?" Nassir asked.

"They are not mine. How do I know that your men didn't put them there?"

Nassir looked to Taj and shook his head in disappointment.

"Director General, you have to believe me. I am not a spy for the Americans, or anyone else, and that is not my Swiss bank account. I have never seen those documents."

"But you do have a Swiss bank account?" Nassir asked.

Durrani intervened before Ashan could answer the question. "Who doesn't have a Swiss bank account? Let's cut through all the crap. We are all intelligence professionals. Every single one of us has at least one Swiss bank account. Those sheets mean nothing."

"I'm afraid it's not that simple," Taj announced. "The Swiss bank account we can handle. As Akhtar said, once you rise to this level, Swiss bank accounts are part of the job. But the American clandestine officer saying that you are a CIA agent . . . that is something that is not easy to undo, even if it is a lie."

"It *is* a lie!" Ashan protested vehemently. "I am not a CIA agent." Looking from face to face Ashan realized that none of them believed him. Even Durrani wouldn't look at him. "Akhtar, surely you don't believe that I would sink so low?"

"You're a better man than the three of us, and I think this all a complete fabrication, but," Durrani said, looking angrily at Taj, "I have no say in the matter, and apparently we aren't going to take the time to find the truth."

It didn't sink in at first. Ashan looked at Taj with confusion. "What is he saying?"

Taj leaned forward and stabbed out his cigarette. "The president called me just before you arrived. I'm sorry, there's no other way to say this. He wants you sacked."

The words drifted over him as Ashan attempted to process the finality of it all. His jaw hung loose and he asked, "Just like that . . . after more than thirty years of honorable service?"

"This is bigger than you . . . it's bigger than us . . . it's bigger than the ISI. It's my hope that you will be proven guiltless of all charges, but the president wants action now. We need to look strong. We cannot afford to look like America's puppet."

"At least let him step down on his own," Durrani said. "Let him make a statement. We could even spin it in our favor. He could say that for the sake of clarity he is going to step down. And then he can say something about an American plot to interfere with the sovereignty of Pakistan."

Ashan was having an out-of-body experience. He watched Taj shake his head and say, "The president is adamant. He wants him fired this morning. I'm sorry it has to be this way, Nadeem. For what it's worth, I think you are a good and honorable man. I'm sorry, but you and the rest of your family will be placed under house arrest until the investigation is over."

Ashan stood, without saying a word. He suddenly felt as if he was going to be sick. He left Taj's office to find a half dozen men in uniform waiting. Arguing would be useless. If the president were involved there would be no fighting his dismissal. He did not understand how his life had been so thoroughly upended. As he walked down the hall surrounded by the men, he told himself to remain calm. There would be time to figure out what had happened, and, he hoped, to discover who was behind this.

CHAPTER 51

RAPPAHANNOCK COUNTY, VIRGINIA

APP and Hurley reviewed the file. Nash, Schneeman, and Coleman had done the bulk of the interrogations, with Lewis providing a brief psychological evaluation. Gould had been very uncooperative, repeating the same things over and over and insisting that he was done talking to anyone other than Rapp. It was total bullshit. The two veterans could smell it from a mile away. Gould was weaving partial truths with outright lies in an effort to hold on to some negotiating chip. From Rapp's perspective none of it mattered. The only negotiating chip that would work with Rapp was the truth.

Unlike the transcripts, which were worthless, the surveillance footage of Rapp that had been shot by Gould before the assassination proved rather interesting. It took just two viewings for Rapp and Hurley to see what had spooked Gould. Someone with less field experience would have missed it. Hurley and Rapp were so attuned to the normal rhythms of a street that the two men jumped out at them.

Rapp took the steps to the basement and hit the buzzer on the metal door. They turned their heads skyward for the camera, and then when he heard the buzz of the lock Rapp opened the door. The room was rectangular, with two large viewing windows for each cell. Gould was in the cell on the left and the one on the right was unoccupied. Big Joe Maslick was sitting at the control desk.

"How's it going, Joe?" Rapp asked.

"Boring as shit. What's with the Zurich trip . . . did I get bumped?"

"Not my call, Joe. Sorry . . . Irene's running the show."

"Is it my shoulder?" Maslick moved his arm around. "It's fine . . . just a little scratch."

Rapp knew that wasn't true. Maslick had been shot at the veterinary clinic in Kabul. Kennedy had told Rapp the doctors were nervous that there might be some nerve damage, but they wouldn't know until he'd completed at least another month of physical therapy. The bigger concern was that his best friend Mick Reavers had been killed in the same attack. Lewis wanted to make sure Maslick was coping before they sent him back out in the field.

"You'll have to bring it up with Kennedy." Rapp took the file in his hand and pointed at Gould's cell. "What's he up to?"

"Nothing." Maslick rocked back in his chair. "He keeps asking to see you. It'd drive me nuts if it wasn't for the fact that the prick probably saved our lives."

"How do you mean?"

"For starters, he could have plugged you the second you stepped out of the vehicle, back in Kabul. After that . . . once the shooting started," Maslick said, shaking his head, "he kept those dogs at bay. If he hadn't been up on the roof with me . . . we would have been fucked."

"You been talking to him?" Rapp asked while he pointed at Gould, who was lying on his bed.

"No . . . not really."

"Keep it that way. What's the status on the video and audio?"

"It's on."

"Take 'em both off-line."

Maslick looked uncomfortable. "Sorry, but Irene said she wants everything recorded."

Rapp was pissed. "Come on!"

"She was adamant, Mitch. She told me you'd want it turned off and that under no circumstances was I to allow that. She also said you need to check your guns."

Turning to Hurley, Rapp said, "What the hell?"

Hurley offered a shrug and said, "Who gives a shit? So she and Doc are going to want to slice and dice your performance? That's nothing new." Hurley drew his 1911 from his hip holster and set it on the desk. "Let's go." Hurley motioned at Rapp to do the same and said, "Come on."

Maslick disengaged the lock and Rapp entered the cell, Hurley behind him. The interrogation table was bolted to the concrete floor, as were the chairs on each side. The bed was also bolted to the floor, and next to it was a toilet with no seat and a small sink. The floor was coated with three inches of black rubber to cushion any falls, and the walls and ceiling were covered in gray foam acoustic tiles that enabled the microphones to catch even the softest whisper.

Rapp set the file on the table and pointed to the chair on the other side. Gould slowly unclasped his hands from behind his head and sat up. "Who's that?" he asked, looking past Rapp.

Rapp didn't bother looking over his shoulder. This arrogant prick was still trying to act as if he was in a charge. Before Rapp could say anything, Hurley answered.

"Who I am is none of your fucking business. You need to be concerned about why I'm here."

Gould rolled his eyes. "Okay, why are you here?"

"I'm here to make sure he kills you this time, and if he doesn't I'll gladly step in and snap your neck."

"Yeah, right," Gould scoffed. "Give it your best shot, old man."

Rapp felt Hurley move past him. Gould was caught in a bad spot on the edge of the bed and underestimated Hurley's quickness. He was halfway up when Hurley smacked him in the jaw with a quick right hook. Gould fell back to the bed and Rapp saw Hurley turn back to him with a pair of brass knuckles on his right hand. Gould was half sitting against the wall holding his jaw. His eyes were closed tight, as he fought through the pain.

"You're not in charge," Rapp said. "So get your ass over here, or I'll let this old man beat the shit out of you."

Gould slowly made his way over to the table, working his jaw as he sat. "That was uncalled for." Addressing Rapp, he added, "That's the way you treat the man who saved your life?"

"Say what?"

"When I got to that building across the street and found out you were the target I could have taken the shot. It would have been easy, but I owed you. I could have run . . . I could have done anything, but instead, I chose to walk across the street and save your ass. And this is how you treat me," Gould said as he held out his arms and looked around the cell.

"Did you have backup for the operation?"

"Excuse me?"

"Backup. Were there people there to support you?"

"No." Gould shook his head. "I always work alone. You know that."

Rapp opened the folder and withdrew one photo and then another. He laid them on the table side by side. "You recognize these guys?"

Gould did, but he shook his head.

"Really? That surprises me. We got them off the memory card you had when we strip-searched you at Bagram." They were photos of two men, both talking on cell phones while manning their posts at each end of the block where the attack had taken place. Rapp laid a third photo on the table, one that had been provided by the Afghan Police. It showed one of the men lying on the ground with a bullet hole in his chest. Rapp made an educated guess and said, "You recognized this guy from your surveillance run and then when you were on the roof you shot him."

Gould did his best to show that he was unaffected. "You may think whatever you like."

"This is really a treat," Rapp said, smiling, "watching you sit here like you did the right thing when we all know you're a piece of shit. You didn't cross the street to save my life . . . you crossed the street to save your own ass. You saw the police show up and you realized you were going to be double-crossed. Your only chance of surviving was to come over and join forces with us."

"You have no idea what you're talking about."

Rapp picked up the three photos and replaced them with two new ones. He had used this trick before. Fathers and husbands were uniquely vulnerable when it came to their wives and their children. Rapp watched Gould. The only sign that the photos affected him was that he looked away after a few seconds.

"I gave you a second chance," Rapp started.

"And I gave you your life in Kabul," Gould quickly added. "We're even."

Anger in this line of work could be an asset as long as it was controlled. Rapp understood this as well as anyone, but this was an exception. This was more personal than anything he had ever dealt with. He made no effort to slow or curb the rage that came rushing to the surface. "You piece of shit. You think I'm that selfish . . . that just because you're so in love with yourself, I must be as well? You dumbass. I would have gladly given my life if it meant that my wife and child could have lived, but I didn't get that choice because you killed them." Rapp leaned over the table and drilled Gould square in the nose with his left fist. Gould's head snapped back, and blood began cascading over his upper lip.

Rapp walked around the table and punched him in the side of the head. Gould moved his arms and hands up to protect his face. Rapp grabbed him by the hair with his right hand and pounded away. "You selfish fuck. I gave you a second chance at life. I allowed you and your wife to live so you could raise that little girl. Do you know what I'd give to spend one more day with my wife?" Rapp stopped punching and yanked Gould's head back so he would have to look at him. "I never got to meet my kid, you idiot. I gave you life. You've spent three years with your daughter. I didn't get one fucking second." Rapp's left fist came crashing down two more times, the thin skin above Gould's left eye bursting. "What are you . . . some kind of a crack addict . . . you need the fix . . . you can't walk away?"

"You don't understand," Gould yelled back. "You're still in the game. You don't know what it's like . . . all of these idiots wandering through life. There's a fucking Walmart in New Zealand . . . did you know that?"

"What in the hell are you talking about?" With the realization that Gould might be nuts, Rapp let go. "You actually think we're alike, don't you?"

"More than you will ever want to admit." Gould took his shirt-sleeve to wipe the blood from his mouth.

"I don't get off on the kill. I don't take bags of cash to do my job. I kill bad guys like you because you not in it makes the world a better place."

Gould wasn't buying a word. "You're lying to yourself. No one can be as good as you and not love it."

"You're wrong. It's a job that I happen to be good at, but I don't get off on it like you do. I don't need the challenge. All I'm trying to do is rid the world of assholes like you . . . something I should have done when I found you on that beach. Do you realize the gift I gave you?"

Gould straightened himself and stared at the surface of the table, refusing to answer Rapp's question.

"You know what . . . they don't deserve you." Rapp walked back around the table and pulled out the photos of Gould's wife and daughter. He placed them directly in front of Gould and then while walking back around the table he drew a second, smaller pistol from the small of his back. "This is your moment of truth." Rapp pressed the barrel into the back of Gould's head.

Maslick's voice came over the speakers. "Mitch, the interrogation is over."

Hurley looked at the mirrored glass, knowing Maslick was on the other side ready to call Kennedy. "Put that fucking phone down right now, Joe." Now Hurley had a gun in his hands as well. "We're going to settle this right now. Either this piece of shit is going to tell us everything he knows, or we're going to execute his ass, and if anyone tries to stop us I'm going to put a bullet in his head."

Rapp forced Gould to look at the photos. "No more games. You either talk and prove to me that they matter to you, or I blow your brains all over those photos and you never see them again. It's an easy choice. What's it going to be?"

"I saved your life," Gould growled through gritted teeth.

"You saved your own ass."

"No, I didn't," Gould shouted.

"None of it matters, Louie. There's no negotiating. You either talk or you're dead."

"I want assurances."

Rapp let go of his hair for a second and slapped Gould in the head. "The only promise you'll get out of me is that I'll let you see your wife and daughter if you tell me everything."

"See them . . . that's not good enough. I want assurances that I will be able to return to my old life."

"As an assassin . . . Are you fucking nuts?" Rapp looked up at Hurley and said, "Can you believe this guy?"

"Don't waste any more time. Just kill him. We'll get Obrecht to talk. We don't need him."

"You're right." Rapp jammed the gun into the back of Gould's head.

Gould wasn't sure if Rapp was bluffing. The man had proven to be difficult to predict. All he needed to do was get through this and then he could negotiate with Kennedy or one of the others guys later. "Wait."

"No more waiting. I know what you're thinking right now," Rapp whispered. "'Is he bluffing or is he going to pull that trigger?' Well, all you have to do is ask yourself one question . . . If someone killed Claudia and your daughter, what would you do? You wouldn't hesitate, would you? The guy would already be dead. So if you think you and I are so much alike, then you know I'll pull this trigger. This is your last chance. We're all dying, Gould. Just some of us sooner than others."

CHAPTER 52

ISLAMABAD, PAKISTAN

DURRANI took no joy in watching Ashan fall. He was a good man and a good friend, but he was horribly misguided. For the ISI to forge a strong future for Pakistan, they could not afford to have someone so weak running the Foreign Wing. Durrani already had his replacement ready to go, a man who shared his zeal for the future of Pakistan. Ashan would survive. After a few months this would blow over and Durrani would do his best to make sure he and his family were treated with respect. He might even be able to arrange for him to keep some of the money in the Swiss bank account.

Durrani shook off the feelings of sorrow over what he'd done to his friend and turned his attention to Rickman. He was troubled by the man's discontent. He had worked hard to make everything fall into place. Only a fool would think that every aspect of the operation should work to perfection. Now should be a time to celebrate, not point fingers and blame each other for what had gone wrong. He recognized now that he might have been a bit aggressive in telling General Qayem that he wanted the assassin killed as soon as Rapp was eliminated, but his heart had been in the right place. The Frenchman's life meant nothing to any of them, and besides, his complicated history with Rapp would serve to further confuse the CIA.

Durrani was prepared to make amends to Rickman. It would be a gesture that would make his co-conspirator very happy. And then Durrani would make sure that Rickman understood that he still had to fulfill his part of the bargain.

The dog was an absolute monster. Durrani had directed the head of his security detail to buy three new guard dogs to help patrol the property. He specifically asked for Rottweilers. The head of his detail did not like dogs, nor did the rest of his men, so Durrani had to pay for a professional trainer to be flown in from Europe to teach them how to handle the dogs. The cost had been exorbitant, twenty-seven thousand dollars and counting, and one of his men had quit after he'd been bitten. Durrani complained openly about the dogs, but he had secretly grown to like them, due to both the fear they brought out in people and the way they jockeyed for his affection. They seemed to understand that of all the people who worked at the compound, Durrani was the one who was in charge.

One of the dogs, a fourth one, was not so cooperative. He was much bigger than the others, older and far smarter. He ran the show, and unlike the other three, this one made him nervous. Durrani had him on a choke chain with a long leash, but he did not use the choke chain for fear that the dog would turn on him and bite him in the groin as he had one of the guards. For this one it was all treats, no punishment.

The beast practically dragged him up the stairs of the guesthouse, and when they reached the main floor, the pudgy nurse took one look at the dog and recoiled in fear. Durrani ignored her as the dog sniffed his way down the hall toward the bedroom. Durrani didn't bother knocking on the door. He pushed through into the room and set the dog free. The beast leaped onto the bed and began licking Rickman's bruised face.

"Jax," Rickman said in a happy voice. He scratched the dog's neck and said, "Did you miss me? I sure did miss you."

Durrani could not stop himself from smiling. He hoped he could have the same special relationship with his dogs someday. "I'm sorry I didn't bring him by sooner, but caution is still imperative. That and I wasn't sure you could handle him."

"Handle him? He's as gentle as a baby around me."

"Yes." Durrani approached the bed. "He is much more cooperative with you than with my staff." The big dog lay down, his head resting on Rickman's lap. Durrani grabbed a chair, pulled it over to the bedside, and sat. "He makes you happy, doesn't he?"

"Very much. Thank you for arranging his disappearance and transportation. When they were beating me I wondered if I'd ever see him again."

"I am more than happy to reunite you." Durrani watched the dog and master for another moment. This was the first time Ajax had looked content in over a month. The timing, he decided, was right. He clapped his hands together and said, "Now, you have many stories to tell me."

Keeping his focus on Ajax, Rickman said, "Not yet."

Durrani's anger flashed, and then he got a grip on it. "You made a promise. I have arranged everything. You are safe in my country. I have even gone so far as to arrange a new identity for you. You must follow through on your side of the bargain. I want the names of the American spies."

Rickman stroked the large head of his Rottweiler. "When Vazir gets back from Zurich, we will see how things are, and then I will decide when and how I will begin sharing that information."

"That was not our deal!" Durrani shouted.

The Rottweiler's eyes narrowed, and he bared his teeth. Rickman calmed him and said, "The deal has changed. You did that when you decided to interfere with my assassin. Now we will have to wait and see."

Durrani was furious. "I could have you killed," he hissed. "Or better yet, I will nurse you back to health and have you beaten to a pulp again. How would you like that, you stupid American? You think you are so smart . . . well, you are not so smart. I hold all of the cards here. I am the one who decides if you will live or die."

The laughter hurt, but even so Rickman couldn't stop. When he finally caught his breath he said, "You think you have me by the balls, General?"

Durrani did not like Rickman's tone, but he was not about to back down. "I could have you killed right now."

"Yes, you could, and then in a month or so you would die as well."

"What are you talking about?"

"You are so naïve, General. Do you think I'm foolish enough to put my life in your hands and not have an insurance policy?"

"You are bluffing."

"No, that's not my style. I plan, I don't bluff. I have taken certain precautions. I've hired multiple lawyers and given them very specific instructions that if they don't hear from me at prearranged intervals they are to mail an encrypted file to Director Kennedy and a few other select people."

Durrani wanted to think it was a lie, but Rickman was devious and untrustworthy. "What kind of information?"

"Very detailed information that implicates you in all of this."

"What could you possibly be thinking? That is reckless . . . what if these lawyers take a look at the information?"

Rickman knew this would drive Durrani nuts. The specter of an unknown number of people possessing information that could expose him, ruin everything he'd worked for and probably get him killed, was too much to absorb for a control freak. It would likely keep him up at nights for years to come. If he lived that long. The important thing for now was to keep him as levelheaded as possible while making him understand that he did not hold all the cards. "It's encrypted, and don't worry, they are people I trust. They have no desire to look at the files. They know they contain information that could get them killed." Rickman scratched his dog's neck and said, "You have nothing to worry about as long as you honor our agreement."

"You are the one who needs to honor our agreement. The senator says he needs the information so he can move against Rapp and Kennedy."

That might have been true, but until Rickman was confident that Rapp wasn't coming after him, Senator Ferris would have to wait. "Let's see how things go in Zurich."

"You are a fool."

"Really," Rickman answered in an amused tone. "I think it is actually very pragmatic of me."

"I'm talking about giving such valuable information to people I cannot trust. It's foolish."

"It's actually very smart, although probably not all that smart considering your history."

Durrani shook his head and scowled. "What is that supposed to mean?"

"It's pretty obvious that you have a habit of killing the people you work with."

"That is an exaggeration."

"Not really, so the fact that I took a few precautions is just common sense. It's not particularly smart."

If Durrani had thought it would solve his problems he would have killed Rickman and his crazy dog, but he needed the American to complete his plan. It was time to change gears and find common ground. "Joe, you must understand . . . you are different. We have discussed this. You understand the stupidity of your country's folly in Afghanistan. You knew it almost from the beginning, but you did your job. You saw the people you despised become rich beyond their wildest dreams, all with American cash provided by you." Durrani pointed at him. "You fought valiantly and then you saw the light. America should not be in Afghanistan, and they most certainly shouldn't be giving money and weapons to the very people who are already turning against them. You saw the injustice and you took the money, but you needed an ally to help you disappear. I am that ally. Your dream could not have come true if it wasn't for me."

"General, I am not disagreeing with you," Rickman said, wondering why Durrani had to take everything so personally. "I am simply saying the timing isn't right. I'm happy to hear that we have a special relationship. And the best way to keep it that way is to make sure neither of us tries to bully the other into doing something that we do not want to do. Surely you must see that."

Durrani was not used to sharing power. He didn't like the lack of control, but until he could find a way to dismantle Rickman's network of lawyers, he would have to play this game. "I see your point," he said, even though he didn't. "But surely you can see where I am coming from. I have put a great deal into this, yet so far I have seen no return for my effort, and if we are to carry out the next phase of our plan and embroil the CIA in scandal, we need to begin passing your information on to Senator Ferris."

This was the one part of the plan that Rickman had never fully embraced. Senator Ferris was a windbag, and although Rickman felt strongly that America should not be involved in Afghanistan, the idea of Senator Ferris getting credit for America changing its policy turned his stomach. Now was not the time to discuss the senator, though. "General, I don't believe for a second that you have seen no return on your investment. I've heard the enthusiasm in your voice. You are very proud, and you should be. You have conducted one of the greatest intelligence operations of the modern era, and I have no doubt that when the proper amount of time has passed you will let the world know, and you will bask in the accolades of your countrymen. But until then, you may enjoy the knowledge, the extreme satisfaction, that you have outsmarted perhaps the greatest intelligence agency in the world."

CHAPTER 53

ZURICH, SWITZERLAND

RAPP'S anxiety increased as the heavy sedan climbed its way up the mountain road. Europe had become a major pain in the ass. Gone were the days when you could slip in and out of a country or a town without being noticed. Now there were cameras everywhere, even in the little hamlets that dotted the Swiss countryside. Customs and law enforcement databases were linked, and everybody was either online or texting or talking on an always available cell phone. Getting into a country like Switzerland wasn't necessarily the problem. Even killing someone like Obrecht was manageable. The problem was what happened in the aftermath. You left a digital footprint as you traveled, and investigators had gotten really good at assembling the puzzle and coming up with a suspect.

The fear of getting caught after the fact was very real, as the Israelis had learned firsthand when they'd sent a team of agents into Dubai to kill Mahmoud al-Mabhouh, a senior Hamas official. Customs computers and cameras, as well as hotel security cameras, had captured the entire team assembling for the operation and then leaving. The lesson was simple: Sneaking into a country to snoop and steal was still fairly easy, but once you started killing people you had better find a way to erase your digital footprint or you were going to have your photo plastered all over the BBC and every other twenty-four-hour news channel.

As a result, operations were increasingly complex. Instead of flying directly into Zurich and having to clear customs, the group landed at Ramstein Air Base, where the appropriate stamps were placed on their passports to make it look as if they had arrived in Frankfurt, Germany, two days earlier. Local assets then moved the group to a nearby private airstrip where they boarded a second jet for the short flight to Zurich. With EU customs already cleared, the group of eight deplaned at the private jet terminal and loaded their gear into two waiting BMW 7 Series sedans. Among them they had six assault rifles, twelve pistols, a pound of plastic explosives, and a wide variety of technical gear. None of it would have made it through normal customs.

The only security camera they spotted was at the gate, and the heavily tinted windows of their BMWs rendered it useless. It was Saturday afternoon, and the advance team had informed them after landing at Ramstein that Obrecht had left his townhouse in Zurich and had traveled to his estate near Lake Constance. They emailed aerial video of the place that had been taken by a small drone. Rapp, Hurley, and Coleman took a moment to review the footage, and none of them liked what they saw. Hurley was surprised by the size of the estate, while Coleman was worried about the number of men who appeared to be guarding the place.

For close to seventy years elements within the CIA had maintained a very good relationship with a Swiss bank owned by the Ohlmeyer family. After watching the surveillance video, Rapp said to Hurley, "I think you need to reach out to the Ohlmeyers and find out what they know about this guy. There's no way he's a simple private banker. If he owns a place like this he must own the whole bank, and if he owns the whole bank, what in the hell is he doing managing someone like Gould?"

The interrogation with Gould had been brief, due to the fact that they had to catch a plane, but they got what they needed in terms of Obrecht. Or at least that's what Rapp had thought at the time.

"I told you we should have brought him along," Hurley said, referring to Gould. "The little shit lied to us."

Gould had told them that Obrecht had been more than his private banker. He was also his handler, setting up contracts and negotiating prices with his prospective employers. "So he knows who hired you to kill me?" Rapp had asked back in the interrogation cell. Gould would not commit to that point, as Obrecht rarely met face-to-face with prospective employers, but he did handle the transfer of funds, which could likely lead to the person who had put the price on Rapp's head.

Rapp looked at the video of the massive estate. It had to be worth at least $25 million. He got the pissed-off feeling that Gould had played them. "There's no way this guy is just your average banker."

"Could be family money," Coleman suggested.

That was when Rapp put Marcus Dumond on the problem of finding out who owned the estate. Dumond, their resident computer expert, was not having a good day. He'd spent the majority of the flight trying and failing to hack into Obrecht's bank's computer system. Rapp had rarely seen Dumond so frustrated.

Rapp had come to the conclusion that Gould had likely lied to them. As to Hurley's point, that they should have brought Gould along, Rapp couldn't bear to spend another second with the man. He made him sick, and if Kennedy was serious about keeping him alive, she needed to keep them apart, because Rapp wanted to kill him.

Even though the prospects didn't look good, they continued on the second leg of the journey. They might not be able to get their hands on Obrecht while he sat behind the walls of his estate, but he couldn't stay there forever. On Sunday night, more than likely, he would have to make the return trip to Zurich. The winding mountain roads would provide the perfect opportunity for an ambush.

Rapp sat behind the wheel and Hurley was in the front passenger seat. Dumond and Hayek were in back, Dumond still trying to hack into the bank while Hayek tried to get a lead on Obrecht's mobile phone with a digitized scanner. Gould had given them a number, but so far they weren't getting a thing, which meant that either the phone was turned off or Gould had lied again.

They met the advance team on the outskirts of a small town called Engwilen. It was a male-female team, which Rapp was happy to see, as it was easier for them to blend in and look like a couple. They had made one pass by the main gate to confirm what the drone had already shown. Four men in dark blue SWAT uniforms were at the main gate, and at least one dog and his handler could be seen halfway up the driveway. Rapp watched the video they had taken and said, "It looks like a frickin' G Eight summit."

Rapp and Hurley stood around the trunk of the first BMW with Coleman and the couple and asked questions for another ten minutes. The entire thing looked hopeless. The couple said they were fairly certain the place had an advanced security system around the perimeter of the property and that they assumed the house would have one as well. Beyond that, they'd used the drone to count a total of eight bodyguards. How many more were in the house was anybody's guess.

They all agreed that the smartest course was to wait for Obrecht to leave the estate and take him on the way back to Zurich. In the meantime Hayek would coordinate with Langley to see if they could get signal interception on the house, and Dumond would continue to try to hack into the bank's secure server.

Coleman took his men into the town to scout things out and see if there was an inn without security cameras where they might be able to spend the night. Rapp and Hurley stood at the rear of the car, neither speaking for a long while. They were both in dark suits with lightweight overcoats. The temperature was in the midfifties, but the afternoon sun was making things warm.

Hurley lit a cigarette and exhaled. He tilted his face skyward and took in the warmth of the sun. "Do you know what's strange?"

"There's a lot of strange shit, Stan. You're going to have to be more specific."

Hurley opened one eye and squinted at Rapp. "I feel good."

"That's nice."

"I mean I'm at peace with the whole thing."

They didn't talk for over a minute and then Hurley asked, "You thinking what I'm thinking?"

"Yeah," Rapp replied. "But they'll have cameras at the gate."

Hurley shrugged. "Who gives a shit . . . I'll be dead in six months."

"Why do you keep talking like that?"

"Because it's true," Hurley said, as if it was the most obvious thing in the world.

Rapp thought about it for a moment and then said, "It might be, but—"

"Don't waste your breath," Hurley said, cutting him off. "You and I don't bullshit each other . . . let's not start now."

Hurley was right. They'd always been honest with each other, at least after the first year or two. Now wasn't the time to start denying the truth. Besides, it was his death. He could choose to deal with it in whatever way worked for him.

"All right, let's go." Rapp pushed off the car. "You have your Interpol creds?"

"Never leave home without them."

"Good. I'll text Scott and let him know."

They climbed into the car and Rapp fired up the engine. He slipped the car into gear and pulled out on the smooth country road.

"Where are we going?" Hayek asked from the backseat.

"Stan wants to knock on Obrecht's door."

"You're joking, right?"

Hurley shook his head. "I don't joke about stuff like this, princess."

"But . . . I thought we were going to wait for him to drive back to Zurich tomorrow."

"We could," Rapp said.

"But it might get messy," Hurley added. "I'm going to knock on the front door instead. You might be surprised how often it works."

"And if it doesn't," Rapp said, "it still might."

"How?" Hayek didn't understand anything they were saying.

"Spook him," Hurley said. "Right now he's comfortable, thinking everything is fine. We rattle his cage and he might turn that phone on that you're trying to get a line on. He might fly the coop; he might do anything that would be better for us than spending the night in some boring town and then finding out tomorrow that he doesn't travel by motorcade back to the city but takes a helicopter instead."

Hayek didn't have a lot of time to consider the new plan, as only a few minutes later they pulled off the road across the street from the main gate to Obrecht's estate. Hurley handed Rapp a set of credentials and checked to make sure his fake Interpol identification was in order.

Rapp looked out the windshield at the four bodyguards. "What do you think . . . rent-a-cops or the real deal?"

Hurley watched the men for a moment and said, "They look like the real deal to me."

"Me too."

"No sense in trying to bully my way, then. I'll make some easy conversation and then leave them a calling card." And with that, Hurley was out the door. "Wish me luck."

Rapp watched him cross the street. No one knew Hurley's exact age, but Rapp guessed he was in his early to mid seventies, although he knew he could easily be off. The man moved like someone twenty years younger but his face showed the wear of someone who had been through a lot of rough stuff.

"Dammit," Dumond barked from the backseat.

Rapp looked in the rearview mirror to see what was wrong. Dumond had attended MIT with Rapp's little brother Steven. The computer genius had run afoul of the Feds for hacking into some of New York's biggest banks. Rapp had Kennedy intervene on Dumond's behalf. Rather than go to jail, the whiz kid decided to come to work for Langley. Rapp had rarely if ever seen him so frustrated. "What's wrong, Marcus?"

"This is bullshit, Mitch."

"You still can't get in?"

"I can't even get close."

"Why?"

"These guys are using heavy-duty shit. Like the stuff the Chinese use, and our buddies out at Fort Meade—I'm talking cutting-edge stuff."

Rapp didn't know a lot about what Dumond did, but he tried to help. "Would it be better if you were back at Langley on a bigger computer . . . faster hookup speed?"

Dumond looked at Rapp's reflection in the mirror with a "don't even try to act like you know what you're talking about" look.

Rapp threw up his hands. "Just trying to help."

Dumond went back to hammering away on his keyboard. "The point I'm trying to make is that this isn't normal. The only people that pay for protection like this are people who are really paranoid, and I'm not talking paranoid for the sake of being paranoid. I'm talking paranoid because they need to hide some serious shit."

Rapp watched Hurley talk to the bodyguards, but was still thinking about Dumond's frustration. Herr Obrecht was turning out to be a far more interesting person than he had first thought. Rapp watched Hurley hand one of the men a card and jog back to the car.

"How'd it go?"

"Nice chap." Hurley pushed back in his seat and straightened his jacket.

"British?"

"No . . . he's one of ours . . . Green Beret. The other two are British, and I think the third one is Polish Special Forces."

"Who do they work for?"

"Obrecht."

"Directly . . . not Triple Canopy or someone?"

"Nope . . . Obrecht brought them on board a month ago."

Rapp thought about the timing. "Anything else?"

"Yeah . . . I wrote down my number on a card and told him to give it to his boss." Hurley pointed across the street. "Look, he's calling him right now." The guard had a handset in one hand and Hurley's business card in the other. "I told him to tell his boss that I needed to talk to him about Louie Gould."

Rapp was surprised. "I like that. If Gould was telling us the truth, that should freak him out."

"You think he'll call?"

"No." Rapp shook his head. "A guy like this will have his lawyers call Interpol and ask about you, and if you check out then he might call, but it's a Saturday, so the earliest we'd hear from him would be Monday."

"Yeah . . . I bet you're right."

They watched the bodyguards for another minute and then Rapp said, "I've been thinking. Marcus is having a hell of a time trying to get into the bank's server. He said they are using high-end stuff."

"Doesn't surprise me. These banks are security conscious now."

"This is different," Dumond declared from the backseat. "Not your normal stuff."

"My point is this," Rapp continued. "Obrecht seems awfully security conscious. Does he seem like the kind of guy who would sit down with someone from the FBI and willingly turn over private information pertaining to his clients' financial transactions?"

Hurley frowned. "No, he doesn't."

"This doesn't smell right. I think someone is jerking our chain." Rapp drummed his fingers on the steering wheel and was about to suggest they head back to hook up with Coleman when he noticed a dark gray Peugeot round the corner in front of them. As the vehicle neared the gate it slowed to a crawl. Nothing too unusual when you thought of the big ornate gate and the armed men standing in front of it. Rapp's window was down and he leaned over the steering wheel to get a good look at the driver and passengers. There were four of them, all with jet-black hair and dark skin. The driver had a thick mustache, but it was the man in the rear passenger seat who caught Rapp's eye. When the cars were almost level with each other, Rapp and the man in the backseat locked on to each other, and the expression on the man's face was one of both recognition and fear.

The other car was gone in an instant, and before Rapp could articulate what was on his mind, Hurley said, "What in the fuck are four rag heads doing sightseeing in the middle of Switzerland on a Saturday afternoon?"

Rapp wasn't sure the men were Afghanis, but he *was* sure the man in the backseat recognized him. Rapp pulled the gearshift into drive and checked his mirror. "Did you see the guy in the backseat?"

"Yeah . . . He looked like he saw a ghost." Hurley snapped his head around. "And they're not waiting around to talk. You'd better whip a U-turn, and step on it."

CHAPTER 54

RAPP pushed the car past 70 mph, popped in his earpiece, and called Coleman's cell. As it started to ring he rounded a corner and caught his first glimpse of the gray sedan. The sedan disappeared around the next corner faster than Rapp would have thought possible. They had to be going close to 100 mph.

"They're in a hurry," Hurley announced.

"You two have your seat belts on?" Rapp asked Hayek and Dumond. They both did. Rapp glanced over at Hurley and saw that he was not wearing his belt.

"Big deal," Hurley said in his angry voice.

"Yeah . . . I know, you're going to be dead in six months, but that's six months from now, so put on your damn seat belt."

"What's up?" Coleman's voice asked over Rapp's earpiece.

"We are in pursuit of a gray four-door Peugeot sedan. Headed your way. There's four guys inside . . . all late thirties or early forties. Looks like they're Afghanis or Pakistanis."

"They're Pakistanis," Hurley stated more forcefully. "I know my Pakis."

Rapp ignored him and focused on Coleman. "Are you at the inn?"

"Standing on the sidewalk in front."

"Get back to the car and get out to the other side of town where we were stopped earlier. The ditch on the south side has some good concealment. Put Wicker in there and have him shoot out the tires on the Peugeot when it clears the town." Rapp could hear Coleman shouting orders to his men.

"Scott," Rapp said, "they're coming fast. You guys need to really haul ass."

"We're on it. Already in the car and moving. Do you want me to stay on the line?"

"No, this road only goes to one place. Get in position and call me, and if you guys get in a shootout, don't kill all of them. We need to talk to a few of these guys."

"Copy. I'll ring you back."

Hurley pointed at the road. "You need to speed up."

"Scott's got things handled."

"What if he doesn't?"

"God, you're a pain in the ass sometimes." Rapp braked and turned the wheel, the tires skidding on the pavement. "You want me to end up in the ditch?"

"I just think you could go a little faster, that's all."

They were on a straightaway now and Rapp pushed the BMW north of 100 mph, only to have a car pull out of a driveway. Rapp swerved into the oncoming lane and slowed. Another tight turn was up ahead and there was no sign of the Peugeot. With each turn he expected to see the car smoking and wrapped around a tree. He didn't need to catch them, only stay close enough to drive them to Coleman.

Three hundred yards on the other side of town, right where the road began to curve north, Coleman pulled over and popped the trunk. Wicker jumped out and grabbed his shooting bag. As soon as the trunk was closed, the BMW took off and Wicker ran across the road, into the ditch, and up the other side. The mistake most people made with vehicle interdiction was that they set up too close to the road. Once you took the shot you then ended up with a five-ton vehicle careening toward you out of control. Wicker went to the edge of the trees, turned, checked out his spot, and dropped his bag.

The former SEAL sniper didn't bother with his camouflage netting, as the trees offered enough concealment. He set up his position against the base of a big pine tree, then marked two signs on the road and their approximate distance. As Wicker eased his eye into position behind the scope, he focused on his breathing.

Less than ten seconds later he heard the roar of an engine and popped his head up to see the gray sedan flying through the middle of town at an incredibly reckless speed. Wicker dropped his eye behind the scope and acquired the target. The guy was going too fast to allow Wicker to get off an accurate shot, but Wicker knew he would have to slow down or he'd never make the next turn. Almost on cue, the vehicle braked hard. Wicker sighted in on the front driver's side tire and squeezed off a suppressed round.

A split second later he heard a pop and then the sound of rubber shredding. The front left corner of the Peugeot dropped down and the back end began to swing around clockwise. Wicker grabbed his rifle and rolled behind the big pine. It was going to be close.

Kassar had been filled with a sense of dread for several days. The only reason he'd accepted the job to go to Zurich was that it would provide him with the opportunity to run if he finally made the decision. He no longer trusted Durrani. He'd seen him kill one too many people to tie up his so-called loose ends. Sooner or later Kassar was going to be one of those loose ends, and Durrani would replace him with one of his fanatical goons, like the three men he was working with today.

Kassar despised them. Durrani had found them in the tribal areas and trained them to carry out his radical plots. They were thoughtless militants who wavered between amazing acts of bravery and stupidity. There was not an ounce of finesse among the three of them. After the first pass of Obrecht's estate, the men unanimously wanted to wait until nightfall and storm the property. Kassar tried to explain to them that the odds of a successful outcome were close to zero, but they would not listen to him.

It was on the second pass that they found a big surprise. Kassar had learned that they liked to question his authority unless he invoked General Durrani, so he had told them upon leaving the embassy that Durrani had been very specific. If they saw Mitch Rapp they were supposed to abort the mission and get back to the Pakistani Embassy as soon as possible. When they made their second pass and he saw the BMW parked across the street, Kassar was curious. Then he saw Rapp behind the steering wheel. For once the men listened to him when he told them whom he had seen and that they needed to go as fast as possible.

For the first half mile it worked, and then Mansur, the self-appointed leader of the three, started talking about setting up an ambush. When Kassar told him no, Mansur wanted to argue and began asking for input from the other two imbeciles. That was when Kassar lost it and pulled out his phone. "I'm calling the general, you idiot. He gave us specific orders and now you want to argue with him." Kassar made a great show of hitting Send and then holding the phone to his ear.

Mansur tried to apologize, but Kassar was not interested. When Durrani finally got on the phone, Kassar filled him in on what was going on and then told him that the men he had sent were incompetent fools who should be reassigned to one of the suicide battalions that the Taliban were so proud of. When Durrani started asking too many questions, Kassar cut him off and told him he would call him back. He ended the call just as they raced into the small town, going so fast that they were out of it by the time Kassar could tell the driver to slow down.

He breathed a huge sigh of relief that they were back among the fields and trees. Kassar had just started to tell the driver to slow down when it happened. The car lurched, slowed suddenly, and then began to spin out of control. None of them were wearing their seat belts, and when the car came out of its first full spin it flipped, and Kassar found himself floating between the seat and the ceiling. Then the vehicle hit something incredibly hard and helicoptered upside down into the forest until it came violently to a stop between two trees.

Disoriented but conscious, Kassar began to feel his way out of the upside-down car. There was broken glass everywhere and he could already smell the petrol leaking and the burnt rubber of the tires. There were other movements inside the car. Unfortunately, the fool Mansur was still alive. The driver was motionless. The thought of Rapp in close pursuit drove Kassar to ignore the pain and move faster. He squirmed out of the vehicle, onto his back, and sat up. He immediately noticed his balance was off, but nothing appeared to be broken. Mansur and one of the other men got out of the car and wanted to know what to do. Kassar stood and looked down the road. To his left he noticed another car and some men with rifles. To his right he thought he glimpsed Rapp's BMW moving through the small town.

Mansur clutched his arm. "We should make a stand here."

Kassar shook his head and said, "I know what we need to do." He pointed into the woods, and when Mansur and the other man turned to see what he was pointing at, Kassar shot them both in the back of the head. He then dropped his gun, put his hands above his head, and walked back to the road.

CHAPTER 55

RAMSTEIN AIR BASE, GERMANY

THE Gulfstream G550 touched down after dark. The president had ordered Kennedy to meet with her counterpart in Pakistan to see if she could find a solution to the brewing controversy at the U.S. Embassy in Islamabad, where four Pakistani nationals were seeking political asylum after having been exposed by Rickman. The crowds were growing each day, the worst and most violent on Friday when a group of radical imams had led a march on the embassy that had resulted in three deaths and Pakistani security forces dispersing the crowd with tear gas and rubber bullets. The imams had promised to return and storm the embassy. Kennedy was to try to find a backdoor solution. If she failed, the secretary of state would be making the next trip.

The G550 was capable of flying nonstop from D.C. to Islamabad, but Kennedy had the plane diverted to Ramstein after Rapp told her what he'd discovered. Kennedy's plane came to a stop next to the other CIA G550, and as soon as the stairs were lowered, Rapp bounded up the steps with Hurley following. Rapp and Hurley continued past the director's security detail and her staff to the back of the plane, where they sat down with Kennedy. With the help of Hayek, Rapp had prepared a briefing folder for Kennedy.

Rapp handed it to her and said, "Look at this on the flight. It's information that you can use to make Durrani nervous, but I don't want you letting him know that we know he's behind this."

Kennedy took the file. "Are you sure he's behind it?"

"Yes. This Kassar is cooperating, and there is no way he could be making this stuff up."

"And he says Rick is still alive?" Kennedy asked.

"Alive and resting at Durrani's private compound. He's slated for plastic surgery on Monday."

Kennedy grabbed her forehead. "I can't believe this." Looking at Hurley, she asked, "Stan, do you trust this man?"

"I don't trust anyone except maybe you two, but he seems sincere."

"I heard he executed two of his own men in Switzerland."

"He did," Rapp said, "but they weren't his men. They were Durrani's, and he claims they were idiots."

"So he just kills them and I'm supposed to think that makes everything fine?"

Hurley and Rapp shared an awkward glance. "It's hard to explain, Irene, but I believe this guy," Rapp said.

Kennedy thought of what Rapp had said to her a few days earlier. "Do you believe him because you want to believe him?"

"That's not it," Hurley jumped in. "This Kassar tells a pretty convincing story."

"Irene," Rapp said, leaning forward, "he's the guy in the tape. The one who walks in and shoots the two guys."

"He told you that?" Kennedy asked in near total shock.

"Yes . . . he told us how he gave Rick a shot right before the final beating that would make it look like he was dead. They staged the whole thing. Including leaving the camera behind for us to find."

"And the beating was real?"

"Yep . . . It was Rick's idea. Kassar said he tried to stop it repeatedly, but Rick would not listen. He said the only way it would work was if they made it look real."

As Kennedy thought of the remorse and recrimination she'd felt over Rickman's beating and death she was dumbstruck. What kind of sick man would go to such lengths?

"And Hubbard was supposed to disappear as well," Hurley added. "It was part of the deal Rick set up. He had arranged for Hubbard to stay behind and feed Mitch the information about the dog and then they would sneak him out of the country, but Durrani thought bringing Hubbard along was too big a risk, so he had him killed and told Rick Mitch did it."

"And Gould?"

"Rick hired him," Hurley said. "Kassar said Rick was obsessed with Mitch. Said he kept telling Durrani that the only way this would work was if Mitch was killed."

"I don't understand."

"Apparently," Rapp said with no joy, "he thinks I'm the only man who ever really got him. Who understood how he thought."

"And," Hurley said, "he was scared shitless of Mitch. Kept telling Durrani that Mitch was the last man at the Agency. That if he had even the slightest inkling that something was wrong he wouldn't stop until he'd tracked both of them down and killed them."

"Which is exactly what I'm going to do."

Kennedy took in a deep breath and leaned back. She could tell by the look on both Rapp's and Hurley's faces that it would be impossible to dissuade them from killing Rickman and Durrani. At the moment she had no objection, but this could be a very complicated operation, one they might not survive. "Why do I get the feeling that the two of you already have a plan?"

"We're still working on it," Rapp said.

"I don't want to rush into this," Kennedy declared. "We should get JSOC involved and do this the right way."

"Irene, you know I love JSOC. No one is better than those guys, but that could take weeks to pull together. Rick can give away a lot of secrets in two weeks. Shit, he can give away a lot of secrets in two days."

"I don't like the idea of sending you two in to handle something like this. If anything goes wrong I won't be able to help you. Durrani is a dangerous man."

"Irene, look at the fallout after the bin Laden raid, and that was Abbottabad, sixty minutes north of the capital, and bin Laden was a fucking Saudi and the most notorious terrorist in the world. Durrani is a decorated Army officer and for all intents and purposes the second-most-powerful man in the ISI, and his compound is on the outskirts of the capital. You can't send the SEALs or Delta Force in there. We'll have a fucking war on our hands."

As much as she hated to admit it, he was right. "How are you going to do it?"

There was another sheepish look between Rapp and Hurley, and then Rapp finally said, "Like I said, we're still working on it."

"That's fine, but I want to hear the broad brushstrokes."

"When's your meeting with Taj, and can you get Durrani to attend?"

"Tomorrow afternoon at three, and I have requested that all three deputies attend, including Nadeem Ashan, who was fired yesterday."

"Good. It would really help if you made sure Durrani was in attendance. He knows three of his men are dead. We were listening when Kassar told him. He freaked out."

"Considering the importance of the meeting, I think I can make that happen."

"Here's what we're going to do. We're going to fly into Jalalabad and then cross into Pakistan via car. The checkpoints are way more lax than the airports. This way we can bring our equipment, and if Kassar makes one wrong move he's dead. I can't hold that threat over him if we fly into Islamabad International or Bhutto."

"How long is the drive?" Kennedy asked.

"Four hours, tops," Hurley answered, "I've done it many times. I also have a few guys in Peshawar who can facilitate the border crossing so things go smoothly. It's the Wild West. With enough guns and money, you can get anything you want."

"That doesn't comfort me."

"Irene," Rapp said, "this shit's never easy—you know that—but if there's ever a time where we need to act quickly, this is it. Durrani still thinks he's safe. We had Kassar check in and tell him that everything is fine."

Kennedy asked him to explain what they were going to do after they got to Jalalabad, and when Rapp was done telling her, Kennedy said, "I need to meet this Kassar before I sign off on it."

Rapp had expected as much. Kennedy followed him from one plane to the other while Hurley decided to stay outside and smoke a cigarette. Kassar was in the last seat on the starboard side of the plane with his wrists and ankles flexcuffed. He had a bruise on his forehead and some cuts on his arms and hands.

Knowing what his boss was thinking, Rapp said, "Those are from the car accident. We haven't laid a hand on him." One of Coleman's shooters, Bruno McGraw, was watching the prisoner. Rapp tapped him on the shoulder and told him to take a break.

Kennedy sat down across from Kassar and said, "Do you know who I am?"

"Yes, ma'am."

"How old are you?"

"Thirty-six."

"And you've worked for General Durrani for how long?"

"Five years."

"Why the sudden change of heart?"

Kassar took a moment to consider his answer. "The general has become a very reckless man. And he does not treat his people very well." Kassar looked up at Rapp.

"Go ahead," Rapp said. "Tell her."

"When he gets what he wants out of them, he has a habit of killing them." Kassar stopped for a second and then added, "And lately I've been the one doing the killing for him. I get the feeling he's running out of uses for me now that he has Mr. Rickman. I know too much . . . so he is going to get rid of me."

"Black Storks?" Kennedy asked, referring to the Pakistani Special Forces' nickname.

"Yes . . . seven years."

"And you were recruited to the ISI?"

"Yes."

Kennedy looked at his haircut and his clothes. His suit was torn and bloody but it was a nice cut. "Where did you grow up?"

"Karachi."

"Slums?"

"Yes."

"And the Army gave you a new life?"

"Correct."

"Religion?"

"Islam," Kassar said, without any passion.

"Not very serious?"

"No."

She wasn't sure if she could believe him even though he sounded sincere. "So what do you want out of this?"

Kassar looked nervously at Rapp and said, "My life."

"That's a good start, but you surely have other hopes and aspirations?"

"I don't think Pakistan is really an option for me anymore."

She understood. "What about America?"

Kassar got a faraway look in his eye. "America would be nice."

"And what do you think of Mitch's plan to go in and get Mr. Rickman and General Durrani?"

"Get them . . . you mean we are taking them with us?"

Rapp intervened. "She means kill." Rapp didn't want this any more complicated than it already was.

"I think it's a good plan."

"All right." Kennedy stared at him for a long time and finally said, "Vazir, I don't treat my people like General Durrani. If you do a good job on this, and everyone makes it out alive, I will make sure you are taken care of. I might even have a job for you, but only if you want it. If you don't, we'll set you up with a new identity and some money and you can start your life over. Does that sound good?"

"Yes." Kassar nodded. "It sounds very good."

"Okay." Kennedy pointed at the flexcuffs and nodded to Rapp. "No more need for these."

After Rapp had cut the plastic cuffs with his knife, Kennedy shook Kassar's hand and said, "Good luck, Vazir, I look forward to getting to know you better when you return."

Rapp followed Kennedy off the plane and walked her across the tarmac. They stopped midway between the two planes, where Rapp asked, "What'd you think?"

"It's impossible to know someone's heart after talking to him for a few minutes."

"Yeah, I know, but what's your impression?"

"I think he's worth the risk." Kennedy looked back at Rapp's plane and then added, "But if he makes one wrong move, if you get even the slightest whiff, I want you to put him down. Are we clear?"

"Crystal."

"Good." Kennedy kissed him on the cheek. "Good luck and don't do anything stupid."

CHAPTER 56

INTER-SERVICES INTELLIGENCE HQ, ISLAMABAD, PAKISTAN

KENNEDY entered Air Force General Ahmed Taj's office with Mike Nash, who had flown in from Bagram. She had briefed him on Kassar back in the embassy's secure conference room. Taj, Durrani, and Nassir were all decked out in their military uniforms, while Ashan was in a suit. Kennedy was pleased to see that Ashan was there, but noted that he did not look well.

The office was a grandiose affair, left over from the Brits, no doubt. It was easily four times bigger than Kennedy's. The walls and ceiling were paneled in a dark wood and there were three large stone fireplaces. Bookcases dominated every wall and there were two flat-screen monitors, one by the large conference table and the other one by Taj's desk. Taj and his three deputies were standing near the fireplace to their right. Kennedy walked over and said hello to each man.

When she got to Ashan she said, "Nadeem, I am sorry to hear of your difficulties. One of the things I would like to clear up today is your situation."

"It's a travesty," Durrani announced passionately.

Kennedy looked at the Judas to her left. She had had ample time on the plane to review the entire Rickman affair and analyze the various motives of Rickman and Durrani. As for Rickman, she had a few guesses about why he'd decided to become a traitor, but Durrani was clear-cut. He wanted Taj's job and he wanted Ashan and every other moderate out of his way. He would use Rickman's information to bolster his status, and within a year or two he would be running the ISI and all of its clandestine operations.

Taj stepped forward with a pained expression on his face. "Director Kennedy, I must caution you. Nadeem is only here as a favor from our president to yours. He no longer works at the ISI and has no official capacity here today."

"Yes, I find it all rather interesting. I think your intelligence agency may have been played the same way mine was, but we will discuss that later."

"Yes," Taj said, not having a clue what Kennedy meant. "Please sit." Taj directed her to a massive leather couch that could seat six adults. It was centered on the fireplace, with couches that ran perpendicular off each end. Durrani and Ashan sat on the couch to the right and Nassir and Nash sat on the other couch.

Taj asked Kennedy if she'd like some tea. She declined and withdrew a briefing folder, signaling to everyone that this was all about business.

"This problem with your embassy," Taj winced, "is very bad for our relations."

"I agree," Kennedy offered quickly.

"Then you should hand those four men over," Durrani said, as if it was the only option.

Kennedy ignored Durrani and directed her remarks at General Taj. "I don't like this strife between our two countries, but something is afoot here, and until we figure out what is going on, those four men will be afforded the safety of the sovereign territory of the United States of America."

Durrani laughed at the preposterous claim.

"General," Kennedy said, turning to Durrani, "surely you don't dispute the fact that the American Embassy is sovereign U.S. territory?"

"No, but I don't think the clerics will acknowledge the fact."

"Then why don't you explain it to them rather than use your political affairs officers to whip them into a frenzy?"

Durrani kept his cool. "I'm sorry, Director Kennedy, but you are misinformed."

"I don't think so, General, but you and I will agree to disagree, as we usually do." Kennedy opened her file and pulled out a series of photos. Like a card dealer, she tossed three sets on the table, one in front of Durrani and Ashan, the second in front of Taj, and the third in front of Nash and Nassir.

"You are all familiar with the abduction, interrogation, and murder of one of my men last week in Afghanistan?" They all nodded and Kennedy said, "A second attempt was made on the life of another one of my people. This was the episode in which twenty-one police officers were killed. It turned out they had been ordered to attack my men by General Qayem, who has since disappeared." Kennedy pointed at the photos. "These two men, one of them was killed in the attack and the other we are unable to locate. Do any of you recognize either of them?"

No one answered, so Kennedy said, "According to Afghan intelligence, these two men are ISI assets."

"What are you trying to imply?" Durrani asked angrily.

"I'm not trying to imply anything. I'm just trying to get some answers. Please, by all means show these photos around and see if any of your assets have gone rogue on you."

"This is preposterous," Durrani said. "You are merely trying to distract us from the fact that despite being our supposed ally, you hold four Pakistani citizens whom you have recruited to spy against us in your embassy."

"I'm not arguing that point, General, I'm just trying to find out who launched a coordinated attack against my Clandestine Service last week."

Durrani threw his hands up in frustration while Taj said, "I'm sorry, Director Kennedy, but we have no knowledge of what you are talking about."

"Maybe . . . maybe not. I have another interesting piece of information for you." Kennedy retrieved the copies of Special Agent Wilson's affidavits with Herr Obrecht. She doled out three sets of copies and said, "Have any of you heard of the Swiss bank Sparkasse Schaffhausen?"

Ashan's face lit up. "That's the bank where I supposedly have a million dollars deposited courtesy of your government."

"I thought I'd heard that. Well, apparently this same bank has accounts for the now deceased Mr. Rickman, and another one of my key people, even though I know for a fact that my people never opened any accounts at this bank, or I should say I know Mr. Rapp never opened an account at this bank, but I can't say the same for Mr. Rickman."

"Why is that?" Durrani asked.

"Because he's dead. I have no way to prove that he didn't." Kennedy turned her attention back to Taj, saying, "The point is, we think this bank has been used to make certain people at the CIA look corrupt when in fact they are not. This disinformation was passed on to the FBI in an effort to jump-start a criminal investigation against the CIA. Fortunately, other elements within the FBI believe this is part of the same plot that involved kidnapping Mr. Rickman and the attempted murder of Mr. Rapp. I find it more than a little strange that this is the same bank that Deputy General Ashan was supposedly storing his ill-gotten gains in."

"I've never heard of this bank." Taj said. "Have any of you?" The three deputies all shook their heads. "It is a rather strange coincidence. Why would someone want to frame Mr. Rickman, Mr. Rapp, and Ashan?"

"That's a very good question, General."

"Have you been able to talk to the bank?"

"No, we have not. I sent some people to Zurich late Friday, and they have had a very difficult time tracking down Herr Obrecht, the man whose name is listed on all three accounts." Kennedy paused and then added, "There was one strange development, however." She opened her file for the third time and pulled out more photos. "My people were parked in front of Herr Obrecht's country villa when a car with four men pulled up. The details are a little sketchy, but a chase ensued and then a gunfight." Kennedy tossed the photos of three dead men on the table. "A fourth man escaped and we were unable to track him down, but we have a good description of him. He had black hair, was dark-skinned, with dark eyes, and he, well—" Kennedy pointed at the photos, "he looked like these three men." Kennedy cocked her head to the side and asked, "What nationality would you say these men are, General Taj?"

The director general of the ISI scooped up the photos and stared at them while a layer of perspiration formed on his forehead. After several painful moments he cleared his throat and said, "They look Pakistani."

"And why would they be in Switzerland trying to talk to Herr Obrecht? Did you send men to talk to Herr Obrecht?"

Taj was embarrassed beyond anything he had ever experienced. "If you will excuse me, Director Kennedy, I think we will need to continue this tomorrow. I need to speak in private with my deputies right now."

"By all means, General. If you need me, I'll be at the embassy."

CHAPTER 57

BAHRIA TOWN, PAKISTAN

As Hurley had promised, the border crossing had been un-eventful. The two dusty, dented late-model Toyota 4Runners made their way through the mountain pass and down the A1, through Peshawar, and into Islamabad in three hours and forty-seven minutes. Rapp drove the lead vehicle, with Kassar in the front passenger seat and Hurley and Dumond in back. Coleman and three of his men followed in the second vehicle. Everyone was dressed in local garb. They were traveling with several hundred thousand dollars in cash, and if they were stopped they weren't going to try to get cute and claim they were working for an international aid organization. They were weapons merchants and they had plenty of samples to show any border agents or Army personnel who were interested.

As it turned out, they burned through just ten thousand dollars in cash, using Hurley's contacts at the borders. After that, they moved unmolested with all of the trucks that were busy carrying supplies back and forth between Pakistan and Afghanistan. They arrived in the nation's capital shortly after one in the afternoon. They had worked on the plan while in flight from Germany to Jalalabad. Coleman and

Hurley had gotten into a heated argument with Rapp over the plan, but Rapp had held his ground. Trying to get the entire team past the guards and into Bahria Town would raise too much attention. Kassar was adamant that this would not work. Hurley said that was bullshit, and Kassar spent the better part of a half hour trying to prove the unprovable.

Rapp, never known for his patience, finally put an end to it. The best chance for success was for him to be smuggled into the compound in the back of Kassar's Range Rover. The guards never searched his car. Wicker could take up a sniper position a half mile from the compound in the foothills just outside Bahria's fence line. Dumond could run aerial with one of the minidrones and the rest of the team would have to roll as a Quick Reaction Force.

When they picked up Kassar's truck in Humak, Hurley tried to state his case one more time. "Let me be the one who goes in."

"Why?" As soon as Rapp asked the question he knew what Hurley would say.

"I'm going to be dead in six months."

"Again with the six months? It won't work this time. I have a good handle on Kassar, and although you're no slouch I'm a little better at this stuff than you are."

"Bullshit."

"And besides, what happens if you have one of your coughing fits while he's talking to the guards? You'll probably need a smoke . . . that would blow the whole thing."

The old spook held up a pack of Nicorette gum. "Funny."

"Look at you. You're like a Boy Scout . . . prepared for everything." Rapp grabbed his gun bag and tactical vest and transferred them from the Toyota to the back of Kassar's truck.

"Why do you have to be so stubborn?" Hurley asked as a last effort.

"I think I got it from the dickhead who trained me." Rapp checked one of the pockets on his vest and then slid it on, saying, "Listen, we don't need to make this complicated. Irene has people watching Durrani. She's going to text us updates and you are going to give me radio updates," Rapp tapped his headset, "in case I'm in a spot where I can't look at my phone. There are two bodyguards at the compound when Durrani's not there. I can handle a couple of bodyguards who are bored out of their minds."

"But why not put another person in the backseat?"

"It's not worth the risk. They key is to get in without anyone knowing what's going on. Then it's easy." Rapp could tell, Hurley was still not buying his plan. "Just keep an eye on Durrani. If he comes back with more than the usual number of men, then you guys might have to bust your way through the secondary gate. Otherwise, I've got it handled." Rapp started to climb into the back of the Range Rover. "And remember, it's just like you said the other day. We're all dying." Rapp pulled up the tailgate and then reached up and started to close the back hatch.

Hurley put his hand up and stopped him. "What if Kassar turns on you?"

"I'll keep an eye on him." Hurley still wouldn't let go of the hatch. "Listen, I'm a big boy. I can handle myself."

The three-car convoy rolled out with Kassar in the lead. When they reached the spot in the foothills where Wicker should deploy, Kassar called Coleman and let him know. The Range Rover continued while the other two trucks pulled over. Wicker jumped out of the last vehicle covered in camouflage netting and disappeared into the underbrush. Dumond grabbed a case from the back of the truck and popped the clasps. The small drone was about the size of a crow. Dumond unfolded the wings, snapping them into place, and then started the prop. The gray device hummed to life, and Dumond let it fly, releasing it as if it were a paper airplane. The UAV dipped a few feet and then steadily began to gain altitude. It was on a preset program to climb to 5,000 feet and circle. Dumond stowed the gear and they all climbed back into the truck and moved out.

Rapp was on his side, curled up facing the back of the truck. He had already warned Kassar that, with all due respect, if anything went wrong at either the main gate or Durrani's private gate, Wicker would shoot him in the head. Rapp also showed him that the small drone would provide his phone with a bird's-eye view of what was going on. Rapp had his pistol in one hand and the phone in the other and watched as they pulled up to the main gate.

The black SUV slowed and came to brief stop before rolling on. Rapp breathed a sigh of relief as they made it past the first obstacle. It took another two minutes to make it to Durrani's private driveway. The guards waved Kassar through, making no attempt to search the vehicle.

"Show me the courtyard," Rapp whispered to himself. On cue, Dumond zoomed in on the common area between the main house, the garage, and the two guesthouses. A gardener was tending to some plants but other than that no one was about. As the vehicle pulled into the garage, Rapp slid the phone into his vest pocket, gripped his gun with both hands, and started his five-second count. That was how much time he had given Kassar from the time he parked the car to open the back hatch. There was a click and the hatch popped up. Light spilled through the two-inch gap between the rear cargo cover and the tailgate. Rapp could see Kassar and then he heard a voice.

Kassar began talking to someone Rapp couldn't see. After about ten seconds the conversation ended and Kassar lowered the tailgate. Rapp slid out of the vehicle but stayed in a crouch while Kassar closed things up. He then led him through the garage in the exact way he said he would. He opened a metal door at the other end and checked things out before continuing down a flight of stairs. Rapp was right behind him as Kassar punched a code into a door lock. Next they were in a long, well-lit tunnel and moving at a trot. They stopped at a second door and, after punching in a code, moved up a flight of stairs. Kassar had Rapp wait on the landing until he could get rid of the nurse.

Rapp radioed Hurley and told him he was in. A few seconds later he heard the nurse moving down the hallway and the front door clos- ing. Rapp came up the last flight of stairs, where Kassar was waiting for him. He pointed down the hallway and with a nervous look said, "He has his dog with him."

"The big Rottweiler?"

Kassar nodded.

This wasn't Rapp's first time dealing with dogs. His M-4 rifle was slung around his neck and off to one side while he gripped his suppressed pistol with both hands. Rapp checked to make sure his radio was in transmit mode and said, "You stay out here. Let me know if anyone shows up."

Rapp started down the hallway, moving silently to the door at the far end. Kassar had described the layout of the room, but Rapp had no idea where the dog was. He should have asked Kassar, and thought about going back for a brief second, but was too eager to push on. He opened the door with his right hand and stepped into the room, sweeping his gun right to left and back again. He heard the dog growl and placed his front sight on the beast's massive head.

"That dog fucking moves and he's dead."

A pale hand grabbed the dog's collar.

Rapp looked at the pulped face, and if it weren't for the fact that he'd seen the interrogation video he would have never believed it was Rickman. "You okay, Rick?"

Rickman couldn't manage to speak for a full five seconds. Then he began to stutter.

"Yes . . . thank god you're here."

"Shut the fuck up, Rick."

"It's just that I can't believe you found me."

Rapp's eyes continued to dart around the room, making sure he didn't miss anything. "I bet you're shocked as hell, since you hired Louie Gould to kill me and you used your fucking dog as bait."

"Mitch, I swear to you, this is all General Durrani. He abducted me, tortured me, and made it look like I was dead so you guys would stop looking for me."

"And then he gave you your dog back to keep you company. You are so full of shit, Rick. And too smart for your own good." Rapp kept coming back to the dog. There was no away around it. He had nothing against the pooch, but he had to go. Efficient as always, Rapp squeezed the trigger and sent a single bullet into the Rottweiler's head. The dog didn't make a sound.

But Rickman did. He was absolutely beside himself. "What have you done? Ajax hasn't done a thing!" Rickman screamed as he wrestled with the dog's lifeless body. "You're a fucking animal. God dammit!"

"And you're one sick fuck," Rapp said calmly as he approached the bed. "Your four bodyguards are all dead . . . one of them by your own hand. Mick Reavers, twenty-one cops, and Hubbard, and you don't shed a tear, but someone kills your dog and you finally show some emotion."

Rickman couldn't respond. He was too devastated by the loss of his dog.

"Any final words?"

"Don't do this, Mitch. I can help you. I can still help Langley. You can debrief me. I know things . . . very important things."

Rapp guessed that he probably did, but there was this little trust thing. Rickman and his big brain would be a nightmare for interrogators. Add to it the fact that his betrayal had gotten some good men killed, and the decision was easy. "Fuck you, Rick." Rapp squeezed the trigger once.

CHAPTER 58

DURRANI was temped to call the mullahs and the imams and order them to storm the American Embassy. He'd even gone so far as to wonder if he dare provide them with a photo of that bitch Kennedy so they could kill her for him. Ultimately, though, he knew he could not move. Taj was furious and he was bound to be keeping a close eye on him. After Kennedy and her man had left the meeting, Taj demanded answers. Durrani knew that the photos provided by Kennedy would be checked against ISI personnel records and eventually all five men would turn up as positive matches. That little fact wouldn't necessarily incriminate Durrani, but the fact that they were assigned to the External Wing would sink his career. And it would only get worse as they began to interview his deputies. Durrani was extremely hands-on, and his fingerprints were all over this mess.

So he did the only thing he could do and admitted to sending the men to Switzerland. "What were you thinking?" Taj asked.

"That my friend had been framed," Durrani answered, with all the sincerity he could muster. "I knew no one else was going to lift a finger, so I sent some men to talk to this banker."

The photos were still on the table and Taj said, "How did they get into a gunfight with the Americans?"

"I don't know."

"What type of men are these? What were they planning to do to the banker?"

The implication was obvious. Durrani had sent some knuckle draggers to rough up the banker. "They were good men. I only sent them to get answers." Durrani could tell that Taj didn't believe him, and Nassir seemed unaffected by the entire disaster. Durrani supposed he was enjoying the fact that his chief competitor had just shot himself in the foot and ruined his chances of replacing Taj. *Go ahead*, Durrani thought to himself. *Continue to underestimate me and I will make you pay for it.*

Ashan, for his part, seemed unusually cool toward him. Durrani would have thought that he'd appreciate the fact that he was trying to help him. The fact that he wasn't meant Ashan was beginning to suspect Durrani's real motives. Durrani couldn't get out of the director general's office fast enough. He needed to talk to Rickman. The two of them needed to figure out what to do.

Now, as his convoy reached the gates of Bahria Town, Durrani wondered if it might not be best to move Rickman to another location. There was a manpower issue at the moment, so security would be a problem, though. Even worse, it might further delay the moment when Rick shared everything he knew about the CIA. That was the part that infuriated Durrani the most. He could replace the men he'd lost in Switzerland, but he could not get the information out of Rickman fast enough.

The cars pulled into the courtyard and Durrani was out like a shot. Raza was waiting for him at the main door, and as Durrani walked past him he heard his butler say, "Kassar is back."

Durrani spun. "Where is he?"

Raza pointed to the smaller of the two guesthouses.

Durrani started back into the house and then decided he did not want to bother with the tunnels. Besides, it was time he took care of something. He marched back into the courtyard and yelled for his men to follow him.

Rapp was standing in the kitchen, watching the feed from the drone. In addition to the video, Hurley was on the radio acting as play-by-play announcer. When Durrani exited his car and started for the main house, Kassar explained that he usually entered the house and then came over through the tunnel. When Durrani came back into the courtyard and started gathering his men, the coms exploded with chatter.

"Everyone calm down!" Rapp barked into his lip mike. He swung his rifle around and handed Kassar his suppressed Glock 19. "Fourteen rounds left. He's on his way over with a half dozen men."

Kassar hustled across the foyer to the living room, where a magazine and ashtray were waiting for him. He sat on the couch and placed the gun close against his right thigh. Rapp retreated to the pantry on the far side of the kitchen and left the door cracked. "Everyone hold your positions."

"We're blind," Hurley announced.

"I'm fine. I'll call if I need help."

"It might be too late by then."

Rapp couldn't reply, because he heard the front door open and then the scuffle of shoes and boots on the marble floor. With his rifle gripped in both hands, he took a look through the crack. He counted six men plus Durrani.

"What in the hell are you doing here?" Durrani demanded. Rapp could see a pistol in his hand. "I told you not to come back here."

"I had no problem getting out of Switzerland. In fact the only problem I had was with those amateurs you made me bring along."

"They were good men and you got them killed."

"They got themselves killed."

"Do you understand the problem you have caused? I just left a meeting with the director of the CIA. She has photos of my men and she gave them to Taj."

"I told you not to send them. I could have handled it by myself."

Rapp watched Durrani raise his pistol. "I no longer have a need for you."

Rapp's right hand pulled the door open. His rifle came up as he moved to the left. The red dot found the back of the first man's head and Rapp squeezed the trigger. The spit of the round leaving the barrel was followed by the man's head exploding across the foyer. Before anyone could react, two more men were down. Rapp skipped Durrani and shot the next man. The last two men were reacting to the shock of their comrades' heads exploding before their very eyes. Their rifles were swinging in Rapp's direction, but not fast enough. Rapp shot the fifth man in the face, and just before he could take out the sixth man, a bullet whistled past Rapp's left shoulder. He pulled the trigger a sixth time and the man collapsed to the floor, blood flowing from the back of his head.

Rapp aimed his rifle at a shocked Durrani and said, "I'm clear. Six tangos down. Slick," Rapp said to Wicker, "anyone with a gun moves toward my position, take them out."

"How *dare* you." Durrani stood shaking in the middle of the foyer, six dead bodyguards at his feet. "This is an—"

Rapp had no desire to listen to any empty threats, so he lowered his rifle's muzzle and shot Durrani in the left knee. The general looked as if a puppeteer had cut his strings. He collapsed to the floor, landing in an ever-expanding pool of blood.

"I am the last man you should have fucked with, you stupid prick."

"You don't understand . . ."

Rapp stopped listening to Durrani as his team started chattering over his earpiece. It sounded as if Wicker was engaging at least one target. They needed to get moving, and Rapp didn't really care to listen to Durrani, so he raised his rifle's muzzle and was about to squeeze the trigger when Kassar said, "Wait."

Kassar stepped over the bodies and looked down at Durrani. "I always knew it would come to this one day."

"I was good to you," Durrani said, clutching his knee.

"You were just about to kill me."

"But," was all Durrani could manage to say.

With calm in his eyes and a steady hand, Kassar said, "I no longer have any use for you." He then sent a single bullet into his employer's head.

Rapp took note of the clean shot.

Kassar turned the pistol around in his hand and offered it to Rapp.

Rapp shook his head and started moving toward the staircase. "You keep it."

CHAPTER 59

AURORA HIGHLANDS, VIRGINIA

WILSON was feeling a little better. It was Monday night and his Redskins were up by seventeen points against their hated rival the Eagles with less than five minutes to go. In Wilson's opinion, there was no worse fan on the planet than a Philadelphia Eagles fan. They even managed to make Yankees fans seem like model citizens. Wilson took the Redskins' advantage as a sign that things were looking up. He checked his watch and finished his beer. It was time for another one of his late-night meetings.

He grabbed the leash and found the dog waiting at the front door, which he didn't like, as he didn't want the damn mutt getting used to this. His wife pushed her chair away from the desk but didn't bother standing.

"Isn't this nice? I love the fact that you two are bonding."

"Let's not go overboard here."

She stood and gave him a kiss, placing her hand on his stomach. "You're going to lose this little belly if you keep this up."

Wilson wasn't aware that he had a belly. He patted himself. "I have a gut?"

"Just a teeny one," she said, holding her thumb and forefinger an inch apart. She kissed him again. "I'm going to take a shower and then climb into bed with nothing on and wait for you to get back." She started up the stairs and said, "Don't be too long."

Wilson thought things were definitely looking up. The temperature had already dropped into the forties, and Wilson decided that he and Ferris were going to have to come up with a different way to meet. He was getting sick of walking this stupid dog in the cold night air. He took his usual route, wishing they could meet in an office on Capitol Hill. He stopped at the prescribed corner and checked his watch. He was on time. Thirty seconds later, he said, "Where the fuck are you guys? I'm freezing my ass off."

At the far end of the street he saw a man standing under a streetlight. A few seconds later the man made his way down the block. When he was within speaking distance, Wilson said, "You're late."

Darren Sickles looked over both shoulders and said, "I wanted to make sure I wasn't followed."

Wilson wanted to tell him that no one gave enough of a shit to have him followed, but he got the impression that Sickles had a very fragile ego, so he kept that thought to himself. The Town Car pulled up a minute later, and Wilson had Sickles get in first. It was a little snug with the three of them in back. Instead of waiting for Ferris to ask for the dog, Wilson simply handed him over again.

"Mr. Sickles," Ferris started, "Joel tells me you're not very happy with your current employer."

"No, sir."

Wilson looked out the window at the passing houses. "He said Rapp threatened to kill him."

"I'd prefer to hear it from Mr. Sickles, if you don't mind."

I'm just trying to speed things along, Wilson thought. *I've got a naked woman waiting for me.*

"Yes . . . he threatened my life, among other things," Sickles said.

"What else?"

"Pretty much every nasty thing in the book."

"When was this?"

"After Joe Rickman was kidnapped. Do you know who he is?"

"Most certainly."

"Well, Rapp blamed me for that . . . said I was drinking the administration's Kool-Aid on reintegration."

Ferris smiled. He couldn't wait to get Sickles to give this answer under oath in front of all the cameras. "But most important, he threatened your life?"

"Yes."

"And what are your feelings about the missing funds?"

"With Rapp and Rickman, you mean?"

"Yes—and anyone else at the CIA."

"The Clandestine Service, in my opinion, is rife with corruption, and Rapp and Rickman are the poster boys for what is wrong with the place. That's why Rickman was taken. But no one wants to talk about how corrupt he was."

Ferris nodded as if he understood all of Sickles's frustrations. "I'm about to announce hearings into this mess . . . probably Wednesday. I might have to compel you to testify. Can you assure me that you will give these same answers when I put you under oath?"

Sickles thought about it for a long moment. "My career is basically over . . . Why not?"

"This is about doing the right thing." Ferris searched Sickles's eyes for a sense of commitment. "I can protect you from them. As chairman of the Judiciary Committee, I can help clean out the rat's nest."

Sickles liked the sound of that. "Okay. I'll testify."

"Good. Now before I announce things on Wednesday, I want you to reach out to Arianna Vinter and Colonel Poole and see if they will corroborate your statements. I understand Rapp was very rude to them during his most recent visit to . . ." Ferris stopped speaking when he heard the sirens. Flashing red and blue lights were bouncing off the windows. The Town Car lurched to a sudden stop and then the doors were opened. Wilson was ripped from the car and thrown to the pavement, as was Sickles. Both men had their arms wrenched behind their backs and cuffed. Sickles was silent, but not Wilson. He was arguing like a madman about his rights.

A man in a dark suit and a dark trench coat approached Ferris's open door. "Senator, please get out of the car."

"And if I don't want to?"

Rapp bent over and showed his face. "Then I'll gladly drag your ass from the vehicle and cuff you."

Ferris sighed and got out of the car. "I know who you are," he said to Rapp. "You have no right to arrest me."

"You're right, but he does." Rapp pointed at FBI Director Miller, who was standing next to a black Suburban, keeping a close eye on things. "If you'd like, you can deal with him, but then everything gets real official and the press will get involved, and based on what I've seen, you really don't want to go that route."

Coleman stepped in and took the dog from the senator. As he walked away, he removed the bug he'd placed there the previous week.

"This way, Senator," Rapp said as he led the man toward Kennedy's waiting Suburban. Ferris joined Kennedy in the backseat and Rapp got into the front passenger seat.

"I don't want you to speak, Senator," said Kennedy. "We have recordings of your little meetings with Agent Wilson."

"Hardly a crime."

"I said, don't speak. Earlier this evening, we confiscated your maid's laptop, which contains some very incriminating emails between you and General Durrani of the Pakistani ISI. By the way, did you know he was shot and killed in his house yesterday?" Kennedy could tell by the surprised look on the senator's face that he had not heard. "Do you know what else they found in his house? No? Well, it's not good. The body of one of my Clandestine Service officers, Joe Rickman. I think you've heard of him. Apparently, General Durrani was behind the kidnapping and was torturing him for information that he was going to use against the United States.

"Now, as this starts to sink in, Senator, I want you to think of two paths. One will involve a great deal of embarrassment and an extremely public trial for treason. None of your colleagues will support you, because I will show them the information I have and you will be completely toxic to them. You will probably be spared execution, since we no longer have the stomach for that anymore, but you will most certainly go to jail, and I will make sure it is the kind of jail that a scumbag like you deserves. The second path you may choose is to show up in my office tomorrow morning at nine a.m. sharp, where you will be debriefed. You may keep your job and your chairmanship and despite your hatred of the CIA you will become one of our most valuable allies of the CIA on Capitol Hill. Do you understand your two options?"

Ferris swallowed hard and said, "I do."

Kennedy looked at her watch and said, "All right. You have ten seconds to decide."

There was only one valid option for a man like Ferris. "I'll take option number two." Maybe later he could figure out a way to undo this mess.

"Good," Kennedy said. "I'll see you at nine tomorrow morning."

Rapp opened the door for Ferris, and when they were a few feet away from the Suburban, Rapp grabbed him by the arm and said, "There is a third option."

"What's that?"

"I sneak into your house in the middle of the night and I snap your neck." Rapp stared at Ferris for an uncomfortably long moment and then said, "Good night, Senator." Rapp walked back to the SUV and climbed into the backseat.

As they were driving away, Kennedy asked, "You still don't like it, do you?"

Rapp rubbed his eyes. "I would prefer to kill him."

"I know that's your default switch for every problem, but sometimes it's a little more complicated than that."

"I know. We avoid all the publicity and we now own the chairman of one of the most powerful committees in town."

They drove in silence for a few blocks, and then Kennedy said, "We have one problem."

Rapp was staring at his iPhone, checking emails. "We have lots of problems."

"What do you want to do with Gould?"

"I didn't think my opinion mattered."

"Don't get all sensitive on me. It doesn't suit you well. You know your opinion matters."

Rapp thought about it for a second and said, "You know what . . . I'm tired and I don't give a shit what you do with him as long as you keep him away from me."

"If we let him go, do you think he'll quit?"

"No," Rapp answered without hesitation. "He won't quit until he's crippled or dead."

Kennedy had to be careful with this next part. Rapp was likely to come unglued. She cleared her throat and said, "What if we put him on retainer?" She watched as Rapp slowly turned his head toward her, waiting for the explosion.

Rapp's jaw was locked in a grimace and then it slowly started to relax. "I'd say we give him a trial run. He screws up, he's dead. He finishes the job, we'll sit down and talk."

"That was unexpected." Kennedy didn't bother hiding her surprise.

"And I know who we're going to send him after."

Rapp thought about all of the tight security around the man and how difficult it would be to kill Obrecht. Just maybe, Rapp would get lucky and Obrecht would put Gould out of his misery and save Rapp from the guilt of doing it himself.

"Who?" Kennedy asked, a bit nervous.

"I think our newest Swiss banker would be a nice place to start."

"Herr Obrecht?"

"Exactly."